T0384217

Girlfriend on Mars

Girlfriend
on Mars

A NOVEL

Deborah Willis

W. W. NORTON & COMPANY
Celebrating a Century of Independent Publishing

Copyright © 2023 by Deborah Willis

For information about permission to reproduce selections from this book, write to Permissions, W. W. Norton & Company, Inc., 500 Fifth Avenue, New York, NY 10110

For information about special discounts for bulk purchases, please contact W. W. Norton Special Sales at specialsales@wwnorton.com or 800-233-4830

Manufacturing by Lakeside Book Company
Book design by Beth Steidle
Production manager: Julia Druskin

ISBN 978-0-393-28591-8

W. W. Norton & Company, Inc., 500 Fifth Avenue, New York, N.Y. 10110
www.wwnorton.com

W. W. Norton & Company Ltd., 15 Carlisle Street, London W1D 3BS

1 2 3 4 5 6 7 8 9 0

For Kris

The fictitious name MarsNow refers in this novel to a fictitious interplanetary mission and corporation. Neither the name of the mission/corporation nor any other aspect of *Girlfriend on Mars* has any relation to, or is in any way endorsed by the owner of, the registered trademark Mars Now.

Michaelis saw with a shock that he was looking at the eyes of Doctor T. J. Eckleburg, which had just emerged, pale and enormous, from the dissolving night.

"God sees everything," repeated Wilson.

"That's an advertisement," Michaelis assured him.

—F. SCOTT FITZGERALD, *THE GREAT GATSBY*

And I saw a new heaven and a new earth: for the first heaven and the first earth were passed away . . .

—THE BOOK OF REVELATION

Nuke Mars!

—ELON MUSK, VIA TWITTER

SEASON
ONE

*MarsNow or
Maybe Not*

AMBER KIVINEN—DRUG DEALER, LAPSED EVANGELICAL CHRISTIAN, my girlfriend of fourteen years—is going to Mars. This is real. This is what I've been told.

Flashback. Interior. Day. Three months ago. Amber sat beside me on the Voyager. "Hey, Kev?" She tucked a blonde curl behind her ear. "You busy?"

Me, clearly not busy, wondering if I looked as stoned as I felt: "What's up?"

That curl bounced into her face again; she tucked it again. "I have to tell you something."

I expected the *something* to be that she wanted to adopt a cat, or that she wished I would get a real job, or that she'd made out with a guitarist or a guy who writes graphic novels. I did not expect her to say that she would soon be on television in a *Survivor*-meets-*Star Trek* amalgam, where she would compete for one of two seats on the MarsNow mission. I did not expect her to say that within the year she would ("hopefully") strap herself into a rocket and blast into deep space, where she would float for nine months like a fetus in a womb before landing on the iron-rich red dirt of Mars. That she would then use the frozen water in the planet's crust to grow her own food and produce her own oxygen. And she would stay on Mars forever, because the technology to come home doesn't exist yet. And even if it did. Even if the technology existed, even if she wanted to come back, she couldn't—her muscle and bone density would have decreased so drastically that Earth's gravity would crush her to powder.

She confessed all this while sitting next to me on our green IKEA Beddinge couch, in our basement suite off Commercial Drive. She used the same voice as she had when she told me, last year, about hooking up with a guy we sometimes sell to, a computer programmer/skateboarder named Brayden. (She "accidentally" went down on him on that green couch, one of our first purchases together—the couch we named the Voyager, because we've taken our best trips on it.)

"So." She spoke quietly and looked at the constellation of confusion that was my face. "This is probably a bit weird for you."

I wondered if I was more stoned than I thought. I waited for her to laugh. But she hadn't been joking about Brayden, and she wasn't joking about this.

"I mean," she chattered, "it's not dangerous or anything. Mostly the ship will be remote-controlled by people in New Mexico. It's sort of like a drone."

"Aren't drones notoriously inaccurate?" I said. "And what about aerobraking? What about solar radiation?"

How did I even know those words? From hours of sitting on this very couch, in a nostalgic stupor, watching *Star Trek: The Next Generation*.

"Will you do something for me?" Amber took my head in her hands. "Will you be a little bit happy for me? For, like, one second? 'Cause I made it to the third round and that's kind of a big deal."

"Since when were you in the first round? And do they know you're a drug dealer?"

"We're not *drug dealers*. We specialize in hydroponics. Which, by the way, will be the technology used to grow food on Mars."

"*By the way*," I said, "we sell drugs."

I remembered when we were kids and she went to summer camp, then mailed me letters addressed to:

Kevin Watkins
105 Amelia Street West
Thunder Bay
Ontario
Canada

North America
The Earth
The Milky Way
The Universe

"Remember when your parents sent you to that weird Bible camp?" I said.

"Kevin." She shut her eyes, opened them. "Are you even listening?"

"Is this like that time you hooked up with Brayden?" I said. "Just to see what I'd do?"

When she shook her head, her hair bounced like it was already on Mars, like her hair already existed in low gravity. "No," she said. "This is real."

THIS IS FUCKING REAL.

Amber is in the makeup room of a television studio and can hear a dull roar—the audience. Someone named Teeghan paints glittery eye shadow on her lids.

"So *cute*," says Teeghan. "Seriously, you're gonna look am*a*zing."

"Is this stuff hypoallergenic? My eyes are kind of sensitive. I never wear makeup, actually."

Teeghan gasps as though Amber had revealed a bomb strapped to her chest. "How do you feel *right now*? Is there *any* irritation?"

"No, fine. Just sometimes, creams and stuff make my eyes water."

"Oh, well that's probably good. If you cry out there. People love that."

"Right."

"Just be natural." Teeghan smiles. "You totally got this!"

Then someone infinitely tall appears, digs her fingers into Amber's hair, and says, "Oh my god, your hair. It's am*a*zing." Holds out her hand. "I'm Manusha. Key hairstylist. What should we *do* with your hair?"

What Manusha does with Amber's hair is add a shimmery spray-in serum, scrunch it, and say, "We'll just let these curls do the work." Then Amber is sent to wardrobe and told to put on a tight black jumpsuit emblazoned with the MarsNow logo. It takes two people—interns?—to zip her into the suit.

"Like wearing an eel's skin," Amber says. "And eels are *brilliant*. Some use the lunar cycle to navigate."

One of the interns—a young man so gorgeous *he* should be on TV—adheres the jumpsuit to her chest with body tape for extra security.

"Some infant eels travel five thousand kilometers, through estuaries and seas, by looking up at the moon," Amber says. The intern is clearly gay and *so* handsome—she wants his attention. His undying friendship. "Crazy, right?"

"Do your nipples feel secure?" he asks. "'Cause no one wants a Janet Jackson out there."

If only Kevin were here—he'd love this dialogue. If only Kevin were still writing screenplays. Or reviews. Or stories. If only Kevin did anything, really.

She takes a selfie and texts it to him with the words: *New Martian lewk! Too much??* Then, before she can stop herself, texts it to some of her back-burner men—Jianju the IT guy from work, Brayden that artsy hottie, Tariq her personal trainer. Out of habit almost texts it to Adam, but he's *here*, somewhere in this studio; he might appear at any moment. The thought makes her queasy, so she emails the photo to her parents along with hugs and kisses, hears back from Brayden (two fire emojis and a request for *more pls*), posts the pic to Instagram (#selfie #smile #picoftheday), and rides the wave of a TikTok dance challenge by shimmying in her eel's skin. Then hugs the phone to her chest. The producers said that this week they should post anything and everything to build momentum for the show, but once people start getting eliminated, and the chances of spoilers increased, their phones would be confiscated. They wouldn't even be allowed to contact family and friends.

After five minutes, she has 124 likes and 11 new followers.

This is real. This is *happening*. She's in the same theater where they shoot *American Idol*—she's more likely to give herself bangs than to watch that show, but *still*. She was once a directionless person, a person who couldn't even stick to being vegetarian let alone vegan, a person who couldn't pay the rent without breaking the law, a person—

A camera is in her face and a guy with slick hair and a fake tan, that producer dude she met during Test Day, holds out a microphone. "For the confessional!" he says. "How are you feeling?"

"Confession?"

And boom, she's twelve again, back in Thunder Bay, on her knees in a kitchen that smells like bleach. Her mother sits silently at the table, eyes averted; her father looms. They aren't Catholics, they pity Catholics, but her father believes that to confess is to be cleansed. Her sister, Caleigh, always admitted to food crimes: *I ate all the Goodie Rings from the package of Dad's Cookies.*

All of them? hisses Amber, who'd now be stuck with the crunchy oatmeal ones.

Amber.

Sorry, Daddy.

Let your sister speak. Unless you have something to say?

Amber shakes her head. Tucks her hair behind her ears. *Nothing.*

Are you sure?

From this angle, her dad looks like a cyclops, like he possesses only one huge, unblinking eye. She suppresses crazed giggles. Focuses on the swirling beige pattern of the floor. The floor her mother swabs every Saturday with Mr. Clean, on her knees, scrubbing until the lino gleams like marble.

You can keep the truth from me, but God sees everything.

There's always something to confess. Caleigh is prone to sloth and gluttony, Amber to envy, lust, and pride. And even if you hadn't done anything wrong, you'd probably had evil thoughts. Even if you hadn't had evil thoughts, your body had bad urges—your body could only be controlled through physical exertion, sweat-inducing saunas, and simple self-hatred.

Even this, her intractable wish to keep her mouth clamped shut, to say nothing despite knowing that her father would force her to kneel until the linoleum's pattern was pressed into the skin of her knees—

"Nothing," she says now. "Nothing to confess."

The slick producer (Nick? Rick? Dick?) laughs. "We call it a *confessional*—that's just TV-speak, baby." He gives her ass a smack—

is that allowed? "Just a quick splice, for our intro sequence. So the people can get to know you."

"Right." She blushes. "Sorry."

"Ready?" Slick producer dude seems to disappear and then there's just the camera, one huge unblinking eye.

She's totally got this.

"Hi! I'm Amber." She smiles. Waves girlishly. "And I don't know about anyone else, but I'm going to Mars!"

AMBER APPLIED TO GO TO MARS, WITHOUT TELLING ME, ONE YEAR and two months ago. She read about the competition online, then sent in a résumé and a two-minute video of herself. The video was filmed in our kitchen—I must have been out buying groceries or picking up lattes or hanging with Marcus, and it must have been summer because her hair catches the sunlight and haloes around her face.

I've now watched the video over and over, in the obsessive way a man might watch pornography that he happens to find on the Internet and that also happens to star his wife. Our laptop is ancient, so the video is grainy and slightly distorted—Amber appears as though she's already looking out through the curved glass of a space helmet. You can see a hint of the sequoia-tree tattoo that wraps itself around her bicep, and there's chipped green polish on her thumb. Her lip ring glints in the light, calls attention to her shimmery mouth.

"I believe that discovery is a universal human drive." She leans forward, showing just enough cleavage. "And I am sure that my athleticism, expertise in the field of hydroponics, and thirst for spiritual meaning will serve me well on the first human-led mission to Mars!"

The panel of MarsNow shareholders and venture capitalists and scientists must have liked what they saw, because Amber beat out over 150,000 other candidates such as Laurie Kalyniuk, housewife in Iowa, and Dr. Christopher Gelt, Germanic literature professor living in Guatemala City.

Round Two involved writing a placement exam that tested your basic math skills, and a thousand-word essay about your motivations/ambitions. Amber must have composed the essay when I was having naps or showers or something, because if I'd seen her writing anything I would have worried. When Amber writes—always in one of those overpriced Moleskine notebooks—it means she has a secret she can barely keep. Like when she bought a single flight to Bolivia using our joint airline points, or applied to work in a fire tower, or ate pulled-pork poutine every day on her lunch break even though we were supposedly vegans at the time and I was subsisting on peanut butter and rice cakes. Writing is often followed by surreptitious texting, generalized anxiety, and finally by the relief—for both of us—of discovery or confession.

But this time she didn't want to get caught. This time she quietly composed her essay and submitted it. This time she told me she was going to meet friends for coffee, when in fact she was being checked by a MarsNow-hired team of medical specialists: cardiology, psychology, osteopathy, and kinesiology.

Of course I noticed that she joined a gym and lifted weights, enrolled in spin and boot-camp classes, hiked the Grouse Grind every Wednesday with her "Active and Out There!" Meetup group, practiced yoga and qigong for mental/psychological well-being, and talked a lot about *maintaining muscle mass*. I also noticed that she started taking a cocktail of supplements—vitamin D, curcumin for inflammation, CoQ10, and cal-mag (same stuff we feed the plants). I noticed that she lost weight and became ropy with muscle. I noticed that she stopped getting her period and her box of different-absorbency-level tampons sat unopened under the bathroom sink.

I noticed, but didn't notice. I lived in my own world, existing mostly in a limited, indoor orbit. (This metaphor only works if you think of me as a small and insignificant planet and our pot plants, glowing under 9,000 lumens of LEDs, as the sun.) And even when she told me—the day before the MarsNow team was set to send out a press release—that she was one of 143 MarsNow applicants worldwide who'd moved on to Round Three, I didn't believe it. Mars didn't seem real.

Here's what's real: Amber and I are thirty-one years old, born four months apart in Thunder Bay, Ontario, but currently living in

Vancouver, BC. She works as a receptionist at the conference center downtown and I work as an extra on film sets (I once met Jennifer Love Hewitt), but we generate most of our income from selling the high-THC-content weed we grow in our bedroom.

Here's what else is real: we've known each other since grade two. She was a little bit scary—playing tag with Amber was likely to get you mowed down on the playground when she came at you with the full force of her YOU'RE IT!—but I liked her. Maybe even liked-liked her. When our class had to draw warm-fuzzies for Valentine's Day, I drew a stick figure of a girl with wild hair and wrote: For Amber, you're pretty and god [sic] at running.

Then I got shy around girls for a few years and didn't talk to her, barely knew her—she was just one of the Christian kids who had to leave the room during sex ed classes. Then she was the girl known for being the gymnastics champ of eastern Canada, particularly impressive in the vault event. The local paper had pictures of Amber shooting off the springboard like a rocket, pirouetting through the air. Then she was the girl whose Olympic ambitions were dashed when she injured her shoulder. The girl who started drinking too much and hanging out at parties with guys like me and Marcus.

The girl who took me outside. Who grabbed my hand and led me to a place that felt like it was beyond the city, beyond time, beyond the border of the life I'd been living—she showed me a hidden lake. A refuge, a paradise.

We lost our virginity to each other two months after that, on her single bed, under a canopy of glow-in-the-dark stars she'd stuck to the ceiling. Afterward she pressed her body against mine and said she hadn't been able to breathe properly since losing her chance at the Olympics, said she felt nauseous because she didn't know what to do with her life—she was only seventeen but already fully heartbroken. She said she liked me because she could breathe when I was around, because I didn't seem to have expectations of her. I said that was true:

I loved her for no reason at all. (It came out sounding dumb, but I meant it in a good way.)

We are officially the only people we have slept with. Unofficially, during the 3.5 weeks we "took a break" in 2006, Amber had sex with a video store clerk and I technically had sex (for about two seconds, in and out) with Tanya Vargas at a bonfire. But other than those 3.5 weeks, we have been together every day for twelve years. We live in a suite as hot as a sauna and like to cuddle on the couch and look at Dino Comics. Our tippy bookshelves are jumbled with my mom's movie collection, the detritus of my post-film-school attempt at becoming "well-rounded"—faded copies of Chomsky and Flaubert—and Amber's old textbooks on botany and nutrition. I call her Slammer (she once spent a night in jail) and she calls me Tater-Toter (don't want to talk about it) and we have a life together. We own one of those four-hundred-dollar blenders that could pulverize your skull, several hardcover luxury cookbooks, and the entire *Get Smart* oeuvre on old-school DVD. And we have our plants.

We started with a few seeds sprouted between wet sheets of paper towel, then planted like an herb garden on our windowsill. We transplanted those into bigger pots that we kept beside our bed like babies in bassinets. We fed them molasses and they grew past our knees, and that's when we started selling. Just to Marcus and Amber's sister and our former friend Brayden and some people I worked with on set.

It was Amber's idea to go hydro. She had a master's in environmental science, with a cross-disciplinary focus on nutrition and health (thesis: "Pacific Northwest Ferns and the Traditional Food Technologies of the Coast Salish People"), but couldn't find work doing anything but waitressing or answering phones. I was going to sell a screenplay someday for sure, but in the meantime I played Member of the Crowd or Guy on the Bus in other people's productions. And the rent we paid for our basement suite, complete with peeling paint and worn-out carpet, was eye-wateringly expensive.

We could have moved to Alberta, where Amber would write dodgy environmental reports for oil companies. Or to Chilliwack or Prince George, where low wages would stretch further. Or back to Thunder Bay, where we'd live too close to Amber's oppressive family and to the bungalow where I grew up with my mom, a house I feel sure is haunted.

Seven years ago, we sat on this couch and considered our options. Amber packed the small pipe I'd bought for her birthday. The glass used to be pale orange with swirls of gold, the same color as her hair, but years of smoke passing through had darkened it to a burnished red. We passed it back and forth, and that's when Amber said, "Or we could stay here and do this."

She said we'd probably produce more marijuana, using less space, if we grew hydroponically.

"Dealing drugs." She leaned against my chest, her eyes half-closed. "It's the best idea so far, right?"

First we cleared it with our upstairs neighbor, Norm, who works nights stocking medical supplies at the hospital. He said our secret was safe, as long as he got to partake of the product—marijuana helps him sleep when he gets home from work in the mornings. So we bought a pH and PPM meter, a water pump, lights, nutrients. We went to a pet store and bought six kitty litter boxes to use as reservoirs. We set up in the bathroom because it has good ventilation, but opening and closing the door and using the shower kept messing with the ambient temperature. We moved our operation into the spare room Amber once used as an office.

It's not ideal to live where you grow. We keep the heat at 28 degrees Celsius, and when the plants are in a vegetative state, we leave the lights on for eighteen hours a day. And there's that skunky, sticky smell that coats your skin and throat. It took some getting used to but this apartment has become my habitat. The heat, the humidity, the stillness, the silence. It's like the Garden of Eden, except better than the original. Every plant here is the Tree of Knowledge, and you can eat from it whenever you want.

So why would Amber want to go anywhere else, especially to a red, dead rock? I thought we had an understanding. We're not married; we don't have kids; we don't have pets. But we have our plants and we have each other. And we're committed to this kind of noncommitment: growing weed in our apartment, ordering pizza from the gluten-free place up the street, watching whole seasons of *Arrested Development* all at once. We sat on this couch and made a decision. We were, I believed, committed to going nowhere. Going nowhere together.

IT STARTED WITH GYMNASTICS, THE EXHILARATION OF SPRINGING off the vault and looping through the air.

Or maybe it started when gymnastics ended: when she injured her rotator cuff and lost her chance at the Olympics—lost everything.

Or maybe it started a year and a half ago when her Outlook crashed at work and she had to call the IT guy. But instead of the old white dude with the gray ponytail, this beautiful Asian kid appeared and said, "Hey, I'm Jianju."

She could only stare at him.

"IT," he said. "You called us, right?"

"Oh my god. Yes."

"Outlook crashed? It's the worst." He leaned over her desk, his fingers on her keyboard. "I just need your password to get into the back end here."

"Into the—back end?"

"You can change it once we're done."

"My password?" She wanted to die. "It's . . . LiamHemsworth1."

He smiled only slightly. "All one word? Capital L and capital H?"

"Correct."

Then he leaned over her, silently worked some IT magic, and she could smell his laundry soap. Could feel the heat from his body. Could see, up close, the smooth skin of his neck.

She had to stop being this person. Because her life was perfect. She loved Kevin. She loved their relationship. Loved that their relationship didn't fit the paradigm. She and Kev were not married because it was an outdated, misogynistic tradition that left women miserable—studies proved this. And she and Kev were not going to have children because she did not want her body invaded by alien life-forms. Plus, the environmental impact of having kids is obscene.

"You're good to go." Jianju clicked her mouse expertly. "You can reset that password now."

But maybe she did want a baby? Sometimes it felt like she did.

"Maybe Chris Hemsworth this time?" Jianju paused on the way out. "Or are you committed to Liam?"

She laughed. "I am committed to nothing."

Afterward, when they saw each other in the hallway, he smiled in a way that suggested he knew her darkest secret, and she smiled in a way that suggested he did not. Then he contacted her through the workplace email directory, and somehow they exchanged phone numbers. His texts lacked wit and punctuation, but her ego was boosted at the thought that a twenty-two-year-old would bother. Then he asked if she would be at the work Christmas party, and she replied, *hell yes and I'll be wearing sequins . . .*

She knew she should stop. But she sat at her desk and watched all the women click by in their heels, wearing their Aritzia blazers or the little cardigans they called "cardis," holding their Michael Kors bags, running their manicured hands through their highlighted hair, stopping at her desk to confide in her—it was something about being a receptionist, you were viewed as *receptive*, a good listener. Amber knew and guarded these women's secrets: they were overwhelmed by trying to organize child care, overwhelmed by work, overwhelmed by in-laws and birthday parties and schlepping the kids to swimming or ballet or hockey. They were addicted to caramel corn or iced caps or Coffee Crisp or wine—which they called *mommy juice* without any seeming awareness of how sad that was. They watched helplessly as their parents demented then died, while dealing with their own cancer scares or Hashimoto's or fibromyalgia. They were constipated since menopause hit; their antidepressants made them bloated; they had insomnia and couldn't sleep more than three hours a night. They were either expected to endure a husband's weekly jackhammering or sexually ignored; one married woman confessed that she hadn't been kissed in over a decade. And of course while Amber's own body sounded its alarm—a subtle whine of *baby, baby, baby*—these women were having trouble conceiving or were accidentally pregnant. Their babies had colic and their toddlers ADHD; their teenage children were anxious and cruel and addicted to their phones; their adult children were depressed and neglectful and addicted to prescription drugs. There must be some joy in it, in "having it all," or at least a sense of accomplishment and job-well-done, but the women didn't talk about that. Amber was only twenty-nine then—*you're a baby!* the women said—but she could see the menacing road toward forty, fifty, sixty . . .

It felt like she was about to be sucked into a black hole and there was no stopping this gravitational force. Before it was too late, she wanted to dye her hair blue or move to Ecuador or hit a sex club. Anything. Anything to feel alive before she got spaghettified.

She started fantasizing about being stuck in the elevator with Jianju. Or him offering her a ride home, then . . .

Her imagination was so *porn-y.*

But sometimes a girl gets tired of the 9 p.m., post-Netflix, pre-teeth-brushing, *I-love-you-I-love-you-too,* mellow-missionary sex at home. And Jianju was so young, was probably rock hard all the time. With Kevin there were always questions. Did his erection flag because of the pot—she'd googled it and daily use *can* lead to ED—or was he just *not that into her* anymore? And why would he be into her when she was always distant, enraged, or childishly cuddly? Also she couldn't be bothered to shave her legs *or* her pits, and who wants a girlfriend with gorilla legs? Plus she was embittered because she always initiated sex, and that bitterness led her to be dry as toast and limp as cold seaweed salad. Once, in a club, a stranger grabbed her by the wrists, kissed her, and said, *Give me your tongue. I want to feel your tongue.* She craved forcefulness—wanted Kevin to press her against the wall, kiss the ridge of bone along her neck, say, *Does this feel good?* Smack her ass while he took her from behind. Though if he did that, they'd probably both burst out laughing. And it's not as if she ever asked what *he* liked.

Usually he liked the usual. Who has time to be creative? Not someone who works full-time, runs a home-based business, and does nearly all the cooking and cleaning. But Beyoncé is probably creative in bed, and she has three kids!

So maybe this is Amber's biggest, most shameful secret: she's good at many things, but as a lover she's a failure. Would it be different if she'd been allowed to take sex ed as a kid? Would she have learned about pleasure and joy? She tended to initiate sex on the Voyager by matter-of-factly rubbing Kevin's crotch to see if he could achieve liftoff—barely bothering to kiss him. Sometimes they launched and it felt so comfortable and real and *right*. But sometimes it didn't work; sometimes he was distracted or uninterested. She told herself it was not a reflection of her worth. But even if it was just the pot, a purely physical issue, wasn't that worse? Because it meant that he loved weed more than he loved her—chose weed *over* her, every single day. But of course he loved pot more than he loved her. Who wouldn't? A woman with a real sense of self, a true feminist, a good and honest and lovable person, would just *talk* to him about it. But talking about it would hurt his feelings, and she couldn't stand that—she loved him so much. Her devoted, funny, sensitive Kev. Wasn't she hurting him less this way? By keeping quiet?

Imagine having simple, empty sex with a stranger. Imagine if it meant *nothing*.

Around that time—the winter of Jianju—she succumbed to food cravings and gave up being vegan, which was an added disaster because eating meat seemed to exacerbate her sex-drive (baby-drive?) problem. She noticed that she was going out of her way to walk past the IT desk every day, and when she saw Jianju she felt a lurch in her stomach, equal parts pleasant and painful, one hundred percent familiar. And she thought: *It's happening. Again.*

She was exhausted. So tired of herself.

That was around the time she read about the MarsNow project. On a whim she wrote her essay, the words pouring out, and submitted a video she didn't even bother to edit. She started working out again; it was a good excuse to get into shape and her body changed from slouchy-secretary to potential-astronaut. She did a phone interview with a woman who sounded like an automaton. She met with a series of doctors who tested her for kidney stones, gallstones, a heart murmur, slipped disks. It started to feel a bit real then, once she was declared fit for space travel despite her weak shoulder. She wanted to tell Kevin, but what was the point of worrying him when Mars was such a distant possibility? She still had to beat thousands of people to even get on the show. Just like the Olympics. Even if you rocked the national championships, even if you made it onto Team Canada, your squad still had to compete with the Americans, the Russians, the Chinese, and everyone else to qualify for the Games—to be in the top nine and move on to the finals. And none of it guaranteed a place on the podium. Failure and humiliation were the most likely outcomes—Amber should know. She made it onto the national team but injured her shoulder before they qualified and was replaced by a girl from Moose Jaw. And that was it. The end. She could have tried for the next Olympics, but by then she would have been geriatric by gymnastics standards. Her father kept saying, *You can do this* and *You're my champ* and *Did I raise you to be a quitter?* But by sixteen, she'd been training hard for ten years and her body felt broken. It wasn't just the shoulder, though that was the worst—there was her wonky knee, her partially torn calf muscle, a rib she broke at age ten.

The strangest thing about losing her shot at the Olympics was that the world kept spinning. Other people's lives continued. And no matter how much Amber stretched, no matter how religiously she did her physio, her shoulder remained weak and tight. No matter how much she prayed for relief, for healing. So she stopped praying. Stopped listening to the sermons at church. Stopped taking her dad's word as the Word. Her injury was the beginning of the end of belief, because what could God do for her now? *Smite me from above,* she used to dare Him. It was funny because she was already smote.

But look at her now. Forsaken, sure, but back in the game. Winning a seat on the Mars mission wasn't only unlikely—it was madness to even try, but a madness she must have missed, a madness that made her feel alive. She had to tell someone about her successes, so she spent more time on the MarsNow private forum, and that led her to Adam, and once they started messaging a floodgate opened. Turned out she craved honesty. Craved a stranger at the other end of an electronic rope, a stranger as distant and mysterious as a priest shielded by a confessional's mesh.

Then she had another MarsNow interview, this time over Microsoft Teams. Six men in suits sat at a table and asked her a series of questions:

Do you ever hear voices telling you what to do?

Would you rather steal something from a store or from an individual's home?

Have you ever been in a fight? Have you ever initiated violence of any kind?

Are you straight, gay, bisexual, or other?

Have you gotten a DUI?

Have you made a sex tape?

Are you on the pill?

Do you have enemies?

Why do you want to go to Mars?

WHY? I ASKED. WHY MARS? WHY NOW?

Because I want to see the Earth from above!

Because it's an amazing opportunity!

Because it's the first mission of its kind!

Amber sounded like a convert to a new religion. Still, I wasn't super worried because I knew this: her parents were coming to visit, and her father—this freaky Finnish guy, a die-hard fundamentalist and yet also an alcoholic—would never allow his daughter to go to Mars.

When we were growing up, her dad coached peewee hockey and would put me in goal without a helmet, which was supposed to teach me to be less afraid of the puck. He still addresses me by my last name, Watkins, and it still scares me. My fear is made worse because I'm in love with his daughter and have a crush on his wife. (This might be the only secret I've kept from Amber, the fact that when her blonde, big-boned mom sat in the bleachers, it made me play harder, skate faster, flinch less when the puck flew at my teeth.) What you need to know about Amber's father is that he hates our cannabis business and blames me for his daughter's life going nowhere.

But now Olav would be my savior. He would come to town, with his vodka and disapproval.

Then they were here, in Vancouver, after driving for a week straight from Thunder Bay because Amber's mother has a fear of heights. (Lydia is unlike her daughter in this regard. In fact, everything in Amber's life, from gymnastics to weed to Mars, can be read as one long attempt to be nothing like her mother.)

We all went to a pub that served burgers and craft beer, and Amber told her parents about her plans to move to Mars.

"Mars," said her father. "You mean the planet?"

"The planet." Amber shifted in her chair. "Fourth from the sun."

"The planet." His accent sounded dangerous. He crossed his arms, leaned back, and I had never loved him until that moment. "Mars."

"Sweetie." Amber's mom bit her lip. "You're joking?"

"It's for real—some billionaire is funding it." I leaned forward, relieved to have people on my side. "She's seriously considering this."

Lydia caught my eye. "How long would she go for?"

"She won't be able to come home," I said. "Ever."

"There's no way to transport or create enough fuel to launch a rocket from Mars," said Amber. "Maybe one day we'll have nuclear power stations out there, but probably not in my lifetime." She took a breath. "There's tons of info on the MarsNow website. They plan to set up a colony, everything state-of-the-art. They've already sent two rovers and an unmanned cargo ship. The show is just to pick the first two Marsonauts, but they'll be sending more teams every two years. The long-term idea is planetary ecosynthesis."

"Planetary what?" said her mom.

"Terraforming. Planetary engineering. Warming Mars like we've done here on Earth, but it'll be a good thing there. Water will flow, plants will grow. In a few hundred years, humans could live on Mars without difficulty. Well, maybe a thousand years, if we take breathable air into account."

"We should probably take breathable air into account," I said.

"What I mean is," said Amber, "it's going to be a *society*, a utopia— this beautiful experiment in how to live." She put a hand on her father's arm. "Dad, it's like the Rapture."

"The Rapture will be God's work," he said. "What about your job?"

He thinks Amber and I are insane to live in a dank Vancouver basement when we could afford a mansion in Thunder Bay. What he didn't yet know was that Amber had already quit her receptionist job.

"The pay for MarsNow is way better than at the conference center," said Amber. "I mean, *way*."

"You'll leave your family?" He'd apparently forgotten that he'd once disowned her. "We'll never see you again?"

She sighed. "I'm not actually going to win, Dad. It's crazy-competitive."

"Right," I said. "So what's the point?"

Olav stared at me, then turned back to Amber. "You could beat anyone."

"It's not that easy."

"Who said anything about easy?"

"It's probably just a fluke that I got this far—"

"When you broke your rib as a child," he said, crossing his meaty arms, "do you remember what you said on the way to the hospital?"

"You've told this story a million times."

"You said, *What about my schedule?* You wanted to get back in the gym. To complete your week's training."

"We're talking about space travel," I said. "We're talking about living on another planet *forever.*"

"Forever." Olav's gaze was on Amber. Finally: the moment he'd forbid her to go. She would be angry, despondent, but also secretly relieved to have an excuse to back out.

Instead, he raised his glass. He was the kind of man who gave speeches when he drank, and he gave one then. He talked about moving from Finland to Canada, believing that he might never see his homeland again. He compared the winter in Thunder Bay to the inhospitable atmosphere of Mars. He mentioned the Franklin expedition, but didn't seem aware of how it had turned out. Then he spoke of his mission trips to Mexico, where he built houses for Mayan people in exchange for their minds and souls—as if Amber would be building Pentecostal churches for Martians. He said he was proud that his daughter was an adventurer, that she came from a long line of explorers.

"We are Vikings." He drank, then slammed his pint on the table. "And we will die as Vikings."

Then he looked over at me and asked if I was still standing around in the background of movies he'd never seen.

"No," I said. "I mean, yes." I wasn't hungry; I pushed aside my chickpea burger.

"Dad?" Amber looked shell-shocked. "You really think I could win?"

Could I even go on? Could I live in this depressing world? A world where a madman who believes that the Earth was created six thousand years ago is somehow considered a source of wise advice and stable parenting?

"If you can't win," he said, "who can?"

Amber started prattling then, as if she'd been drinking something harder than soda water. Told us about ice at Mars's equator, about a landing parachute that can withstand 65,000 tons of force, about an organization called the International Potato Center that's creating a variety of everyone's favorite starchy tuber that will thrive on Mars. Olav drank three more beers and Lydia seemed to go into a trance—stared slack-jawed at the darts players on the pub's television sets.

Cut to when we got home and her parents went to the hotel they'd booked (they can't stand the heat in our place) and I rolled a joint as thick as my finger. I wanted to be brain-dead, body-stoned, obliterated. I wanted the kind of high that tears you right out of your skin.

I lit the joint, listened to the paper crackle, inhaled. Amber did crunches and push-ups, and beads of sweat rose on her freckled skin like blisters.

"Can I come?" I said, holding the smoke in my lungs.

"Where?" She wasn't even breathing hard.

"Mars." I exhaled, toked again. "Fourth from the sun."

"You missed the deadline." Her body moved up and down, up and down. "You didn't apply in time."

"We could have applied together. They probably want couples."

"I didn't think you'd be into it."

"They probably want people to, you know. Propagate." I giggled. "Name the animals, that sort of thing."

Amber finished her push-ups, sat back on her heels, looked at me. I didn't like that. I didn't want to see her seeing me. I closed my eyes.

"It's really competitive." She stood and walked past me to the bedroom, her stride cutting the humid air. "So, yeah."

SHE STRIDES ONSTAGE, SHOULDERS THROWN BACK, SMILING LIKE A maniac. Stands between Zach from Hong Kong and David from Norway—Adam is at the other end of the stage. When he glances her way, she pretends to be focused elsewhere. It's not that she doesn't want to meet him. But they've been in touch on the MarsNow forum for over a year, since the early days of eleven hundred competitors, messaging each other regularly despite the Israel-Canada time difference. They sweated together digitally, each round wondering if one of them would be cut, and recently switched from DMing on the forum to texting over WhatsApp. His full sentences, distinctly emoticon-free, flooded her brain with dopamine day after day after day.

But now he's here, IRL, and it's too much. Too real.

Anyway, there are so many people—not just Adam and the other contestants but a huge crew. Wires, cameras, lights. She feels as if she's already in space, dodging debris, and the lights remind her of how blinding the sun will be without Earth's atmosphere to protect her from its rays.

The sun will be brilliant when I am in space. The sun will be brilliant when I am in space.

She's been trying this out lately, positive thinking, mantras, manifesting. A return to her father's days of "positive confession," saying the right words with the right faith. When Amber was a teenager, her dad briefly embraced the Prosperity Gospel and bought himself an ATV, a five-thousand-dollar barbecue, and a Buick Enclave. He was mildly manic, perhaps spending too much time with Becca—the church's young, sparkly admin—and working almost constantly. But this phase was more fun than the usual negative confessions, especially because he also bought Amber twelve pairs of high-top Chucks in twelve colors, Caleigh got sessions with a dietitian and a teeth-bleaching kit, and their mother got a diamond tennis bracelet that she never wore because she didn't want it to slip off while she was doing dishes—what if it got sucked down the sink's drain? Worrying about such a stupid thing, laughed her father, only proved the weakness of his wife's faith.

You are moving toward a new activation of glory, the sermons-on-tape assured them all. *You've got a long way to go, but look how far you've come.*

Amber has a long way to go until Mars, but as her dad used to say when she was training: *Eyes forward.* Or as Coach Rodney used to say, *One step at a time.* That's about as far ahead as Amber can think. She can't truly imagine being chosen for Mars but can envision making it through the first eliminations and on to the next episode. Minimum. Hopefully she'll get to episode five.

And she *has* come a long way. Seems like a hundred years ago that she was invited to Test Day in Los Angeles. Test Day! A huge deal in the MarsNow universe. Test Days were held on every continent around the world, and if you couldn't get yourself there, you were automatically eliminated. She told Kevin she was going away for the weekend for work, to a team-building retreat in Whistler.

"*Team-building retreat* always sounds like code for *orgy*," he said. "Are you having an affair with your boss?"

"With Suzanne?" She kissed his chin. "You wish."

She was picked up at LAX and driven to a nondescript hotel. She knew Adam was finishing his own Test Day across the globe and wanted to text him, but her phone was confiscated at the hotel's front desk. Hundreds of people milled in the lobby, where she was told to wait.

"If anyone asks why you're here," said the tired and hunched young woman who escorted her into the lobby, "tell them we're shooting a movie."

"What movie?"

"A 3-D remake of *Schindler's List?*" The young woman wore a fanny pack and a name tag that said *Linnzy.* "Make something up."

Amber sat on the grimy carpet, eyed the other people in the room. Some were reading. Some talked in confused whispers—*I'm not sure how long, they just said to wait.* Some slept on the floor. At one point a group of remarkably tanned men walked around, singling people out and telling them they could go home. This nearly caused a riot—*But we've been waiting for hours! I came all the way from Salt Lake. Give me one good reason you're eliminating me!*

"'Cause you're ugly, my friend," said one of the tanned guys.

Then an older man in a white coat walked around the lobby sticking needles into everyone's arm. *He's a doctor,* said the rising tide of whispers. *He's testing us for STIs.*

"STIs?" said Amber. "This isn't *Love Island.*" No one seemed to hear her and she wondered if she was dead, a ghost among ghosts. Was she in hell?

Linnzy reappeared and herded Amber and a dozen others into a suite where they were miked up, then told to sit in front of a camera and talk about themselves.

"I'm not good at talking about myself," said Amber. "I'm Canadian."

A slick guy who said he was a producer—Nick?—laughed. "Awesome, hon. Exactly. What else?"

"What do you want to know?" It came out flirtatious. "Height? Weight? Bra size?"

She acted like a moron. Only figured out after she left the room that it had been a screen test. Then Linnzy led her to another suite where a middle-aged woman in a suit said her name was Dr. Meynard-Gonzales. She administered three personality tests: Myers-Briggs, the Winslow Personality Profile, and the Rorschach. The testing took hours and Amber was starving.

"Can I get a granola bar or something? I haven't eaten since I left Vancouver."

Dr. Meynard-Gonzales held up one of the Rorschach drawings— its black dots and dollops swam in front of Amber's eyes. She saw nothing but images of food in the inkblots—a roasted chicken, a plate of pasta—then was escorted to a hotel room, given a soggy egg-salad sandwich and told to "sit tight."

She was alone, it seemed, for the first time in her life. She scarfed the sandwich's innards and even some of the bread, so hungry she was willing to risk the gluten. Then listened to the overhead lights buzz, looked out the window at an air-conditioning unit. There was no television or radio in the room. She had one book with her—*Why I Am Not a Feminist: A Feminist Manifesto*—but had finished it on the plane. When was the last time she'd endured even five minutes without media? She tried to meditate. Cried for no reason she could fathom. Fell asleep and drooled on the lumpy hotel pillow, even though it looked like someone else had already slept in the bed. Went into the bathroom, splashed cold water on her face. Applied and reapplied lip gloss until her mouth shone like Venus on a clear night.

Then she saw it: a telephone. They had forgotten to remove the landline! Maybe they'd assumed she wouldn't recognize this ancient technology. She grabbed the receiver, held it to her ear, heard a dial tone.

She had only two phone numbers memorized: her parents' and Kevin's. She could call him. He would see a Los Angeles number, so she would have to tell him the truth. *I'm not at a team-building retreat.*

Easy. No problem. Why hadn't she told the truth before? Kevin was her boyfriend, her partner; he would understand. And if he didn't, what was the big deal? She was a strong woman, living an independent life. She would just move on. Wasn't that what the women at work always said? *Move on, honey. You can do better.* That's what she was supposed to do. What everyone is supposed to do. Better.

She pressed the receiver to her ear, grimy plastic against waxy cartilage, dialed all but the last digit of Kevin's number. Then heard a knock at the door.

Slammed the phone down, caught her breath. "Come in!"

Linnzy handed her an envelope that contained an inch-thick stack of paper.

"Your contract." Linnzy was eating an apple and the juicy crunch of it blurred her words. "We need it back ASAP."

"I made it? I'm on the show?"

"Nope, not yet." Linnzy handed her a pen. "They won't do final selections for a while."

Amber flipped through the papers. "But I sign the contract now?"

"It's just a formality. So we know you're serious. We'll get in touch about the next steps."

"But can you tell me—"

"I'm a PA, I know jack shit." Linnzy chewed the apple. But she must have taken pity on Amber because she whispered, "Not everyone is being asked to sign a contract. So that might mean something."

Amber skimmed the pages, hardly reading a word. Signed with a flourish on the last line.

"Anyway, you can go now." Linnzy gathered the papers, popped them back in the envelope, the half-eaten apple hooked to her teeth. "We need this room."

"Thank you. Thank you so much for—"

But Linnzy was gone and the door juddered shut, inching along the cheap carpet.

A contract? It was like she'd been flirting with Jianju, keeping it fun and innocent—then suddenly ended up half-naked with him in the elevator. Or like she'd planned a simple tuck jump but instead found herself executing a Produnova vault, huge forward momentum propelling her through a handspring into a double front flip with a blind landing.

She wanted to text Adam. Wanted to call Kevin.

Oh god. She would have to tell Kevin.

She would do it right when she got home. Or next weekend, when they had some downtime. Definitely as soon as possible.

Kev, she would say. *You busy?*

She hugged her torso, then lunged into the cramped bathroom and vomited the masticated remains of the egg salad.

AFTER AMBER'S PARENTS' VISIT, OUR PLACE NO LONGER FELT LIKE a garden—everything was too damp, too muggy. The quiet between us felt wet and heavy, a thing that could drown you.

She set up a Facebook page ("Amber's Off to Mars!"), Twitter, TikTok, and Instagram accounts (@AmbersQuest), and a blog where she posted about her training. She rarely slept at the same time as me—normally we put the plants to bed, turned off those LEDs, curled up together and drifted off in the pitch-dark of our bedroom 'cause all our windows are blacked out. But she started staying up at the kitchen table, the laptop open and shining its pale, alien light over her skin. She was chatting with other applicants on the MarsNow forum. They would share tips, argue, or comfort each other as more of them were eliminated in the pre-televised assessments.

I know this because I looked at her browser history, clicked through a few pages of her conversations. Here's a sample from a few months ago:

> **AmbersQuest:** Anyone out there? Can't stop thinking about life on Mars tonight.
>
> **FirstMan34:** Living on Mars = unimaginable. I think what appeals is that the simplest things will be extraordinary, u know?
>
> **AmbersQuest:** For sure. Eating a meal. Taking a shower!
>
> **FirstMan34:** Going for a walk. Watching the sun set.

I wanted to punch that FirstMan34 guy. But I told myself to *let it go*, to appreciate having Amber around, even if she was always in another room, 'cause soon I wouldn't even have that meager comfort. Soon I'd only see her on TV. Thursdays at 7 p.m. (Pacific Standard) on CBS and streaming on EyeSite, the social media platform owned by that douchebag billionaire, Geoff Task. Guy who owns Almanac, parent company of the biggest search engine on Earth. (You know the type: white guy, middle-aged but in denial about it, walks around embodying the zombie brain of the neoliberal economy.) EyeSite is his only failure, an imitation of Instagram/Snapchat/TikTok, a social media site nobody wants to join. I guess he's hoping that Mars-Now will make it happen. And he's promised that MarsNow will be the *most real* reality TV we've ever seen. He can't do anything without "disrupting" it, so he's poured almost half a billion into production. They'll film and edit the show almost in real time: each episode will be shot over a period of six days, with teasers posted to EyeSite every night. This is supposed to ensure that the show isn't scripted; there's no planning, no shaping the story. It also helps, in this age of constant connectivity, to reduce the chance that some dumbass crew or cast member will post spoilers all over Twitter. So the show will be edited in record time, by people in control vans on location, and the episode will air immediately after filming wraps, on the seventh day. Very biblical. Then they start all over again the next week, and this goes on for twelve weeks. I truly feel for the poor schleppers, the grips and caterers and assistants, on that set.

Flashback. Interior. Day. Two months ago. I was still processing that Amber had applied for MarsNow when I got a call from their director of Casting, Communications, and Commitment, Helena Slora. She said she was phoning everyone close to Amber to do a background check. "You are Amber's boyfriend, no?"

"I am Amber's boyfriend, yes."

"As you know, we at MarsNow are narrowing our field and Amber is one of our strongest competitors. As we approach the date of filming what will be the biggest television event since the moon landing, we need to ensure that each potential star meets our stringent requirements."

I filled my lungs for the first time in months. "Are you aware that she's a drug dealer? I mean, *allegedly*. Allegedly we grow marijuana in our apartment and allegedly we sell it."

"Thank you for this information," said Helena Slora. "Is there anything else I should be aware of concerning Amber Kivinen?"

"She cheated on me. More than once." Amazing to say that out loud. "Her whole self-confidence seems wrapped up in—let's call it the male gaze? Male approval? She has daddy issues, trust me."

Helena Slora took notes—I could hear the tippity-tap of her keyboard. She said things like, "Mm-hmm. Anything to add?" And I went on, telling and telling and telling on Amber.

Reader, I sabotaged her.

When I hung up, I felt light-headed with happiness. I would get to keep her. She wouldn't be going anywhere.

It hadn't occurred to me yet that this is *reality television*. They want personality. They want instability. They want, more than anything, attractive women with daddy issues.

The first episode airs in a few days and Amber is one of twenty-four competitors, two of whom will be eliminated every week. After the first week in LA, where they're filming B-roll footage, the show will be shot in stunning locations around the world, the idea being that the competitors will see the breadth of what Earth has to offer before two of them are chosen to abandon this planet forever. Season two will feature the "winners" being shipped off to become space dust.

It's hard to sleep lately. It's hard to eat. So I cancel my so-called acting gigs—why stand around as an extra on set, day after day, now that Amber's making the big bucks? With my newfound freedom, I should excavate some of my old screenplays, see if any still have potential. I have the distinction of receiving a couple of contest placements along with sixty-four rejections from LA and Vancouver agents—capitalist shills. I was partial to my experimental buddy comedy, where I exclusively used dialogue stolen from the mouth of my friend Marcus. And *Awaken*. Or *Awoken*? I could never decide.

About zombies who look just like ordinary hedge-fund managers and fossil-fuel execs, and keep their brain-eating urges under control in public—but in private, they gnaw on the flesh of their immigrant staff. (It's a metaphor for society. Get it?)

I leave the apartment only once, to buy groceries and lottery tickets. But being outside, away from the warm jungle that Amber and I grew together, makes me feel like my head might detach from my neck and float away into the atmosphere. I decide to forgo lottery tickets and to sign up for an organic grocery delivery service called Good Food for Good People Box. Did you know it was that easy to become a Good Person? Me neither.

A few clients come over to purchase. Brayden, that graphic designer/skateboarder who once had his cock in my girlfriend's mouth but thinks I don't know about that and now gets charged double. And my best bud Marcus, who also moved to Vancouver after graduating and who suggested that I followed him out here. (Not true.) (I followed Amber.) And a girl named Bronwyn who always brings me and Amber homemade, raw, vegan desserts.

Cut to Bronwyn standing in the entryway, holding a Tupperware of sweets, waiting for me to invite her in. What's my deal with this chick? She's nice enough and god knows I could use more friends. Also, I shouldn't notice this 'cause I have a girlfriend, but Bronwyn is cute in a hippie way: white-girl dreadlocks piled on her head, loose sweaters that show her bony shoulders, leggings that outline the shape of her legs. But she's got these huge brown eyes that always seem to X-ray through my cranium.

She leans against the doorframe. "I heard Amber's gone—"

"For a bit."

"—for, like, ever?"

We face each other in awkward silence until she holds out the Tupperware container. "I made you some coconut-almond macaroons. They're vegan."

"We're actually not vegans anymore."

"Oh. Did you—?" She laughs nervously. "People always think they need more protein, but you can get everything you need . . ."

What is wrong with me? She stands there, chatting, and instead of saying, *Thanks so much, Bronwyn, come on in,* what I actually say is: "What about B vitamins?"

She sways for a second, mouth hanging open. "There are some plant sources for that, and I take supplements—"

I turn, go to bag up a gram of bud for her, all while going on about how *Amber's in training, it's pretty hard-core, so she needs animal fats as fuel, etc. etc.,* then hand Bronwyn the pot, pocket her cash, grab the macaroons, and close the door in her face.

See? I am not a pushover. I am not a doormat. I am a big man who doesn't let women boss him around.

Then I yank open the door. But because I'm a dumbass who slammed it on a pretty girl, the hallway is empty.

THE FIRST DAY OF SHOOTING HAS WRAPPED AND ALL TWENTY-four finalists are ushered onto a bus that takes them to an apartment building covered in graffiti and cracked, faded-peach stucco.

"This is Hollywood?" Amber hauls her duffel bag into the entry-way and one of the American competitors laughs—a guy with a man bun and remarkable bone structure, an engineer who invented a way to make superstrong fabric out of the bamboo he grows on his Austin, Texas, property. Logan?

"You thought it'd be glamorous?" he says. "You're thinking of the Hollywood Hills."

Ramesh, the guy from India, says, "On *The Bachelor* they stay in a mansion with a pool."

"'Cause that's where they *shoot* the show," says man-bun bamboo-guy. "This is just where we sleep."

"Yeah, except you don't have followers who expect you to post to your Stories." Tish is a Pilates instructor/Instagram micro-influencer who goes by the name @tish.to.the.core. She's almost six feet tall, willowy, with hair dyed not blonde but silver. "I say good-night to one hundred and seventy thousand people every night, and I can't exactly—" She points to a smeared stain on the wall by the elevator. "I need a *background*."

"You can't post shit," says man-bun Logan—pretty sure it's Logan. "It's in our contract."

"I can't post *spoilers*. I can't post about my progress. But this week I can post about my outfits, and my makeup, and about mansplainers like you."

Amber moves away, leans against the wall, closes her eyes. Wants to avoid meeting Adam's gaze—she saw him at the back of the bus, and can sense his presence now in the entryway, but can't muster the courage to talk to him. Too tired. For over two hours they shot a five-second sequence, again and again, from every angle: the group of them leapt into the air, fists held high, shouting *Mars! Now!* Her calves ache.

"Are you Amber?" It's a cute woman with Princess-Jasmine-from-*Aladdin* eyes. "I'm Pichu. I think we're roommates?"

"We have roommates?"

"I think so?"

Amber feels enormous compared to this person. "Are you from India too?"

Cute chick laughs. "Canada."

"Shit. Sorry. They put the Canadians together." Amber holds out her hand. "Vancouver."

"Eastend, Saskatchewan. Well, that's where I'm from. I live in Calgary now."

"East End? That's a place?"

"Completely is. Nicer than this shithole." Pichu smiles. "I think we're in apartment 216, roomie."

The apartment is small but clean, with beige walls, two identical bedrooms, one bathroom, and a stocked kitchen—milk, coffee, Earl Grey tea, packages of instant noodles, boxes of cereal and par-boiled rice, a freezer filled with chicken thighs and hot dogs and fish sticks.

"I feel like someone else lived here," says Amber, "then died five minutes ago, and we moved in."

Pichu is unpacking one of her suitcases, which seems to be filled with sachets of spices and Ziploc bags of legumes. "I brought my own food 'cause—" She waves to condemn the fish sticks.

"I should have thought of that."

"That's my motto. *Think of everything.* 'Cause once we're on Mars, we will not be ordering from Amazon." Pichu pulls a small pressure cooker from her suitcase. "Do you like dal?"

"Love it." Amber leans on the counter and watches her roommate rinse the lentils. "Why do you want to go Mars? You look like you're twelve, by the way."

"I'm thirty-six. And I'm an author, YA sci-fi. I write about brown girls traveling to distant planets, so—" She shrugs. "Makes sense, right? Might as well."

"*Might as well?*"

"Also my mom died, and I had surgery that left me feeling worse than before, and my marriage ended, and my fourth novel is stalled in that swampy first-draft phase. So I was like, *fuck it.*" Pichu puts the lentils in the pressure cooker with a generous handful of salt, a pour of oil, and what looks like an improvisation of spices. "You?"

"I'm a failed Olympian. And now they're going to legalize marijuana, so the business I run with my boyfriend is maybe screwed. And I can't seem to love people in any normal, adult way. So I was like, *fuck it.*"

"I think we're going to be friends, Amber-from-Vancouver."

"Maybe we'll go to Mars together." She knows they'd never send two women—the rules state that the winners will be one man and one woman—but going to Mars with this adorable person seems about as likely as going to Mars at all. After meeting some of the other competitors, like the Japanese woman whose robotics designs are *already* being used by NASA, Amber has lost hope. Still, she must make it to episode three. Anything less would be too mortifying.

"The way I see it, they have to send someone who's not white so they don't get accused of racism—that could be me," says Pichu. "And they have to send someone who's white so white people tune in. That could be you."

"Two women, though. Not happening."

"Doing research for my last book, I read that men suffer from vision problems in space but women don't have the same issues." Pichu stirs the steaming lentils. "Our eyeballs hold up. So they *should* send two women."

"But they won't."

"I wrote a book called *Diversitas*, about these two sisters who are born on a spaceship, but shit happens and the whole crew dies, including their parents, so the sisters continue the mission on their own, they find Planet Diversitas—which seems chaotic at first, like a riot of color and overrun with these alien beings, creatures sort of based on the Hindu gods, you know? Also Muhammad, Jesus, everyone. But instead of colonizing the planet like the crew planned to do, the sisters make friends with the inhabitants, learn from the aliens, go home, and use their new technology and philosophies to eradicate war on Earth."

"That sounds amazing."

"You can read it. I brought copies." The pressure cooker whistles and Pichu pops the lid. "You said the word *boyfriend*. He must miss you."

"Not sure. He probably won't realize I'm gone until next week." Amber refuses to feel bad about leaving Kevin. Refuses. "He's a writer too, actually. Or used to be. Mostly screenplays that never got produced, but he published lots of film reviews that were super smart and hilarious. And wrote these cool stories for me."

"Then he got a real job?"

"Not exactly. Depression, I guess. Kinda gave up."

"Common sitch. Afraid of failure?"

"I guess." Maybe it'll help him to see Amber on TV, risking everything to achieve her dream. Maybe she hasn't *left* him—she's *inspiring* him. "Aren't we all afraid of failure, though?"

"Failure has always already happened, or is already in progress. I'm an optimist! Things can only improve. A few years ago I was so depressed I went three weeks without brushing my teeth, and now . . . somehow I'm on TV?"

"I'll tell Kevin that. Things can only improve. I want to help him, 'cause he's really talented—"

"That's sweet, but you can't." Pichu scoops dal into two bowls. "We should have rice with this but I'm too tired."

"Insane. You made dal in five minutes." Amber takes a bite and the lentils are creamy and perfectly seasoned. "This is giving me a foodgasm."

"See? Don't you want an Indo-Canadian author on Mars with you? My job will be to cook and tell stories."

"Seriously. You're miraculous."

"Not sure what you'd do, white girl. Stand there and look hot?"

"Grow the lentils hydroponically."

"Holy shit, my friend. We're a dream team."

IT OCCURS TO ME AS I STARE OUT AT THE EMPTY HALLWAY, THE
place where Bronwyn stood, that Amber is gone, my girlfriend has
left me. She's been trying to get away from me, from the knee-deep-
in-mud feeling of *us*, for years. It's a bit like the climate crisis—I'm
aware of it now, finally *seeing* it, but it was happening in front of my
face for a long time.

Okay, but maybe not? Climate change is real, but it's tough to
believe that my girlfriend is going to Mars. And I'm a failed screenwriter; unbelievable narrative leaps are my specialty. Thing is,
Amber has tried to leave me before and it never stuck. How can
you leave your best friend? Your home away from home? The only
human on Earth who truly knows you? For example, I know that
Amber is right now in bed, twisting and turning until the sheets are
wrapped around her legs like ropes, blaming herself for not being
able to fall asleep.

Or maybe she's in a hot tub with a bunch of other reality stars,
about to have an orgy? I call her, just to check, and her phone rings
four times. Then her sleepy voice: "Hey Kev. I can't sleep."

Bingo.

"*Ah oui.*" In my terrible French-philosopher accent: "I am also
experiencing late-capitalist dread mixed with angst *de* relationship."

"I'm sorry. It's my fault."

"Entirely."

"How are the babies?"

"Growing up so fast."

"What about the toddlers? You'll have to taper their nutes soon."

"Daddy knows."

I can hear her shift in bed and imagine that she's rolled on her
side, snuggled into my chest.

"I have a cool roommate," she says. "She made us dal. And said there'd be chai with ghee in the morning."

"I could make you chai with ghee."

"What did you eat today?"

"Are you asking because you think I'll starve without you?"

"I'm asking because it seems like a neutral conversation topic."

"I ordered white-boy sushi favorites. California, Dynamite, yam tempura roll. I love that fake-crab stuff."

"There's sushi at the craft services table. So good."

"Haven't I been extolling the wonders of craft services for years?"

"You spoke the truth."

"So you can't sleep, even though you're living the American dream. Want me to sing to you?"

She laughs. "Please don't."

"Want me to tell you a story?"

"Please do. Hey, Kev, my roommate is a writer! I told her about you and she said—"

"There once was a hummingbird named Amber Kivinen. If she stopped moving, she would die."

"That's terrifying. It's not even a story."

"But you are a hummingbird. And I love that about you." That's true. I envy her ambition and bravery. She envies my patience and stillness. Is that why people fall in love? Because they want to absorb the other's qualities? It's basic science: two electrons repel each other, but a proton and an electron make electricity. Or something. "How is electricity created again?"

"What? It's the transfer of electrons between atoms." She yawns. "I gotta sleep, Kev. You can google it."

"Goodnight, Slammer."

"Goodnight, Tater."

I use an old Bic pen to scratch a line into the bedroom wall. That's how I'll keep track: scratch one pained line every evening, to represent each day that Amber is gone. I like the image, very filmic. When

Amber comes home, the wall will be covered in scrawled lines and I'll be skinny and weak, reaching for her with a shaky hand (it's, like, the 1880s or something in this fantasy—bear with me), and Amber will be all, *I should never have left you, my love. If only I'd known . . .* and she'll weep in this beautiful, Kate Winslet way while I die of diphtheria or typhoid.

If only.

In a week, it'll be time to switch out the plants' water solution. That means I need to age the water starting tomorrow, allowing the chlorine to off-gas. This is another reason to keep track of the days: I vowed to myself that I would keep our children healthy and happy until their mom comes home.

Amber is the brains behind the operation; she has dominion over these plants and she taught me everything I know. But I'm the patience; I'm the stillness. And patience is key to a successful grow-op. It's tempting to overfertilize to try to speed up the growth process, and it's tempting to harvest early to get at the product faster. But harvesting too early will give a dark, depressing high. And too late will make you feel like you've been brained by an asteroid. I'm waiting for that perfect time because I want a Goldilocks high—not too heavy, not too light.

Patience. Stillness. Either Amber will see that the Mars project is insane and dangerous and so pointlessly absurd that it might as well be one of James Franco's conceptual "art" projects. Or she'll get eliminated. Kicked off the show and forced to come home.

And in the meantime I'll taper the nutrients until they're down to zero. Feed the plants distilled water for a few days to get rid of any chemical aftertaste. Then wait. Wait some more. Wait until the leaves curl and fall off the plant, scattering softly on the floor. Until the pistils turn a shade I can only describe as "amber."

SHE WAKES AT 5 A.M. FOR THE NEXT DAY'S SHOOT AND CAN already tell that the chai with ghee will be the best part of her day. The shoot is endless, exhausting, but by evening she feels like she was born in the studio, born for the studio. It's strange how you get used to having a camera two feet from your face. How the camera becomes invisible, but you're also constantly aware of its presence. It's like when she still believed that God was looking down upon her—her every word, action, and thought are once again monitored and important, and therefore altered. It must be happening to all of them. When she runs into Ramesh, the computer programmer from India, he says, "What motivates you to get to Mars, Amber?" in this team-player voice that she can tell is a heightened version of his real self.

"My Insta handle is @AmbersQuest, and I really do feel like I'm on a quest." She says this ostensibly to Ramesh but really to the entire world. "I'm looking for meaning, adventure, and freedom. Isn't that what we all want?" Pause for effect. "My dad always says I'm a seeker. I'm a badass, probably-totally-insane seeker." She laughs, to show that she's modest, and Ramesh laughs too, to show that he's friendly and awesome and gets along with everyone.

Again she avoids Adam. It's getting ridiculous now, but she can't bring herself to wave or even smile at him, though they both steal glances. The problem is, this means something. It's real. She's never met anyone who understood her so fully—they're practically the same person. She grew up in an evangelical household in Canada; he grew up in an Orthodox settlement in the West Bank. She found refuge in gymnastics, vaulting through the air; he found refuge through a strange and lenient rabbi who encouraged his interest in sports. They both escaped their upbringing: she moved from her frozen, conservative home to the Left Coast, discovering feminism and the biological sciences and the capacity of her own mind; he left his community when his yeshiva declined his request to practice martial arts, telling him that physical exertion would interfere with his religious studies. Her father briefly disowned her when she was nineteen and "living in sin" with Kevin; his family hasn't spoken to him since he left the Haredim and said goodbye to God. Leaving their families, joining the real world—they both agreed it felt like landing on the moon.

The hardest thing to get used to, he once texted her, *is the loss of meaning.*

She coped by embracing a full and irredeemable rebellion: growing and selling weed. He coped by focusing on a different type of study, completing college preparatory courses and discovering a talent for math and sciences that led him to study medicine. She took shelter in Kevin and their predictable world of two; he found stability in the IDF, rising to the rank of Captain.

And now the thought of meeting this man who knows her story, who understands her loneliness, the thought of having a face-to-face conversation—what if they don't click? What if he doesn't like her? She might puke on her jumpsuit.

He approaches when they get a break. Of course it happens when she's grabbing handfuls of gummy worms from craft services, justifying it by telling herself that they're full of collagen.

"Amber." He's tall, with close-cropped dark hair. "I'm happy to see you."

"Oh god. Adam?"

His face, his voice, his body—is it possible that he's even fitter up close than in her imagination?

"I saw you yesterday," he says.

"I looked for you!"

"I tried to talk to you but they were filming your intro—"

"It was a busy day."

"I was nervous to speak with you."

"Me too!" She laughs. "But we're talking now and it's not weird. Right?"

"I'm struck by how natural it feels." He looks into her eyes. "I don't connect with people easily."

"Me neither," she says, although that isn't true. "I'm the same way."

"Dudes. Why are you flirting *off*-camera?" Pichu is suddenly beside them, grabbing Doritos. "You wouldn't just urinate on the floor, amirite? Hold it in until the appropriate time."

"You're Pichu?" He holds out his hand. "I am Adam."

"Oh, I know you." Pichu curtsies adorably. She's *good*. Good at playing herself. "The guy from Israel."

"You're correct that we should show everything to the cameras," he says. "I did research before arriving. One piece of advice was: *The audience wants only one thing.*"

"Nude pics?" says Pichu.

"*Your soul.*"

"Crap." Pichu laughs. "I don't have a soul."

"And I am unwilling to give mine away," says Adam. "What will we do?"

"Fake it?" Pichu gives him a little shove. "You should go get texturized or whatever. They want everyone's hair touched up before they start rolling again."

"Amber," he says before striding off. "Which apartment is yours?"

"Number 216."

"I can visit you later?"

"Yeah." She's sweating, can feel the foundation sliding off her face. "You can visit me later."

"Girl," says Pichu once he's left, "that hot Jew-man *likes* you."

TONIGHT MARCUS COMES OVER BECAUSE HE SAYS THERE'S THIS new video game called *Soccer Mom* that we have to play. He arrives with a joint tucked behind his ear and a bag of that caramel- and cheddar popcorn, the stuff that makes you believe in God.

"So *Soccer Mom*." He lights the joint like it's a cigarette. "You gotta get the kids out the door, hit a yoga class, grab a macchiato, make cookies for a bake sale, pick up the kids from school, get dinner ready, do bedtime—all while stopping these ISIS terrorists from blowing up the suburb *and* these white-power assholes from shooting up the school. It's fucking sick."

"Sounds intense."

"Where's Amber, man? She'd like it. It's all feminist and whatever."

"Amber's gone. Remember? Mars."

"Oh right, *Mars*," says my oldest and stupidest friend. "Shit, dude." He's exactly the same as he was in high school. The ape-like arms, the studied nonchalance. "Did you know they faked the moon landing? You can YouTube it."

"The moon landing was not faked. That's a gateway conspiracy theory, Marcus. Next you're going to be a Holocaust denier."

"That's not gonna happen, though. She's not going to Mars."

Whenever people tell me not to worry, that Amber's definitely not going into space, I have this weird, contradictory urge to defend her. *I guess you don't know Amber.*

"The idea is to launch from Earth, then land on Olympus Mons." I've spent too much time on the Internet researching Mars the way you might flip through guidebooks to plan your next vacation. Did you know that there are formations on Mars that resemble volcanoes, valleys, deserts, and polar ice caps? I say "resemble" because the surface of Mars is geologically dead, no volcanic activity to recycle chemicals and minerals from the interior to the exterior. Other facts: dust storms cover the entire planet for weeks at a time, and only 43 percent of the sunlight that reaches Earth gets to Mars. "Olympus Mons is this massive mountain," I say. "Way bigger than Everest, and it has this huge red crater. Twice as deep as the Grand Canyon."

"Olympus Mons." Marcus crashes onto the couch. "Like the biggest, warmest vagina in the universe."

I understand, for a moment, why some people think getting stoned is boring.

"Mars isn't warm, actually. It's cold as fuck."

"But not cooler than you, my bro."

"Sure."

"Seriously." Marcus looks at me. "Why do you stay with her, man?"

OF COURSE ADAM WOULD KNOCK ON THE DOOR WHEN AMBER AND Pichu are wearing terrycloth robes, their faces smeared with blue enzyme masks.

"Shit," whispers Amber at the door's peephole. "It's him."

"Own it, honey," says Pichu. "We're TV stars. What does he expect? We should offer him a face mask. Men never take care of their skin. Or their fingernails."

Amber opens the door, grateful that Pichu is already yelling at Adam: "Did you bring beer?"

"Sorry." He smiles. "I only drink clear, distilled liquor or organic, sulfate-free wine."

"I wish you weren't so good looking," answers Pichu. "Then I could thoroughly hate you."

"I came to see if you two wanted to join me in the sauna I've set up. I brought five infrared bulbs and have placed them in my closet."

"Is that the punch line?" says Pichu. "Or is there more?"

"It's a real thing," says Amber. "It helps with muscle recovery. I used near-infrared when I was a gymnast."

"Neato," says Pichu. "But *no gracias*."

"Come with," says Amber.

"I'm not going to sit in a *closet* with two people who so clearly want to bang each other."

"I have a boyfriend," says Amber.

"She has a boyfriend," says Adam.

"Are you guys leaving soon? 'Cause I don't know how much longer I can keep a straight face."

Amber rinses off the enzyme mask, changes into shorts and a tank, then follows Adam up the stairs—Jesus, look at his muscular back. They enter his apartment, as beige as the one she shares with

Pichu, but his room is unnaturally tidy: he made his bed military-style, the corners perfectly tucked. Inside the closet is the make-shift sauna. Shyly, without speaking, they lie side by side and close the sliding, mirrored doors. It's pitch black until he switches on the power strip and the tiny room fills with red light.

"Close your eyes," he says. For sure he's going to kiss her. But then he settles beside her and says, "Some people say the infrared wavelength is healing for the eyes, but others say it's dangerous. Research is inconclusive."

They lie there, glistening like those hot dogs served at gas stations.

At first she's conscious of his body next to hers, his breathing, her own heartbeat. Conscious of Kevin, at home in Vancouver, sunk into the couch cushions. Will he have made himself dinner? Remembered the compost and recycling? Fed the plants? And conscious of the residue of her day, her whole life, a scum that seems to stick to her like sweat: competition, confession, guilt, shame, love. Proving herself, hiding herself, winning, losing, wanting, striving.

To the one who conquers, I will give a place to sit with me on my throne . . .

But then: the carpet under her skin is velvety, soft like Mars's butterscotch earth. The red light reminds her of the way Martian dust will reflect the sun's weak light. And behind her closed eyes she can see specks. The star-like Earth. Its orbiting moon.

"This is what it will be like," she says, and Adam must know what she means, because he reaches out and takes her hand.

WHY? WHY DO I STAY WITH HER? WHEN MARCUS LEAVES, THE question circles in my head, crashes against my skull like a light-bulb-drunk moth.

I stay because I want to feel sorry for myself? Because I'm afraid of being alone? But what's wrong with being alone? I envy Pluto, out there on the edge of the solar system, so independent and unassuming that it's not even considered a planet anymore. I use my empty Bic pen to scratch another line into the paint, to represent this dull day's passing.

Maybe I stay because Amber pulled me out into the world? That first afternoon when we skipped school—*wanna get out of here?*—and later when we walked endlessly through Thunder Bay: Trowbridge Falls, Soldier's Hole, Mount McKay. We wandered, which was new for both of us. I was used to hiding indoors with my mom, and Amber was used to being driven from one obligation to another—practice, school, gymnastics meet, repeat. In Thunder Bay, I associated "nature" with freezing winters, or with lakes and rivers that were in various states of post-industrial death—polluted, murky, dangerous. But with Amber I noticed the vast sky above us, the sunlight on my skin; there was beauty out there and it seemed to belong to her, to be created by her.

Then we arrived in Vancouver after driving across the country in an old Ford Galaxy that barely survived the trip, and the city seemed absurd to us, so idyllic it made us laugh. I remember Amber getting out of the car, dropping to her knees, and kissing someone's lawn. *It's so green it hurts!* You didn't even have to go anywhere special to be overwhelmed by growth: even our lawn now, in front of this shitty house, is a marvel of the blowsiest dandelion, the most fecund clover, the tallest spruce.

With Amber, I discovered that the world isn't a hostile place, or isn't wholly hostile; it's a place where you can sometimes feel at home.

Speaking of home, I don't have much interest in going outside now, without Amber—not that we did much wandering during these past years. Since my mom died, I lost interest. And it depressed Amber too much to visit natural spaces; she couldn't see anything but the effects of climate change. When you're in mourning, everything is loss, everything a reminder of death. So we stayed inside. We watched nature shows.

Now I'm happily sitting down to a *Twin Peaks* marathon when Bronwyn knocks at the door. She isn't holding any treats, which is disappointing 'cause those macaroons were good. Normally Amber would have taken them to her office for the sad women who work there. Amber doesn't consume sugar herself, of course, because it's a dangerously inflammatory drug, and it's given to *children*. She wrote a paper in grad school arguing that sugar—with its history of slavery and its link to obesity and countless deaths from diabetes— is the closest thing humanity has ever encountered to "pure evil" in the form of food. Her prof gave her a B, the worst mark of her academic career, because it was "inappropriate to include moral judgments in scientific discourse." Amber was furious—if you couldn't make moral judgments based on evidence, when could you make them? I read the paper and thought it was well argued; Amber wasn't wrong. But still, two days ago I ate that entire box of macaroons in one sitting.

"Hey, Kevin." Bronwyn looks different. Not wearing leggings and a tank top, but a dress that seems to have been ripped on purpose, tights that seem to have been ripped on purpose, army boots, lipstick. Like a hot, urban sorceress.

"Hey, Bron, you look nice." It just comes out of my mouth.

"I was in the neighborhood, so." She beams. "One of my friends played a gig at Bandidas. Thought I'd drop by?"

"It's, like, midnight."

"Yeah, but I just had this intuition that I should visit. 'Cause last time you seemed kinda." She shrugs at me. "Lost?"

"Sorry about that. About being a dick."

"No, I get it. My relationship with Atticus, you remember him? I'm *still* processing that." She leans against the doorframe. "I know it's not the same, we were only together for a couple of months. But it really messed me up."

She's definitely going to tell me about it, so I say, "Did it?"

"He was mean. Like, he told me once that I was *skinny-fat*. Have you heard that term?"

"That's a shitty move." This whole conversation reminds me of being a kid, comforting my mom after she went on one of a zillion crappy dates. "And it's not true. You have a great body."

She blushes. "Thank you."

"Do you want to come in?" It feels inevitable now. "I was just going to smoke a bowl."

"Are you sure?" She's already inside. "I can't stay long. I work tomorrow."

"What do you do? For work?"

"I'm starting this import business with my friend Yamuna." She props her umbrella against the door and unwinds her scarf. "Last year in Guatemala we met these craftswomen who make such incredible woven stuff—hats and bags. So we're working with them to sell it at markets. Fair trade, obviously."

"Obviously." I wait for the rest of it. If you ask someone who lives in Vancouver what they do for a living, you might as well settle in.

"And I work at Café Deux Soleils during the lunch rush. I also host their poetry slams."

"Of course."

"And I do zodiac readings. Sort of freelance. I *love* helping people. Everyone is dealing with, you know, questions about the future."

"You tell people their horoscopes." I sit next to her on the Voyager. "Freelance."

"Ascending sign, moon sign—I need my charts. It's way more complex than people think. Like, what's your sign?"

I finish packing the pipe. "Pisces."

"Knew it. Wow. I'm an Aquarian."

"Wow."

"Do you mind my asking? What's Amber?"

"Born in August. I think she's—"

"Leo? Oh my god. No wonder."

I light up, inhale. "No wonder what?"

"No, that's just a really tough combination. You guys being together this long is amazing."

I pass her the pipe and she tokes, eyes closed, and tells me that Mars will soon be in retrograde. Then says, "Oh shit. Sorry. Didn't mean to mention Mars."

Which strikes me as so ridiculous that I laugh, and she laughs, and for a second I'm happy she's here. Then I immediately wish Amber could see how happy I am.

"Do you do palm readings?" I hold out my hand and Bronwyn puzzles over my life line as though it were an olden-days paper map. Honestly, I just want someone to hold my hand.

"I don't know much about it," Bronwyn admits. "But my friend Carlos is a palm reader. It's such a deep practice."

I make listening noises while Bronwyn chats, and at around 1 a.m. she says, "Well, I've got work tomorrow, so."

Then she gives me an intense hug at the door, pressing the length of her body against mine.

THE SECOND WEEK IS A BLUR: HAIR, MAKEUP, WARDROBE, THEN shot after shot of the competitors running, laughing, strutting while the AD yells, *Stay fierce, people!* Flirting with Nick the producer, 'cause Amber wants him to like her. (She wants everyone to like her, especially Linnzy, who doesn't seem to like anyone.) Helping Pichu with her jumpsuit, which fits awkwardly over Pichu's layers of shapewear. Saying her own name so many times—*I am Amber Kivinen*—that she begins to experience a distancing of self from identity, an ego death like those sixties psychedelic hippies were always on about. But she just manages to sidestep that, to stay out of her own head, out of her own way—as an athlete, she trained herself to be in her body, to move instinctually, to rely on muscle memory and put aside all thoughts. If you become self-aware, you choke.

And when it's unstoppable, when she starts to get anxious, she crouches in a corner to pray. Like when she was a teenager, shoulder in a brace, and prayed to be healed so she could compete at the Olympics. Also prayed to remain injured so she wouldn't have to risk public humiliation, couldn't possibly lose. Ironic that she's at it again, begging the Lord to help her get to Mars, considering that space travel is a God-like act. And part of the reason she wants to go to Mars is to show God—that irritable, judgy, unhelpful bastard—who's boss. To beat Him at His own game. To win.

Because if she gets to Mars, she'll begin the grandest creation ever imagined by humanity: planetary ecosynthesis. Mars's atmosphere is 2 percent nitrogen, 2 percent argon, trace amounts of oxygen and carbon monoxide, and—most importantly—95 percent carbon dioxide. Which happens to be what plants breathe. Martian soil is a mineral-rich regolith—all you have to do is remove the toxins—and the Martian atmosphere contains 100 percent humidity, so plants could potentially drink water from the air. Flora is likely to thrive, given the right human-led circumstances. Within a few decades, as her plants inhale CO_2 and exhale O_2, Mars could become warm and humid and she could grow the garden of her dreams. Chaotic, overgrown—nothing like the tidy, hydroponic rows she keeps in the apartment. She would create Eden.

During her undergrad, she wrote a paper for her History of Science class called "The Importance of Scientific Failure: William Pickering and a Botanical Vision of Mars." She was trying to come to terms with failure, to understand it as essential for human advancement—she was, basically, failing to come to terms with failure. But she felt such fondness for Pickering, alone in his Jamaican viewing station during the First World War, sending out florid dispatches describing what he believed he saw of Mars through his telescope: blue coastlines, marshes teeming with vegetation, sheets of rain nourishing the ground. No civilization, no conflict, only pristine wilderness. A peaceful fantasy.

She could make it reality.

But she'd have to win and that seems insane. She's constantly sizing up the other competitors: Gabija from Lithuania, slight but ferocious; Marion from France, no clue how that one got here; Agneta from Sweden, some sort of pop star; Bernita who defected from Cuba to be on the show by crossing to Florida on a goddamn dinghy—probably tough as hell; Sergey from Ukraine, a chess master who must already be strategizing three moves ahead; Fernando from Argentina, unbelievably tall, maybe from all that Argentinian beef; Ramesh from India, super sweetheart and likely a mad genius; Ebad from Pakistan, has a stunning smile and will probably make a surge; Tish from New York, complete waste of time; Logan with the man bun, from the US, never shuts up; Adam from Israel, possible future husband; Pichu from Canada, pure gold; Tamiko from Japan, always talking about the designs she pioneered at MIT and perfected upon returning to Tokyo; Cawaale from Somalia, a mechanical engineer and the most beautiful person Amber has ever seen; Sarah from South Africa, an ex-con who currently performs as a contortionist in a circus; Justine from Alaska, a weight lifter and hunting guide who could probably put a bullet between your eyes; David from Norway, poker face, plays the ukulele; Jalal from Lebanon, total BDE; Steve from Australia, surfer's body, thinks he's funny; Adiya from Saudi Arabia, possibly a literal princess; Ying Yue from China, a geneticist and concert pianist; Zach Chan from Hong Kong, game designer and ballroom dance champ with amazing posture; Ha Joon from South Korea, skinny and reserved but likely a wild card.

And her. Amber Kivinen from Canada. How do the others see her? How does the world see her? She knows from going online that she's liked, but doesn't trust it. Is it just that she's hot? "Hot" doesn't last—especially since the makeup and crappy food are already making her break out and get *so* fat. And even if she keeps a grip on her looks—"maintains" the "natural" beauty that a woman isn't even supposed to be aware of—the conservatives are likely to dox and abuse her soon enough, once she starts opening her mouth and having opinions. And lately the progressives keep cultishly excommunicating their own—that's one of her fears: being canceled, disowned by her leftist tribe. How soon until everyone hates her? Until the public turns on her? Until they see that she's needy, sad, ambitious in that unlikable, Hillary Clinton way. *God sees everything.*

Not if you work hard enough. She learned that in gymnastics. If you focus all your energy, push your body until it nearly breaks, even God can't keep up.

FOR THE REST OF THE WEEK, THE ONLY HUMAN I SEE IS THE GOOD
Person who delivers my Good Food Box. Turns out he's not only
Good but also Cool. He helps run an organic farm near Tsawwassen.
Bastiaan from Tsawwassen. All those doubled letters make my day,
so I invite him in. He's unbelievably tall—I'm five nine, so he must be,
I dunno, eight feet?—and looks gigantic when he sits on our worn-
out Voyager. He tells me he has four kids, is married to a woman
named Cedar, and owns part of a racehorse.

"Which part? The ears?"

"I own a share. Such a beautiful animal. I almost don't care if he
makes us any money."

Bastiaan from Tsawwassen is a beautiful animal. Can a straight
guy say that about another guy? I have a man crush on Bastiaan, this
dude with a real wife, a real family, a real job—he's a *farmer*, for god's
sake. He's so tanned and healthy. He probably wakes up at six in
the morning, willingly. He probably knows how to forage for morels.
He probably writes earnest books about being Good, like Wendell
Berry. I feel like less of a loser just seeing him on my couch.

"Do you want to smoke a joint?" I say.

"I should get going. Got more deliveries to make." Bastiaan from
Tsawwassen gives me a little salute. "See you next week, my friend."

Once he leaves, I feel newly lonely. Even though I fry up leek and
kale and other Good Food for dinner, afterward I don't sleep properly and wake in the middle of the night gasping for air.

This used to happen when I was a kid, but when I opened my
eyes, my mom would be stroking my hair. *I'm here, honeybun. I'm
here.* Then she'd tell me a story.

*There once was a little alien named Kevin and he lived with his best
friend, a big old alien named Mommy. They were the only beings on their*

planet, which they called Home. They could circle their planet in three big skips. They could dance and run and spin through the air, because there was no gravity on Planet Home.

Now I get out of bed, scratch another line into the wall, then make some of Amber's herbal tea (organic tulsi, whatever that is) and try to read. *The Great Gatsby*, my desert-island book. Ticks all the boxes: party scenes, pretty girls, pathos. If I were still a writer, I'd want to create something like *Gatsby*: a story ostensibly about love but really about soul-crushing decadence. Ostensibly about decadence, but really about love.

Back in my early twenties, I had big plans to write a killer screenplay, then a best-selling novel. This is a common fantasy—screenwriters believe that once they make millions in the movie biz, they'll settle into their Cabo retreat and write a book. How hard can it be? Just words on a page! And book writers always think they can whip off a screenplay for kicks and cash, but instead end up with reams of beautiful scene description, soggy dialogue, and a story that goes nowhere. At least my stories *traveled.* (That might seem ironic, since now I don't leave the couch—but the brain is wider than the sky.) Amber used to love reading my stories and screenplays because *it's so fun to coast along on your weird imagination.* It was foreign to her, to make things up. Her singular focus on gymnastics meant that she had to forgo parts of childhood, including—she claimed—her imagination. So I created stories for both of us. And a couple of weeks ago, she asked me to write something for her.

"Write something? Just like that? The way balloon artists whip up sausage dogs?"

"I'm serious. It would make me happy." Then her true motivation: "It could be a fun project for you while I'm doing my Mars thing."

"Sorry, let me get this straight. While you're competing on a reality show that would allow you to depart from Planet Earth for all eternity, I'm supposed to sit down and write? As if I won't be distracted by the fact that my life is falling apart?"

"Life isn't falling apart." She rolled her eyes. "Life is . . . expanding."

"You sound like an Instagram post written by a white woman who's built her online brand selling whimsical cutlery or botanical-infused footwear or plant-based bras."

"See, that's funny! Write a story about that."

"Please don't treat me like a child who needs an assignment."

"I honestly feel like our lives are in flux, and it's stressful, but we need to *harness* it." She raised her hands to her head, pulled her hair in that adorable, anxious way. "Everything happens for a reason, you know?"

"Also don't use the phrase *everything happens for a reason*—Amber? For real. It's offensive to survivors of rape, abuse, murder . . ."

"Oh yeah." She snorted. "We wouldn't want to offend 'murder survivors.'"

I won't be writing her a story. Not going to happen. Because years ago, I wrote and wrote but never found an audience. When only two people think you're gifted—and those two are your mom and your girlfriend—you gotta get real with yourself. And when one of those two people dies . . . In short, I gave up. Instead of stories, I dedicated my life—this one and only life—to my sweet, loving Zelda.

Put another way: I realized that Amber is a planet, and I'm a moon in her orbit, and I'm okay with that.

Hey, fun lunar fact: if I were on Mars, awake during a dark night like this, I might look up and see two small moons. Mars's moons are believed to be made of the primordial matter of the solar system, the stuff that existed before anything else: water, sticky tars and oils, amino acids. Their names—Phobos and Deimos—mean *fear* and *terror*.

THEY HAVE ONE DAY OFF. AMBER TRIES TO SLEEP IN, EATS A COBB salad for breakfast, has an Epsom salt bath, then visits Adam.

When he opens his door, he has only a towel around his waist. His shoulders—they're so . . . *shoulder-y*. Muscled, masculine. She's used to Kevin, slim and cute with his big, tousled hair, green eyes, ears that stick out a bit, wrinkled T-shirts. Adam's ears are minuscule. His muscles look like they've been carved from stone. His dark hair is clipped short, nails bitten to the quick, clothing never creased.

"Is it too early?" she asks. "I can come back."

"I have been awake since five."

It's 8 a.m. and Pichu's still sleeping; Adam says his roommate, Steve the Australian, is out surfing. Amber waits while Adam gets dressed and realizes that no one knows she's here. Not her roommate, not Kevin, not the cameras that now follow her even in dreams.

They lie in Adam's closet again, under those heat lamps, and her jaw unclenches, her shoulders drop. It's strange how quiet they are together, despite how well they know each other. For the past year, they monitored each other's ketones and glucose levels through their shared Nutrit app, tracked each other's runs and bike rides on Strava, sent each other endless photos and links and Spotify playlists. Communicating via text, they confessed everything: Adam said that when he'd left the Orthodox community, he had to break off his engagement to the girl his parents had set him up with, whom he'd met only once. He missed his family, his brother most of all, but what woke him at night was wondering about that girl. Malka. Had she found another husband? Or had his abandonment ruined her chances? Was she now deemed damaged goods?

And Amber confessed about her relationship: that Kevin was probably depressed but she didn't know how to help him; how the more she tried, the more helpless he seemed to become; how she veered between worrying about him and resenting how he made her worry. But she must have been depressed too—how else to explain that she'd worked as a receptionist and drug dealer for over eight years when she had a master's degree?

She also confessed that it felt like her whole life, even the failures, were leading her to Mars. If she hadn't injured her shoulder, she wouldn't have moved to Vancouver for school. If she hadn't been depressed in Vancouver, she never would have stayed home and learned about hydroponics. If she hadn't learned about hydroponics, she wouldn't have made it onto MarsNow.

Did it feel that way to him? Inevitable?

Yes, Adam wrote. *We have been chosen.*

But now, with him in the same room, she feels tongue-tied and timid.

"So you do CrossFit, right?" As if she doesn't already know. But it's a start. "Incredible, right?"

"I did an Israel-wide competition two years ago. I'm addicted."

"I'd love to compete. But my shoulder."

Gradually conversation blossoms in the closet: they talk about how the paleo diet changed their lives. About the other contestants—how Tish and Steve are perfect for each other. The rumor that Justine gave herself a Brazilian wax *by herself*, spread-eagled on the bathroom floor and propping a mirror in front of her vag. About Sarah, the contortionist, hooking up with Fernando—it was *so* obvious. About whether a drug test would pick up microdoses of LSD. About California and Israel and how scary it is to be in a desert when the whole planet is about to burn. About how maybe they don't have to worry about the climate crisis anymore, since they might get off this sinking ship—and is it evil to have thoughts like that? Yes, absolutely evil. But seriously, for *real*, they think MarsNow might actually *help* the environmental movement because the show offers an enormous platform to recognize the importance of science. Plus, most of what we know about climate change is thanks to space-based observation; climate action and astral exploration are not in conflict.

She tells him about that seminar course she took for her master's degree, the one that altered her life. *Ethics at the End of the World: Ecological Practice and Principles in the Era of Climate Change.* "We debated everything. Do humans have the right to eat other animals? Do wealthy countries owe reparations to poorer ones disproportionately affected by climate change? Do developing nations have the right to emit carbon to pull their citizens out of poverty? Should Canada give land back to Indigenous people?"

She learned why Kyoto failed—because of an ascending neoliberal ethos that gave rights to markets instead of living beings—and most devastatingly, learned what it meant if humanity acted and if we didn't. What it might mean if the world warmed by 2 degrees, or 3.5, or 5.

Flood.

Fire.

Drought.

Famine.

Pandemics.

War.

She wasn't an idiot. It wasn't the first time she'd given thought to global warming. But it was the first time she'd understood it. Felt it. *I was blind, but now I see.* Her childhood terrors—engendered when her father gave deep-voiced readings of Revelation—were coming true, but not thanks to any god. Thanks to human beings. Thanks to *her.* So she began one of her many flirtations with veganism. She attended rallies. She schooled people on Facebook when they posted photos of their new cars or beach vacations. She refused to fly home for Christmas, even though it broke her mother's heart. She started growing vegetables on the back deck, started to learn about plants. She became pure and resolute and uncompromising and it felt *good.* For a while. Until she faltered. Went on a run, forgot her water bottle, and in a fit of dehydration bought a single-use plastic water bottle flown in from fucking Fiji. Then promptly had a panic attack on the sidewalk and only avoided total public mortification by remembering that she had an Ativan in the pocket of her windbreaker.

She went home that day, sat on the Voyager in her sweaty clothes, listened to the ticking of the fridge, and understood that she was nothing. Powerless, weak, unable to stop the inevitable, unable to even curb her own sinful desire for imported water. The fridge's clicks, in the otherwise silent apartment, sounded like a clock ticking down to extinction.

She should have been out doing fieldwork. Measuring, counting, tagging. Trying to save what was left. Instead she would soon become a receptionist at a goddamn conference center, a gardener who ignored her containers on the deck and let the veggies die, because what was the point? The problem was so big, so overwhelming. A few consumer choices weren't going to cut it, but what else could she do? *Choices* were the problem. Humans must make them, and every choice involves loss. Every choice is a death. And we hate death, are terrified of death, will do any depraved thing to avoid even its shadow. We are unwilling to sacrifice. Unable to cooperate. How to fight our own nature? It was over. The end.

She was Wile E. Coyote: she'd been running, so fast and focused, but now—she'd looked down. Saw that beneath her feet was nothing but air. She fell and fell. All winter, Vancouver's gray sky wept tears that mirrored her grief for this dying world. This world that she herself had killed.

"It is bad, yes," says Adam, his skin aglow under the red lights. "But we can only help in ways that are possible, that match our capacity."

"I know." She loves this about him, the way he remains logical even in the face of horror. She used to be like that too; at her strongest, as an athlete, she could compartmentalize any thought that did not serve her sport. And the Mars endeavor is helping her regain this superpower. She's emerging from years of despair. "You know,

I compost. Bring reusable bags to the grocery store. But sometimes I just want to escape. Find a safe place. A calm place.". She used to imagine herself in some wet, idyllic, West Coast refuge—maybe on a Gulf Island—growing her own food, raising chickens. But it's gone too far now; there is nowhere without danger. She was haunted for months by the words of a scientist studying the effects of intensive forestry on wildlife. *Birds used to be able to escape the clear-cuts, to find shelter elsewhere, but now the forest is so fragmented. There's nowhere to go.*

There is nowhere safe on Earth. No shelter from what will come. From what has begun.

"Is it wrong?" she asks. "To want to escape?"

"No." Adam kisses her forehead, like a priest bestowing a blessing. "You deserve safety, Amber. You deserve peace."

She closes her eyes, breathes. "I keep having this fantasy. This idea for a Martian garden." It's embarrassing to admit how clearly she sees this vision. "But if we genetically engineer plants to withstand more radiation, less atmospheric pressure, less nitrogen than on Earth—in just decades, Mars could be like a jungle. And plants produce oxygen, so eventually the planet would become habitable for us." She sits up in the closet. "I know it's not that simple, but Mars used to be warm and wet, right? As far as we know. It's not meant to be arid and frigid, so we'd be righting something that's gone wrong."

Returning what has fallen to a state of grace.

"Rather than engineer the whole planet," Adam says as he sits cross-legged, tilting toward her under the warm light, "we could genetically modify our own bodies. Reengineer human lungs and blood cells to split the carbon atom from the CO_2 molecule. Code humans with genetic material to allow us to withstand radiation."

"I never thought of that."

"We already use this technology to cure disease," he says. "Why not to improve human performance on Mars?"

"It makes total sense."

"At the very least, we should be changing human egg and sperm cells to allow our progeny to flourish on Mars."

He blushes, maybe at his mention of *our progeny*. Amber smiles, looks down, examines her hands. "Totally."

When they're done in the closet-sauna, they drink kombucha and eat grass-fed beef liver pâté with flax-seed crackers, roasted cauliflower sprinkled with za'atar, and halva that Adam made himself using raw honey, bee pollen, and sprouted sesame seeds.

They compare biceps and abs and the muscle definition of their quads; they arm-wrestle; they grapple playfully on the floor. They end up panting and laughing in each other's arms. She thinks for sure he'll kiss her now, but instead he says, "Do you do yoga nidra?" and they lie awkwardly on his bed to listen to a meditation track.

Relax your tongue in your mouth.

Relax your eyes in their sockets.

Relax the right hemisphere of your brain.

Now the left.

She falls asleep around the time the voice asks her to *imagine your vagus nerve, running from your cranium all the way to your colon*, then wakes to see Adam smiling at her.

He brushes hair from her eyes. "You're tired."

Maybe because he's a doctor, she finds herself admitting that she has heartburn all the time lately, that she's taking a laxative before each day's shoot, that she isn't sleeping well.

He nods gravely and rummages in his suitcase. Then comes back with a whole kit: Betaine HCL to help her digest and access nutrients. A spore-based probiotic. Some 5-HTP and GABA supplements for sleep. A prescription for low-dose naltrexone, which will bring down inflammation. A small vial of CBD oil, not detectable in a drug test, to calm the endocannabinoid system. And—if all else fails—a couple of sleeping pills and a handful of little ampules of pure caffeine to add to her chai in the mornings.

"Thank you." She's not used to being cared for. She's usually the strong one, the tough one, the one who keeps the op running, the one who plans the meals and travel and sex, the one who nags Kevin to put the weed away and get up off the couch, the one who says things like, *This weekend we need to clean the bathroom or I'll blow my brains out.* "This is—you're wonderful."

"It's nothing. I took a Hippocratic oath."

"Yeah, but—" She might burst into tears. "I should go. Pichu and I planned to watch the first episode together. You want to join?"

"No, thank you. I can't watch myself on a screen. It will only make me act unnatural."

"Seriously? You're not going to watch at all?"

"I am also self-conscious about my chin."

"You have a fantastic chin." She smiles. "But I get it. It's probably better to just pretend we're not on TV."

"I pretend I'm doing military exercises—the repetitiveness, the long days, the hierarchy. I'm too comfortable in such situations."

"I think it's cool. I mean, you're driven." Amber holds the bag of supplements and meds in one hand and waves with the other. "Anyway. Thank you."

"Of course. We are a team."

They high-five, which they both find hilariously platonic. Then he holds her to his chest. Her cheek against his T-shirt.

"Go now, Amber," he says. "I want to keep you, but I can't steal from Pichu."

I PACE THE APARTMENT—GETTING MY STEPS IN!—AND EXAMINE what Amber left behind. The MarsNow people advised her to pack for "all eventualities," so she stuffed a duffel with a bathing suit, shorts, thermal underwear, yoga pants, dresses, sweaters, tank tops, hiking boots, sneakers, sandals, a coat, mittens, and a tuque. But everything else she owns is here, with me. The set of weights I got for her birthday, stashed in a corner of the living room. Her yoga mat, dirty from years of use. The pens and highlighters and half-filled notebooks from her student days. The graveyard of dead iPods and phones she always means to recycle but never does. The seashell she took home from Mexico when we spent Christmas there with her family. The jade apple her friend Reza gave her for good luck, shiny and cool to the touch. Her bookshelf: George Monbiot, Naomi Klein, bell hooks, Margaret Atwood, Brian Greene, Yuval Noah Harari, Michael Pollan, Doris Lessing. A history of her mind. And the CDs she couldn't bring herself to get rid of, dusty in a box at the back of the closet, a compendium of junior high girl crushes: Portishead, Dixie Chicks, Tori Amos. Her vibrator, in its little linen pouch. Her pillow, which still smells of her hair.

I hate her for leaving. Maybe I should pretend she's dead? Let her lie in her Martian grave.

Except then her sister calls, which doesn't help me to forget about my girlfriend because Caleigh has the same vocal inflections as Amber, the same impatience, the same laugh. Though she's not laughing now. She opens with, "I could kill her, Kevin. I actually want to destroy my sister."

"Is that . . . new?"

"Going to *Mars?* I'm sorry, but it's embarrassing. And it's stressing my parents out so bad."

"They seemed cool with it when we saw them. They were all blasé."

"Can you *not* speak French to me right now?"

"Why don't you get your dad to talk to her? She'd listen to him."

"You know them. They trust in the Lord. They paid some You-Tube preacher five hundred dollars to pray for her." Caleigh sighs. "I'm mad at you. You should have stopped her."

"Have you ever tried to stop her? From doing anything?"

"It's all going to fall on me," says Caleigh. "*Again*. Like when she ran away with you to Vancouver and my dad had a breakdown."

Caleigh remembers it as a painful time for her parents. I remember it as devastating for Amber. Her father disowned her. Said to Amber: *I don't have a daughter. My daughter is dead.* Forced her to choose between her love for him and for me—and I'll never forget that she chose me.

"How's Starbucks?" I ask, because Caleigh manages a Thunder Bay location and this connects us—the fact that her parents consider us both to be losers with no ambition.

"Everyone on my staff is either sixteen years old or acts like it," says Caleigh. "Does she ever think about anyone but herself?"

"Are we back on Amber?"

"Maybe when she's gone to Mars, my parents will finally notice that I'm alive. Maybe they won't think the sun shines out her ass anymore."

When she's gone to Mars. After Caleigh hangs up, I pace the apartment again, picking up Amber's belongings. Each item seems to pulse with life, with use, with love. It was the same after my mom died: I paced her house, the one I'd grown up in, surrounded by her DVD collection, her filmy flowered blouses, the jumbo bottles of ibuprofen, the books with titles like *The Arthritis Solution* and *Anti-Inflammatory Recipes*. And the relics of her pre-pain days: cracked leather boots she wore when she was into punk music, her framed diploma in architectural drafting, photographs of her holding me when I was a swaddled newborn. And the chaos—I knew she'd been feeling bad, had gone on disability, but thought she was coping okay. Until I saw the garage stacked with pizza boxes crawling with flies. Wilting grocery-store flowers in a vase on her kitchen counter. Dirty dishes piled in the sink. The bathroom drain so clogged with hair and toothpaste-sludge that it smelled of rot.

How long had she lived like this? I should have visited more, called more. Because who was around to help her? To stop her?

And when did it start? When did she lose hope? When her immune system started attacking her own cartilage? When her bones began to shift out of place? When her body no longer felt like home.

I sat on the couch in our living room. There were practicalities to deal with: probate, paying funeral costs, emptying the house. But I was unable to stir for hours, my body and brain frozen. I knew I should cry but no tears came. Sunlight moved along the floor, illuminating dust in the air. Could I go on? Could I live in this world? A world where my mother died in a house full of dirty dishes and TV dinners?

But Amber's not dead yet. And I keep replaying that moment in the pub, with her parents, when she said, *I'm not actually going to win.* If she doesn't believe in her own endeavor, why should I? I do not accept that she's abandoned the hoodie with the silkscreen dinosaur, the one she calls her "cozy." I do not believe she's forgotten her jade apple. In fact, surrounded by her stuff, I come to a decision: I will not leave this apartment, this shrine to our life together, until my girlfriend comes home. It's like not shaving your beard for the playoff season, except even more nonsensical. I will stare at these walls with their faded rental-white paint job. At the grease-splattered stove in our galley kitchen. At the scratchy brown carpet. My only outdoor view will be of East 12th's sidewalk. I might seem slothful and reclusive, but I'm doing important work. I am refusing to leave the garden. Hoping that my loyalty, my stiff-necked stubbornness, will convince Yahweh to let Eve back in. I will summon her—my interstellar traveler, my rebel, my girlfriend of fourteen years—through stillness.

WHEN AMBER RETURNS TO HER APARTMENT, PICHU'S ON THE
couch eating chips.

"I know it looks like I'm being lazy," says Pichu, "but I'm actually practicing my Kegels."

"Don't work too hard."

"I'm trying to give you privacy, but I can't take it anymore. What's going *on?*"

"What do you mean?"

"I wake up and you're not here," says Pichu. "You're gone all day. Then you walk in looking all flushed."

"Those infrared lamps are great for your skin too."

"Is Mr. Universe a good kisser?"

"Nothing happened."

The chip bag flies across the room. "What?" Pichu pouts. "But *why?*"

"I've turned over a new leaf and am trying to be a good human. No more cheating on my boyfriend."

"Don't mean to state the obvious, but if you're going to Mars, what does it matter?"

But Amber probably isn't going to Mars. A conclusion based purely on stats: her odds of winning are one in twelve, which equals only an 8.3 percent chance. She must assume that at some point she's heading home.

And maybe she wants to go home. Part of her misses him.

"Anyway." She throws herself on the couch. "Adam said he doesn't want to sully our connection by starting off in a morally compromised way."

"He said the word *sully?*"

"He said he's *seeking purity* at this point in his life."

"Oh, what a waste. If that tall drink of water were interested in me, I'd be all: *Tie me up, Leonard Cohen.*" Pichu slides off the couch and crawls toward the chip bag. "I was never into bondage when I was married—like, why make the metaphor literal?—but now I keep wondering about it."

"He also kept talking about *directing the energy.* Said that I should try to harness our erotic charge and focus it on my relationship. Said that's what he would want me to do if I were his girlfriend."

"That's . . . generous?"

"Said, *You can't control your feelings, but you can control what you do with those feelings.*"

"So much talking."

"Also said we shouldn't let our mutual attraction distract us from the Mars mission."

"Mm-kay."

"Do you think that's possible? To channel this erotic energy into my relationship? I mean, I want to be a good person. What if I only have a couple months left on Earth? For once in my life, I want to do it right."

"You've been fucking Kevin since high school, correct?"

"And he's great. No one makes me laugh like he does."

"Since *high school.* And now you want to have grown-up-woman sex with him? Good luck with that."

"What if I end up on Mars with someone horrible? Like that Australian guy. What if this is my last chance to have hot sex before I die?"

"Welcome to my life. Every straight woman over thirty-five is asking herself that question all the time." Pichu pours the last of the chips into her mouth. "Well, you've broken my heart. But guess what airs in t-minus one minute?"

Amber sits on the couch. "I might throw up."

"Puke in this." Pichu passes her the empty chip bag, then flips on the TV.

MARCUS ARRIVES WITH A PLAN TO GET "SUPER BAKED" BECAUSE the show airs tonight. He also brings a rotisserie chicken from Safeway, tortilla chips, salsa, and a jar of that orange cheese dip that tastes shamefully good when you microwave it. "I know you don't drink anymore, but I brought beer," he says. "Special occasion."

"Don't fuck me up. Drink it all yourself or take it home when you go."

"No problemo, amigo." Then he hesitates. "But Amber's gone. So you can do whatever you want, right?"

I gave up drinking a few years ago when Amber went booze-free to protest the hypocrisy of a government that allows the legal consumption of the most emotionally, physically, and financially harmful substance in the world—alcohol—but doesn't let people with cancer smoke a joint to ease their pain. Her sobriety was kinda like Gandhi's hunger strike. And once Amber had gone off the sauce I followed her lead because she became hypersensitive to it; when I drank, she'd say things like, *You smell like someone pickled you. I wonder if Lenin's body reeks like this.* I just wanted my girlfriend to kiss me, but I don't know if she ever appreciated my sacrifice. During the era of craft breweries, I gave up booze for her.

I crack a beer now and Marcus throws his fist in the air. "Yasssssss!"

We smoke a bowl and Marcus tries to talk about things that matter more than Amber: Brad and Angelina's divorce, Bieber's abs, illegal wildlife poaching.

Then it begins.

Typical shit: loud music, flashing lights, a hostess with unbelievable hair (Amber is always drilling into me that all the hair on TV is fake). Then CGI representations of a future colony on Mars—a bustling metropolis under inflatable domes—and a parade of talking heads. Scientists from NASA, Neil deGrasse Tyson, an astronaut named Dirk Riley who speaks from on board the International Space Station to tell us that *this is the most thrilling mission humanity has ever attempted!* There's a live audience of shrieking people that makes you think that perhaps some sort of mass human-extinction event would be a good thing.

I could have been in the audience. Isn't that what MarsNow director of Casting, Communications, and Commitment Helena Slora offered? I could sit front row, holding an *I [heart] Amber* sign. I could cheer and smile as MarsNow tries to steal my girlfriend forever.

I refused this once-in-a-lifetime opportunity.

Helena Slora also suggested that I might make a donation to MarsNow via PayPal and receive a small replica of the Lockheed Martin MarsNow Lander to show off to my friends. Or I could have my name printed on one of the landing parachutes. Or perhaps I'd like to virtually travel alongside my girlfriend via my own Mars selfie?

"Here we are, Marsonauts!" says the host, Bridget. She can't move most of the muscles of her face, but she can widen her eyes in imitation of human empathy. "How's everybody feeling?"

No one is eliminated tonight because the first episode is our chance to meet the competitors; next week we have the pleasure of seeing two of them—one man and one woman—get their dreams crushed. The idea is that "the citizens of Planet Earth will choose the Marsonauts," meaning audience members call in to vote for the people they most hate, the people they most want eliminated from the ranks. This makes no sense: we should vote to eliminate the ones we love so that they won't be sent light-years away from us. (Typical. People are always voting against their interests.)

A message flashes along the bottom of the screen, classy like an infomercial, telling us to visit www.marsnowandforever.com or to call 1-900-Mars-Now to cast our votes.

I admit it's pretty good TV. I already have some favorites. Tamiko, thirty-nine, from Japan: a yoga instructor with a PhD in astronautical engineering. She's also super hot, so there are tons of shots of her doing sun salutations.

Ramesh, twenty-six, from India. He has a good story, which he illuminates on his website: "I am a computer systems analyst, mentally nimble and intuitive. Working at my parent's *vada pav* stall since age nine, I found time for my studies at night. My motivation for flying to Mars comes from being an out-and-proud gay man, but being told for many years by my own country that I was a criminal. I wish only to be unrestricted in my soul. I also do stand-up comedy acts."

Marion, forty-six, from France. A hairdresser who happens to have a photographic memory; Marcus predicts she'll be better than all the others at remembering flight procedure and physics.

Sergey, fifty-one, a chess champion from Ukraine and the least TV-appropriate of all the contestants—his gray hair sticks up and his accent is ridiculous and he says things that don't quite fit into sound bites. "I would like, on Mars, to create a more logical society, free from judgment and hatred. This will be difficult. This will be the true challenge. Technology cannot solve this."

Pichu, who seems to have no qualifying attributes other than being adorable. But then she assures her own stardom by grabbing Zach, the shy ballroom dancer from Hong Kong, and doing a waltz—the moment goes instantly viral.

And of course there are a bunch of douchey guys. Logan from the US, that know-it-all type of dude; he's got a man bun, strong jawline, some sort of bamboo farm. And Steve from Australia— do I even need to describe him? There's only one type of guy from Australia: tanned, loud, probably drunk. And then there's Adam, from Israel. In his own words: "I am a physician who believes that a healthy mind and body is essential to self-actualization. I served in the Israeli Defense Forces, trained to work in avionics. I want to increase human flourishing: spiritual freedom, bodily autonomy, and intellectual liberty."

Adam, from Israel. Soulful brown eyes and smug cheekbones. I don't know why, but I hate that guy.

And amid them all is Amber Kivinen. Passably charming, incurably dishonest, sexy as hell. I have to admit: she's got it. You know, *it*. Hard to take your eyes off her. She has a look, like some sort of hippie Amazon. The wild hair, the toned muscles, the tattoo, the lip ring, the freckles. And she has an instinct for how to sell herself. Hers is a conversion narrative: she was once a failed gymnast, an underemployed millennial, a criminal who'd been charged with marijuana possession, a woman edging toward her (gasp!) unmarried mid-thirties. According to her one-on-one intro clip, hosted by a guy we might as well call Ryan Seacrest 'cause he comes from the same factory, before MarsNow Amber was depressed and "going nowhere." Yes, she had a loving family and a boyfriend (that's me!), but "something was missing." Her story might not be any better than yours or mine, but raised in her father's church, she knows how to sell it. *I was lost, but now am found.*

"This is what I'm meant to do with my life." She speaks breathlessly, in fast-cut TV segments. "This is real. I can feel it."

"*This is real*," says Marcus in a high-pitched voice. "*I can feel it.*"

I go to her Instagram. She now has over 200,000 followers. Strangers—men, women, and children—telling her that she's beautiful, that they love her, that they remember her from gymnastics camp, that they're obsessed with her hair, that they'd love to partner with her to expand their market reach, that they wish the camera would pan down because her feet are probably "crazy erotic," and that she is a KWEEN! I could scroll forever. They keep sending her *so much love* and *all the vibes* and *good luck!!!!!!!!*

Now *I* can feel it: this might be a problem. A dilemma. Amber might not get eliminated for some time. Or ever. And therefore, I might not be able to deal with this whole Mars phase by waiting around for a week or two on the couch and scratching a dozen lines on the wall.

I pick up my phone, which is the best and only course of action in the modern world, and text Amber: *Will you marry me?*

I do this every year or two, ask her to marry me. And she usually says something like, *Careful what you wish for!* and both of us are relieved and pretend it never happened. But this time I wonder: Will she say yes? If only 'cause it would be a great story arc for the show?

I wait; Marcus talks at me; I wait some more. No reply.

So I text Tanya Vargas, of the two-second sex at the bonfire: *Hey.* Then: *What's up?* Then, feeling inspired: *You keep blazing into my thoughts. Burned into my mind. Haha.*

She doesn't text back. Obviously.

Marcus is pretty drunk by now and I'm pretty stoned but somehow the pot isn't working—I'm still feeling it, that low-level pain, that cramping in my gut that seems to keep time with my heart: *she's gone, she's gone, she's gone.* The Mars show is over, so Marcus and I are watching some soft-core European crap on Bravo, and my phone is resting in my upturned palm. It's hard to know what to blame—technology, loneliness, my own dumb hands?—but for some reason, I text Bronwyn, of the vegan macaroons.

Hey.

LH͟ //

"OWEE, OWEE, OWEE," MOANS PICHU ON THE FLIGHT TO MANAGUA, Nicaragua.

"Are you sure about this?" Amber yanks another gray hair from Pichu's scalp. "Maybe you should dye them?"

"This is cheaper."

"Are you poor?"

"Pull them out." Pichu grips the armrests. "They need to learn a lesson."

Amber wants to squeeze this delightful person—it's been years since she had a real female friend. Her relationships with the girls at gymnastics were constricted and competitive—and after her injury, how many of them visited or called? Then she had fitness buddies and a university clan, but avoided them during her embarrassing receptionist years and those friendships withered like the veggies neglected on the deck. And the ladies at work don't count.

There's something wrong with Amber, something other women can smell, something that warns them away.

The only real girlfriend she ever had was Evie at summer camp. Evie, with her flyaway hair like someone had rubbed her head with a wool mitten. She and Amber used to wander around in matching cutoffs, arm in arm, laughing breathlessly at inside jokes. Until gymnastics took over Amber's life, they attended Big Belief Evangel Kids Camp for a week every summer, and between camp sessions, exchanged letters that borrowed the passionate language of the church to express their obsessive friendship. Amber's missives would open with *My beloved!* and end with exhortations for Evie to *feel Jesus's presence, I'm residing with Him too, and I've been counting down. Camp starts in seven months and three days!*

Weird. Amber hasn't thought of Evie in years. Or of Big Belief and the brief, bizarre era when Amber was the star of Bible camp. When she happily pledged to fight the war against abortion; when she paddled a canoe to nearby campgrounds and handed out leaflets titled *Have You Met the Light of Jesus?* When she preached to the other kids in the dining hall that doubled as the worship hall, lifting her hands and channeling her father's voice. *Faith is a gift! But it's not given for free. You must walk with Him!* The others, even Evie, seemed to worship her.

"You're all done." Amber brushes Pichu's gray hairs from her palms. "What next? Need me to pop any zits?"

"Help me apply hemorrhoid cream?" Pichu props a pillow against Amber's shoulder. "JK. I'm going to sleep."

Soon Pichu snores peacefully against Amber's shoulder, and Amber posts a photo of them to Instagram (#friendshipgoals #sleepy #cute #travel) that ends up being her most popular post to date. Which is good timing, because as they're landing, Linnzy walks down the plane's aisle with a large steel lockbox that has an opening in the top like a piggybank.

"Listen up, guys. It's time. All your phones in here please."

"How long will you hold on to them?" says Tish, who always travels in a pair of silk pajamas because she has a sponsorship deal with some organic loungewear company.

"They're *confiscated*," says Linnzy. "Gone. Until you get eliminated or you go to Mars."

"Oh my god, it was a question." Tish grips her phone to her satiny chest. "What if there's, like, an emergency?"

"Tish." Because they're filming even now, Amber makes her face *fierce*. "You think you'll be checking your follows from space?" Then she unclips her seat belt, stands, and struts down the aisle toward the lockbox, like she's in *The Matrix*. Who even *is* she? Amber holds out her phone. Stomach-clench: it feels like her umbilical cord will be cut. All nutrition lost.

But this way she'll have an excuse for why she hasn't answered Kevin's text.

What's worse? That he asked her to marry him via *text message* or that she hasn't replied?

"I'm not here to get followers. I'm not an influencer," Amber says. "I'm down for the cause. I'm here for the mission."

She drops her phone in the box, and everyone on the plane gives her a round of applause.

AMBER'S BEEN GONE ONE WEEK AND I FOCUS ON RUNNING THE OP.
Keep the lights the correct distance from the roots, maintain the
water's pH at 5.8, feed the plants a homemade cocktail of nitrogen,
phosphorus, potassium, and magnesium in the form of Epsom salts,
along with a teaspoon of micronutrient mix that contains copper,
zinc, iron, molybdenum, chloride, and manganese. Just living my
life, not thinking about the fact that I have a date with Bronwyn. A
"date." A date-like event. Obviously not a real date, because I have a
girlfriend.

Bronwyn brings over ramen from Noodle Head, and I suggest we
watch a movie.

"Sure." She has a sweet, lopsided smile. "What do you want to
watch?"

"Only the best dance film ever made: *Dirty Dancing.*"

Which *is* my favorite movie because I grew up watching it with my
mom, though I'm also aware that straight women respond to Patrick
Swayze fervently and you can sometimes just stand in the way of that
fervor and it'll get transferred to you. (Not that I'm angling for Bronwyn's sexual passion. The idea of *doing it*—having total, actual sex—
with someone other than Amber feels about as plausible as letting a
helium balloon carry me to Mars. But. If Bronwyn flirts with me, I'll
flirt back, which is not illegal.)

Slurping the ramen is a bit like how I imagine it would feel to
eat worms, but not in a bad way. We sit on the couch, and just that,
sitting on a couch beside a woman, makes me feel that old, familiar
comfort—that *rightness*. I have an urge to hold Bronwyn, to cradle
her dreadlocked head against my chest.

Flashback. Interior. Evening. To when I was a kid, basically every
time my mom didn't feel well. I'd make a big pot of Kraft Dinner or

teriyaki chicken from a jar, and we'd rent a bunch of movies. Then I'd sit beside her on the couch, and roll her cigarettes or massage eucalyptus oil into the joints of her hands and wrists. We sometimes spent whole weekends inside, blinds drawn, watching one VHS tape after another. Each movie held us rapt. When one ended, we emerged from the dream together—long enough to open a bag of Oreos, rewind and eject the tape, and choose another movie. If we liked the film, we'd write the title on our ranked Best Ever list. If it was a "turkey"—Mom's word—we'd talk about how to improve it: different casting, different ending. We might hear distant sounds of kids having snowball fights or racing around on bicycles, and Mom would say, *You should go play outside, honey*, but she never meant it. I would snuggle against her side, her arm around me, both of us under the same quilt. *It's just you and me against the world, honeybun. Isn't it?* she would say. And I knew that it was: the world was a shit place. In the world, out there, her bosses wouldn't give her sick leave, so she'd have to take days without pay—and that brought more problems because the world, out there, was also full of banks and credit card companies and utility firms that had no understanding of a single mom doing her best. The world, out there, also harbored her parents, who'd never helped her in their lives—just drank too much and made each other miserable. The world also contained her brother, that tight-ass who lectured her every time she asked for a bit of assistance even though it was a *fucking loan*, she'd pay him back. And the world, out there, contained my father. Somewhere. He'd been a trucker for a forestry company who (in the one story my mother told of him) learned she was pregnant when she called him long distance. *Then he hung up on me. I was nineteen and fully heartbroken. Could barely get out of bed. I kept meaning to make an appointment at the clinic for a termination but time kept passing, honeybun, and I couldn't move.*

Then what happened? I'd ask, pressing myself against her, grabbing a handful of her soft belly.

Well, you got bigger and one day you got the hiccups and it made me laugh. I pictured you all safe and snug in that little amniotic sac. And I knew you'd come to save me.

I made my mom laugh—saved her entire life—before I was even born. So what happened at the end? Why couldn't I save her then?

Anyway. Sad-mom memories are not appropriate for this date-like event with Bronwyn (which I may have orchestrated out of an immature need for revenge on Amber). I pop in the DVD because we still own a DVD player for exactly this purpose: watching *Dirty Dancing*.

Then Bronwyn and I sit stiffly while two beautiful people fall in love and have great sex on-screen. I say some of the lines along with the actors—*I carried a watermelon*—and Bronwyn does me the favor of laughing. I nearly cry toward the end, mouthing the words along with Baby:

Me? I'm scared of everything. I'm scared of what I saw, I'm scared of what I did, of who I am, and most of all I'm scared of walking out of this room and never feeling the rest of my whole life the way I feel when I'm with you.

When the movie's over, Bronwyn says, "This was fun. Thanks for inviting me."

"Thanks for coming. Like, really. 'Cause I don't leave the house."

She laughs because she thinks I'm joking. "So . . . did you watch the show the other day?"

"What show? Oh, you mean the Mars thing?"

Bronwyn scoots a little closer. "I'm just curious 'cause—are you guys together? I mean, is this a date? Or?"

"Do you want it to be a date?"

"I guess so. Do you?" She fiddles with one of her dreads. "But I don't want to come between you and Amber, 'cause she's my friend, and." Bronwyn puts the dreadlock in her mouth, which doesn't seem sanitary. "But if you're not together anymore?"

"I mean, we haven't really defined things."

"But how do you feel about her? About her maybe going to Mars?"

How do I *feel?*

I stand up, offer Bronwyn my hand. "Nobody puts Baby in the corner." I dance her around the Voyager, wondering what Amber is doing right now, wondering if it's Bronwyn's hair or skin or soul that smells like patchouli—

Then she kisses me, and I kiss her back, which is definitely illegal.

Our tongues inside each other's mouths remind me of the ramen, but not in a bad way.

WHEN THEY LAND, THE COMPETITORS ARE RUSHED THROUGH CUS-
toms, then greeted for a photo op by Nicaragua's president and his
wife, who arrived in separate Rolls-Royces. Then the competitors are
piled into vans and taken to the foot of a volcano. Each is assigned
a pack to carry and told that their first test will be to navigate and
climb their way to the top, while also collecting soil, rock, flora, and
water samples as if they're on an exploratory Mars mission. They're
split into teams and given checklists of organic and inorganic matter
to find. The first team to reach the top and collect the samples wins.

"This challenge doesn't just test your data-collecting skills," says
host Bridget, cameras hovering around her. "It will also prove your
resilience and grit. The most important qualities required to become
a Marsonaut."

A stroke of good fortune: Amber has Pichu and Adam on her
team. Along with Marion the Frenchwoman, Fernando from Argentina, and Jalal from Lebanon.

"Solid team, team!" says Pichu, who's bent double with the weight
of her pack. Adam offers to carry her tent, and Amber takes some of
her water.

"We've totally got this," says Amber, to convince herself and the
cameras. The heat is so intense that she keeps looking down at her bare
calves, certain that the skin is sizzling like bacon. "We can do this."

Amber looks at her team; the Mars endeavor is so inclusive.
They're coming together from all over the world with a shared goal—
that's Nobel Peace Prize material right there.

Well, most of them will be eliminated. But still.

They start trekking. Sergey is way too old and struggles with the
incline. But his teammates Ebad and Ramesh—the heat doesn't
bother them at all—take Sergey's arms and drag him forward,

Ramesh encouraging him with lies like, *Only half an hour more, my friend, and we will be sipping tea with our feet elevated comfortably.* Marion plows onward, sweat rolling off her face, speaking to no one, stopping to collect samples without even glancing at the checklist. Fernando sings *cuarteto* songs. The mansplaining man bun, Logan, expounds to Bernita from Cuba on the ways the Sandinista revolution differed from the Cuban one. Gabija from Lithuania and Agneta from Sweden walk with their teammate Justine; the huntress strides faster than you'd expect, since she's only about five two. Tamiko looks fresh and dewy like she's in an ad for Dove lotion. Cawaale starts running up the hill, actually running. Then Tish gets swarmed by wasps.

"I think they're attracted to my laundry soap." She breathes slowly and deliberately. "It's organic."

She takes off her shirt, stands in her bra with arms outstretched like some fantasy-femme version of Jesus on the cross. Her silver hair glimmers like chrome in the sunshine; her spray tan is flawless. Every camera turns toward her and Amber thinks, *This girl might not be so dumb.*

"Don't worry," says Adam. "I am equipped with a first-aid kit that includes an EpiPen."

"Thanks, doc," says Steve the Australian, looking around as if he said something witty. "But stick to your own team. We're sorted here."

Amber and her teammates trek and trek. They veer off the path looking for clays and mosses—Amber has a good eye for the flora samples. But they get lost. Dehydrated. They go through all the fruit bars provided in their packs and worry that the MarsNow people are trying to starve them. Then Pichu remembers that she bought a sachet of guava-flavored Tang at the airport. She pours it into her water bottle and shares it around—the calories feel heaven-sent. Amber already cracked at the sight of gummy worms, but now Adam crumbles too. Breaks his no-refined-sugar rule.

Trying to find the main path, they end up in a village, where the camera guys assigned to follow their team capture the unimpressed, confused faces of the locals.

Pichu says, "I feel like those people are thinking: *Fools.*"

Then their secret weapon: Fernando negotiates in Spanish with one of the village kids to act as their guide. The boy climbs the mountain like a goat, and keeps looking back at them, bored.

They pass a herd of cattle who stare, wide-eyed and silent. Pichu says, "I feel like those cows are thinking: *Fools.*"

They trudge up, up, up. It's hell and Amber loves every minute. The sun sets and they still haven't reached the top, but when they summit this beast of a volcano, Cawaale and his team are already there—he ran the whole thing, didn't get lost, found half the samples, and had time to cook a rice pilaf for everyone. Amber's team is so hungry that they don't mind coming in second.

Once the other teams reach the summit, Bridget and Nick arrive with even more camera crew in a horse-drawn wagon. Bridget's hair and makeup are perfect and she smells like wealth. "You guys! You did it! Achieved your first challenge." She clambers down from the wagon, two male crew holding her hands, then adjusts her mane of hair. "But you knew this moment had to come, Marsonauts. Two of you will be eliminated tonight."

"Now?" says Pichu. "Can we eat first?"

Amber can imagine the GIFs. Pichu with her bowl of rice, rolling her eyes. *Can we eat first?*

They are not allowed to eat first. They must set up their tents in the dark, while being filmed. Amber's tent ends up on such a steep incline that she worries it'll slide down the slope.

Then they sit around the fire Cawaale built, and Bridget says, "You're here in Nicaragua, having sweated and survived your first challenge. How do you feel?"

How do you feel? Amber is rarely asked that question. Never asks others.

They go around the circle: Tamiko feels proud of her achievement and "ready for whatever comes next." Logan feels "awesome to be here, man, wow." Bernita can't believe it, she'd never traveled outside her country and now she's seeing the world! Pichu feels like she smells so stinky. Amber says the truth: that she's happy, for the first time in a long time. Tish tips her head back, looks upward: "I've never seen stars in real life before." Then: "What? I'm from Manhattan, guys."

When all twenty-four of them have summed up their mental states, Bridget says: "Many of you have known each other for a while. Audiences at home might not realize that you met on the Mars-Now forum months ago. But there are rules to this game." She looks around, meeting their eyes. "Two of you must say goodbye tonight."

Pichu squeezes Amber's hand.

Adam presses the toe of his hiking boot against Amber's ankle.

"Our international audience has voted," says Bridget. "It wasn't easy for the people at home and it's not easy for us."

There's an interminable pause while the camera guys circle, capturing their nerves from every angle.

Finally the focus is back on Bridget, who says: "David, you came to us all the way from Norway. You impressed us with your stoicism and determination. And Agneta, from Sweden, you wowed us with your energy and we are so proud to have had you on the MarsNow team." Another pause. "David, Agneta, I'm sorry—you're going home."

David nods. Agneta looks . . . relieved? Then they're taken aside for their final In the Moment confessionals.

"That *sucks*," says Pichu. "Being the first ones."

"Sweden didn't even seem upset," says Amber.

"She wasn't in it to win it," whispers Pichu. "I heard she was on Sweden's version of *The Voice* and wanted more exposure." She turns to the crew. "Are we actually sleeping in these tents, or was that just for show?"

One of the camera guys laughs.

"Damn," says Pichu. "I guess that's a yes."

They gratefully eat the cold rice pilaf—Adam breaks his no-grains rule—then Amber crawls inside her pup tent, inside her sleeping bag, braces her feet against a rock so she won't slip down the mountain. Breathes. Whispers a prayer of thanks because today she felt that old certainty. Determination. The *rightness* that she once associated with gymnastics and thought she'd lost. Maybe she'll always be able to rely on how her muscles kick into gear when it counts, how they seem to gather power under duress, how it feels almost spiritual and righteous to work this hard. Every cell, every brain wave, every breath sharing a purpose, her whole being narrowing to a single point of light: *the top.*

$\cancel{||||} \ \cancel{||||} \ \cancel{||||} \ ||||$

THE SECOND AND THIRD WEEKS GO BY FAST, SINCE I'M FORTUNATE
to spend them with a group of highly accomplished pot plants—
which are all excelling by the way. Our babies are healthy and meeting
their milestones. When Marcus comes over, I tour him through the
grow room and he says, "Wicked. You haven't killed them yet."

"I'm not going to kill them. That's not even a possibility."

"I completely believe you."

"Let's just watch the show."

Episode three opens with Dirk Riley, astronaut aboard the ISS.
"Hey Marsonauts!" He floats cross-legged and looks like a round,
bald space-Buddha. "I'm watching from way up here and wishing you
all the best." He does a slow spin while waving.

Because carbon emissions are no object, the MarsNow competitors
were flown from Nicaragua to Scotland, and the second "challenge"
consists of a Scottish-themed obstacle course. The competitors engage
in a game of tug-of-war, throw shot puts, leap over tartan-patterned
pylons, even darn socks—because on Mars they'll be responsible for
repairing their own clothes. They also speed-eat haggis, presumably
because on Mars they'll eat to live, not to enjoy themselves. And they
play a hole of golf—because on Mars they'll organize their own cor-
porate golf events? Whatever. Let the games begin.

They scamper through the obstacles, and Amber is near the front
of the pack just like in Nicaragua. She reaches the finish line right
after Tamiko, Adam, Logan, and Ramesh—who darned that sock
like a pro.

"But there's one more challenge, Marsonauts," says Bridget, whose
only qualifications seem to be breasts that defy gravity. "Based on the
beloved tradition of the Highland Games."

A massive red Scotsman steps forward to demonstrate. He drags a tree trunk behind him and points to a streak of chalk on the grass. "You must get your caber past that line." He grunts, lifts his tree, yells something in a terrifying brogue, then throws the tree. The trunk flips end over end twice and lands past the line.

"You have just one hundred and twenty seconds to complete this challenge!" says Bridget, giving the Scotsman's bicep a squeeze.

How does tossing a tree relate to being an astronaut? Your guess is as good as mine.

Ramesh just manages to lift and toss that tree.

"Throws like a girl," laughs Logan, the talks-too-much American with the perfect jawline.

"Hey," says Steve, the talks-too-much Australian with the perfect pectorals. "Don't pick on him just because he's gay."

"Some of my best friends are gay. Just saying, that was a girly toss."

As if to prove this theory about girls correct, Adiya can't even pick up the tree.

"Dang," says Marcus, spread-eagled on my couch. "Saudi-princess is ooooooouuuut."

"He never said we had to throw the tree by ourselves." Tish jogs over to Adiya. "Just that we had to get it over the line."

Together, Tish and Adiya carry their trees past the chalk. But Amber, who hates accepting help—of course Amber tries to do it on her own. She strains, lifts the caber a few inches, then there's a terrible popping sound. Her right shoulder, the same injury that cost her a gymnastics career. She drops the tree and breathes in short gulps. But she doesn't cry. I have never seen Amber Kivinen cry. (For that matter, she's never seen me cry. Unless crying during movies counts?)

"She's okay, man," says Marcus, anticipating my next move. "It's just a TV show."

But I know Amber's face better than my own. That's real pain. She isn't pretending.

I pick up my cell to call her, even though she's not allowed to take calls anymore and her phone will probably just ring uselessly in a trailer somewhere. It rings and rings as I watch Adam from Israel drop his own tree—abandoning his chances at winning—and run to help her. I watch as he uses his medical training to force her shoulder back into its socket, which causes another horrible *pop*.

"Looks like an alliance has formed," says Bridget, in her tiny kilt.

On the screen, Amber bites her lip, emitting a low growl as she clutches her arm. In my ear, her voicemail comes on. *You've reached Amber. I'm not living on Mars yet, so leave a message!*

"Let the joint settle," says Adam. "You'll need to ice it." He lifts his T-shirt to wipe the sweat from her brow, exposing his cut abs. Then puts an arm around her waist. "Amber? Talk to me."

"Uh-oh," says Marcus. "This bro's going all McDreamy on her."

The camera is tight on Amber's face. "I'll never get there," she says. "I'll never get there now."

"Look at me." Adam takes her head in his hands. "You're already there. It's not outside of us." He touches her chest, his hand over her beating heart. "Mars is in here."

Then it hits me, and I can't believe it took this long: Adam = First-Man34, from the chat forum.

No wonder I can't stand him. Adam from Israel, with his smug cheekbones. If this situation isn't resolved, he'll be *the one*. The one Amber will be locked up with inside a space capsule for months. The one who'll fondle her pliant flesh in zero gravity. The one she'll get space-married to. The one who will father her Martian children. And I'll be here, on a planet with breathable air and koalas and ballpoint pens. Oil spills and snowfall. Spruce trees, sinkholes, pine beetles. I'll be here, alone.

I say nothing into the phone. Let her voicemail record my silence.

A SEAR OF PAIN AND FAILURE, LIKE THE FIRST TIME SHE INJURED her shoulder. She was on the parallel bars performing a Khorkina, a move she'd done hundreds if not thousands of times before. But somehow, at an international meet, in front of the whole goddamn world, she twisted too far during her release and grabbed the bar with only one hand. A disaster. Felt her shoulder joint tear apart. Didn't even come close to sticking the landing. Collapsed to her knees. Destroyed her own life.

Lost her faith.

Lost, on some level, her father's love.

Is that true? Did he stop loving her when she was no longer competing? When she was no longer his little champ? Surely not.

But he couldn't quite forgive her for fucking up. Or maybe it was just logistics, scheduling: without gymnastics, her dad no longer drove her to meets and practices. No more hours in the Enclave or in Tim Horton's, passing Bible quotes back and forth.

"Here's one for you, kiddo. *For you formed my inward parts; you knitted me together in my mother's womb.*"

"Easy." Amber would grin. "Psalm 139."

"Next line?"

"*I praise you, for I am fearfully and wonderfully made.*"

Maybe her body *is* wonderfully made, because now the doctor says Adam did a great job of setting her shoulder and the physio says her muscles are firing so quickly that within a few days she'll be back in business.

"You mean I can still do the show?"

"Of course!" The physio's jaunty ponytail bounces with each word. "You're doing great!"

So she's cleared by the MarsNow medical team and given a bottle of Tylenol 3s that rattle in her suitcase, calling to her. She usually travels with her own painkillers, as a kind of insurance policy—she can convince herself that she won't dislocate her shoulder if she's always prepared to dislocate her shoulder. She has a stockpile at home: Tylenol 3, Demerol, Oxy that she bought off Tariq after his knee surgery, and enough Ativan to subdue a tiger. She never takes any of it—okay, rarely takes any of it—just feels better *having* it.

But she hadn't packed any pills with her, believing it a sign of maturity to forgo her old, irrational belief. So of course, *of course*, she's gone and dislocated her shoulder. The surprising part is that she's survived, that she's still in the game; in fact, the injury—especially the fact that Adam came to her rescue—seems to be regarded as a good thing. Slick Nick keeps telling her that she's *giving great story*, as if she did it on purpose. Yesterday he loved their "dialogue" so much that he made Adam and Amber film and refilm their exchange— *Mars isn't out there. It's in here*—until she pointed out that she truly had dislocated her shoulder, was in *reality* in agony, and should probably take a break. Now it was supposed to be their day off, the rest of the cast had been released, but Slick Nick thought Adam and Amber should get one more scene. She and Adam are brought to a hotel room that's far nicer than the ramshackle "safe house" in a suburb of Glasgow where they're actually staying.

"Okay, guys," says Nick in his producer voice. "We loved what you did out there. So we're thinking, *More*. More tension about the shoulder, more tension about your relationship. Can you do that?"

Adam gives her a look that she can barely interpret. Fear?

"Adam, Amber's icing her shoulder, you're going to check on her. And Amber." Nick stands too close, his hand on her lower back. "You're worried. You've got this injury. You don't know if it means you're done or not. Big nerves, got it?"

Amber yawns. Those Tylenol 3s. "Got it."

Adam disappears, then reappears a few seconds later, solicitous at the door to Amber's pretend hotel room. "Amber? Can I come in?"

"Of course, Adam."

"How are you?"

"I feel okay."

"Cut! Sorry," says Nick. "But no, not *okay*. Anything but *okay*."

Adam nods, goes back outside, knocks again, comes inside again.
"How are you?"

"Not great. It really hurts." She pauses, turns to Nick. "Honestly,
I would never say that."

"I feel like we need something here." Nick calls over his shoulder.
"Linnz, honey, can you get me a lemon? Sliced?"

Nick takes Adam aside, talks to him in that bro-to-bro way, then
comes over to Amber. "Thing is, baby doll, we need a bit of will-they-
won't-they. You know? Like Ross and Rachel."

"So we're a sitcom?"

"And Adam might have something he needs to tell you." Slick
Nick raises his eyebrows. "About himself."

She turns to Adam. "What do you need to tell me?"

But Linnzy appears with a slice of lemon, and Slick Nick says,
"Perfect, thanks, doll," then tilts back Amber's chin and squeezes
juice into her eyes.

"Jesus!" She wipes at her face. "What the hell?"

"More of that passion, exactly." He pats her knee, speaks softly.
"You need to *wake up* and generate some scenes. Got it, cutie-pie?"

Adam goes out of the room and knocks on the door. "How are
you?" he says again, and Amber blinks at him, tears blurring her vision.

"Fine." She could stab that Slick Nick. "There's nothing wrong
with me."

Adam scratches his head, as if trying to remember his line. "But
you dislocated your shoulder, Amber. This is serious. I keep thinking you might get sent home. Back to your boyfriend." Meaningful
pause. "And I might never see you again."

Of course. Of course Slick Nick would spring her *boyfriend* on
her. She's supposed to blubber about how confused she is, how *she*

doesn't know what to do. She's supposed to take shelter in Adam's arms. They're supposed to share their first intimacy on camera. She's supposed to throw Kevin under the bus.

Instead she throws the bag of ice at Adam's chest.

"Don't you *ever* give up on me." She stands, shoves him backward. "I won't break this easily."

Adam fights back a smile.

"This same injury kept me from the Olympics but it's not going to stop me now." She glares red-eyed at Slick Nick, then at the camera. "And I am not going to cry about it."

WHEN BASTIAAN FROM TSAWWASSEN COMES WITH MY NEXT
delivery, I practically drag his huge body inside. "Come in for a bit.
Have some tea." I already made a pot because I just know that Bastiaan is a sencha guy. He probably also plays the banjo. He probably
spends his evenings in front of a fire, singing folk songs with his
well-adjusted children.

"Whoa, my friend," he says. "You must have quite the business here."

Right. This apartment stinks of weed. I can't smell it because I never
leave, but the suite is full of cut buds, which give off an odor that's
wet and mulchy and alive. A smell that always reminds me of Amber's
pubic hair, of opening her up and putting my tongue inside her.

"Just a little side operation."

"You sell this stuff? I could maybe find customers for you. On my
route, I mean."

"Like we'd be partners? Business partners? And friends? I think
we could be friends."

"Sure. I'll feel it out. See if there's any interest." He looks around
the apartment, collapses onto the couch. "Love your place. Reminds
me of my single days."

"How old are you?"

"Thirty-five. Goes by fast. Make sure you appreciate this time,
know what I mean?"

"You're thirty-five? And you have four kids?"

"I haven't experienced quiet like this in years." He laughs. "This
couch. Brings back memories of my party phase. My wasted youth."

Because he's four whole years older than me and very wise, I ask
his advice. Should I call Bronwyn? Text her? What is the dating
etiquette when you've got a girlfriend but she's maybe on her way to
Mars? And when you like a person but they freak you out? Some-

times I feel like Bronwyn's eyes might be too big for her face, like she's some sort of extraterrestrial. Do Bronwyn's eyes probe my brain?

"Tough situation, my friend." Bastiaan nods thoughtfully. "I think you know the answers better than I do."

Which is completely what a wise, banjo-playing farmer *would* say. And I do know the answer: I will not punish her, this innocent young woman, by luring her into my jungle lair to ease my loneliness and offer me a refuge from heartbreak, even if Bronwyn does have a nice body. No. I'll be a good person and sulk in my lair by myself. Ease my loneliness by subtly and passive-aggressively punishing Amber the next time I see her.

Except as soon as Bastiaan leaves, Bronwyn texts me. *Hey Kevin, how are you? You just popped into my mind so thought I'd see what you're up to this weekend.*

And listen, if she hadn't used full sentences and correct grammar, I would have ignored her message. I would have saved her from herself. But there's something erotic about that well-placed comma. About a woman who does not confuse *you're* and *your*. About a woman texting me, pretending she's all casual about it. *You just popped into my mind.* A woman chasing me for a change.

THE SCENE IS IN THE CAN; THE CREW IS PACKING UP; AMBER IS blinking lemon juice from her eyes.

"Hey Nick?" She smiles sweetly at him. Jesus Christ. She's walking a tightrope with this guy, has been since she'd met him during the screen test and said that line about her bra size. "Have a minute?"

"Sure, baby, what's up?"

Amber steps closer, whispers. "Can I get access to my phone? For, like, a second?"

"Are you kidding?" Nick laughs. "Not happening."

The crew are loaded up, Linnzy is gone, and Adam hovers by the hotel room door. "You coming, Amber?"

"I'll meet you in the van." She turns back to Nick. "I just want to call my parents to tell them I'm okay. They'll be freaking out about my shoulder."

"Not my problem. They'll see you on TV like everyone else."

She pouts theatrically. Puts a hand on his arm. "Honestly, five minutes. One phone call?"

"No way, love." His eyes hover on her breasts. "There are rules."

"Okay, I get it. Somehow I thought you were kinda . . . in charge? But whatever. It's fine."

"I am. In charge." He takes her elbow. "But that would be a serious violation. I would lose my job."

"How would anyone find out?"

"Are you crazy?"

"I wouldn't touch social media. Wouldn't even log on. I'd make one phone call."

"Forget it."

But the next day on set, Nick puts a hand on her lower spine and passes her an envelope. "You owe me," he hisses in her ear. "Big time."

His hand travels downward and cups her ass. A jolt. Of anger. Arousal. Like when she was fifteen and fell asleep on the bus after a meet and woke to find Coach Rodney beside her, his hand on her thigh, fingers reaching inside her shorts. She'd squeezed her eyes shut. Terrified. And morbidly curious about how far his hand would go.

"Thanks, Nick. You're the best."

"Catch you later," he says, then lopes off to talk to the crew.

She'd shifted subtly away from Coach Rodney, pretending she was still asleep. She didn't want to embarrass him: he was the best coach in northern Ontario. But now that she's a public figure, she should #metoo his ass—the other girls on her squad would definitely back her up. That was one of their favorite topics of whispered conversation: how gross Coach Rodney was. His wandering eyes and inappropriate jokes.

But the whole case would be undermined by Amber herself, because later she had that flirtatious email correspondence with him during her first year in Vancouver, when she was lonely and missing gymnastics and he was having problems in his marriage. Never mind that she was nineteen and he was forty-six. She always opened each email with *Hey coach ;)* and signed off with *xoxo*.

Had Rodney helped her in some way? Was she allowed to think that? Those emails had momentarily made her feel less broken, at a time when she believed she'd be defined by that shoulder injury and the failure it represented. And isn't it convenient that Slick Nick finds her attractive? It means he's forgiving if she's a bit late to set or needs an extra minute to deal with her hair. It means she has her phone. Is she allowed to dislike Nick and to flirt with him?

Kevin always says that hypocrisy and cognitive dissonance are the defining features of the modern world: you want to save the planet but there's no way to visit your family except by car or plane; or you want to be a powerful woman but the only option is to "lean in" and become as sociopathic as the men. So you feel trapped and hypocritical and guilty. But you can't tell anyone, because all your friends on social media seem righteous and outraged and pure. So you nurture shame, and this shame keeps you from blaming the real culprits, the 1 percent who built this world and who are profiting off your inner turmoil by selling you alcohol or OxyContin or online porn.

Anyway, whatever. She has her phone.

"Hey Linnz?" she calls out. "Just gonna use the bathroom."

"Ten-one or ten-two?" Linnzy holds a walkie-talkie to her mouth, ready to announce Amber's bladder or bowel activity to the entire crew. Is that necessary? They're treated like children. Or prisoners. Every minute accounted for.

"Ten-two," says Amber, to buy herself time, and the other contestants stare at her enviously. None of them are shitting lately—constipation is rampant on set, thanks to all the travel.

"Lucky bitch!" yells Pichu.

Amber's heart pounds as she walks to the porta-potty, locks herself inside, turns off her mike, and slips the phone from the envelope. And there it is, in all its idiotic glory: *Will you marry me?*

How dare he? How dare he trigger that dormant desire, the wish of every good Christian girl—to be a wife and helpmate, to embody purity, to be chosen and beloved. She doesn't need that crap anymore. Because being a reality star is exactly like being a bride: she is no longer an ordinary woman but instead a performative, sanitized, admired, envied emblem.

Fuck him. *You're dead to me.*

But her shoulder is strapped to her side, immobile and sore, and it's like some Pavlovian response: Kevin saved her life—repaired her spirit—after the first injury, and now she feels like her body won't heal properly without him. Superstition. As ridiculous as praying to a big man in the sky.

She said this to Adam last night as they again lay in his closet, under the red lights. He adjusted one of the bulbs so it shone directly on her shoulder, and she admitted that she missed her boyfriend.

"I know I shouldn't be talking about this with you," she said. "I'm sorry."

"We are free to express anything to each other."

She closed her eyes. Felt better when she couldn't see Adam's face, when they were each other's anonymous confessors. "I know it's stupid, but I just need to hear his voice."

"If someone loved me the way your Kevin loves you," said Adam, "I would never let that person go."

MAYBE I'M GIVING THE IMPRESSION THAT AMBER'S ADVENTURES on TV are what absorb me most. But as I clip the buds and lay them out on newspaper to dry, I'm careful, almost reverential. With Amber gone, the pot plants are my companions. Friends who will never abandon me. They shelter inside our shared habitat, inhaling carbon dioxide and exhaling oxygen while I do the opposite: I breathe in oxygen and exhale CO_2. In this way, we create each other's air; we know each other inside out; we breathe each other into being.

See? I'm becoming a freaking shaman over here, so no, I don't think much about Amber or MarsNow. What garbage. All the MarsNow contestants are now fully inhabiting their roles: Tish the pretty ditz, Ramesh the sweet queen, Logan the man's man, Tamiko the beautiful bitch, Pichu the adorable best friend, etc., etc. They're worshipped like a pantheon of gods, secular society's answer to the saints, the charismatic faces of our real religion: individualist consumerism. And Amber's role—tough, hippie badass—has expanded. The injury and possible romance with FirstMan34 has made her a star. Ellen even had her on the show:

ELLEN

So, Amber Kivinen, you're gorgeous, you're fit, you're maybe going to Mars, and . . . you deal drugs? You used to deal drugs? I don't want to get you arrested.

AMBER

(laughing)

Yeah, we deal drugs, but Canada is about to legalize pot—I like to think I was ahead of the curve.

ELLEN

So it won't be illegal anymore for you to sell weed? You'll be legit. Portia and I could visit and smoke the ganja?

AMBER
(laughing)

Not that simple. I won't be one of the licensed distributors, so technically the weed we sell won't be legal—

ELLEN

Technically it's illegal, Your Honor.
(laughing)
Are you stoned right now?

AMBER

I'm not! There was a time, though . . .

ELLEN

Before you found Mars.

AMBER

Exactly. I was kinda lost. I think a lot of us can relate to that. But now I just want to be really *clear*, really present.

ELLEN

'Cause you're competing, and it's not physically or mentally easy, I imagine.

AMBER

Not just that. I want to be present now, when I'm talking to you. I want to be clearheaded for all of it. This whole thing means so much to me.

ELLEN

That's fantastic. An inspiring story.

AMBER

It's not just about space travel or science or even status, accomplishment—I am a goal-oriented person, but—

ELLEN

It's more than that for you.

AMBER

There's something about the journey, exploring a new world—it's about starting anew. Being reborn.

Clear. Present. Amber has publicly sworn to focus, to cut all liabilities from her life, to be *reborn*. But she still calls me. Or called me. Last night. From a porta-potty in Glasgow. Supposedly because she needed me to look in the medicine cabinet to remind her of what brand of acid inhibitors she uses.

"Won't they have state-of-the-art Tums on Mars?" I said.

"Fuck off, Kev, please. I'm serious."

"You just got the no-name kind from Shoppers," I said. "Extra strength."

"I can feel my stomach acid all the way up in my throat," she said. "I can feel it in my head. It's burning my eyes."

"Is that even possible?"

"Is it? Do you think it can get into my brain?"

"Slammer, your stomach acid can't reach your brain."

I was sitting in the bathtub, which is the place Amber and I go to cool off. The ceramic was cold against my back. "Anyway, you're going to Mars. The landing will kill you first."

She couldn't help but laugh.

"You're fine," I said. "Take a breath, okay?"

"Okay. I'm doing it. I'm breathing."

"And you look hot," I said, "in that little uniform they make you wear."

"Oh god." She laughed. "Thanks. Thank you."

And it occurred to me that even if Amber gets to Mars, even if we do live light-years apart, we'll still watch the same sun set.

||||| ||||| ||||| |||||
/

SHE'S IN A WET UNDERWORLD, ALMOST WEIGHTLESS, FACE-TO-
face with a pregnant bull shark. The shark—Amber has named her
Diana—moves languidly, gently. Swims close, takes a curious look,
and nearly brushes Amber's suit with her sandpaper skin.

Amber smiles. Signals at Ha Joon, her diving buddy and teammate
for this challenge. He returns her OK sign. They've spent the past
three hours underwater, wearing puffy MarsNow suits and gloves,
circling a sunken model Lander to repair a broken valve. They finished
with time to spare on the clock, and this is her first chance to look
around. No sound but the hiss of her scuba equipment. Has she ever
felt so calm? She doesn't notice the underwater camera crew. Doesn't
care what her body looks like in the suit, or that hair is tangled in her
mask. Her heartbeat has slowed; she is nothing but breath. Inhale,
exhale. A school of fish glides around her. A loggerhead turtle, alien
and incredible, runs along the ocean bed, kicking up sand.

The current is getting stronger—she clutches a rock to keep
still. Dusk. The sharks will be hunting soon, and Ha Joon gives her
a thumbs-up. She could stay down here forever, but he's right. Her
flippers propel her upward, through silence, toward sunlight.

They break the surface and she's back in the human world. Pulled
onto the boat by the scuba crew, a camera in her face, Slick Nick saying, "How was it, baby doll?"

"Amazing. Perfect."

The crew helps remove her space suit, then Slick Nick unzips her
wet suit—she is filmed while she fights her way out of it, an awkward
striptease.

Bridget says, "Amber, you've now repaired the MarsNow Lander
in time to escape the deadly bull shark. You kept calm under pressure. You survived the challenge!"

Amber feels like she emerged from a mythical world. A sea creature dredged up.

"The sharks were beautiful," she says. "I think one of them was pregnant."

A sudden tightness in her chest, as if she's still underwater and the oxygen has stopped flowing. Sadness. That habitual heartbreak that lately she's been able to ignore, thanks to the distractions of Adam, Mars, fame. But microplastics, agricultural runoff, warming temperatures. What future exists for that shark pup?

. . . and a great mountain burning with fire was cast into the sea, and the third part of the sea became blood . . .

There's no hope. No beauty without regret; no wonder without fear. Humans have changed the planet so deeply that it is no longer anyone's true home.

She cannot let this in.

Ha Joon is pulled onto the boat and it's his turn to be bombarded. She steps away, looks for her towel, feels a nip against the skin of her shoulder—did Slick Nick just *bite* her? No. Snapped the strap of her bathing suit, like he's in high school.

"Nice job down there," he says. "By the way, have you forgotten something?"

"Have I?"

"The phone. Our deal was that you'd have it for five minutes and it's been two days."

"Oh yeah, of course. I forgot I still have it. I'll bring it tomorrow?"

"Tonight. You can stop by my trailer."

Gross. She'll have to sprain an ankle or have a mental breakdown. She'll have to find a good excuse—an endless number of good excuses—to never stop by that trailer. "For sure." She smiles at his smooth, burnt-umber face. "No problem."

"Uh-oh, look." He runs a finger down her spine. "Goosebumps."

THE BUDS ARE ALMOST DRY, NEARLY READY TO BE WEIGHED AND
bagged. And I'm baking the leaves, then soaking them in Bacardi
and honey. I have a plan to expand the business, to produce a potent
Green Dragon. And I have a text correspondence in progress with
Bronwyn, who updates me on her latest vegan baking adventures
with promises that *you'll taste my avocado brownies soon!* ("Avocado
brownies" is not code for some sexual act/position. I looked it up.)
What I mean is: I have a lot going on. So it doesn't concern me when
Marcus says he can't watch the next MarsNow episode with me
because he had to switch his Uncle Fatih's Pizza shift. I probably
wouldn't bother to watch the show either except that I'm not really
the story here; I'm Nick Carraway to Amber's Gatsby, and you gotta
give the people what they want. So here's the update: the eighteen
competitors who made it through the first three challenges are flown
from Costa Rica to the Los Alamos National Laboratory in New
Mexico, best known as the location where the first atomic bomb was
created. Now the home of MarsNow.

The contestants are toured through rooms of young men in
hoodies, hunched over computers, headphones strapped to their
ears as they design a new Internet for Mars. Laboratories, offices, a
24/7 cafeteria, a MarsNow pub where the scientists poached from
NASA and the programmers from Silicon Valley keep to their
respective tables.

Astronaut Dirk Riley, still aboard the ISS, makes an appearance
on the show to remind us that MarsNow is "the most ambitious
space program ever conceived!"

Then the contestants—I cannot bring myself to call them
Marsonauts—meet Geoff Task, that doughy douchebag billionaire who uses the profits from Almanac to invest in projects that

satisfy the bullied high school nerd within: manufacturing bullet-proof SUVs and marketing them as the best vehicle for the coming sociopolitical-environmental collapse; building a "smart suburb" in Quebec that will collect and sell endless data on its inhabitants; running a space program that is officially named the MarsNow Mega Project; marrying and divorcing a series of blonde actresses.

At Los Alamos, Geoff Task stands in the desert, wearing all black, his thinning blonde hair artfully arranged, his glasses self-consciously hip. He's slim and pale, with a regal neck only a guillotine could love, and his sleeves are rolled up to reveal a tattoo: *amor fati* in black script. (Which part of his fate would be difficult to love?) His eyes are gray like concrete and his skin disturbingly smooth—there are rumors that he's pioneering an experimental treatment for aging that involves transfusions of blood extracted from children. I can tell from looking at him that he's the kind of person who confuses business success with spiritual enlightenment. That he uses the word *ask* as a noun and the word *gift* as a verb.

The MarsNow contestants stand behind him in their shiny uniforms. (And of course when I check the MarsNow official Instagram account, I see a picture of Amber temple-to-temple with Douchebag Billionaire, captioned: *Our Marsonauts made contact with this genius! #solucky.*)

"This is the most important thing humanity has ever undertaken," says Douchebag Billionaire, because he's forgotten about the time we liberated the Nazi camps. He says that the Lockheed Martin MarsNow Lander will be boosted by something called the Super Intense Rocket (you can't make this shit up), which will have forty Raptor engines to provide more than thrice as much thrust as NASA's Saturn V, bitch.

Speaking of thrust, the starship-rocket thingy looks predictably phallic. It gleams in the desert sun; the Marsketeers admire it and cheer. What has happened to my girlfriend? Amber went from contributing money to land defenders to . . . celebrating her own techno-feudal serfdom?

Douchebag Billionaire stares at his rocket. "This is the most beautiful creation I've ever encountered," he says, because he's clearly never seen the haunting grace of a beluga whale, not even on TV. "This might sound nuts, but we are planning to launch in less than six months. We will soon be inhabiting other worlds!"

The MarsNow contestants whoop like women on *The View*.

"This project is a necessity, as our own planet degrades." Douchebag Billionaire's face takes on a practiced Jean-Luc Picard look. "For a sustainable future, we as a species must become interplanetary."

I guess being a billionaire means that you don't need to think about any species but your own.

I close the laptop and wonder if there might be an epically long German word to express exactly what I'm feeling: profound shame at being part of humanity. Can I go on? Can I live in this insane world? I might throw myself out the window if I'm not careful (and when you live in a basement, that could result in bruises), so I text Bronwyn and invite her to watch another movie. She texts back: *Now? Sure!* Turns out she's in the neighborhood. Turns out she's having a slow day on the freelance-zodiac-readings front.

She brings over pecan squares, which we eat from the pan while watching *Beau Travail*—no romantic comedies tonight because I want to cleanse my brain with filmic poeticism. But Bronwyn must not be a fan of exquisite cinematography, 'cause she talks through half the film, saying banal things like, "You really like movies, huh?"

"My mom and I watched so many when I was growing up. She was mostly into rom-coms."

"That's so great. You seem to know a lot."

"Did a semester at the Vancouver Film School. Wanted to be a screenwriter."

"What happened? You didn't pursue it?"

I hate talking during a movie—Amber knows not to break the spell unless it's an emergency. Also I don't want to relive those first years in Vancouver, which are irrelevant. Two years studying English at UBC before I transferred to VFS. A time of youthful promise, when I woke in the middle of the night with script ideas, when I was determined to reclaim the word *entertainment* from its association with passivity—I would write scripts that made people laugh *and* think. Scripts that connected audience to creator in mutual, intelligent, comedic delight. Scripts that made people feel less alone.

When I wasn't writing, or thinking about writing, or talking about writing, I collected movies to watch with my mom over Christmas break: *Bringing Up Baby, His Girl Friday, The Producers, The Man with Two Brains.* For two Christmases running, I traveled home to Thunder Bay on the Greyhound through a frozen Canadian landscape, reading *Anna Karenina* or George Saunders, carrying some BC bud for Mom in my backpack. Amber was the best girlfriend in the world back then—even though she was busy at UBC, she researched rheumatoid arthritis and discovered studies showing that marijuana could help with arthritic pain. The first seeds of our future were planted, and life seemed expansive and bright.

See? I can't talk about those years because I'd have to mention Amber. How during that semester of film school, when my mom didn't make it to Christmas, Amber's laugh, Amber's body, Amber's voice—her whole self—saved me. I was twenty-one years old and fully heartbroken.

"I just didn't want to be fifteen thousand dollars in debt," I say to Bronwyn now. And that's part of the truth. "You know how it is."

"I think you'd be such a good writer. Maybe you could take some courses now—"

"Nah. I feel crappy enough without failing to be brilliant."

"Then write for fun! I think writing is so magical."

"My writing was never 'magical.' The best thing I wrote was a buddy comedy about me and my friend Marcus getting drunk."

Plus everyone's a fucking writer these days, furiously composing emails, texts, posts. Everyone is doing this work, unpaid, for a handful of corporations—a handful of Geoff Tasks—who innocently encourage us to "share" and "connect." And in the background of all this writing is another text, the data that the writing produces, a story that is bought and sold with the aim of advertising to us, suppressing our votes, or activating our violent fears. I will not add to the information apocalypse, this dystopia of never-ending content. Screw it. Writing has become meaningless performance, just a way to engage users—a way to keep them using. I'm doing myself and the world a service by staying silent. I'm not sharing, not connecting—not writing—and that is my rebellion. I have withdrawn my labor.

"Well, I'd like to read it," says Bronwyn. "Your buddy comedy."

"Here's some advice," I say. "Do not *ever* offer to read an unpublished writer's work. It's dangerous and unsafe and could result in spending your precious time on this planet reading pleonasms like, *It's dangerous and unsafe.*"

Bronwyn looks at me with those X-ray eyes. How can I possibly be more interesting than Claire Denis's film? I'd be even less compelling if I were a writer, one of those cyborgs with a keyboard attached to their hands. One of those functional alcoholics who are always going on about how *challenging* it is to *create characters*, how *deep* one must go to *embody other souls*. I met too many dicks like that in film school. As if writing is an extreme sport, requiring phenomenal levels of—not egocentrism and selfish determination, of course not. Only *curiosity, imagination,* and *empathy*. Trust me, I could write if I felt like it. I've been training for fourteen years. What is a relationship—what is love itself—if not an Olympian feat of curiosity, imagination, and empathy?

"So you don't write anymore, but you work as an extra?" Bronwyn asks.

"Being an extra suits me. I get to be on set but not responsible for anything. I'm, like, *adjacent*. Being adjacent fits my values."

"But sometimes you have to be a hero, you know. Dive in."

I can tell she wants us to get it on, but I cannot bring myself to disrespect the film by making out. Though I'm also thinking that her line—*sometimes you have to be a hero*—followed by a passionate kiss? That shit would be romantic-comedy gold.

Then it hits me. I know what to do. I was raised on eighties rom-coms—how have I not thought of it before? I should burst out the door, sweat through the streets (or maybe just hop in a car2go, for the sake of efficiency), run through the airport to buy a last-minute flight to New Mexico from a pretty airline clerk who will smile when I say, "I'm chasing love!" (Except of course there are no smiling airline clerks anymore and I'd have to buy the ticket from a kiosk, but you get the idea.) Then let's skip past the boring part where I'm sitting on a plane drinking ginger ale from a plastic cup and get to the climax: I find my way into the Los Alamos dorm building or whatever, and security chases me but they're not very fast, and there's some sort of surprising but surmountable challenge right before I somersault from a balcony, or crash through a window, and see her. Amber. Who stares at me in awed disbelief.

Then I drop to my knees: "I love you—"

She finishes the sentence: "—for no reason."

And we hold each other.

Cut. The End.

It all flashes in front of me, perfect and whole and narratively satisfying. I know what to do. I need to be the hero. I need, first of all, to leave this apartment.

But then Bronwyn leans against me, wraps my arm around her shoulder, and says, "Want to smoke a joint?"

ON SET, NICK GRABS AMBER FROM BEHIND, HIS ARM AROUND HER
waist. "You didn't show last night. Or the night before."

"I had a bout of *turista*, Nick. Maybe from the salad in Costa? It wasn't pretty. I'm still nauseous."

"I need that phone back."

"It's in my room."

"Go get it."

"Aren't we about to start shooting?"

Thankfully Linnzy appears and says, "Nick? Talk to you for a sec?" and he forgets about the phone—is too busy yelling at the crew about some real or imagined crisis. Then the shoot begins and they all tour the MarsNow facilities: the mock-up of the MarsNow Lander, labs filled with people in MarsNow-branded white coats, the cafeteria and foosball tables and nap rooms and rebounder stations. It's like the American megachurches Amber's family visited each summer, in New Jersey and Texas and Arizona. Their church in Thunder Bay was a plain brick building with pale moldings and uncomfortable pews, but they made pilgrimages to churches that felt like neighborhoods—leafy and winding streets, parking lots full of glittering cars, restaurants that served the best steaks, gyms and basketball courts and football fields, stores that sold Jesus merch, and "devotion centers" that held thousands of rocking bodies. This Mars-Now campus feels like a place of worship.

The most incredible part is outside: a vast field of rovers and full-scale replicas of the Settlement Structures where the Marsonaunts will live and work, inflatable homes that provide fifty square feet of private space and two hundred square feet of communal space. The Martian city of the future.

Or maybe the labs are the coolest. Amber watches Tamiko

talk tensegrity with one of the designers. Ramesh chats with the software developers. Logan goes on about mining iron ore, nickel, cobalt, platinum, and gold from the asteroid belt—"Some of those puppies would be worth hundreds of millions of dollars!" But when they reach the cool, moist air of the Aquaponics Room, this is Amber's moment.

Tiny shoots of kale, lettuce, and chard grow out of cups that could fit in the palm of her hand, glowing under purple light. A modified hydroponics that seems to use some sort of porous substrate.

"As you can see," says Geoff Task, who has taken time out of his week to appear on the show, "we're using state-of-the-art technology to ensure that our Marsonauts never go hungry."

"I'm curious." Amber steps forward. "Are these plants hand-pollinated?"

"For now, we use fans for air circulation," says one of the botanists, in her white coat. "But we're thinking about whether bees could be transported, while hibernating. We are absolutely taking pollination into account."

"And how are you dealing with the challenge of Mars's low gravity? How do you keep water from saturating the roots? It looks like you've suspended the plants in—" Amber peers closer. "Wet clay?"

"It's a work-in-progress, to be honest." The botanist steals a nervous glance at Geoff Task. "We're using mechanical means right now. We're thinking of exploring hanging plants."

"It's impressive." Amber can imagine growth chambers like this on Mars, buried underground to protect against radiation. "This is aquaponics scaled way *up*. I love it."

"Thank you, Amber," says Geoff Task.

"But it isn't food security," she adds. "Not for the long term."

Task goes tense around the mouth, as if he isn't used to bad news. "How so?"

"Lettuce won't keep us fed. Simple as that. We need food that's calorie- and nutrient-dense."

Geoff Task crosses his arms, tilts his head. Heat travels to Amber's cheeks as every camera swivels toward her. "The biggest problem with growing food on Mars is the high levels of CO_2 in the atmosphere," she says. "We know, from Loladze's work studying Earth's changing climate, that the more CO_2 in the atmosphere, the bigger plants grow—but these large plants are sugar-dense and nutrient-poor. A source of carbohydrates, but not much else. The natural equivalent of junk food."

Geoff Task stares at her, jaw clenched.

"If we're really going to colonize another planet," she says, tucking her hair behind her ears, "we'll have to find ways to develop portable, renewable, sustainable proteins and fats."

Geoff Task nods. "I'm listening."

"Crickets, ants, beetles—are there ways to use CRISPR technology to create a super-insect, edible, that can live and reproduce even in extreme cold?"

"We're already on it," says Task. "Looking into mealworms, grasshoppers, and crickets. We're also exploring meat grown in petri dishes."

"There's also the possibility of livestock farming, perhaps bringing frozen embryos with us from Earth," says Amber. "Like on Earth, healthy soil needs fertilizer from animals."

"Frozen baby cows?" Task laughs.

"I would suggest chickens or rabbits, animals that breed quickly, don't require much feed, and are negligible in terms of carbon footprint. Though of course this would require temperature regulation. Some sort of passive system." She spent months using the UBC interlibrary loan system for just this moment. Considered the possibilities of breeding Antarctic lichen, quail, cockroaches, dandelions, seaweed—felt like a student again, open and curious and courageous. "I'm also thinking about waste products. We can perhaps grow root vegetables and mushrooms in our own feces, like in that movie *The Martian*. But there's also the CO_2 we'll be exhaling—it's old research, practically forgotten, but in the 1960s NASA found that CO_2 could be converted into nutrients, including protein, by microorganisms called hydrogenotrophs."

"There's no shortage of carbon dioxide," says Task.

"Exactly. And the efficiency—we'd only need a few fermentation tanks—it's mind-blowing."

Task stares at her, face eerily blank.

"Fermentation holds huge possibilities," she continues. "For food production and storage, keeping ourselves and our living environment clean, regulating the internal microbiome in a harsh and foreign environment."

Geoff Task's silence is unnerving. She glances at Adam, who gives her an almost imperceptible nod.

"My goal, if I'm chosen for the MarsNow mission, is to partner with the brilliant researchers here." She gives her sweetest, I'm-smart-but-I'm-also-pretty smile. "Together we can develop ways to feed the Marsonauts and future generations in a sustainable and equitable way."

Then, Visionary Geoff Task nods. "I like the way you think, Amber Kivinen."

AFTER THE LAST EPISODE AND GEOFF TASK'S UNCONVINCING PER-
formance as a human being, I can't face MarsImminently alone. I
also can't face Bronwyn, the human being I seem to be leading on.
So I invite Marcus over and we watch footage from Amber's twelve
hours spent in a sensory-deprivation tank, thanks to night-vision
cameras à la Paris Hilton sex tape. This challenge is to ensure that
they can handle the intense boredom and isolation of space travel.
Amber's assignment is four hours alone, four hours with Ramesh,
four hours with Tamiko. Alone she lies perfectly still until she
can't handle it, then splashes and hums. She does better with
company. Ramesh and Amber talk about winters in Thunder Bay
and Ramesh's early twenties spent hanging out in comedy clubs in
Mumbai. Then they sing every Taylor Swift song they can remember. Which is a shocking number of Taylor Swift songs.

With Tamiko, Amber tries conversation—"So, MIT? Must have
been amazing?"—but Tamiko says nothing, just lies back in the
mineral-rich water and floats with total equanimity.

"Why do you hate me?" says Amber, during the second hour.

"You're so self-absorbed. Why would you make me feel anything
as extreme as hatred?" Tamiko lifts her head from the water, looking
like a Japanese Brooke Shields emerging from the Blue Lagoon. "It's
a simple fact: under the circumstances, we are enemies."

The enemies are going to keep battling it out because neither
Tamiko nor Amber is eliminated. Sarah from South Africa is eliminated; Zach from Hong Kong is eliminated. This after Ying Yue
from China and Jalal from Lebanon were eliminated. But Amber
Kivinen—drug dealer, former vault champ, singer of "Hot Legs" at
karaoke—remains.

"She's an Energizer Bunny, man," says Marcus. "Takes a lickin' and keeps on tickin'."

"Are you aware that you just combined references to two of the most iconic advertising campaigns of all time? Our brains have been colonized."

"What?"

"Energizer batteries and Timex watches."

Marcus stares at me. "Coolio, daddy-o."

Our favorite part is when they go inside the MarsNow Lander Simulator, a module built to mimic the constraints of space travel. We watch as all sixteen Marsplorers wear space suits and live out a normal day: blood samples drawn for analysis—fucking FirstMan34 does the icky medical stuff—then air quality and pressure checks, two hours of working out on a treadmill or exercise bike, a lunch of dehydrated chickpeas and vitamin gel, more treadmill, more system checks, some "personal time." Then they zip themselves into sleeping bags, which they strap to chairs to sleep sitting up.

The best part is when they use the toilet, they position themselves on the seat using leg constraints, these awkward thigh-bars. Each Marsplorer has a *personal urine funnel*; they attach one end to a hose and the other to their own anatomy; then fans suck their piss into a wastewater tank.

"Is that how they'll take a shit too?" says Marcus. "Get it vacuumed out of their assholes?"

Pichu has this mischievous smile when using her personal urine funnel. "Wow. Not bad. I have a vibrator that works this way too."

"I love that chick, man," says Marcus. "She's hilare."

"Should we get Team Pichu T-shirts made?"

"That would be awesome. Send a pic to Amber of you flipping the bird, wearing that shirt." Marcus lazily punches my shoulder. "I heard you and that Bronwyn chick are hanging out."

"Who told you that?"

"She's talking, man. Telling all her friends that you're dating or something."

Shit. We kissed once. A couple of times. In Amber's world, that's just how people become acquainted. "Bronwyn and I are friends," I say, 'cause I thought we were on the same page, agreed that those kisses were . . . marginalia. A scribble, in pencil, between the lines. "We're not dating."

"Oh yeah?"

"Yeah. We just make out, eat food, and have awkward conversations."

"Dude. I'm pretty sure that's the *definition* of dating."

"NICE WORK, SUPERSTAR," SAYS PICHU WHEN THEY'RE BACK IN
their dorm room. "Who knew? You're not just a pretty face."

"You think that was okay?"

"More than okay. You gave that nerd a science-boner."

"Or he'll just steal my ideas and leave me down here to rot."

"What would you do?" asks Pichu. "If you got voted off?"

This is a possibility that none of the contestants ever dares mention. But they must all be living in two mindsets at once; Amber can't be the only one convinced that traveling to Mars is within the realm of possibility, while also feeling that her fragile human brain can't even comprehend such a move. It's like believing in the Rapture: you feel that one day you'll be lifted away from this fallen, degraded world—but you still make mortgage payments, just in case.

"No idea." Amber could confess that some days she wants to get voted off, because Mars is terrifying. Other days, she wants to win so bad she aches—sees herself standing on a MarsNow podium, biting down on a gold medal. "I have nothing else going on," she says. "Quit my job. Put all my energy into this."

"Anyway, they won't vote you off. Not after today. Plus you have great tits."

"You won't get voted off either. You're a writer. We need someone to record the journey. To make sense—"

"Please. Spare me."

"What would *you* do? If you got—?"

"Eliminated?" Pichu wraps herself in the ratty dorm-room blanket. "Move home to Eastend? I mean, my ex is living in our Calgary place, and I can't afford—" She groans. "Also I can't live there 'cause I had four miscarriages in that house and I just—"

"You had four miscarriages?"

"If you tell anyone, I'll die. I was worried the producers would find out and broadcast it. Like, I've shared about my dad dying. I've shared about my mom's breast cancer. But my babies aren't a commodity."

"I won't tell. I'm good at secrets."

"It's weird that no one can see anything wrong with me. Sometimes I *want* people to know, so I can get some fucking sympathy, 'cause my ex had none."

"He sounds like a terrible person."

"He's an engineer." Pichu shrugs. "My dad died in the middle of all these miscarriages. I started spotting and cramping at his funeral, actually. I knew what was happening, I was this old pro by then, but I was like, *You must be kidding me, I'm not going to miscarry at my dad's funeral.* Then I did."

"Jesus Christ."

"Then I finally got a diagnosis—endometriosis—which basically means most doctors want to stick me in a room with padded walls."

"That's awful."

"But I've been mostly keeping up on the endurance and strength stuff, and I'm doing okay mentally—I was suicidal for a minute, I know that sounds melodramatic. But this Mars stuff makes me feel alive. Like my body's not broken."

"Your body is *not* broken."

Pichu reaches across the table. "I feel like you're a little bit my sister, Amber-from-Vancouver."

"You're a little bit my sister, Pichu-from-Eastend. As if that's actually a place."

Amber grips Pichu's hand and thinks of Evie from summer camp, of their last conversation. *What's your problem?* Amber grabbed Evie's arm on their way to the mess hall. *Why are you ignoring me?*

Evie tugged herself from Amber's grip, looked her in the eye and said, *Because you're not a good friend.*

"One of us has to make it," says Pichu. "To Mars, I mean."

"I hope it's you."

"No you don't." Pichu squeezes Amber's hands. "Let's say a prayer together."

"Sure, but that's not fair 'cause you have way more gods than me."

"More gods and great hair. Hindu girls have all the things."

Amber closes her eyes. "I'm ready."

"Okay, say it with me, sister," said Pichu. *"One of us has to make it, and I hope it's me."*

But before they have a chance to entreat the spirit realm, there's a knock at the door.

"We're having a moment!" screams Pichu. "Unless this is a very handsome Israeli, please leave us alone."

Adam opens the door. "I feel chosen."

"You're always welcome here," says Pichu. "Especially if you're not wearing a shirt."

Adam massages Amber's shoulders. "She was the star today, wasn't she?"

"Major X factor," says Pichu.

"No I wasn't." Amber gets up from the table and tosses herself back onto the narrow bed.

"Okay." Pichu stands. "I'll leave you two alone."

"You can stay." Amber hops up on the mattress. Jumps. Her shoulder feels better; she's still taking half a Tylenol 3 every eight hours, and managed to get a refill on her prescription—for her collection—but she doesn't need to baby the joint anymore. "Seriously. Stay."

"Oh but I *want* to walk through the desert." Pichu puts on her jacket. "Because I love nature, LOL."

When she's gone, Amber says, "I didn't come across as a know-it-all? Or insulting?"

"Geoff Task noticed you. Which means the world noticed you." Adam climbs up beside her, bounces along with her rhythm. "We witnessed." Jump. "Not just your beauty." Jump. "And your strength." Jump. "But your mind."

Amber collapses onto her back, lets the mattress catch her like a net. Then pulls Adam down beside her. "Why haven't you kissed me yet?"

"Because I have military training." He smiles. "Which gives me particular expertise in self-denial."

"See? This is why we should go to Mars together. Our skills complement each other perfectly."

"How so?"

She presses her mouth to his, knocking their teeth together. Then pulls back, laughs, meets his lips more softly. They take a synchronized breath.

"I see what you mean." He tugs a handful of her hair, just enough to make her whimper. "We'd make excellent colleagues."

THE NEXT TIME BRONWYN COMES OVER, I'M STOKED TO SHOW HER
this Cuban film, an artsy, passionate, political flick that might mitigate the ol' we're-just-friends convo I plan to initiate. Anyway, Bronwyn comes in carrying a plastic clamshell of strawberries and some chocolate for fondue—which is *insane* because the movie I want to watch is called "Strawberries and Chocolate" in Spanish. This coincidence makes me feel like I'm living the correct life, whereas normally I feel like aliens abducted me, used their superior technology to suck out my soul, then dropped me back on Earth in the wrong body, the wrong place, the wrong era.

"You'll never guess the name of the movie I was thinking we'd watch," I say. "You're gonna freak. *Fresa y Chocolate*. Such synchronicity, right?

But then she goes, "So I had an idea."

"I love ideas."

"You know how we always watch stuff? What if we put the screen away for tonight?"

"And just get high?"

"Have you ever tried Tantra?"

"Is that . . . related to tantric sex?"

"It *is* tantric sex. I mean, it's not really sex. It can *involve* our Western definition of sex, meaning penetration." She smiles and blushes. "But I was thinking more like an intro session tonight."

"I thought that was a seventies craze. If people want to explore their sexuality these days, don't they just pay webcam girls to masturbate with oversized dildos?"

"You're funny, Kev. But want to try it?"

"I am not averse to kinky exploration."

Listen, I've officially only had sex with one person, and even though I think that one person is gorgeous and smells nice, doesn't mean I haven't also been curious. Once Amber said we should fulfill each other's fantasies, and I was intrigued. But her fantasy was to have sex with two men at once—*no, but Kev, you'd be one of them!*—and mine was to be kept as a pet by the girls from *Broad City* or to make profound, literary love to Zadie Smith. So that never really went anywhere.

"Tantra is about connection," says Bronwyn. "A way to know each other, inside and out."

"That sounds terrifying." Not that I don't appreciate connection. I do believe that sex is most powerful combined with love, and that instead of growing tedious, can deepen over time. Woefully old-fashioned, I know. "I don't think you want to know me inside and out."

Bronwyn looks me in the eyes. "Kevin, before we start, I just want to say that I am here for you no matter where we go on this journey. I am open to you."

"Okey-dokey."

"If it feels right to you, you can speak those words back to me."

"Sorry. Say what back to you?"

"That you're here for me no matter where we go on this journey."

"Cool cool, yeah, of course. We're here for each other."

"Ready?" Bronwyn sits beside me on the Voyager. "We have to face one another."

"Do we have to take off our clothes? Thing is, I'm definitely going to get back into running and weights and stuff, but at the moment I'm not very fit."

"I . . . gathered that. But no, we keep our clothes on."

"Do we have to breathe funny? 'Cause that yoga stuff makes me dizzy."

"Just breathe normally. Can you feel your breath entering your nasal cavity? Traveling down to your lungs? Can you find enjoyment in a single inhale and exhale?"

"Is this really happening?"

"It's all about pleasure and joy. Being in touch with the body and each other."

I close my eyes. Inhale, then exhale. "Oh yeah, see what you mean. Super joyful. Love it."

"Kevin? Look at me, Kev."

Her huge brown eyes remind me of a sad puppy's.

"Whoa." I'm trying to be chill. "There you are."

She smiles. "Here I am."

"What next?"

"We look at each other. For two full minutes. Think of it as a soft gaze, into my eyes."

"Can I blink?"

"Of course."

"Two minutes?"

"Don't overthink it."

"Is this a spiritual practice? 'Cause I don't want to be accused of cultural appropriation."

"The idea is that we truly attempt to see the other person, take them into our being through the visual sense."

"Do you set a timer—or? How does this work?"

Bronwyn takes out her phone and sets the timer for two minutes. "Ready?"

"Yep."

She gets me to sit cross-legged, which is not something my man-hips handle well, then we look at each other. *Into* each other.

I make it twelve seconds. Then suck air into my lungs, pound my fist against my seized chest. I might be having a heart attack. "Is this dangerous?"

"What if we try a different way," she says. "We gaze, but also hold hands. So we're co-regulating our nervous systems."

I miss Amber. I miss sitting on the couch, my arm around my girlfriend, her head propped against my chest. All our conversations were conducted this way. We didn't *gaze* at each other. We already knew each other. There's something relaxing about already knowing someone. There's also something relaxing about being with someone who's always trying to get away, instead of trying to get close.

"Kevin?" says Bronwyn. "One more try?"

"Yeah, yeah." I stand up, do a few jumping jacks, a bit of air-boxing. "I'm pumped, I'm ready, I'm a contender."

Bronwyn pulls me to the couch. Then takes my hands and stares into my eyes, and I stare into hers. I'm sweating as we look at each other's eyeballs. That word keeps going around in my head: eyeball, eyeball, *eyeball*, eye*ball*. Her eyes are *enormous*, her lashes so long— what if she can read my thoughts?—and she holds my hands and we breathe in and out, in and out, in and out and then—something happens. For a few seconds, two or three at the most, I *see* her. See her seeing me. And I'm okay. Not joyful, but okay.

Then I'm sweating again, and pull my hands from her grip. "One minute twenty-two seconds!" I raise her phone in the air. "That's a record." I flip on the TV. "I think we should be pleased with our results. Quit while we're ahead."

IT'S ALL MOVING FAST, SIXTEEN-HOUR DAYS, THE CAMERAS CON-
stantly in their faces and no one really learning anything—the
MarsNow producers promise that the two final people selected will
do real training, but it's too boring to show on TV.

Filming episode six, they float in the Neutral Buoyancy Pool,
wearing full gear, and work on a replica of the MarsNow Lander
as if they're on a space walk. Then Gabija from Lithuania and Ha
Joon from South Korea are eliminated, meaning they will miss New
Mexico's final challenge: zero gravity. The experience they've all been
anticipating in hushed, reverential tones.

Amber imagines that the remaining Marsonauts will be brought
into a temple-like space, white and bare and clean, where somehow
the force of gravity has been removed. And once the doors are sealed,
they'll float and spin and wheel through the air. Like how Adam
described the Dead Sea, the water cradling you like a beloved child.

But she knows she's being a tool, totally dumb—there's no such
thing as a "zero-gravity room," just like there are no angels soaring
through the heavens. And indeed they're all squished inside NASA's
KC-135, a jet plane that climbs into the air at a steep angle and intense
velocity, followed by a high-speed nosedive, then another climb. The
weightless effect starts as the climbing plane slows before the dive,
and again when it tilts upward. They do thirty of these sixty-five-
second parabolas, feeling weightless for twenty-five seconds each
time. Screaming, gripping each other's hands, laughing like maniacs.
Ramesh spins like a slow torpedo. Sergey giggles. Pichu pukes down
the front of her shirt.

It's amazing, loud, disorienting. But Amber's real zero-gravity
moment happens later, after the shoot is done, when she meets
Adam on the dorm's roof.

There's almost nowhere they can go that's private—everyone shares a room because TV producers are inexplicably cheap. But Adam and Amber climb onto the dormitory roof, stand in the desert twilight, make out under the distant stars.

Adam says again that they should remain, as much as humanly possible, celibate. Sex will hinder their athletic performance and mental sharpness. "I also don't feel right about it. Because of your Kelvin."

"Kevin."

"Yes."

She doesn't feel right about it either, but wishes it felt more *wrong*. Her love for Kevin seems like a whole and separate entity, unbreakable, distinct from her feelings for Adam. As a kid, she'd been told that one day she'd fall in love and form a sacrosanct union with one man; this relationship would be the most intense and rewarding of her life, would produce children, would bring her closer to God. But her adult reality has been so much more complicated, a layering of contradictions. Life would be kinder if you only felt one thing at a time.

"He's my Kevin and you're my Adam." She lifts Adam's T-shirt over his head. "And right now—" She kneels and starts on his buckle. "You're here."

He laughs, but grabs her wrists to stop her. "Amber Kivinen." Drops beside her on the roof. "I like the way you think."

Doesn't he want her to go down on him? She's good at it—wants to prove herself. But instead, he unzips her jeans, slides his hand over the seams of her underwear.

"Where are you most sensitive?" he asks. "Do you like this?"

What does she like? Other than being liked?

He lays her down on the hot tin, slips his fingers inside her. Above her the stars are endless, ancient, and for a moment she forgets him. Forgets herself. His mouth grazes her neck and he's nothing but damp breath and heat against her skin. She arches her back, soars toward the moon.

AFTER OUR EYEBALL-GAZING, BRONWYN AND I EAT THE STRAW-
berries and fondue, smoke a bowl, say goodnight. But the next
evening, courage restored, I invite her over and we have non-tantric
sex. Our first time falls under the venerable tradition known as Cis
Straight Hipster Sex, except that we aren't drunk—I'm sure Bronwyn wishes we were. Me: nervous and awkward and too focused on
not coming prematurely and/or maintaining my own erection. Her:
docile and forgiving and too focused on maintaining my ego and/or
emotional well-being. Let's assume, for the sake of reality, that her
orgasm was faked.

Then she's lying there naked, sort of languid and spent (or pretending to be), and I realize that she'll want to sleep over. In the bed
that belongs to me and Amber. Bronwyn is even lying on Amber's
side, using Amber's pillow.

"Are you working tomorrow?" I sit beside her. "If you have to go
home 'cause you need to be up early, I understand."

She smiles. "I don't work until noon, actually. Why? What are you
up to tomorrow?"

"Sort of a big day for me. A lot of maintenance stuff I need to do
around here. And a few clients coming over."

"Do you like your work? You must meet interesting people."

"I love the plants." I put on my boxers, stand up. "Actually I better
put them to bed."

Bronwyn follows me, entirely naked, into the spare room while I
flick off the grow lights.

"I give them a breather." I always like this moment, standing in
the dark jungle. "It's a literal 'breather'—plants focus on respiration
at night. Use the darkness to catch their breath."

"I love that." Bronwyn leans against me. "We all need restorative time."

"I'm on a sixteen/eight cycle now. Sixteen hours of light, then eight of darkness."

"So you switch it up?"

"Depending on what growth phase they're in."

She asks me more questions—about nutrients, cycles, harvest—and I sound like a professor when I answer. Or like a father. I've spent so much time learning from Amber that it never occurred to me that I also know my shit. These plants are my children as much as hers.

"You must get so attached," says Bronwyn, who has a way of reading my mind. "There's something sacred about plants, right? They have a wisdom we lack."

"Yeah, they're better than human companions. 'Cause they're so quiet." Then I see the look on her face. "I didn't mean that. I like listening to you talk."

"*Listening to me talk?*" She walks back to the bedroom, puts on her T-shirt, hides her face behind her dreadlocks. "I assumed we were having a conversation."

"You know what I meant."

"I never know what you mean." She pulls on underwear, then puts the full force of those eyes on me. "I don't even know how you feel about me. I don't know if I'm your girlfriend or just some side piece until your girlfriend comes home."

"I don't know if I have a girlfriend." I sit on the bed, stare at my lap. At the gray cotton boxers. "She's there and I'm here. But we're not broken up."

What I can't quite say is that Amber and I don't do that: we do not break up. It all comes down to the daddy issues. When Amber's dad disowned her, he didn't speak to her for thirteen months—not until he had a mild heart attack that put things in perspective. And that long silence taught her that nothing, not even parental love, is secure. So she puts us through these tests to prove the relationship's strength. It's like creating a superbug: slam the system with antibiotics and see what survives. I keep thinking that if we get through Mars (and our little dalliances) she'll see that my love is real. My love is a superbug.

"We're still officially together." I lie down, cover my face with a pillow and speak through the memory foam. "But then again, she might be leaving me forever. So you see why I'm confused."

"Oh my god. Kevin."

"What?" I remove the pillow from my face. "I'm telling the truth."

"I know," she says. "That's what's . . . fucked about it."

"Isn't it? It's existentially fucked."

"No, I mean—why don't you just talk to each other?"

WHEN AMBER ARRIVES BACK AT HER DORM ROOM, PICHU IS WEAR-
ing pajamas with a pattern of what looks like shit patties.

"Is that a . . . shit-patty onesie?"

"They're *latkes*! My favorite food. I keep meaning to have a latke
convo with Adam. Compare recipes." Then Pichu's eyes widen. "Oh
holy lord and Lady Gaga, something happened. With Adam."

"What? How did you—?"

"It's so obvious. Bloggers are going to be all over it. You've under-
gone a *glow-up*."

"Oh, I love reading about glow-ups. Always makes me hopeful."

"I know." Pichu wiggles under the bedcovers. "Don't you think
Angelina is so due for a post-Brad glow-up?"

"Overdue. Are they divorced yet?"

"Don't avoid the subject. You finally hooked up with Adam."

"Finally."

"I'm so happy because do you know what this means? Now you
must choose between two guys. Your life is a YA novel!"

Amber throws herself on her bed. Choice is loss. Choice is
death. "If you were writing my story," she says, "what would you
make me do?"

"I don't tell my characters what to do. Those fuckers dictate to me."

"But Amber the character, if you were advising her—who should
she choose?"

"YA is all about empowerment, finding yourself, so she'd probably
have to choose neither. Go off and become a solitary space warrior or
something."

No boyfriend. And no God. No man to kneel to? Amber buries
her face in her pillow. "That's not an option."

"Hey. I'm writing this story."

"What about both? Could she choose both?"

"Both?" Pichu gapes at her. "Like, she's got the wife here on Earth and a mistress on Mars? That's not YA. That's erotica. Maybe New Adult."

"No, just two boyfriends? At once? Like, why couldn't that *Twilight* girl have the vampire *and* the werewolf?"

"You are blowing my mind."

"I always thought Katniss should just be with Liam Hemsworth and the other one, what's-his-name. Then she wouldn't have to be all angsty. She'd just get on with the revolution."

"I know polyamory exists. In theory." Pichu scrunches her face. "But does it actually work?"

"Does monogamy work? Does anything work?"

"I mean . . . for women."

"Yeah. There's that." Amber slouches into the bed. "The patriarchy."

"Honey, I'm sorry, maybe because I come from a traditional family, or because I'm clued in to reality, or because even writers have failures of imagination—" Pichu shakes her head. "I just don't think there is any world, in any universe, where a woman gets to have both."

BRONWYN PUTS ON HER BRA AND UNDERWEAR AND I FEEL A WAVE
of relief—this awkward night is almost over—but then she says, "I
know this sounds crazy, but do you want to go for a walk?"

"Right now? In the dark?"

"It's so hot in here and I just feel kinda—" She fans her face.

"Sorry. About the heat."

"I get it. It's your work." She puts on her shirt and jeans. "But want
to? It's a nice night. We could walk around Trout Lake."

I used to go for walks. Years ago. With Amber. *Wanna get out
of here?* I'd traipse behind her through wet forests, slipping in mud
while Amber leapt over creeks like a deer, or bent to inspect mushrooms, or foraged for salal and salmonberries. She was always bringing home weird, wild food that she'd force me to eat—plantain leaves
for salad, clover for tea—because she was determined to survive no
matter what apocalyptic future comes. Personally, I'd rather throw
myself off the Granville Street Bridge; if it comes down to chewing
dandelion roots or bowing out of existence, I'm firmly in the *sayonara*
camp. But I did enjoy the hikes and walks—I even planted my ass in
a kayak a few times, and I could identify my share of species. Like
the spruce tree outside our door—Amber taught me to recognize its
whorled branches and four-sided needles. I became . . . not one with
nature, but comfortable there.

So I could make the effort now. I could go outside. Walk upstairs,
unlock the door, kick open the screen, and be outside. Go for a walk
with Bronwyn—no big deal. It might even be pleasant.

But it's impossible. Since Amber left—and these have been the
longest six weeks of my life—I've yet to leave the apartment. This
is an epic vigil, a Penelope-waiting-for-Odysseus saga. (Without the
fidelity part, I guess.) It would be insane to stop now.

Anyway, since Mom died, the world hasn't felt too friendly, and since I spread my mom's ashes, the outdoors seem overrated. I stood beside Amber in the fall sunlight and tossed Mom's remains onto a field, only to watch them get kicked up by the wind. Then I inhaled and choked on human ash in a real-life homage to *The Big Lebowski*.

"I can't go for a walk," I say. "At the moment."

"Why?" Bronwyn laughs. "Are you busy?"

"I'm—in mourning."

"What?"

"My mom. Yeah. She just died."

"Are you serious?"

"Weird, right? But it's okay. She'd been sick for a while."

Bronwyn's eyes are saucers. "When's the funeral? Are you going home?" She stands up, her jeans still unzipped. "She was in Thunder Bay, right? Is your dad okay?"

Finally, something truthful comes out of my mouth: "I never knew my dad." But this truth is followed by a doozy of an improvisation: "And I can't go back to Thunder Bay because . . . my mom requested that we not mark her passing, except by—"

Flashback. Interior. Day. My mom's funeral. I was twenty-one and Amber held my hand while we all listened to "I Wanna Dance with Somebody." My uncle Terry showed a clip from *Harold and Maude*, the part where Maude throws the ring into the water and says, *Now I'll always know where it is*. Then Amber nudged me to go to the front, to say a few words, or to peer into the casket and say a private goodbye. No. No thank you. I would not look at the body. I refused to see, refused to cry. Felt dry and lifeless as ashes in an urn. Then Amber linked her arm in mine and steered me out of the funeral home, back to Uncle Terry's place, for the kind of random dinner my mom was famous for: BBQ ribs, artichokes dipped in butter, pineapple chicken from the Chinese place, coleslaw, Oreos. *If things are good on their own*, she used to say, *they'll be even better together*.

Cut to the best sex of my life, the night after the funeral. In my childhood bedroom, on my childhood bed, my face between Amber's thighs for what felt like hours, the pungent smell of her in my nose— Amber was wet, breathing, alive—circling her clit with my tongue until she squirmed and said, "Kev? Kevin. I'm kind of going numb down there." *Numb.* It was the right word. The room was pitch-black and I couldn't see myself, couldn't feel my limbs moving through space. Only Amber existed, though I couldn't see her either—could only brush against her smooth skin, smell her damp neck, feel the bones of her wrists under my hands. There was nothing but *Amber, Amber, Amber,* and slipping inside her was like crawling inside her skin. Her lungs swelled and ebbed for us. Her heart pumped for us.

"Your mom didn't want you to mark her passing, except by?" prompts Bronwyn.

"She, yeah. Requested that I look up at the moon every evening, and wish her a good night, before I go to sleep."

Bronwyn walks over and wraps me in her arms. "That's so beautiful, Kevin. Your mom sounds like an incredible person."

"She was cool."

She was also melancholic, judgmental, resolutely and dishonestly cheerful. Prone to weeping at movies but never in real life. She smelled like lavender shampoo and cigarettes and dryer sheets. Her laugh filled the whole house.

I try to do this every so often. Remember the details. Restore my mom in my mind—otherwise the film becomes grainy and faded.

"I'm so grateful you shared that with me," says Bronwyn. "So appreciative of your trust and openness."

"Totally."

Bronwyn takes my hand, leads me to the window. The moon isn't exactly visible behind the low clouds, but we look upward anyway.

"Does it feel right that I join you in this ritual?" says Bronwyn. "Please don't hesitate to tell me the truth."

"The truth? Oh yeah. It feels right. It feels great." I give her a thumbs-up. "Let's do this thing."

THEIR LAST NIGHT IN LOS ALAMOS, THEY'RE BROUGHT OUT INTO the desert sunset and told to sit in a circle.

"Marsonauts," says Bridget. "You survived training. You are qualified to be on board the next mission to Mars. How do you feel?"

Justine says she feels that same satisfaction as after a good hunt and particularly clean kill. Ramesh says he feels "light-headed, yes, very amazing, thank you for asking, dear esteemed host Bridget." Pichu says she wishes she hadn't wrecked her T-shirt.

Amber has a hard time answering. On the one hand, she feels wonderful—powerful, heady, slightly crazed. Can still feel Adam's breath on her neck, his lips at her hairline. Obviously she should choose Adam: he finger-banged her into existence. But they've gone back to being shy—haven't spoken since their session on the roof and can barely make eye contact. And she keeps thinking of that article she read when she took a primatology elective at university. Buried amid all the studies by men on the fascinatingly familiar violence of male chimps, there was research by a female primatologist who worked with apes in captivity. This woman pointed out that unless new males were introduced into the group every three years, the females became listless and depressed. When a new male came into the enclosure—Amber remembers the exact phrase because poetry was rare in these dry research papers—*the females' instinctual selves seem to awaken from somnolence.*

Is she just a lady-ape in a Homo sapiens's body?

You can't say that—*my instinctual self has awakened from somnolence*—on television.

And is that even true, anyway? She feels excited, but in a sick-to-her-stomach way. Guilt? Fear? It's only a matter of time until the MarsNow cameras catch her and Adam in some compromising position. And it'll be broadcast everywhere. And Kevin will be forced to watch.

With the others—Jianju, Tariq, Brayden—she almost wanted to get caught. It was a destruction fantasy: Kevin would find out and it would be the end of the world. Total meltdown. Relationship apocalypse. But the kind of apocalypse that offers redemption and rapture. *Repent, for the kingdom of heaven is at hand.* She and Kevin would finally be able to talk. Finally be honest. It would destroy everything but they would emerge from the wreckage healed. They would walk, together, into paradise.

"Amber?" says Bridget. "How about you? How do you feel?"

These "sharing circles" are becoming impossible as more competitors are eliminated. She just wants to focus on the daily challenges—not think about the possibility that this week could be her last. *One step at a time.* And Nick keeps trying to make eye contact; he wants that phone back so bad she can smell it through his cologne. Her strategy lately has been to never, ever be alone because he won't mention the phone if other people are around—but she can't avoid him forever.

Amber used to have panic attacks as a kid, what her mom called *spells*; they felt like a bellyful of small, scurrying rodents. The spells only went away once she started competitive gymnastics. But maybe they never did go away? She can feel the rodents now—curled inside her, still dozing. But rousing, stretching their rat-limbs.

"I feel grateful," she says. "To be here with all of you."

God, she's full of shit.

"This moment is never easy," says Bridget, "but no one said life was meant to be easy."

They all nod. Bridget can get deep sometimes.

"Ebad." The host turns to the bioengineer from Pakistan. "You came to us shy and quiet, and you've blossomed out of your shell."

Amber can imagine Kevin at home, exasperated by the mixed metaphor.

"And Pichu—"

Amber's stomach seizes.

"Pichu, you've been a delight from the moment you arrived." Bridget reaches for their hands. "We'll miss you both, but I'm sorry to say: Ebad, Pichu, you're going home."

"What?" Amber stands. "Was there a mistake?"

Bridget smiles, makes an *awwww* face, then says, "The citizens of Planet Earth have spoken."

"But everyone loves Pichu. Everyone."

"Chill, Amber," says Pichu. "It's okay."

"It's not okay. I think they should do a recount."

Adam puts a hand on her shoulder. "Amber. Calm down."

She shakes him off. Hates his patronizing tone even more than Slick Nick's wandering hands.

"I didn't have a chance anyway." Pichu smiles in that don't-show-the-pain way. "There's only room for one chubby brown girl on TV and Mindy Kaling already took that spot." She looks around. "Why do you guys look so sad? That was a funny line." To Bridget: "We need a laugh track."

Later, in their dorm room, Amber lies on her narrow bed watching Pichu pack. "It's suspicious. You're cut but useless Tish is still here? It doesn't make sense."

"It does if you recall that Tish is white." Pichu's phone pings, a sound so unfamiliar now that it makes them jump. "Okay, that's me," says Pichu. "Uber to the airport."

"I can't believe they make you leave right away. I can't believe they make you order your own Uber."

"Things move fast in showbiz." Pichu shrugs but looks like she's battling tears. "One day you're at the top of the world, next you're bagging groceries at your cousin's store in Swift Current."

"But they should at least let you stay a few more days, to rest and—"

Pichu shakes her head. "My ex works in oil-and-gas and it's the same when you're laid off. Security escorts you to your desk, you pack your stuff, you're gone within half an hour."

"But you're a celebrity, sort of—"

"Can you stop? This is post-2008 and we're all expendable. Tiny cogs. Tiny cogs overreaching in a desperate attempt to become medium cogs."

"But you'll be okay?"

"A-okay. Now I'm single and barren *and* the girl who lost an international popularity contest."

"Text me. All right? As soon as you get home."

"Baby doll," says Pichu in her best Slick Nick imitation, "you don't have a phone, remember?"

Amber opens her suitcase. "Don't tell *anyone*." She holds her phone with the same solemnity a Catholic would behold a relic.

"I don't even want to contemplate what you did to get that," says Pichu. "You are a bad bitch. See? That's why you're still here and I'm kaput."

"Untrue. I'm nothing special."

"Please. You're the real deal." Pichu steps closer. "Honestly, I wasn't in it to win. Not really. I mean, it was fun while it lasted, but come on."

"Me neither."

"You neither what?"

"Sometimes I wonder if I should just go home and have a baby."

What did Amber just *say*? To a woman who's had four miscarriages? "Oh god. I'm so sorry."

"Don't be." Pichu takes her hand. "If that's really how you feel, you should quit. Go home and have that baby."

But then Amber would become flabby and weak. And who would she have this hypothetical baby with? Kevin? Stoner, barely employed Kevin?

Most essentially, she can't imagine bringing a child into this world. Epidemics, floods, fires, pine beetles, market crashes, wars, genocides, rising sea levels, literal plagues of locusts. In this era of chronic emergency, how do people hold their children in their arms without despair? How do they find hope?

"The worst thing is regret," says Pichu. "The what-ifs. *Maybe I should have eaten better or not worked so hard or not waited so long. Trust me.*"

The door opens and Amber hides the phone under her pillow. Tamiko walks in carrying a backpack. "Pichu's still here? They told me she was gone and I had to move in."

"Hey Tam!" says Pichu. "So glad we get to say goodbye."

Tamiko rolls her eyes. "Which one is my bed?"

"The one that appears to be bereft," says Pichu.

Tamiko drops her backpack on the mattress before leaving. "I'll be back with the rest of my stuff."

Pichu grabs her own bag. "She loves me."

"She's my new roommate?"

"Ridiculous. She reminds me of my ex's new fiancée. Scary women are always taking my place." Pichu's phone buzzes again. "Damn, I have to go."

Tamiko reappears with two more bags, then leaves without a word.

"Instead of having a baby, I could be like that one," says Amber. "A femme-bot with a successful career."

"Why do we always have to choose?" Pichu puts on her jacket and sends a text. "I just told the Uber driver to calm the ef down, I'll be there in a minute."

Does Amber have to choose? Other women choose; other women sacrifice. But she was once the kid who missed classes to practice and compete but who excelled in school too. The teen who went to the gymnastics center for two hours before class started, then stayed late after school for Model UN club. The one who managed it all. Could she become that person again?

She sees herself tossing a baby into the air, watching him float high, then drift down giggling into her outstretched arms. The first child born on Mars. No rising sea levels, no locusts. Nothing but possibility.

"Maybe I do want it," she says. "To win, I mean."

Pichu smiles. "Good then. Do it for your homegirl." She hands Amber a signed copy of her novel, then they hug hard. "Going to Mars would be the craziest adventure. Your life wouldn't be a YA novel. It would be a legend."

Amber feels those rodents in her gut again. "I'll miss you."

"As Israeli Officer Adonis would say: *Channel that energy, Amber.*" Pichu grips her suitcase. "Channel that energy into kicking Tamiko's ass."

AFTER SAYING GOODNIGHT TO THE MOON, I COULDN'T VERY WELL ask Bronwyn to leave. Not now that I'd lied about my mom's goddamn *death*. And of course Bronwyn wants to hold me, and of course I want to be held because I'm supposedly grieving, and honestly the heat in this apartment makes a person lazy—so we end up in bed, me on Amber's side, me using Amber's pillow.

Bronwyn falls asleep and I sit up. *Sorry I lied about you, Mom.* I imagine my mom smoking her menthols, looking down on me from the celestial sphere and finding it all pretty hilarious.

You never stop making up stories, do you, honeybun?

Maybe I'll make up another yarn, to help me sleep, like I did when I was a kid. A dinosaur story. Or robots. I used to make up stories for myself, unspool them for days, adventures that would run through my mind as I was on the playground or in a classroom or at hockey practice.

The most far-fetched story I told myself was the one where my father showed up. That was one I never shared, my secret story: my father knocks on the door, tall and handsome and ready to be my dad. Ready to love my mom.

But eventually that story seemed pathetic, even in the privacy of my own mind. The character of my father became a villain. Then he faded into the background, took on a supporting role, became nothing but an extra. Stranger in the Crowd.

Around that time, I started to tell stories to calm Amber's panic attacks. Later still, I wrote screenplays and shared them in workshops, listening to overearnest feedback. I sent my scripts to contests and agents—managed to get some honorable mentions, some "your work has potential"-type letters. Once I was a finalist in the Big Break screenplay competition, and my mom printed the announcement, framed it, and hung it on the wall beside my high school graduation photo. There was a literal shrine to me in her house and maybe that's why writing made me feel like a god, in control of characters and conquering worlds. But once my mom died—and the house was gone, the shrine destroyed like the Temple at Jerusalem—writing made me feel small, incompetent, an impostor. And there was Amber, always wanting me to *get back into the writing*. She has her father's understanding of art, as something that people do for the usual reasons: to find glory, to make money.

Nothing comes to me now. No new stories. It's been this way for years. I used to be the kind of person who'd carry a notebook everywhere. Now I only get ideas when I'm stoned, and never remember them when I sober up.

I could scratch lines into the wall—I'm a couple of days behind. Or I could keep reading *The Great Gatsby*. Lie languid in the heat of my apartment like Jordan Baker, both of us with our pleasant, contemptuous outlooks. But Bronwyn's sleep deepens and I don't want to disturb her. She has a nose whistle—such a delicate, adorable sound. When her eyes aren't focused on me, aren't trying to see inside me, she's exceptionally pretty. Nice skin and these sexy, full lips.

I lie beside her and we share a moment of—I'm going to say it—serenity. She doesn't want anything from me; I'm not thinking about Amber. I close my eyes and feel Bronwyn's body next to mine, warm and soft and strange.

AMBER CAN'T STAY IN THAT DORM. TAMIKO OPENED THE WINDOWS as if to exorcise a ghost and is now arranging some sort of minimalist shrine on the windowsill, so Amber goes to Adam's room. When he opens the door, she moves to hug him but he steps backward.

"I know it's difficult," he says, "but we can't make love."

"I didn't come here to have sex with you." She almost laughs. "I wanted to see you because—" The rodents claw at her stomach. "Tamiko moved into my suite. It's like Pichu never existed—"

"It's not cost-effective for them to house us when we're no longer—"

"But kicking her out *tonight*? It's nearly midnight. And she's *Pichu*."

"Some people win and some people lose."

"Thank you. I'm aware of what a competition is."

"But you seem to think—"

"It's called being *sad*."

He grips her shoulders. "We will encounter far greater pain on our mission."

"Are you for real?"

"This is nothing." He practically shakes her. "Without gravity, the fluids in our bodies will pool in our heads, swelling our sinuses and putting pressure on our optic nerves. Our hearts will be under more stress than during an Ironman. The wasting of our muscles—"

"Thanks. Got it."

"We will combat loneliness, homesickness, motion sickness, claustrophobia, disruption of circadian rhythms—"

"You don't get it." Amber pushes him away. "I might never see her again. Or if I do, it won't be the same. We shared all this time together, and she made me laugh, and I could *breathe* around her—"

"You were acquainted with her for seven weeks."

"What if?" Amber takes her hair in her fists, pulls hard. "What if I've lost her?"

"The weakest link in space travel is the human mind."

Amber stares at him. "You just called me *weak?*"

"I want to hold you tonight." Adam takes her hand. "Do you think we could sleep platonically side by side?"

"Is it just sex with a woman that enfeebles you? Or are you not even going to masturbate this whole time?"

"This conversation began wrongly. I take responsibility."

"I do not want to sleep *platonically side by side.*"

"Yes. Save the endurance tests for when it matters."

Was that an attempt at a joke? "I want be alone," she says.

"I hurt you. We should discuss it. You shouldn't go to bed angry—"

"No, you're right. I knew her for a few weeks. I'm being—crazy."

"Amber, if there's something you need to express—"

"I don't need to *express* anything. I get this from my mom. Every once in a while she'd get so dramatic—" She remembers her mother convulsing on the kitchen floor, ululating in tongues, while her father shouted, *Get out, Satan!*

"You never talk about your mother—"

"Because it doesn't matter! She'd get all weepy, and say she was unhappy but didn't know why. A day later it was over."

"That must have been frightening, to hear your mother say—"

"It's *fine.*" Amber steps away. "I'm fine."

She thinks of all the male chimps she read about in those journal articles: stalking each other, forming war parties, smashing each other's skulls. All that primal rage—it lives inside her too. And she'll need it. She'll have to use it. Winning might be unlikely, but she can at least make it farther than Adam. She can at least triumph over this robot who called her *weak.*

"You're right," she says. "Some people win, and some people lose."

BRONWYN LEAVES THE NEXT MORNING AFTER A BREAKFAST OF muesli and almond milk, and I feel such intense loneliness that I clean the apartment. Scour the tub and wash the soap scum from the tiles and put the toilet paper roll on the holder instead of leaving it on the tank. Wash the dishes, including the Tupperware and Mason jars Bronwyn left behind. Change the sheets on the bed, swap out the towels, sweep the floors.

I must feel guilty. Like when I forgot Amber's twenty-second birthday and didn't show up to the pub for drinks with her friends until 11 p.m.—I was chilling with Marcus and just sort of ... blanked. Or the time we were bird-sitting for our friend Mariella— all we had to do was feed this squeaky budgie for a couple of weeks while Mariella was in Hawaii. But one day I forgot that the window was open when I unlatched the cage, and Frederick flew away into the blue sky. We bought another budgie and tried to pass it off as the original, but Mariella knew right away that it wasn't Frederick and burst into tears. Then Amber made it worse by saying, *I guess he wanted freedom?* But I knew that a budgie wouldn't live long out there in the bad world; the crows had probably already torn him limb from limb. I'd killed a beautiful thing. So I scrubbed the floors and washed the walls.

Maybe ... I shouldn't have slept with Bronwyn? I probably shouldn't have slept with her in our bedroom, in our bed. What if Amber is eliminated tonight? What if she comes home and finds out? There was a chance for us before, but Amber has never been forgiving—

Screw that. What's to forgive? Amber's gallivanting around with some killer from the Mossad. And maybe she'll feel awful. Maybe she'll be pissed. And I can be all: *See? It sucks, doesn't it? It sucks to be* made to feel undesirable, worthless, replaceable. *It sucks to find out that the person you love is duplicitous and cruel. It sucks to love them anyway.*

But what if Amber doesn't care? What if she's relieved? Or never finds out? What if I don't tell her, no one tells her, and when she comes home, I get away with it? That wouldn't be good. That wouldn't be right. Because I am not like Amber. I might not be ambitious, I might not be successful, I might not be fit—but at least I'm honest. At least I understand loyalty and love. Right?

I light a joint, suck in some solace, pace the apartment like it's a (relatively clean) cage. I'm tempted to take the cushions off the Voyager and build a fort, hide inside it until this Mars absurdity is over. Have I entered Howard Hughes territory? Maybe I just feel weird 'cause I haven't been outside in almost two months. Probably just need some vitamin D.

I look at the closed door of my apartment. Aware of the possibility of opening it. Of putting on shoes and a jacket and stepping outside. But who are we kidding, this is Vancouver in winter—we might as well be on Jupiter when it comes to how many UV rays reach us through that ceiling of gray cloud. And who needs real sunlight anyway, when one has full-spectrum LEDs in one's own home? Who needs real weather when the thermostat is kept at a balmy 28 degrees? I put on my trendy UV-filter glasses and head into the spare room, with its buzz of high-intensity light. Then I open the door to the closet, which we call *the nursery.*

"Hey, little dudes."

These are the babies of our brood, only eight weeks old, hardly knew their mother before she left to be a TV star. They glow purple under the LEDs. I lie next to them so the light falls on my skin too.

Sometimes I wonder if I'm having some sort of parental urge. I've never really considered it because Amber doesn't want kids, though sometimes I think we'd make good parents. She'd be the Type A mom who forces our fetus to listen to Mozart, and has a non-medicalized birth on a paddleboard in the middle of the ocean, and enrolls our kid in gender-neutral sports classes, and encourages him/her/them to become an activist-entrepreneur by age twelve. And I'd balance it all by being the cereal-and-cartoons-on-Saturday-morning dad, the let's-wander-to-the-library-and-take-out-age-inappropriate-books guy, the dude who makes Mommy laugh and ensures that every once in a while she takes a fucking nap. It sounds kind of fun. And I can imagine Amber pregnant, strong and stunning like one of those ancient fertility-fetish sculptures.

I try to picture having a child with Bronwyn; I can barely fathom going for a walk with Bronwyn. But I guess sometimes I think about being a dad, a better one than I had. A dad who's actually around. One who—when his kid scrapes their knee or gets mocked by jerks on the hockey team or, I dunno, gets their heart crushed—a father who says, "I'm here."

Amber might already be packing her stuff, because they wrapped the shoot hours ago. She might already be on a plane, flying toward me.

I try to imagine going back in time, to the Amber era, when I wasn't allowed to drink beer or eat macaroons, when I'd only officially had sex with one person, when I'd never experienced the enlightening practice of Tantra. I try to imagine Amber here, in these rooms. Sitting on the Voyager, sleeping in the bed I shared with Bronwyn. My Odysseus, my Daisy Buchanan. The one I most want, and most dread, in the universe.

WHEN AMBER WAKES THE NEXT MORNING, TAMIKO IS LYING OVER A bolster, an eye mask covering her face, earbuds popped in her ears. She's probably been up for hours. Probably already showered and massaged expensive cream into her exquisite skin. Brushed her luscious hair a hundred times. Just this woman's existence, the fact of her, feels like a reproach. Is this how Kevin feels, living with Amber?

She opens a bag of pumpkin seeds, shakes them in Tamiko's serene face. "Want some?"

Tamiko sits up. "I practice intermittent fasting and do not consume food before eleven a.m. or after six p.m."

Amber crunches her seeds noisily. "Studies on rats show that's not actually an appropriate diet for females—"

Tamiko lies down, replaces the eye mask over her lids, the AirPods back in her ears.

Does observing someone else as she enters deep relaxation—watching the infuriatingly calm rise and fall of her rib cage—count as a form of meditation?

Amber's skin feels like it's crawling with ants. She grabs her stuff and goes to the gym, keeping an eye out in case she needs to dodge Nick. Doesn't listen to music on the elliptical, just lets this refrain play in her head: *my fault, my fault, my fault.* Amber must be to blame for Pichu's elimination. Amber is being punished for what she did on the roof with Adam. Punished for enjoying it. Punished because this incident is far worse than her other flirtations—this is real. It means something. It's a true betrayal because she could see herself *with* Adam. Oh god, it was embarrassing, but she could imagine *having Adam's baby.* Why could she never imagine having a baby with Kev? Why was she imagining having babies at all?

As her father said: *God sees everything.*

But another voice in her head—Kevin's? Pichu's?—says: *Isn't that a little self-involved? A little self-obsessed? Two hundred species of plants, mammals, insects, and birds are going extinct every day—God doesn't give a shit if you cheated on your boyfriend.*

But maybe He does.

Is fearing God the same thing as believing in Him?

And I gave her space to repent of her fornication, and she repented not . . .

But what is there to feel guilty about? What did she *do* exactly? Mingled saliva and let someone touch her labial folds—who cares? Sex and love are renewable resources; it's not like she's going to run out and have no supply left for Kevin. But that would entail having *both*, and that's not allowed. Not unless Kevin got some action on the side too. She'd almost welcome that—wants him to feel as alive as she does. Maybe he'd be able to write again.

But Kevin has no interest in other women. He's loyal like a puppy, which is his best and most frustrating quality.

So. Fine. Kevin's at home smoking pot. Kevin's rent and their insane electricity bill is being paid with her MarsNow paycheck. What Kevin doesn't know can't hurt him.

But does he, on some level, *know*? Can he sense it, even from afar? When people love each other, are they connected on a spiritual plane?

She already sounds like someone who's spent too much time in LA.

She does squats and dead lifts until her muscles are shaky, pulsing with lactic acid and pain. Then grabs some chocolate milk and two tahini chicken wraps from the cafeteria, and because it seems a bit hilarious, also purchases a Mars bar. Consumes it all in a frenzy, then again regrets breaking her no-sugar rule when her calves go into spasm. Wishes the MarsNow people thought to provide a massage therapist on set. Goes for a walk through the desert and contemplates how difficult it is to find meaning in anything anymore, even the natural world, when there isn't a camera following her. Wishes she were doing something, anything, other than starring in this degrading reality show. Wishes she were still a goddamn reception-ist. Checks her privilege and remembers that some people are refu-gees, some people lose their homes to foreclosure, some people have epilepsy—come on, stupid cunt, get a grip.

Feels those rodents chewing her stomach lining, like when Evie was hauled up onstage at camp, during worship, and made to confess. *Evie, don't let sin fester inside you!* So said the pastor as he stood over Evie, age eleven, because Amber had told him what her friend had confided in private: that sometimes Evie couldn't feel God's presence. Sometimes she didn't believe in Him because she couldn't see Him. That she'd read—and loved—the *Harry Potter* books. Worst of all: Evie was still secretly in touch with her nineteen-year-old cousin in Toronto—the cousin who'd left her husband and now worked as a waitress. *Let go of Evie! Let her go, sin! In the name of Jesus, we bind you, Satan, and command you leave!* Evie stood frozen onstage, eyes locked on Amber the betrayer.

Why had she done it? The same impulse that caused her to tattle on her sister at home: if someone else's sin is revealed, your own stays hidden.

For months after Evie's exposure, Amber drew the plagues of Exodus. On her jeans, her arms, the pages of library books, the backs of her binders.

Blood.

Frogs.

Lice.

Flies.

Fire and hail.

Boils.

Locusts.

Pestilence.

Darkness.

Death of every firstborn son.

Now, evening falls. Amber goes back to the dorm room and

finds it mercifully empty. First things first: she steals a handful of Tamiko's tampons; Amber isn't working out as often lately and her period is bound to make a comeback. Then she takes a shower, patches up her manicure, trims her bush, puts on PJs. Stares at her pores, squeezing out blackheads with tweezers. Her forehead is too wide, her nose asymmetrical. Her smile is okay—thank god her parents sprang for braces—but wrinkles are forming at the corners of her eyes. Fuck. She "borrows" Tamiko's derma-roller and slathers on Tamiko's glycolic serum. Then lies on her bed and stares at the ceiling. Everyone is probably gathered in the common room, watching the episode. Amber refuses. Will not bear witness to the injustice of Pichu's elimination. And doesn't want to see Adam right now. He's right; of course she overreacted. But his cold, analytical attitude—is that normal?

She hears something buzz. Her phone. She still has her phone! Locked inside her suitcase, wrapped in a dirty T-shirt. She searches the bedside drawer for the suitcase key, fumbling with that tiny idiotic lock, ripping the unwashed clothes from the case until her hands find the comforting rectangle of plastic and glass.

A text from Kevin.

I can't believe they voted Pichu off!!! (Sorry, I know we can't be in touch but I think this counts as an emergency.) WTF were people thinking?? Humanity is the worst.

She clutches the phone to her chest, eyes squeezed shut. She can breathe.

Why do you think I want off this bullshit planet? she replies. Then hesitates, adds a heart emoji, hits send.

49

HOW DOES SHE HAVE HER PHONE? AND WHAT AM I SUPPOSED TO make of that heart? If it was green or blue or purple or—god for-bid—yellow, I would read: *friend zone*. If it was black, I would read: *dark, morbid mood*. But it's red.

I've considered these questions for days. I've written a PhD the-sis on these themes. I've stared at Amber's heart for so long that the tiny muscles supporting my eyeballs ache—it isn't lost on me that I'm having tantric sex with an emoticon.

Why do you think I want off this bullshit planet?

I've written and deleted several replies:

I slept with Bronwyn, you know the vegan chick, and it was weird.

Can you come home now?

I miss you.

What I actually send: *Remember the hidden lake?*

Flashback. Interior. Day. Grade twelve. We were in the cafeteria, at a long table covered in candy wrappers and half-eaten sandwiches. The bell was about to ring and Amber turned to me. "Wanna get out of here?"

At first I wasn't sure she was addressing me. She and Marcus were once sort of a thing, almost dating, so I figured she'd never consider me more than his sidekick. I'd chatted with her at a party a few weeks before, but hardly knew her.

"You mean skip class?" I said. "I have a math quiz this afternoon." As if I cared about quizzes.

"Those are only worth one percent of your mark," she said, "so even if you miss or fail nine of them, you could still get an A-plus."

"I'm sitting at a solid B-minus right now." I stared at her. "Where do you want to go?"

She grabbed my hand and we started running. One step, then another, a push through the heavy doors—and we were outside.

It was a cool spring day; the wind cut through the cotton of my hoodie—cooled me as we ran away from school, the end-of-lunch bell sounding in the distance. After a couple of blocks, we paused to catch our breath and my brain caught up: Amber Kivinen had chosen me.

I'd kissed two girls drunkenly at parties, and sometimes heard through complicated rumors that I was considered "cute," but never felt much of anything romantic other than deep, desperate crushes on actresses (Minnie Driver, Gillian Anderson, Neve Campbell . . .). But here was Amber Kivinen, who'd been on my radar for years, a crush so real that I kept it secret even from Marcus, maybe even from myself. And we were ambling through Westfort, under a huge sky.

Westfort was my own neighborhood but it suddenly looked shameful—those small, run-down bungalows on their skinny patches of lawn—because I knew that Amber lived on 20th Side Road. Marcus had been there, had described it: a lot that was probably half an acre, with a newly built house that looked like something from a movie set—an estate practically, right out of a wealthy American suburb.

"I didn't think you ever skipped class," I said.

"Does everyone assume I'm some goody-goody Christian?"

"I guess. Aren't you?" I snuck a glance at her. We were, inadvertently and subtly, talking about sex. Virginity. But I was still a virgin too, despite no religious beliefs. I would have been terrified to have sex. "Are you gonna do the whole *good-girl-rebels* thing, where you get addicted to drugs and sleep around? I've seen way too many movies with that plot. There's got to be a better way."

"I could start a zine," she said. "Or a band?"

"Yeah! Or, like, volunteer at an abortion clinic."

We walked and walked, the sunlight bright in our eyes, and arrived at the Kam River, brown and nearly stagnant, its water clogged with an old ship rusting in the sun. We headed toward the swing bridge, though I'd spent my life fearful of bridges, my mom warning me from the time I was a toddler to avoid them because "bad kids" hung out underneath them like trolls. She said similar things about poorly lit streets, parking lots, and most of the city's parks. The world, I'd been told my whole life, was full of broken bottles and shitty people and aggressive dogs. But right then, beside Amber, I walked without fear. This was the world, and I felt at home in it.

We headed to the bridge, crossed the river; we balanced on the train rails, our arms outstretched. "Watch this." Amber raised her hands, then did a perfect cartwheel as if the metal rail were a balance beam.

"That's crazy! You're amazing."

"It's not amazing, you freak!" She laughed. "It's a *cartwheel*."

"If I could do that, I'd call myself champion of the world. Do you refer to yourself that way? *I'm Amber Kivinen, Champion of the World.*"

She shoved me off my own rail. "As if. Shut up about it."

"About how you're amazing?"

"About gymnastics. Gymnastics is over."

"Well." I shrugged. "Fuck gymnastics then." That seemed to make her happy. She gave me another little shove—was she touching me a lot?—and when I pretended to tumble to the ground, she grabbed my hand and pulled me to my feet.

"Fuck gymnastics," she said. "Fuck everything."

I wanted to kiss her then but was nervous, so picked up some pebbles and tossed them at that old, rotting ship—felt a thrill of triumph each time a rock pinged off the rusted metal.

We walked and walked until we stopped at the Reserve gas station to buy Cokes and a bag of Hickory Sticks. Then Amber led me along an overgrown road, past a dead industrial building she said was the old water-filtration plant, and into the bush, on a trail so wild that we sometimes had to push our way through walls of coniferous needles. We seemed headed toward Mount McKay.

"Where are you taking me?" I swatted at mosquitoes. "You know we've been walking for almost two hours? That's the length of an entire movie."

"We're almost there. You're so impatient."

"Only when I'm exercising."

"You consider this exercise?" She laughed. "Are you, like, the most intense lazy stoner? Or just pretending?" She looked back. "You're secretly some sort of rocket scientist or into lizards or beekeeping or whatever, right?"

I could barely keep up with her. Spiderwebs stuck to my face. "Do I seem like I'm into beekeeping?"

"You seem mysterious."

"I do? That's funny." It delighted me. Almost made up for the fact that branches scratched my arms, flies buzzed by my eyes, and my runners were coated in mud.

"Yeah, you seem quiet and, I don't know. Nice, I guess."

Nice? Did she want a guy who was nice? I leaned into the mystery thing. "I guess I do have a secret. I'm sort of a film geek."

"Ew, did you just call movies *films*?"

"I'm trying to confide in you. About my mysterious life."

"Sorry. Tell me more, mystery man. About the *films*."

So I did. Told her I wanted to write my own movies, maybe even direct them. Told her that my mom had bought me a used camcorder and Marcus and I recently made a documentary about the ugliest places in Thunder Bay. The strip malls, the sludgy parts of the lake, the abandoned grain elevators. "It's like a PSA. Suicide prevention."

"How does filming ugly places prevent suicide?"

"It's a warning system. Don't go to these places; you might kill yourself."

"Can I see this film?"

"Depends. Are you dragging me into the wilderness to murder me?"

She gave me another shove—she *was* touching me a lot, mostly my arm, sometimes my chest. I shoved her back and we kept at it:

bounced off each other, tripped each other, giggled and grabbed each other. I stumbled over tree roots. I was sweaty, out of breath, and would have been miserable if I hadn't been with her.

"This is fun," I said. "While simultaneously being hellish."

"It's like this is your first time outside."

"In fact, it *is*."

We seemed to be going up the fucking mountain, then down the other side of the fucking mountain, and it made no sense because from my perspective in Westfort, the mountain was the end of the world. But then the trail expanded, the ancient rock of the Canadian Shield came into view, and we arrived at an expansive lake.

Clear, blue water. Untouched trees. Sunlight glinting off the water's surface.

At the time, I didn't know this place was called Loch Lomond, or that it had been the city's reservoir. I was dealing with the shock that this sanctuary existed so close to my monotonous street, my embarrassing mom, my high school that smelled of rank gym strips. All this time, paradise had been so nearby.

"Holy shit. This is—" I couldn't risk getting poetic. "This place is cool."

"Told you. Sometimes I say I'm sick so I can skip church, then come here."

"You come all this way by yourself?"

"Is that weird?"

I learned later that she came to the lake often, striding through the forest, propelled by rage. Being out there was her way of coping with her church, her creepy coach, her injury. She liked to launch herself into the water, the colder the better.

"Not weird," I said. "Awesome."

"Do you want to swim?"

It was like a scene in a movie: she took off her shirt and shorts. She wore only a bra and panties—a purple bra that looked too small, that rode up her back and cut into her muscular shoulders. A pair of cotton underwear, the elastic around the legs overstretched, the waist-band yellowed from her sweat. She was so beautiful I could hardly breathe.

"Stop staring," she said, then ran into that crystal water, disappeared below its surface. The air was punched out of my lungs, as though a few seconds without her were too many. She reappeared in the middle of the lake. "Come on, chickenshit!"

It was every teen boy's dream, and it was happening for real. Life was unfolding like a romantic comedy. Except that I could barely swim. I could float, paddle around, but I couldn't travel any distance—she bobbed too far away. I couldn't even remember the last time I'd gotten my head wet in anything but a shower.

"It's chilly at first," she called, "but then it feels soooo good!"

It had to be done. If I drowned, it'd be worth it. I peeled off my sweaty clothes, stood at the lake's edge in my underwear. Took a step into the water, then another. Jesus, it was cold.

"Dive in!" She treaded water. "Be one with nature!"

"The thing about nature," I called back, "is that it's quite messy and unwelcoming!"

"Did you just call nature *messy*? Like, *Hey, nature, clean up your room!*" She laughed. "Don't your parents have a camp? Didn't they at least take you to Sandy Beach when you were a kid?"

No point mentioning that I didn't have parents the way other people did; I had a mother, and she was sick all the time. Also no use mentioning that my mom never took me anywhere. "Obviously my parents took me to the beach," I said. "Then I cried until they took me home."

"You're so pathetic I can't even stand it. I kind of *do* want to murder you." She swam a few strokes toward me. "Are you gonna cry now?"

"Only if you ask me to." The icy water stung my thighs. "I'll cry on demand if the Champion of the World requests it."

Then she dove under again, swam toward me, leapt up, tackled me. I splashed backwards into the water as she pressed her wet, blue mouth against mine. Her skin felt slimy and cool, like an eel's, and it was all I could do to keep hold of her.

SHE'S IN A SAUNA IN LATVIA, THOUGH THE SAUNA HASN'T BEEN
turned on. A fog machine gives the illusion of steam and the Marsonauts have been sprayed with fake sweat made from glycerin and
water. A round, elderly Latvian woman was hired to beat them
with wet birch boughs, and there's nothing fake about the beatings.
When it's Amber's turn, the woman slams her with enough force to
cause welts.

Amber likes it. Deserves it.

When it's over, she sits on the wooden bench, the fragrance of
birch wafting from her reddened skin. If only she really could sweat
it out, the sadness and rage and self-disappointment. Has she always
felt this way? From the moment she was born? If it wasn't your
actions, it was your thoughts. If it wasn't your thoughts, it was your
unruly body. This guilt existed underground for a while, when she
had a goal or project, but always resurfaced. Ate away at her like an
acid. The only thing to do was to mistrust every single one of your
actions and thoughts, to be vigilant, to *not fuck up*. That was her sister's strategy; Caleigh lived alone, was obese to the point of disability,
had never left Thunder Bay, had never had a partner of any gender—
had cushioned her own soul, imprisoned it within pounds of flesh, to
keep it from straying.

Or you could take another tack: you could go ahead and do something *bad*. Because if you were going to feel guilty anyway, you might
as well sin.

"Okay, team," says Slick Nick. "Let's get a few lounging-in-the-
sauna shots. This is your chance to relax. It's hot, your muscles feel
good, you're finally seeing each other almost naked. Got it?"

He looks at Amber when he says the word *naked*. Because her
strategy has changed: instead of hiding from him to keep her phone,

she has made herself and her phone essential to him. Sent him a selfie. Nothing incriminating, no nudity, just a close-up of her glossy mouth. He replied, *That lip ring. Hot. Did it hurt?* Exactly what she'd hoped for. An opening for conversation. *Got it pierced so long ago, I don't remember. You have piercings or tattoos?* He sent a pic of his pectoral, fuzzily tattooed with an eagle and the words: *The slaughterhouse of failure is not my destiny.*

This communication with Nick is a small price to pay for a bit of Pichu in her life. Last night, Pichu texted that she'd sold her novel-in-progress for over four hundred thousand dollars. *Literally four HUNDRED times what I made on my last book!*

Amber replied: *That's crazy! Amazing! Cra-mazing!*

Pichu sent a GIF of a toddler dancing on a picnic table, then wrote: *Gonna pay off my credit cards and buy a condo. Gonna be urban and literary and wealthy like a mofo.*

Now the Marsonauts arrange themselves on the sauna's benches; Manusha the hairstylist sprays their hairlines with water; Teeghan spritzes more fake sweat over their bodies. Amber closes her eyes—she was kept up last night by Tamiko tapping furiously on her laptop's keyboard. Tamiko is, of course, still running a lab and supervising thesis projects in Tokyo. She's *that* brilliant and indispensable—MarsNow had to bend to her will and give special permission for her to go online for two hours a day. She never abuses the privilege. Never even takes five minutes to look up the latest in the Brad-Angie divorce.

"Okay," says Linnzy, chewing an apple—this time a Granny Smith. "Rolling."

Steve the Australian stares at Amber's breasts, which Teeghan thoroughly beaded with pretend-perspiration. Amber wipes glycerin onto her hand and flicks it at him.

"Feisty," he says.

"Quit it." She closes her eyes, can't even look at him. "You're not funny."

"On the rag today, huh?" says Steve. "Or should I say, *eh*? You're on the rag, eh, Canadian girl?"

"If you don't shut up, I'm going to kick you in the balls."

"Feisty Canadian girl is getting too *hot*."

She stands, slams him in the scrotum, then sits on the bench while he writhes. Adam stares at her wide-eyed, probably appalled; Ramesh bites his nails; Tamiko raises one sculpted eyebrow; Tish gasps and covers her mouth; Justine whistles; Sergey shakes his head; Marion says *putain* under her breath. But screw it, this is who Amber is now. Clear, focused, present. Or at least, angry.

"Cut." Slick Nick bursts into the fake sauna. "Perfect, you two. That was awesome." Then, with a wink, "Amber, keep bringing it, baby."

BUT WALKING TO THE LAKE WITH AMBER WAS A LONG TIME AGO, IN a galaxy far, far away. In my current reality, Bronwyn comes over almost every day. Instead of Amber-type food (goat milk kefir, collagen peptides, "activated" pumpkin seeds), the fridge is full of Bronwyn-type food (almond milk, vegan cheese, peanut butter that we eat with a spoon when we're stoned). Bronwyn's toothbrush lives here now, sits in the water-stained glass next to mine. Her clothes hang in the closet next to Amber's, though I have an OCD tendency to keep Bron's apparel from touching Amber's.

This is our routine: Bronwyn brings food, always including a treat that we eat in a munchies frenzy. We drink white wine spritzers and cook a meal, a pasta or stir-fry that includes some of my Good People Box veggies. Cooking gives me joy. Because after about year seven, Amber refused to cook with me, or to even let me in the kitchen. Apparently I drip sauces on the floor, or leave dirty spatulas on the counter, and that means she has to follow behind me cleaning all the time. So even if I offered to give her a break and cook for her, that was more stressful than her cooking alone.

"Or you could just chill about it," I once suggested. "Not worry so much about the damn spatulas. Maybe try that?"

"Don't you understand?" Amber looked so desperate that it shocked me. "Don't you understand that if I don't clean it now, it'll harden and take twice as long to clean later?"

So it makes me feel manly and capable when Bronwyn says, "How about you cut the carrots?" and even leaves me in charge of making quinoa, which is a superfood that Amber and I enjoyed together circa 2009, a superfood I wasn't allowed to cook because I often let the pot boil over or burnt the bottom layer to a black crisp. Maybe I did it unconsciously, for some Freudian reason? Because these days I seem able to cook quinoa just fine.

After dinner tonight, Bronwyn and I smoke an Indica-dominant blend, then she reads my charts and tells me my horoscope—I'm destined for long periods of solitude, surprise! We have sex, which thankfully has improved since the first time. I'm becoming more adept at putting aside my mixed feelings re: betraying Amber (guilt, vengeful triumph, more guilt), and I'm not as nervous that, after Bronwyn's presumed exposure to huge hippie cock, she'll find my penis unsatisfactory. (Men who wear sarongs and porkpie hats out in public must have big dicks, right? Where else would such absurd overconfidence come from?) Everything about Bronwyn's body is soft: silky skin, tender breasts, muscles that seem to melt under my hands. The sex is nice. And there's nothing wrong with nice. Amber's presence was often both overwhelming and too familiar, and my powers (such as they are) would occasionally fail me. Sometimes I did nothing but worry about whether my scrawny body turned her on. And I gave up seducing her the day she told me that the concept of having sex every day, or even every week, is inherently sexist. That if it were up to women, there'd be no pressure to have sex regularly—couples would only engage in coitus during the pre-ovulatory and ovulatory days of a woman's cycle. During that special time, couples would make love up to six times a day.

"If men paid attention to their partner's cycles," Amber said, "everyone would be a lot less miserable."

So I let her be in charge, and I think she appreciated it? But Bronwyn doesn't seem to mind when I turn to her, cup her chin, pull her toward me. She also doesn't seem to mind if I'm not in the mood, if I just want to relax. She likes to lie with her head in my lap; during movies she often falls asleep, which is great because then she doesn't talk through the film. Afterward, I nudge her awake and we move to the bedroom. She holds my hand while we "say goodnight" to my mom. This process involves standing at the bedroom window, lifting the blinds, staring up at the moon in appropriately reverential silence. Bronwyn always seems to expect something from me—tears? A eulogy? It's like I'm going through it all again, and the second mourning period is like the first: I smoke a lot of weed and feel a lot of nothing. Except swelling in my elbow joints, tightness in my shoulders, brain fog every morning that clears around 3 p.m. Every time my mom dies, my body adopts her illness.

Tonight Bronwyn and I stand at the window and I try to say something deep: "Wow. The moon is big."

"It's a waxing gibbous moon." Bron leans against me. "That means now is a really good time to finish an important project."

"Is there ever a bad time to finish an important project?"

Honestly, I need to focus on the project of breaking up with Bronwyn. How can I be with a person who thinks my mom died two weeks ago? And how can I tell her the truth? There's only one way out of this maze now: I must burn all the corn to the ground.

"You know, my dad—when my mom left him, he went downhill." Bronwyn chews on her dreadlock. "Now I only hear from him, like, twice a year. And he's always hammered."

I put an arm around her. "That sounds hard."

She snuggles against me. "I sort of know what it's like to lose a parent."

We've been doing this lately, talking about real life, and the result is that every night I fail to break up with Bronwyn. Instead, we get into bed and lie on our sides, covered by a sheet, Bronwyn holding me. Amber's a stomach sleeper, so this is the first time I've experienced someone spooning me. And I get it now. I see what the hype is about.

IN LATVIA, AMBER CAN'T BELIEVE IT: CAWAALE AND JUSTINE ARE eliminated. Cawaale was a superhero, Justine a pit bull—and Amber has outlasted them? The losers cope by getting gloriously drunk with a group of shop owners while Amber lies on the floor and coaches herself to breathe.

She's tempted to text Pichu about the eliminations, but knows that would be playing with fire. And she doesn't want to mess up now that her phone seems secure in her possession: Nick texts her every night, with complaints about the executive producers, the AD, the crew, the other cast members. She's his confidante.

Things look good. Smooth sailing ahead. Except that she and Adam haven't spoken since New Mexico, since he called her *weak*.

After Cawaale and Justine go home, the remaining competitors are transported out of Latvia in a rickety old military plane. They land on the desert steppes of Kazakhstan. The Baikonur Cosmodrome, once the secret launch site for the Soviet space program, has a single runway made of deteriorating concrete and lined with Kazakh officials. The Marsonauts hug the kids, then are loaded onto a bus and driven along rutted, patched roads—past crumbling Soviet-era apartment buildings, huge cracked satellite dishes, a statue of Yuri Gagarin with his arm straight up in the air.

"This place is disturbing," says Logan.

"Omg," says Tish. "That's *so* racist."

They're brought to what seems to be a palace. The officials who met them at the airport lead them into a building with crystal chandeliers, marble floors, Jacuzzi tubs, and a dining room with pressed white tablecloths, fine bone china, and a flat-screen TV playing what seems to be an old Russian movie. A pot of borscht steams at the center of the table, along with a plate of roasted meat, potatoes covered in butter and dill, cheese, sausage, pickles, slices of salted pork fat that Sergey calls *salo*. Many bottles of vodka.

"Even C-listers live like kings in Kazakhstan," laughs Slick Nick, downing a shot. "Dig in, everyone. Just keep in mind, the moonshine'll put hair on your chest. And that there is horse meat." He shoots back another tumbler of vodka, then turns to Amber and Adam. "You two. Come with me."

They follow him outside into the dry, cold air.

"I feel like we're losing track of the love story," says Slick Nick. "We need another will-they-won't-they."

"Can we not?" Amber feels no need to converse with Adam. And the question of "will-they-won't-they" must be torturous for Kevin. "I'm starving."

Slick Nick laughs, suppresses a burp, winks at Adam. "She's got an appetite, huh?" Then gives Adam a light punch on the arm. "Maybe you have something you want to tell her?"

"If we do this quickly," says Adam, "it'll be over quickly."

Their mikes are adjusted, their hair and makeup touched up, then they walk arm in arm down Baikonur's frozen street. They pass rusting cars. Dogs digging through heaps of garbage. The occasional stray camel, swaggering slowly down the road. There's an eerie silence here and Amber can't think of anywhere better to pretend to be in love.

GATSBY GATHERS DUST ON THE COFFEE TABLE WHILE I DO SOME reading online. Think pieces about how more people are voting in the MarsNow polls than ever vote in political elections, and this proves that democracy is doomed. Think pieces about how we can't get our shit together to reduce carbon emissions but we *can* band together, globally, to ensure that Sergey doesn't get eliminated despite being totally physically inappropriate for the mission. Think pieces about how the show only includes one token LGBTQ+ competitor. Think pieces about how the show's structure, eliminating one man and one woman every week, reinforces a rigid gender binary. Think pieces about how the show objectifies women's bodies. Think pieces about how the show *also* objectifies men's bodies, which is supposedly feminism. Think pieces about the conspiracy theories the show has spawned (that Amber and Pichu are secretly dating, that Sarah is pregnant with Fernando's love child, that Tamiko is a highly realistic AI robot built to sabotage the mission). Think pieces about how none of the competitors has children, even though most parents have at least one moment a day where they want to say to their families: "Peace out, I'm off to Mars." Think pieces about how Adam from Israel should be eliminated since there are no Palestinians participating. Think pieces about how Adam will never be eliminated because he's the Internet's new boyfriend; Adam is everybody's Sexy Spock (as if OG Spock wasn't way sexier—don't @ me). Think pieces about the lack of Indigenous competitors and how that perpetrates stereotypes. Think pieces by Indigenous writers who are all: *We don't need to play at "being eliminated" because we've already experienced genocide. Also we have better things to do, like stopping pipelines.*

I read them all. When Bronwyn isn't around. And Amber still calls me, have I mentioned that? Usually for less than a minute, at strange times of day. She's somehow managed to hang on to her phone, and she calls now in the way she used to call those other guys, the skateboarder or the video store clerk—because she can't stop herself. Because I'm the secret she's keeping from everyone on this planet.

"Hey, Kev," she says.

"Hey, Earthling," I answer.

Usually we talk about the weather wherever she is, and the food. Costa Rican passion fruit, Latvian pickles, that sort of thing. I ask for details about life on set, because I almost miss being an extra, and get to hear anecdotes about Linnzy and Tamiko and the crappy dorm rooms and hotels.

So far Amber has never called when Bronwyn is here—weird, right? Reminds me of the multiverse theory. I'm paraphrasing here, but the idea is that every version of yourself is living out every possibility for your life simultaneously. It's all possible and it's all happening. And the weird thing is that these two particular strands—Amber and Bronwyn—don't seem incompatible. If I'm careful, I might keep them in precarious balance forever.

As soon as that thought hits me, the doorbell rings and my stomach lurches. It must be Amber or Bronwyn. A woman wronged, here to destroy me.

But hey! It's Bastiaan, holding a bouquet of collard greens, a bison steak wrapped in butcher paper, and a bottle of wine. "Hey friend," he says. "Do you mind if I crash here? In a bit of a situation."

Turns out all is not idyllic on the farm with Cedar and the kids. Bastiaan and Cedar are polyamorous but have one rule: no falling in love. They can hook up casually with the people in their organic farming community and beyond, but they do not allow themselves to have long-term relationships. So what did Cedar do? She spent six months Facebook messaging with her junior high school sweetheart, Freddy, who lives in Saskatchewan, works in potash, enjoys watching hockey, and wears a baseball cap *every single day*—he is the yang to Bastiaan's yin. Bastiaan's been at home, growing kale and other hardy crops, tending to the chickens, and listening to improv jazz. Cedar's been homeschooling the kids and fermenting kombucha, while also "falling for" a guy who drives a Ram truck. Crazy, right? Love is impossible.

I hear Bastiaan's story over a dinner of lightly seared bison and collards cooked in butter and garlic. Apparently what Cedar likes about Freddy is that he "gets shit done without having to constantly talk about everything." She feels like she's parenting five children— Bastiaan plus the four that traveled through her birth canal. She says Bastiaan "hooks into women's energy and uses that energy for himself." She says Freddy is a person so divorced from his body, so lacking an inner life, it's as if he barely exists. In the best way! He doesn't need her to hold his hand through every decision—he just makes decisions! He doesn't require her to investigate her feelings for him, just wants to know if he makes her wet. He's nothing but dick pics and compliments and cute jokes. He "replenishes" her.

"Guy sounds like a loser," I say, though I get it. When my mom was sick and alone and needed me, it got to be too much. Especially when I was a teenager. Flash-fucking-back. Interior. All the damn time. I'd come home from a party, or from skateboarding with Marcus, or from a walk with Amber, and find my mom in the middle of a flare, embedded in the couch cushions. Like a big, lumpy mushroom growing out of the trunk of a felled tree. "Oh, you're home." She always sounded relieved. "Come sit with me."

"I have homework." But her eyes snagged me, stopped me—her eyes were like two exposed nails. "You hungry, Mom?"

"Some tea?"

I'd boil water, put a chamomile bag in a mug. "Numb or sore?"

"Bit of both. Mostly tired." She'd rub her eyes; the rheumatoid arthritis would inflame the sclera and she always looked like she'd been crying. "And I had one of those sinus headaches."

Steep the tea, put the cup in her swollen hands.

"Thank you so much, honeybun. You're the most wonderful boy in the world."

"It's *tea*." Jesus Christ. "Not a big deal."

Maybe I didn't run away to Vancouver to be close to Amber, but to get away from my mother. Or maybe I adore Amber because she's capable, healthy, fit—she requires nothing from me. Which is good, because I am not reliable. I wasn't there when my mom needed me most. You could even say I killed her. (Long story.)

"So what should I do?" Bastiaan pours us each a glass of Malbec from the bottle he brought—a bottle with a real cork because he's a real adult. "Is this an indication that Cedar and I need to make more space for each other? Should we try a separation?"

"Definitely separate." I have visions of Bastiaan cooking for me more often. "You could move in here. We could be roommates."

"She wants to go to Saskatchewan to visit Freddy. Should I allow that? Is 'allow' the wrong word? Should I *encourage* that?"

"That would be brave."

"Should I go with her? Leave the kids with my parents for a weekend? Then all three of us could have a conversation. Part of the problem is the triangulation. She talks to me, then she talks to Freddy, and so much is lost in translation."

"You think?"

"Or should Cedar and I go away for a weekend on our own? A dirty weekend? No talking about feelings or the farm or the kids?"

The questions, the possibilities—we discuss them until three in the morning. My eyes keep closing but Bastiaan seems ready to stay up all night.

"Is this a breakup or a breakthrough?" he asks for the fourteenth time.

"Possibly a . . . break*down*?"

"Do you think it's true? That I hook into women's energy?"

"Like I said, it's hard for me to judge 'cause I just met you." I slide to the floor, close my eyes. "Maybe you should go back in time about twenty years and kill Freddy before he has a chance to meet Cedar in junior high. That would be simplest."

"If only that were possible, my friend." Bastiaan pours himself another glass of Malbec. "Is this a wave we're riding, Cedar and me? Or do you think we should separate?"

"Do *not* separate," I say. "Definitely not."

Flashback. To all the times Amber and I almost broke up. The worst was when I came home from set late one night, covered in goopy fake blood—I was an extra on *iZombie*—and Amber told me she couldn't take it anymore, my lack of drive, my depression, whatever it was. She said: *You were going to write a revolutionary zombie movie but now you're an extra on someone else's set? Someone else's vision.* The bloody gashes and wounds on my body seemed real, appropriate, externalizing how I felt. We were twenty-seven and the closest we've come to a real rupture.

But the next morning I made her a card with an eel on it. She loves eels because they use lunar cycles to navigate as they swim. The card was a takeoff on *Us Weekly*: "Eels—they're just like us! They look up at the moon."

Inside I wrote: *Thank you for making me look upward. You are my vision.*

IN KAZAKHSTAN, MARION AND RAMESH ARE ELIMINATED. AMBER hugs Ramesh but hears her dad's voice: *Don't let this in. Stay focused, champ.* For her In the Moment, she says, "I'll miss Ramesh, but I cannot think about that. Eyes forward."

That evening she eats so much salted pork fat that it oozes from her pores as she dances with the Kazakhs. They insist she down a shot of vodka, which makes her woozy, so she drags herself to her room. Tamiko is doing a headstand. Amber leans her own head against the doorframe. In her gymnastics days, she was the girl who skipped parties, went to bed early, avoided fun. Spent her Friday nights stretching and sitting in ice baths. That is the path to success, so why was she just dancing with a bunch of bearded, kinda cute, corrupt officials? Upside-down Tamiko makes it clear: Amber is a loser.

"Are you going to be up for long?" she asks. "I need to crash."

"My pranayama practice will be complete in twenty minutes," says Tamiko.

Amber lies in bed and listens to her roommate's long, loud breaths. When it's over, she says, "Do you like your life?"

"Of course." Tamiko changes into her pajamas, which startle Amber every night—they're fuzzy and girlishly pink. "What a strange question," says Tamiko. "If I didn't find joy, contentment, and challenge in my life, I would make a change."

"You're not scared of change?"

"Existence *is* change—why fear what's constant and unstoppable?" Tamiko sits on her bed. "Is it true that you're a Christian?"

"Not exactly." Must they discuss this? Why rehash how even as a kid, some teachings seemed ridiculous (a virgin birth?), and when she became a teenager they became even more absurd (no really, that virgin-birth story—Mary was clever, right?). For a while, Amber tried out a few other religions: Buddhism, Kabbalah, even attended services at the Anglican and United churches because she appreciated that the pastors didn't publicly shame their congregants. But then she hit university, learned about colonialism, understood that her brand of Christianity had alienated her from the natural world and her own body. Arrived home from anthropology class and said to Kevin: *God is dead to me.* Then called her parents and explained that their trust in an anthropomorphic god infantilized them.

This was the unforgivable line that led to her being disowned, since her dad was already pissed that she was having sex before marriage. Such a thrilling, terrifying moment. She was nobody's daughter and felt fully alive. Didn't yet know how much she would miss her parents. Didn't understand how much it would hurt when they wouldn't return her calls. Didn't yet know that no matter how definitively she renounced the church, how intensely she tried to slough it off, religion is what app developers call *sticky*—it would cling to her forever.

"I was raised in an evangelical church and left at age nineteen," she says now, her go-to line. "Can we just talk about celebrity gossip or something?"

Tamiko stares at her. "I'm fascinated by irrational belief."

"What about your yoga? I've heard Ashtanga is a cult."

"It's an energy practice."

Amber turns to face the wall.

THE NEXT MORNING, the remaining competitors—only Amber, Adam, Tamiko, Logan, Tish, and Sergey are left—take a plane from Kazakhstan to a place that is equally barren, isolated, forlorn: Winnipeg. At the airport, they crowd into a bus, the kind with tinted windows and plush seats, the kind that usually spits out confused tourist groups. On the bus, Adam is two rows ahead, talking with Tish about anti-Semitism in Paris, which is her "fave city outside NYC." Then they discuss the club scene in Tel Aviv—as if Adam knows anything about clubs—and he talks about growing up in "Samaria." *You mean the Occupied Territories?* Amber wants to yell. She tries not to hear his deep, monotonous voice. They haven't spoken since they filmed their will-they-won't-they and she asked him for more sleeping pills.

"I cannot in good conscience give them to you," he said.

"I thought you took the Hippocratic oath."

"You're angry with me, and I am here if you want to talk about it. But I'm a human being. Not a pharmacy."

The sight of his retreating back left her breathless, doubled over, the rodents in her belly roiling. As if they'd never met, as if she didn't exist. *I don't have a daughter. My daughter is dead.* She misses her boyfriend. She's used to Kevin's way of dealing with her rages, his annoying habit of hovering: *Can I make you tea? Do you want guacamole? Did you see that new SNL skit? There's a new doc about GMOs—want to go on the weekend?* Endless, pleading questions that all translated as: *Have you forgiven me yet? Can we go back to normal? Can we pretend this never happened?*

She was always telling the women at work: *I wish he'd leave me alone! Give me some space.*

Now she has space.

The only man in her life is Slick Nick; they're "friends." Maybe even . . . friends. He has confided in her: that he's from Wheeling Island, West Virginia, and his parents are deliriously proud that he works with MarsNow; that kids called him Saint Nick when he was a teenager, because he was rotund like Santa Claus; that when he was twenty-eight, his girlfriend-at-the-time was diagnosed with leukemia and he saved her life by donating bone marrow. That one threw Amber for a loop. Slick Nick is capable of love and sacrifice? But last night he drunk-texted her gibberish:

what r doing?

nakedd?

goodzf girl please lol

She replied with a kissy-face, then turned off her phone.

The bus carries them seventy kilometers north of the city and stops at a place called Brokenhead. Amber's never heard of it, despite being Canadian, since it's cheaper and easier to get from Vancouver to China than to arrive here. The weather is unseasonably warm; a campfire is lit and Amber sits near the flames, under a vaulted ceiling of stars. No challenge today, only what Slick Nick calls a *breather*. A moment when the contestants and audience alike will relax. Slick Nick is always going on about *pacing*, and it reminds Amber of when Kevin studied story structure. In a better world, Kev would be running this show.

A man named William Napakist greets them and says he'll be teaching astronomy—from Cree and Ojibwe perspectives.

"I learned from elders, who carry these stories for us," he says. "They are our living memories. Without our stories, we would lose ourselves."

Amber looks upward. Sees a bright dot that might be Venus or might be a satellite.

"You all know that the Earth orbits the sun faster than Mars," says William Napakist. "Sure you do. But at certain times, it appears that Mars does a circle in the sky."

"Oh my god." Tish reties her scrunchie—her roots are growing out, dark in contrast to the silver ends. "Mars retrograde. It's the worst!"

Napakist laughs. "We call it *kitom pampaniw*—circles back. Or *mooswa acak*—moose spirit. Because when a moose startles, you know what happens?"

They do not know what happens.

"A moose will run in a big circle, then continue on his journey."

He directs them to look at the stars. "In Cree, the Milky Way is called *Neepin Pinesisuk Meskinaw*, meaning 'the summer birds' path.' In Ojibwe, it's *Pinesi Miikana*, 'the thunder bird's path.' Other stories call it the Wolves' Road or the Path of Souls."

Path of Souls. Her father would like that phrase, if it weren't what he'd call "pagan." Amber hugs herself, shivers inside her sweater, moves closer to the fire. Closer to Adam. The cameras notice. The cameras behave like vampire bats—can sense heat.

"Many genesis mythologies say that the stars are where we originate," says William Napakist. "We come from these stars; they are our relatives. And once we finish what we are here to do, we return to the stars."

She feels peaceful, at ease, happy to be outside at dusk, the prairies stretching out around her. But she doesn't trust this. It would be the perfect moment for Bridget to spring an elimination circle on them. If it were up to Amber, Tish and Adam would be cut.

The firelight illuminates Adam's tired face.

What is *wrong* with her? He's her only friend here. The only person she knows and trusts. Why would she want to eliminate him? Her mother used to hold Amber's hands before bed, close her eyes, and say, *Dear Jesus Christ, our Lord and Savior, we ask you to help Amber with her temper.* Because Amber once threw a toy truck that gave her sister a black eye; once pushed Caleigh down the basement stairs; often screamed *Leave! Me! Alone!* then slammed her bedroom door so hard the floorboards juddered under her feet.

She wishes Adam would put an arm around her. At least look at her. She should lean into him and say she's sorry. For what? Why are they fighting?

Oh, right. He called her *weak*. Who gives a shit? Everyone is weak and desperate and vulnerable. It's called being alive.

"So even if you don't go to Mars, you will all one day ascend to the stars." William Napakist seems to be talking directly to her. "You will go home."

MARCUS CALLS TO SAY HE CAN'T TAKE IT ANYMORE. HE CAN'T
watch the show with me tonight because it's too hard.

"It's hard for you? She's *my* girlfriend."

"Yeah, but you're my best friend."

"Isn't that why you should be here? Slogging through this sewage with me every step of the way?"

"I just think . . ."

I picture him wincing. It's painful for everyone when Marcus thinks.

". . . it's getting kind of pathetic now," he says.

"Harsh, man."

"Why don't we play a few rounds of *Soccer Mom* instead? Or grab a beer? You need to get out more. You'd feel better."

"I have to go," I say, because MarsNow is about to air. "Talk to you later."

"Hey," he says, "don't be a bitch about it."

I hang up, even though I know he's right—it sometimes happens that Marcus is right. A few months into this debacle, most people would admit defeat. Would grab a beer with their friend and reenter real life. *Reality.* Whatever that is.

But I also know Amber. Even when FirstMan34 is on-screen with her, she looks miserable. I keep thinking about that scene, way back in episode three, when Amber threw a bag of ice at FirstMan34, shoved him away from her, pushed his perfect body out of her orbit. Was that for my benefit? The scene where she said, *Don't you ever give up on me.* It's a good line, if you're Nicholas Sparks.

If this were the third act in a Nicholas Sparks movie, Amber would have boarded a ship to sail back to her upper-class fiancé instead of living in a shack on the beach with me, her humble fisherman, but then—the next shots are from my POV—we'd see her waving, weeping, climbing up onto the railing! Diving into the ocean! Swimming fiercely! Desperately! Screaming, *Kevin, I made a mistake!*

And I'd tear off my shirt, reveal my rock-hard chest, and run into the water. It'd be like when we skipped school and jumped in the lake, except that I would know how to swim. I'd reach her, hold her. Grip her wet hair and kiss her wet mouth.

Just as this fantasy is giving me a semi, the door bursts open. Maybe this *is* a Nicholas Sparks movie, because I jump up from the couch way faster than I normally would, saying, "Amber? Babe?"

In my doorway are six men. In police uniforms. They have a dog on a leash.

"This is a raid," says one of them. "*Babe.*"

Then another cop grabs my arms, cuffs them behind my back, tosses me on the couch like I'm a throw cushion. "No!" I hear myself say. "Please no!" I roll off the couch, hit my head on the coffee table. The eyes on the *Gatsby* cover see it all. So does the guy holding a television camera. *Global News.*

Another officer points with a truncheon at our spare bedroom. "That's the north-facing room."

"There's nothing in there." I stumble to my feet, lurch toward the closed door, before remembering the truncheon.

The officer who cuffed me, who looks like a Ken doll with a beer gut, shoves me back onto the couch. "Stay, Rover."

"Nothing in here?" A third officer kicks open the door to the spare room—why didn't he just turn the knob? "Then you won't mind us taking a look?"

The LEDs blare out, blinding. The officers slide special goggles over their eyes, then go inside. They look like they're entering another atmosphere. I turn away, fling myself onto the couch, bury my face in the Voyager's cushions rather than watch as they tear out our plants, carry our children bruised and battered to their cruiser.

"More in the closet," I hear one of them say. So they've found the babies too.

When I look up, the camera is in my face. "Jesus, get away from me."

"You invited us, man," says one of the police officers. "By illegally growing marijuana in your home."

"Then your girlfriend blabbed about it on the TV," says another officer, with that disapproving, learn-to-control-your-woman tone.

"This is fucked." I watch the dog sniff the Mason jars of Green Dragon. One of the officers starts dumping it all down the sink. "This is so, so fucked."

"I could also charge you with resisting arrest," says the Ken doll.

"No! No, no." I wiggle away from him, get to my knees, tumble from the couch and hit the floor hard again. "It's legal. Pot is *legal*. Almost."

"It won't be legal for *you* to be selling it, son." And to the camera, for the benefit of anyone watching at home, Mr. Police Man adds, "If Canadians believe that we won't still be enforcing Canada's strict marijuana regulations, think again."

Just as I've started to scream into the pillow, the whole scene breaks as if a director yelled *cut*. The camera guy stops filming, gives a thumbs-up. "Great. Thanks, everyone! Is that everything?"

The police officers slouch, like normal people bored on the job.

"Nah, we're good here," says the Ken doll. "Thanks for joining us today."

Global News leaves as the last officer emerges from the den, the last of the babies tucked under one arm. "It's, like, twenty plants." He removes his goggles. "Basically nothing."

"Hey!" I scream after the camera guy. "Did you catch that? He says it's nothing!"

"Don't push us, kid." The Ken doll laughs. "We aren't planning to press charges—unless you got some fentanyl you're hiding?"

"What? No." I slump against the couch. "So this was all just for show?"

"We aren't *planning* to press charges." The Ken doll gives me a noogie, like I'm his little buddy. "But we could change our minds."

"Please don't." I have an innate understanding—gleaned from watching my share of police procedurals—that if they were to press charges, I'd be taken down to the station for paperwork. I'd be forced to leave the apartment. Give up my vigil. Also, incidentally, a criminal record would ruin my life. "Can you uncuff me, please?"

"Well, since you said *please.*" The Ken doll unlocks the cuffs, then presses another noogie into my skull and slaps my balls.

"*Ow.*" I clutch my crotch. "Okay, I get it."

"Do you?" He slaps my balls again; I wince but keep my mouth shut. The other officers laugh as they file out of the apartment.

Then I'm alone. In this desecrated Eden, this garden of ashes.

WILLIAM NAPAKIST IS ADDING WOOD TO THE FIRE WHEN SLICK NICK comes toward her saying, "Amber, baby doll, check this out." Holds out his phone.

She knows it's bad from the excited look on Slick Nick's face, from the fact that the cameras circle her as he puts the screen in her hand.

"It's tagged #marsnow," says Slick Nick. "Trending for the past hour."

The video is of her apartment being raided, of Kevin being cuffed, then flailing like a fish on a hook, falling to the floor, screaming a high-pitched *please no!* She watches it twice. She might puke—the plants, gone. And Kevin saying: *Amber? Babe?*

"He's great, isn't he?" she hears Slick Nick say. "So emotive. Can we get him on? For a guest spot?"

Go home. She must go home. William Napakist—who is obviously super wise and intuitive—looked right at her when he said it.

She runs. Fast. Speeds away from the fire pit, along the road. The cameramen can't keep up as she races toward a gas station. Toward a man who's just finished filling his truck. Young guy, hair hitting his shoulders, wearing a black button-up shirt and jeans.

"Hey," she calls out. "Hey! Wait!"

"Damn," he says. "You're a fast runner."

"Are you going into town? Would you take me for fifty bucks?"

"I'm heading to the Peg anyway," he says. "But I'll still take the fifty." Then he nods to the men hauling cameras, trying to catch her. "They coming too?"

"No." She opens the driver's-side door, dives into the truck, crawls to the passenger side. "Come on."

"Are you in trouble? Am I going to get arrested?"

"It's not illegal to take someone to the airport."

"It better not be." He gets in, starts the engine, and they're driving. He says his name is Troy. Once off the gravel, he blasts down the highway admirably fast. The MarsNow bus is following, surely filming footage, but not close enough to catch up.

"Wow," she says. "I feel like OJ."

"You kill someone?"

"That's not what I meant."

"I actually know who you are. From that reality show, yeah? You're Tish?"

"Amber."

"Sorry. You all look alike to me. Can I get a pic with you?"

They take a scary, speeding-down-the-highway selfie. Then signs for the airport appear. This is madness—if she gets on a plane, she's throwing away her chance at Mars. But could she really win? Is she meant to travel light-years away? William Napakist said she should *go home.*

"Which terminal?" says Troy.

"Domestic. Can I e-transfer you the fifty dollars?"

"You got cash?"

"Just my phone."

"Forget it, girl. It's on the house. I'm going out salsa dancing anyway."

"Salsa dancing?"

"Never heard of an Indian salsa star?" He laughs. "Now you've met one."

"*That* would make a good reality show."

"Sure you want to go to the airport?" He flashes a smile. "You could come out dancing with me instead."

Salsa dancing. With this handsome one. You only live once—and what if she does end up on Mars? God knows there won't be any dance clubs.

But then she remembers that police officer, his gut protruding, his voice like Darth Vader: *Your girlfriend blabbed about it on the TV.* And Kevin, flailing on the couch. *Amber? Babe?*

She never meant for this to happen. She assumed he'd have the plants—and he loved them more than he loved her anyway. She never meant for him to be alone.

"I'm such a fuckup." She covers her face in her hands. "You'd better take me to the airport."

MARCUS COMES BY WITH GIFTS: AN ASSORTMENT OF CHIPS (BBQ,
Ketchup, Spicy Taco), an eighth of weed, and a baggie of mushrooms.
Because the only response to losing your stash of illegal drugs is to
restock your apartment with illegal drugs.

"Don't worry, man," says Marcus. "I got you covered."

Bronwyn drops by too, bearing my favorite macaroons. "Are you
okay? That looked awful. Police brutality."

Marcus laughs. "I wouldn't go that far."

"They were so *aggressive*," says Bronwyn. "They could have just
knocked on the door and had a reasonable conversation." She pats
my arm. "I would have freaked out too."

"Not as much as he did." Marcus swallows a stem from the baggie
of shrooms. "*No, please no!*" he screeches in the voice of a deranged
grandmother.

"What do you get out of this toxic masculinity, Marcus?" Bronwyn pops a stem in her mouth. "I'm genuinely curious." She sounds
genuine too—Bronwyn is so sweet it makes me ache. "When you
mock Kevin for being affected by his loss, it sounds like fear. Are you
afraid of your own vulnerability?"

Marcus sits on the couch beside us. "I guess so?"

"It's hurting you more than you realize. It limits your relationships with others, but also with yourself."

And maybe the shrooms are hitting him fast, 'cause Marcus tilts
his head back, looks at the ceiling, and says, "Whoa. That's so true."

"I'm going to get stuff ready for tea," says Bronwyn. "If we're going
on a psychedelic journey, I'll want ginger tea when I'm coming down.
Makes the landing softer."

When she's in the kitchen, Marcus gives me a punch in the arm.
"She's dope, man. Super cute."

I have nothing to say, no words. My plants are gone and I might be in shock. The apartment feels empty; an extinction has occurred. There goes my business partnership with Bastiaan. My shared creation with Amber. Flashback. To our first sprouts on the windowsill, fragile, the leaves nearly transparent when the sun shone through them.

I reach into the baggie and grab a stem and a cap and another stem.

Marcus says, "Hell yeah, my boy's going hard."

Twenty minutes later I'm watching the ceiling turn into a swirl of stars, the Milky Way dancing above me. Then Bronwyn is beside me, her face too close, her skin see-through. I can watch the blood flowing through her arteries. I keep thinking: *That's Bronwyn's blood.* Then: *Amber has blood.* Then: *We all have blood.* I can feel it—liquid, intelligent, alive—moving through my veins.

Then Bronwyn's eyes swell like balloons, pop right out of her head. "The thing is that you didn't lose the plants. Kevin?"

"I didn't?" For a second I feel such relief—I didn't lose the plants!

"No, because our cells are *made of plants*," she says, eyeballs goggling. "You *are* a plant."

And Marcus, still on the couch with his mouth hanging open, grabs Bronwyn's arm. "Whoa," he says. "That's so true."

I feel my mom's presence. She's inside my left ear, which is warm, tingling, inhabited—my mom is borrowing my ear to listen to Bronwyn's "mellow chillax" playlist. I can feel Mom's wonder and happiness when a Soap&Skin song plays.

Later—probably hours, but my sense of time is messed—I hear Bron and Marcus giggling in the kitchen, trying to open a bag of chips.

Then Amber's here, looming over me, looking like a cardboard cutout of herself. Tall, a giantess, glowing. If Amber were a constellation, she would shimmer like that in the sky.

"I can't believe how beautiful you are," I say.

"I can't believe you're high." She gives me a swift slap across the jaw. "I can't believe I fucking bothered."

I reach to touch her leg—she's real. My brain starts scrabbling and reaching for a foothold. My brain tumbles around inside my skull like clothing in a dryer. "I'm not that high." Saying it makes it almost true. "I mean, I'm definitely coming down."

Marcus and Bronwyn stumble out of the kitchen with mugs of tea and a bag of chips.

"Is that Amber?" says Marcus. "Kev, are we tripping in an alternate dimension?"

"I'm really here," says Amber. "So it'd be great if you could leave."

Marcus and Bronwyn dissolve into giggles.

"Sorry—it's Bronwyn, right?" Amber's smiling her best I'm-sweet-but-I'll-stab-you smile. "Listen, it's *super* nice of you to support Kevin, I'm glad he has friends around, but I need to talk to him."

"Amber, you should get on our wavelength," says Marcus. "'Cause you're killing the buzz."

I manage to stand up. My feet are on the ground. My neurons clicking into place. "Bronwyn, Marcus." I sound like a television host. "You're out. You're going home."

Marcus laughs. "Dude. Stop fucking around."

"This isn't a joke." What does he expect? After he spent all night flirting with Bronwyn right in front of me? "You need to leave."

"Whatever." Marcus shakes his head. "This is bullshit."

Bronwyn doesn't say anything. Just sways for a second, staring at me. Her eyes are back to their normal size but it still hurts to look at them. To be seen by them. She places her mug of ginger tea on the coffee table—careful to use a coaster—and walks out.

AFTER MARCUS AND HIS GIRLFRIEND LEAVE, WHILE KEVIN NURSES his post-shrooms headache on the couch, Amber paces the apartment. It's like she's been gone forever, light-years, and the place is alien to her. She turns the heat down to a normal temperature. Tears the plastic sheets off the floor and rips down the window coverings. Opens the screen in the bedroom to get some air. The apartment smells different already. Less like skunk-stink, less like mildew. The usual low-level rage and exhaustion she feels at home is gone. She didn't realize until now the burden she'd been carrying. The burden of the future. She paid the bills on time, worried about the plants' health, planned and cooked the meals, budgeted the money, agonized over the shared line of credit. Most of all, she was the one who lay awake at night worrying about getting busted, while Kevin slept peacefully beside her. During those nights, she resented him *and* the plants—admit it, it's been a while since she cared for the plants out of anything but duty and financial need. At first she nurtured them like they were infants, but over the years they became just an investment, a monocrop, and sometimes she wondered if she was abusing them by keeping them cooped up in an apartment she herself could barely stand. There was nothing wild about the plants. Nothing passionate. She often wondered: Why do I risk prison for entities I don't even love? She might as well go legit, get a job with Tilray or Broken Coast, use her expertise to grow excellent and legal bud. But what about Kevin? What would he do?

Now it had happened, the event that tortured her, the outcome she'd most feared.

"Maybe it'll be a good thing," she says aloud. "A blank slate."

"You mean losing the plants?" Kevin calls from the living room. "Are you out of your mind?"

"Possibly. I can't believe I'm here." Why did she come back? To check on him? To hold him and keep him safe? She could have just phoned. It was insanity. Stupidity. The MarsNow equivalent of dislocating your dumbass shoulder when you're on the cusp of competing at the Olympics.

But that's why she had to see him. She knows what it's like to be disgraced in front of the whole world. To lose everything.

Her phone vibrates. Slick Nick again—he called fourteen times while she flew from Winnipeg to Vancouver. She sends him a text: *I'll be back on set early tomorrow. Had to check up on some things. Promise.* Then adds: *xoxo.*

Is that true? Will she go back to the set? She could meet up with the cast and crew in LA—she already looked up flights in a nauseated panic during her cab ride from the airport. She could go back to MarsNow and hope to be forgiven. Or she could stay here. Stay home.

She wanders into the kitchen and opens the fridge, hoping Kevin might have some food other than potato chips. Feels that familiar, heart-sinking disappointment when there's only a Tupperware half full of quinoa, one sad little apple, a bunch of wilted greens, a jar of peanut butter, and— "Kev? You bought almond milk?"

"What?"

"It takes, like, ninety liters of water to grow *one* almond, and every harvest is a Holocaust for pollinator bees." She takes the container out of the fridge, reads the nutritional info. "Plus this stuff is full of sugar and unpronounceable—"

"Well, you weren't here," he says from the couch. "So I thought I'd try something different."

"What's wrong with what we normally get?" She puts the almond milk back, takes out the apple. Slices it, then pours two glasses of water. "You live with someone who has a master's degree in nutritional health." She walks into the living room. "But never listen to a word I say. Or you do, but don't remember it."

"I remember everything." He sits up slowly, takes the water, and drinks. "I remember that we soak and sprout our legumes to make them more nutritionally available. I remember that we eat full-fat dairy because we believe in whole foods. I remember that we eat organic for environmental reasons and because GMOs can interrupt the shiki-boom-boom pathway."

She sits beside him on the couch. "It's the shikimate metabolic pathway."

"I remember when we swam in Loch Lomond when we were seventeen. When we went night-tobogganing at eighteen. I remember that you wore a dark blue, shiny dress to grad. I remember the friendship bracelet you made for me at summer camp. I remember how much you loved *The X-Files*. I remember our anniversary, every fucking year. And I forgive you, every fucking year, when you forget."

She stares at him, her living memory. So that's his burden: the past. He is carrying their stories. If she loses Kevin, will she lose herself?

"I'm sorry," she says. "I shouldn't have—"

"Doesn't matter." He closes his eyes. "You're here. That's what counts."

She takes his hand. "I'm here."

Why does she always want *more* or *different*? Why can't she appreciate the boyfriend she already has? Isn't this the problem, the reason the planet is burning—because no one is ever satisfied? Look at her. Insect populations are plummeting, Arctic ice vanishing, and she's worrying about which man to choose? Feeling unfulfilled because she can't have them all?

They drink their glasses of water side by side, saying nothing. With the plants gone, the window open, she can breathe. There's finally space. This apartment, this relationship, this planet—she might be home.

What if she made this her mission? To be here. To love this person. To recognize that she doesn't yet know him, and will never discover everything about him. A human being is a mystery, as dark and expanding as the universe.

MY HEART POUNDS IN MY CHEST—WHERE ELSE WOULD IT BE?—AS Amber walks through the apartment. What if she sees Bronwyn's clothes in the closet? Bronwyn's toothbrush in the bathroom? The almond-milk conversation nearly gives me a heart attack, then fills me with rage when she says, as if she still lives here, "What's wrong with what we normally get?"

(A digression: what we *normally get* is goat's milk, because Amber says that the molecular structure of goat dairy is the closest thing to human breast milk and that goat products are more environmentally sustainable than cow dairy.

But Bronwyn says that all animal products cause cancer and perpetrate cruelty.

Conclusion: date a couple of women in Vancouver and you'll never innocently enjoy a bowl of Kraft Dinner again.)

But Amber doesn't notice any Bronwyn evidence, which makes me question what kind of scientist she'd be on Mars. She stomps through the apartment, tears up the spare room, opens the windows. Don't get me started on how jarring it is for sun and cool air to burst, unwelcomed, into this apartment—it's "triggering," as the kids say. Reminds me of when the police kicked in the door. But I let it go because I have a post-shrooms hangover and what's the point of a fight? Amber could be gone as quickly as she arrived.

If you've made it this far, you've probably lost hope that there will be any good sex scenes. But after the almond-milk comment, after she wrecks the apartment, Amber straddles me on the couch and kisses me hard, her mouth so familiar and wonderful that I want to dive into it, let it swallow me—her mouth a deep lake. Her mouth a supernova.

Then her hair in my hands. Her muscular legs, her ass. Her

skin. Her smell—she must have the healthiest, sexiest microbiome on Earth.

She unzips my jeans, slides my underwear down my hips, runs to the bathroom to grab a condom and tears the wrapper with her teeth. I lift her shirt, kiss her freckled chest, circle her areola with my tongue. Pull down her leggings and slip my fingers inside her, like digging into warm, wet soil. Then she kneels, slides the condom on, climbs on top and guides me in, squeezes that crazy-strong pelvic floor. I press hard, then soft-soft on her clit until she says, *oh god, oh god,* and we come together in our practice-makes-perfect way.

Then we pant into each other's necks.

"I love you," she says.

"For no reason." I hold her tight.

Sex with Amber is sometimes like this, a phenomenon, like seeing the Northern Lights. It's especially good when she's met someone new. When she's cheating on me, or thinking about cheating on me.

There. I said it.

She kisses my neck, slides off me, goes to the bathroom to pee. Comes back and curls half-naked next to me on the Voyager. She's shaved her legs, even though the hair that grew there was fine and soft.

"Nice to have you home," I say.

"Nice to be here." She points to the pile of empty growlers. "What's that?"

I tell her about my plan to produce a sweet cocktail that I would call Living Green Dragon. Kombucha with cannabis-infused vodka, sold hipster-style, in growlers. My entrepreneurial spirit must impress her, because she stares at me and says, "I almost wish we had some weed right now."

"Marcus brought over an eighth." I point to the baggie on the coffee table, resting atop *Gatsby*. "I smelled it and don't think it's ours— he must have another source."

"That fucker." She goes into the bedroom, rummages in a drawer, and comes back with our small glass pipe. Sits beside me, fills the bowl with a few buds, lights up, inhales. Her chest rises and falls; smoke slides from her mouth.

"Oh my god," she says. "Those Mars guys must be shitting their pants. And if they saw me now, I'd be fired."

I suppose she means the producers and shareholders, the guys in suits. The ones who are raking in advertising dollars while our relationship implodes like a dying star. "Fuck them," I say, and Amber laughs in a throaty, raspy way. Then passes me the pipe. It's damp from her lips.

The weed is too wet and the smoke singes my throat. Not up to our standards, but the buzz isn't bad. Our spines melt into the Voyager's cushions.

"In New Mexico, one of the engineers said he hoped we'd find precious metals on Mars," she says. "And carbon compounds. Stuff we can eventually ship back to Earth." Her laugh is cynical this time, the bitter disappointment of the true believer. "*The space economy.* That's what he called it."

"Told you. They want to turn Mars into a garbage dump, just like home."

"It might be good for preserving the Earth?" she says. "Because down here we're running out of cobalt, copper, all of it."

"Someone always makes money." I imagine slaves mining the asteroid belt the way they used to pick cotton. "And someone always suffers."

"I guess."

"And some of us benefit and suffer at the same time." It surprises me that Amber hasn't considered this. But she has always believed in absolutes. Right and wrong, good and evil, heaven and hell. She was never satisfied to just grow weed—she had to attend legalization rallies, had to post on Facebook about the medical benefits of cannabis, had to try to convert the whole world. "Nothing changes," I say. "Nothing will ever change."

"Change is constant and inevitable. That's what Tamiko says."

"Are you friends with her now?"

"I guess I thought we were going for some grand reason," she says. "For the mystery of it."

The side of her body touches mine, flowing over my skin like honey. I pass her the pipe and she sucks smoke into her lungs.

"There's a face on Mars. Did you know that?" she says. "In the Cydonia region. A human face." Her eyes are closed like when her dad would say grace around the table. "Why?" She turns to me. "Why a face? Is it just a random rock formation? Or is it a sign?" She touches my arm. "You know? Why is there something rather than nothing? Why are we here?" She laughs. "Shit, I sound like I'm stoned."

"'Cause you are."

I want to understand her. Comprehend this desire to escape, to see the Earth from above. To see what God sees. Would she stay if I could understand her? If I could climb inside her, know her inside out? Is that what I want? To give myself over, to become her, so I'll never be alone again?

Beside her, my body light as air, I say, "Maybe this is what it's like. Zero gravity."

Amber shakes her head. "No." A smoke ring leaves her mouth and floats through the living room. It dissipates, disappears. "Zero gravity is a trip," she says. "Way better than this."

SHE ALMOST FUCKED HIM WITHOUT A CONDOM. ALMOST THOUGHT: *Why not see what happens?* Let her body make the decisions, because her brain is an idiot.

And when they smoke a joint it feels like old times, like forever, sitting on that worn-in Voyager. The couch soft as mud, rooting her to the earth. For a moment, she can just *be*. She's in the garden.

If she loses him, she loses herself.

But we weren't meant to stay in paradise. Soon that feeling of old times, of forever, makes her restless. She sees Kevin's red-rimmed eyes—how could she even consider having a child with him? So she wrecks everything, just like she always does. "Zero gravity is a trip," she says. "Way better than this."

She feels Kevin's breath stop.

"Way better than this?" He turns to her. "Than being home? With the person you love?"

"That's not what I meant."

"Then what did you mean? Please explain."

"Can we chill?"

He stares at her. "I've been wondering lately: Why don't we talk to each other?"

"We're talking now."

"About real shit. Our feelings."

"Our *feelings*?" She laughs. "Yeah, you love discussing feelings. I've only been trying for ten years to get you to see a therapist about your mom."

"What about my mom? She's dead. Therapy doesn't change that."

"About your messed-up relationship with her. About the fact that you pretty much grew up in a house with an agoraphobic hoarder who, like, imprisoned you."

"Oh, is that what she, *like*, did? You grew up inside a cult, so maybe you shouldn't talk."

"I'm just saying, you're so much like her. Sitting here committing a slow suicide."

"Do not speak about my mother. Ever again. From the start you were a snob who hated coming to my house 'cause you grew up in a McMansion with a double garage and a big lawn that your dad cut with that stupid mower."

"This is what I mean, Kevin." What does her family have to do with anything? "You say you want to talk about feelings, but instead you make fun of my dad's lawn mower."

"It was like a little Shriners' Circus car! He looked ridiculous. And what kind of so-called Christian is he, anyway? I thought Jesus wore rags. Your dad disowned you because you weren't a virgin, but he lives in a house with a sauna *and* a hot tub, and drives an Enclave. That doesn't seem insane to you?"

"Ever heard of the Parable of the Talents? Why are we even talking about my dad's vehicle?"

"Because it's the same old bullshit, Amber. Now you worship this idiotic billionaire who cloaks his selfishness in pseudo-spiritual language. Geoff Task says he's *allowing humanity to fulfill its destiny*? He's encouraging us to *reach for the stars*? Are you kidding me?"

"At least Geoff Task is trying."

"Trying to what?"

"Save the world!"

"By sending two naive dumbasses to Mars? That saves the world exactly how? It's human hubris, Amber, capitalist bullshit. You said it yourself. *The space economy.*"

She curls her body away from him. She came home for this?

"If you love the world so much, why are you going to Mars? Why not stick around and do something useful on your home planet?"

"Like you?" She turns. "It's as if you're still a teenager who thinks that sulking in your room is cool, and everyone who's trying to *do* anything is lame."

"I have to stay home and sulk," he says, "to offset your carbon emissions."

"I just wish you'd support me."

"Does FirstMan34 support you?"

"Wow. You spied on my browser history? That's classy, Kev."

"You know what's classier? Running away from your problems by moving to another fucking *planet*."

"So I'm supposed to just sit in this apartment for the rest of my life?" She might tear out her own hair. "I want more, Kevin. I *want* things for my life."

"Like a riding mower and a big lawn?"

"Maybe a job that fulfills and challenges me. Maybe—" She stops herself. She'd been about to say *a family*. Maybe she wants a family. Maybe she wants a child. Intensely, selfishly, full-heartedly. Maybe she wants it all, no compromises. "MarsNow isn't just hubris or capitalism. It's also *science*, Kevin. And science is knowledge. Historically, it pulled us out of ignorance and superstition—"

"That's how you justify yourself?"

"I don't need to justify myself. Especially to you."

"Yeah, 'cause I'm no one." He laughs. "Definitely not one of the VIPs competing against you to travel to an uninhabitable hellscape."

"If you feel insecure, don't blame me for that."

"I don't blame you for anything." He takes a pillow from the couch and crushes it in his hands. "You're just a fame whore like everyone else. You can't help it. It's the culture. Fame whores get lots of likes."

She stands. Why put up with this? From a guy who probably hasn't showered in a week.

"But that's only one part of you." He reaches for her hand. "The made-for-TV part. I know the other parts. I *know* you."

"I have to get to the SkyTrain station. I have to catch a flight."

"You're leaving? You're going back?"

"I never planned to stay. I wanted to see if you were okay, and clearly you're fine."

She opens the apartment door, scales the stairs to the front entryway, kicks open the screen door. Rain pours down. She wishes she had her jacket.

"That demagogue *wants* us to fight each other, so we don't rise up in a revolution." Kevin is beside her. "You wanted adventure, fine, and attention, fine—but admit that's what this is. Be *real* for once."

The sky is gray and the grass that West Coast neon. She remembers when she and Kevin first arrived in this city: they couldn't believe how lush it was, even in winter. The day they arrived, she knelt to touch wet grass. *It's so green it hurts!*

"You don't have to go back, Amber."

She stands on the threshold. *One small step for woman . . .*

"Let's go for a walk, like we used to." Now he's on his knees, as if he's about to propose. "Remember the hidden lake? It could be just like it was before."

"What are you talking about? What lake?" Then it hits her: the afternoon at Loch Lomond, a day he insists on celebrating as their anniversary but which she barely remembers. She went to Loch Lomond so many times, and only dragged Kevin there in a moment of weakness—she'd been lonely, injured, bored. "I don't want to relive the past."

"Okay, go to Mars. Do what you need to do." He grabs her hand. "But don't leave like this. Do not leave without telling me the truth."

About Adam? What would she even say about Adam? "What truth?"

"That this Mars thing is nothing but a billionaire's pet project."

"I don't see you turning down the money, Kevin." She zips her hoodie. "Who pays your rent?"

He's as manipulative as his fat, weird mom was—wants to keep Amber captive, to force her to share his depressing life so he doesn't feel bad about going nowhere.

"So *I'm* supposed to have integrity?" he says. "In a system where twenty-two men own more wealth than all the women of Africa combined, I'm taking what I can get from Geoff Task."

"Is that how you justify yourself?"

"Just admit it. You came home because, on some level, you don't believe in this Mars crap. On some level, you want out. Right?"

"Let *go*, Kevin." She rips her hand from his grip, steps onto the sagging porch, rain hitting her hair. Sucks in oxygen.

"You know that MarsNow is morally bankrupt," he says. "You know it's wrong."

She takes a step, then another. Can't look at him. Cannot let this in. Feels that same nausea she felt when she signed the contract. When she puked up the egg salad sandwich.

"I need to hear you say it," he calls from the doorway. "Amber! Please. Tell me you don't believe."

But she's running now.

I STAND IN THE DOORWAY FOR LONG MINUTES, THE WIND HITTING
me, because I expect her to march back—jaw tight, arms stiff at her
sides. *Fine*, she'll say. *You win.*

Because surely it's not *over*. Surely she's not simply *gone*. Fourteen
years. Surely she hasn't chosen Mars over reality?

I want more for my life.

But not that. Not a Martian wasteland. She can't possibly want
that—or she wouldn't have come home.

Can you blame me for thinking it means something? For thinking that since she came all the way to see me, and was willing to get
high—to risk that the next MarsNow-administered drug test will
show traces of illegal substances in her blood—it means that she's
done with Mars?

I saw her hesitate. I saw her pause at the door.

I wait in the entryway. Wait and wait, until rain hits me in the
face. The fucking outdoors. Fucking Amber. I slam the apartment
door, punch the Voyager's cushions, then google MarsNow. How
did I not think of this before? I pick up my phone and dial the 1-900
number that flashes along the bottom of the screen.

"Hello, and welcome to the MarsNow hotline," says the pleasant, automated voice of a woman. "Please listen carefully to the following options: If you want to purchase MarsNow products and
memorabilia, please say, 'I want to make a purchase.' If you want
to vote to eliminate one of the MarsNow contestants, please say, 'I
want to vote.'"

My turn to exercise my democratic freedom.

"I want to vote," I say.

"Thank you." The voice has a slight accent, and I imagine it
belongs to Casting, Communications, and Commitment director

Helena Slora. "Your number has now been recorded in our televoting system. Please say the full name of the contestant you wish to vote for."

"Amber," I say. Then, more clearly: "Amber Kivinen."

"I have recorded your vote for: Amber Kivinen." The machine pronounces it *Am-bar Kiv-eye-nen*. "Thank you. And do not forget to visit our website at www.marsnowandforever.com."

"Okay." Somehow I thought it would feel better, more satisfying, to try to save her from herself. "Bye."

But I stay on the line, and the voice starts up again: "Please listen to the following options." They're the same choices that were available to me before.

"What I'm wondering about is *why*?" I say to Helena. "Why are we here? Why bother? The world is a disaster. Love is a fiction. Everything is shit. Then we die."

"I'm sorry," says my automated friend. "I cannot understand your request."

I realize this might not be Helena after all. This might be the voice of God.

"If you would like to return to the main menu," says God, "please say, 'Main menu.'"

AMBER JIGGLES HER LEGS; HER EARS POP; SHE NEEDS TO PEE BUT the guy in the aisle seat beside her is asleep. Why is it so impossible to sit *still?* Everyone else on the plane seems happy to nap or read or play Candy Crush.

The recycled air feels dry in her nostrils and stale in her lungs. She didn't cry when she left Kevin, but she's crying now, facing the airplane window, tears streaming down her face in the privacy of her aisle-mate's snores. The way she used to cry after a bad meet, in those moments when she wanted to give up: in the darkness of her room, away from her sister's needling, her mother's worries, her father's low-voiced questions: *Did I raise you to be a quitter? Amber, you can stop if you want—if you need to. But ask yourself: Where does this weakness come from?*

She knew what he meant. The weakness came from her mother. Her mother and Caleigh. The other team—with their tears, their soft bodies, their breakdowns. She wasn't like them. Amber was different. His champ. His gold-medal girl.

A fame whore? Her goal is immortality. She'll show Kevin. She'll save the fucking world. She spent too many years feeling hopeless and angry. About glyphosate, industrial agriculture, logging practices, tar sands, fracking—the list is endless. She spent too many years on the couch with Kevin doing nothing, feeling despair. But now she has a new vision: she imagines herself striding through the MarsNow colony, past gleaming Settlement Structures, on her way to run the most advanced hydroponics lab in the universe. Creating Eden. And decades in the future, she'll be celebrated as the woman who grew a garden on Mars. But not just that. The woman who developed Martian technology to capture and use CO_2 to make food. The woman who refused to patent her tech, but sent it home to the suckers still suffering. The woman who saved Planet Earth.

When the plane lands at LAX she has seven texts from Slick Nick explaining exactly where they are, Van Nuys Airport, Gate B-14. The others completed their Winnipeg challenge (were they tied to trees and forced to escape like Houdini before the mosquitoes ate them alive?), then flew to LA, and are now about to charter a private plane. There's room for her, if she gets there on time, though Slick Nick can't guarantee that the audience will be so forgiving.

If you're not here by 7:55 pm honey you're not getting on this flight FYI

She replies: *Thanks, Nick. I know you work SO hard and I haven't made your life easy! Just landed and am on my way.*

He replies with a simple thumbs-up, which makes her realize that, shit, he's really pissed. But then he adds: *sorry to be such a hardass this job is a lot of pressure.*

I believe you! she replies, as she gets into a taxi. *But you're so good at it, seriously!!!*

And when she arrives at Van Nuys, there are cameras waiting for her outside—not just some of the MarsNow crew, but also paparazzi. They follow her into the airport, flashes blinding—so *this* is why celebrities wear sunglasses inside—and scream a barrage of words.

Amber, your boyfriend, is he going to jail?

Are you quitting MarsNow? Can't handle it? Why'd you run away, Amber?

What about Adam? How many boyfriends do you have?

You're beautiful when you smile, Amber! Look this way, Amber!

At security she escapes them, then runs to the gate, her shoulder aching again. When she reaches the others, more MarsNow cameras are rolling. Logan crosses his arms and shakes his head in a thou-shalt-not-pass manner. Tamiko doesn't even glance up from her laptop. Tish, in her silk loungewear, speaks too loudly: "I hate when *some people* think they can just do whatever they want. When *some people* act like they're not part of the team."

Adam strides toward her and she half expects him to discipline her like an army officer. Or maybe, even worse, he and Nick planned some romantic reunion. If he acts all fake and lovey-dovey, she won't stand it. She'll turn and walk right out of the airport and back into her real life.

Tell me you don't believe.

Adam puts his arms around her, hugs her like he's missed her. But there's no rehearsed speech, no big gesture.

"Ignore them," he whispers. Squeezes Amber tighter, his mouth next to her ear. "Remember: Give the audience *one thing*."

He's been strategizing. Thinking about their future. And suddenly, in his arms, she feels safe.

She squeezes him back, then faces her fellow competitors. "It's true, I pulled a runner. I went to see my—Kevin. Because he was in crisis, and if there's one thing I'm known for, it's loyalty." She glares at Tish. "Even when it hurts me, I'll be there for you."

"I call bullshit," says Tish. "I think you got scared."

Adam shoots Amber a look.

One thing.

Her soul.

"Maybe I did feel some doubt. Maybe I—got scared." The private tears from the plane threaten to return. "Maybe I lost faith in myself because of my injury, and the police raid, and sometimes I don't . . . I just wanted to go home, to feel normal, to have my life back."

Sergey and Linnzy nod. "I think we have all felt this way," says Sergey.

"But we didn't act on it," says Tish.

"My dad," Amber continues, "my dad emigrated and was dirt poor, never finished high school. But he started his own concrete business, oversaw million-dollar projects—he's the toughest person I know."

Adam reaches for her hand.

"My dad says that if you don't feel doubt, then your faith is untested. Your faith is worth nothing." She grips Adam's hand, her palm sweaty. "He used to say that doubt is a shape-shifter. When doubt is conquered"—she meets Adam's eye—"it becomes power."

卌 卌 卌 卌
卌 卌 卌 卌
卌 卌 卌 卌
卌 卌 ||||

IT TAKES DAYS TO GET AROUND TO IT, BUT I FINALLY STRAIGHTEN out the destruction Amber wrought: roll up the plastic sheets that once covered the floor and tuck them in a corner, black out the windows. Then I watch Amber run on the beach and drink protein shakes in Trinidad, lift weights in a former prison yard in South Africa, do complex math and eat live beetles in Mexico, and "share" during "group" with her fellow competitors in Kenya. Sergey from Ukraine is eliminated. Tish from New York is eliminated. I'm still not over the fact that Cawaale from Somalia, basically the most competent person on Earth, was eliminated—and I can see in astronaut Dirk Riley's face that he's concerned too, even though he feigns cheerfulness aboard the ISS by doing a zero-gravity boogie. Engineers and Pilates instructors and concert pianists have been eliminated. But Amber Kivinen—drug dealer, former vault champ, onetime president of the Thunder Bay *Calvin and Hobbes* Fan Club—remains.

She runs away, proving her lack of dedication to the endeavor, and the audience loves her more.

The Cut features a "retrospective" of her "edgy girl-next-door" style. *People* magazine publishes a piece about her diet regimen: *The meal plan that will take Amber into space!* (Kale smoothies, grass-fed yogurt, bone broth, omega-rich fish, low-fructose fruits, veggies, and—you guessed it—the occasional indulgence: a square or two of dark chocolate.)

She isn't just reality-TV famous. She's now part of a celebrity power-couple. Adam-and-Amber. *A-squared*, to their fans. The sexiest space cadets since Buzz Aldrin. They have yet to kiss on-screen, but in this era of porn and hookups, their modesty seems to make them even more fascinating. Instagram accounts are dedicated to boomerangs of Adam and Amber hugging, holding hands, smiling at each other.

Hilariously, I too become a celebrity. Yep. Your Kev. The police raid doesn't bring me what I want (Amber), but it does bring me what everyone else wants (fame). 'Cause the video of me getting busted goes viral; millions of people watch Amber Kivinen's boyfriend/ ex-boyfriend hug a couch cushion like it's a teddy bear. Apparently it's adorable and funny and heartbreaking to watch a grown man have a meltdown. A GIF of me looking up, stunned and hopeful— *Amber? Babe?*—becomes the default GIF to express desperate optimism in the face of utter hopelessness. Bustle.com puts out a list of "Five Things You Need to Know about Amber Kivinen's First Love," illustrated with photographs scalped from her Instagram account as well as that GIF of me flopping around on the couch and smashing my face on the coffee table:

1. He's hella loyal and started dating Amber when they were only seventeen!
2. He lives in Vancouver's hippest neighborhood
3. He's super sensitive and we are HERE FOR IT
4. He and Amber were adorable together, and he's pretty cute on his own too
5. He's appeared in way more movies than you! (But only as an extra)

A surprising number of women message me on Facebook, saying they live in Vancouver and are looking to meet a nice guy. People from film school get back in touch: Clara the punk chick who became a successful showrunner and now looks like a bag of dust; Jeremy with the tattoos, who gets all the grants now because he conveniently discovered that he was *of Latinx descent*; and the only real friend I ever made there, a mature student named Gloria who has a puff of white hair and used to hoot while reading my scripts, "Too clever by half!" She wrote films about menopause that were so raw and intelligent they will never be produced. I have a few nostalgic text conversations, scared I'll disappoint these apparitions from my past—they haven't seen me since my youthful, idealistic days. Or maybe not. Maybe being famous, even for no reason, cancels out my failures. *The Georgia Straight* interviews me over the phone about the best places to get stoned in the city (answer: anywhere close to a Japanese grocery, so you can have fast access to Pocky and wasabi beans and that dehydrated, shredded squid stuff). *Vice* invites me to pen a guest column called "Bongin' It," and I write one half-baked (haha) article about combining a good hit of weed, one glass of Merlot, and one shot of espresso to create what we in the know call "the perfect buzz."

Anyway, I can't keep up the momentum, can't parlay my fifteen seconds (well, five and a half days) of fame into a career. I could have stretched it out to at least a week. I could have monetized it. But I don't post to Facebook or Instagram, don't reply to the messages from the hopeful women, don't return the calls from LA bros claiming they're agents and can do for me what Scooter Braun did for Justin Bieber. Instead I'm spending my time going over that last conversation with Amber, thinking of brilliantly skewering/seductive lines—in other words, squandering my chance to "be a presence." I guess I'm too attached to my mundane, complicated self, unwilling to hack away at my inner life until it becomes a brand. Because if you go out to sell your soul, you never know who's buying: I get emails from guys saying they've seen the viral video and they know *how it feels, man.* These are invariably white dudes who believe that their livelihoods are being stolen by brown people or women or vaccinations. I become a favorite of incels, who believe that my story is an example of *how the world has become a place of worshipping females like gods even though they're just evil slut-whores who even if they do give you access to their skanky cumdumpster bodies will eventually leave you for dead!!!*

I wish I could go back in time, to the innocent era of last week, when I didn't have to think about the existence of incels. Back in time, to before I felt the dark pull of their way of thinking. Before I had a horrifying second of understanding how easy and violent and satisfying it would feel to make myself into a victim and put all my energy into blame. Back in time, to when I had my plants and therefore my purpose. To before fame had touched me and left me lonelier. Back in time, to before I'd left Bronwyn for dead.

THIS PLACE IS INSANE! IT HAS A *MOAT*.

After their ultimate challenge, a survival trek, they are hiking to the most glorious property Amber has ever seen. Well, they make it *appear* as though they're hiking, for the cameras; Teeghan and Manusha cover them with fake dirt and sweat. In reality, they take a helicopter—the place is that remote. A 479-acre property on New Zealand's Southern Island, a former sheep station. Miles of rolling green that belong to Geoff Task.

Only four left now: Amber, Adam, Tamiko, and Logan. And for a special bonus episode, they've been invited to stay at Geoff Task's home. Tonight, for the pleasure of the cameras, the four of them—plus Bridget and Nick—get to live like billionaires in a house called the Ark.

From the helicopter, the house, designed by boss-bitch Zaha Mohammad Hadid, looks like an enormous ship. The sloping roof appears to be billowing sails, and there's a dreamy, mast-like tower with what appears to be a lookout at the top. Once the helicopter lands, a man in a butler uniform drives them in a Range Rover from the landing strip, over the moat's drawbridge, to the front gate. A screen outside the gate scans their eyeballs, like in a movie! Inside the gate is a garden, and inside the garden is a Damien Hirst sculpture of a fetus floating in an amniotic sac.

Then the door to the house opens and there Geoff Task and his wife stand. Amber can't help it—she loves them. Because Geoff Task isn't the boring, exploitative kind of billionaire who parties on yachts and has orgies with underage girls. Or the creepy, secretive kind who funds anti-choice groups and gay-conversion camps. He's a classy billionaire. An intelligent billionaire. A visionary billionaire. Geoff Task wears a black shirt and jeans but they're somehow more than that—they are the ultimate, exemplary, simple-yet-stupendous black shirt and jeans. His hair is artfully styled. And Talia Annabelle Lorne is hugely pregnant, wearing a flowing raw silk dress that makes her look like a hippie angel, her blonde hair elaborately braided. Amber wants to get a selfie with her—Kevin would pass out if he saw it. She's one of his favorite actresses and that's probably why Kevin hates Geoff Task. Jealousy.

Talia Annabelle Lorne hugs each of them. "Welcome! We're so happy to have you here." She says, "Call me Tali, please." She says, "Make yourselves at home." She holds Geoff Task's hand like it's no big thing to be married to a visionary billionaire. The cameras eat it up, and Amber can't take her eyes off them. Feels envious of their unborn child—wishes *Geoff* and *Tali* (omg!) could be her parents.

Then Geoff shakes her hand and says, "Here she is. Amber Kivinen." Smiles behind his architectural glasses. "You have such a purity of energy, Amber. I'd love to pick your brain."

Geoff Task wants to pick *her* brain?

Adam looks at her, raises his eyebrows—as close as he gets to being expressive—and she buries her face in his chest, not caring that the cameras catch her so starstruck. Everyone laughs indulgently and Tali says, "Oh, you're adorable," then takes Amber's hand. "Let's get you guys settled in."

"Let's!" Bridget grabs Tali's other hand. Throughout the helicopter flight she talked nonstop about how Tali was a "good friend" from "way back in our struggling-artist days."

Tamiko and Logan are staying in the west wing of the house, and Adam and Amber in the east. Amber's room has a king-size bed, a trickling fountain, and a meditation corner with a Himalayan rug and a quartz singing bowl. It feels like a colossal accident that she's inside this space, and also as if it's meant to be. This is the safe, calm shelter she's longed for.

She goes into the en suite and her bathroom includes a glass-paned shower for two and a huge, crystal-encrusted, circular tub with a smaller circular footbath attached. It almost looks like—

"Adam!" She bursts into his room next door. "My bathroom has a tub shaped like a *hydrogen atom.*"

He takes her hand, leads her to his bathroom, and she nearly falls over. A bathtub shaped like a double helix.

"Can we just die now? Because it's not going to get any better." She tosses herself on the bed. "I want to text Pichu, but would that be cruel?"

"I can't believe you have your phone. You get away with everything." Adam lies down beside her. "FaceTime Pichu. Then she'll feel like she's here with us."

When Pichu appears on the screen, Amber says, "We're in Geoff-fucking-Task's fucking house!"

"Fuck me," says Pichu. "And fuck you."

"And Adam's room has a bathtub shaped like a motherfucking double helix."

"It does not!"

"And his wife, remember Talia Annabelle Lorne from that cheerleading show? Her skin is *so* flawless."

"Do they have robots as servants?"

"No," says Amber. "They have a human *butler.*"

"Listen, you bitches, I'm at Safeway, about to buy kimchi, frozen pizza, and cupcakes for dinner—" Pichu turns the screen so they can see the automated cash register, then flips it back to her face. "So I need some vicarious living. Text me a list of every single item of food that you're served, and include whether or not it was brought to you by a butler. Otherwise you won't be my friends anymore."

"Consider it done," says Amber.

Then there's a male voice in the background, and Pichu giggles. "I *am* that Pichu. The one and only." She brings the phone close to her face and whispers: "Did you hear that? I get hit on all the time now. I deleted Bumble! I meet people in real life."

"That's awesome," says Amber. "Anyone special?"

"Nope, but I've decided to have a baby the old-fashioned way: by sleeping with the entire town. The men of Calgary don't know what hit 'em."

"That's actually how humanity is meant to reproduce," says Amber. "Your cervix will do the work—sift through the sperm to block the feeble and welcome the strong."

"I love you. I love that you're using science to justify my slut phase."

"You're not a slut," says Amber. "But you should probably lay off the cupcakes."

"Sweet Jesus, am I *already* pregnant?" Pichu's eyes widen. "I've been craving the weirdest food."

"You're going to be such a loving mom."

"Don't jinx it." Pichu shakes her head. "You two need to beat Tamiko and Logan and win those seats to Mars."

"Consider it done," says Adam.

The human butler knocks on their door and announces that dinner is served.

"We gotta go," says Amber. "Buy a pregnancy test and text me."

THEY WALK INTO the dining room to find Dirk Riley in the flesh, his bald head gleaming like the moon.

"Surprise," says Geoff Task. "The man himself is back from setting the world record for longest time spent in space."

"By an American," says Dirk Riley. "Let's be accurate."

"Absolutely." Geoff Task seems oddly intimidated. "Apologies."

Tali jumps in. "He was just telling us about reentry into Earth's atmosphere."

"Knocks your socks off." Dirk smiles. "Want to see something?" He lifts his pant leg to show them an emaciated shin and calf. "The technical term for this is 'chicken legs.'"

"It's *so* cool that you've joined us," says Amber.

"Rather be with my family, but what can you do?" Dirk winks at her. "One of my aims is to promote NASA's work to the public. So here I am."

The meal opens with an appetizer of grilled Mediterranean octopus served with green garlic butter. Next is swordfish encrusted with Maldon sea salt, Russian caviar, caramelized golden beets, kelp and wakame salad. All served by a squadron of human butlers and hardly a single bite consumed. Amber stares at her plate, wanting to *eat*, to lift a forkful to her mouth, to feel the butter melt against her tongue, the salt crack between her teeth. But no one actually eats on camera—too messy, too ugly, too risky. You could get something pasted to your gums and then what? Everything you worked for ruined because a flake of dill got stuck on your incisor. She wonders what will happen to all this nourishment. Will the staff eat it later? Will it be scraped into the compost? They move food around their plates. Lift their forks, smile, lower their forks. She almost wishes she were at home, in front of a *Seinfeld* rerun, eating kimchi and cupcakes.

"This is a beautiful meal," says Tamiko. "Very Japanese in its inspiration."

"You can thank my wife for that," says Geoff. "She found our chef and is always searching out recipes for him to try."

Tali puts a hand on his shoulder. "Geoffrey would eat McDonald's every day if he could."

Everyone at the oblong table laughs pleasantly.

"I don't like to waste time thinking about what to have for lunch," says Geoff. "I just eat what's easy."

"Actually," says Tali, "whenever I go away—"

"She leaves me sometimes," says Geoff. "Can you believe that? For days at a time. Even though she knows it's dangerous."

"It is!" Tali laughs. "The last time I went to a primal-screaming retreat, I came home and he'd acquired three new start-ups."

Geoff leans over and kisses her neck. "How else am I supposed to fill the void?"

God, look at them. They're happy. Not restless, not dissatisfied, not constantly sabotaging their own good fortune.

"Anyway, as I was saying, when I go away"—Tali strokes his arm—"he eats like an astronaut. Just dehydrated fruit and protein drinks."

"By choice?" Dirk Riley shakes his head. "All I've dreamed about for the past six hundred days is real bacon. And fresh fruit. And chicken soup like my Oma's."

"We'll work on that for you. Bacon in space."

"Nah. How about you focus on getting these kids to Mars safely?"

"See, this is why sharing ideas is so important to me," says Geoff. "Because Tali said that one day, *he eats like an astronaut*—I think we were in Saudi and you were chatting with MBS, right, pumpkin? Anyway, it stuck there in my brain. Got me thinking that there must be others like me, people too rushed to think about what they're putting in their mouths."

"Like every TV showrunner ever," says Slick Nick.

"That's how the line of MarsNow protein and energy bars began," says Geoff. "Because I feel that the new technologies we develop at MarsNow shouldn't just benefit people on Mars, but all humans on Earth."

"That's so great," says Amber. Her ideas for CO_2 sequestration, and a rewilding program on Earth inspired by her Mars Eden, are *not* hubris—no matter what Kevin claims. "I've actually been thinking about how MarsNow could benefit everyone." She glances at Dirk, hoping for an ally, but he's busy eating what's on his plate, not giving two shits about the cameras.

"We'll be licensing dozens of space-age technologies," continues Geoff, "making business-to-business partnerships to create products that will improve American lives."

"That idea I told you about, to harness CO_2 and turn it into food?" says Amber. "It could help combat climate—"

"Absolutely." Geoff nods. "That's what private enterprise is about. Solving problems."

"Right, so—"

"Products such as the MarsNow sprouted rice drink and the MarsNow freeze-dried vegetable bars will improve human health and human lives."

"But—"

"Prototypes of these are already being served in elder-care homes across the United States. And will soon be available in stores."

"He never stops," says Tali, petting his skull. "He never, ever stops thinking."

BASTIAAN COMES BY WITH MY BOX OF GOOD FOOD AND ASKS IF HE can come in for a toke. He's distressed because Cedar has started using the word *divorce*.

"We run a farm together." He sits on my couch and stares at the ceiling. "We have four children. It's logistically impossible for there to be any separation between us."

"I wonder if that freaks her out. You know? Maybe she just needs space." I lift the blinds slightly to let in some light—don't want Bastiaan to think I'm some sort of weirdo. "Sometimes people want to quit their jobs, but really they just need a vacation."

He nods. "That is good advice. You're a wise person, Kevin."

Which unsettles me, because he's supposed to be *my* wise farmer.

"How's your dilemma?" he asks. "Have you talked to your girlfriend yet?"

"Which one?"

He smiles. "My eldest is eleven and obsessed with that show. I should bring her over to meet you."

"It's still possible Amber will come back. We had a good talk. I don't think she's really committed to Mars."

I know how deluded I sound. I suppose you could call it *blind faith.* Or addiction. She's my false object, my incorruptible dream; I'm addicted to Amber the way other people are addicted to Twitter.

Or maybe it's not Amber herself? Maybe it's the feeling she gave me when she took my hand and pulled me outside—that life could be welcoming, that the world could be home.

"What I'm learning, when it comes to marriage," says Bastiaan, "is that you have to observe and accept the other person the way you would the natural world. Women are like nature. Unpredictable."

"Can I write your dialogue down?"

"What does Amber most want? Figure that out, and maybe she'll come back."

I know what I want. Don't I? For her to be here. To be my home. My shelter in a hopeless world. Instead, she's been gone months and I'm alone, inside, hiding from reality. Living off her e-transfers, which she must continue to send out of guilt and shame and love.

"She wants perfection," I say. "Paradise. She's impossible to satisfy."

"Tell me about it." He shakes his head. "Maybe it's time to let her go, my friend." Is this the wisdom I've been waiting for? "Or maybe not. Maybe you're meant to be. You've been together so long. How can she consider a divorce?"

After he leaves, I replace the blackout coverings. Reenter my bunker. Not that we need blackouts now that the plants are gone, but sunlight is so bright, ostentatious. The clouds have cleared, sunshine is pouring all over Vancouver, and I just know everyone's walking around going, *Isn't this so weird? New normal, right?* but secretly enjoying it, the warmer weather, and excited for an extra-long patio season. It's convenient that I don't leave the house anymore because I have no interest in participating in this sham, this *Brave New World*–level fakery where we all pretend to be human beings but in truth are commodities in a highly competitive marketplace—walking our designer dogs and going on Tinder dates and posting pics of our salads and ditching anyone who seems even remotely *toxic*. Marcus used that word when I called him up. "You're, like, verging on toxic, dude."

Which was a good clue that he's been talking to Bronwyn, so I said he was a traitor and a crappy friend and that I'd been playing *Soccer Mom* without him and his stupid avatar.

"Barbara is not stupid." He didn't even bother to insult my avatar, Cheryl, a kick-ass operative who knows Costco like the back of her hand. "I don't know why you would say that."

So now I call Bronwyn. I expect to leave a message on her voicemail, but she picks up. Live, from a basement on East 12th, I am forced tell her that I sincerely didn't intend to be an asshole.

"You were beyond an asshole," she says. "You *eliminated* me."

"I was high. You and Amber were both here and I didn't know what to do—I freaked out."

Silence. I hold the phone to my ear, wonder if it's true that the wavelengths are giving us both brain cancer. Speaking of *toxic*, even inside the apartment I can feel the solar radiation melting my gray matter. Mold infiltrating my lungs. Polluted air seeping through the walls.

"What happened after I left?" Bronwyn says.

"Nothing. We talked. She went back to Mars."

"Did you break up? Are you together? Do you have any information at all?"

I'm not proud of it, but I say the words: "We are not together." And tell myself that's technically true, since Amber and I are literally *not together*—she's off in Casablanca or Nunavut or wherever, and I'm in East Van.

But Amber didn't say goodbye. And she never answered my question. Never said aloud: *Yes, I believe in the MarsNow project. I believe in my own destruction.* And it's not possible—surely not possible—that she does.

And there's something else. Last night I found her stash. In a shoebox in our bathroom. The painkillers she collects. She never travels without them, so I know she intends to come home.

"You're not together?" says Bronwyn. "For real?"

"For real."

AFTER THEIR FAKE DINNER, THE CAST AND CREW SNACK ON SOME
prototype MarsNow protein bars that taste like wood chips, then
Tali rubs her bump and says she's "just pooped."

"Oh, sweetie, you *must* be," says Bridget. "You're *enormous.*"

Tali kisses Geoff on the cheek, then heads to bed. Tamiko and
Logan go to their rooms too, and Amber links arms with Adam,
walks through the concrete-and-glass labyrinth toward their
bedrooms.

"I feel like I'll never sleep again," says Amber. "Stay up with me?
A little while?"

She puts her arms around his waist. Adam kisses her, sliding his
hands down to take hold of her butt, and she thinks: *Finally.* How beautiful would it be to consummate their relationship here, in paradise?

Adam releases her, opens the door to his room, says, "We have our
final shooting day tomorrow. We need rest."

"You're killing me."

He gives her another long kiss, one that reminds her of her first
years with Kevin, when they used to make out behind the school,
leaning against the cold brick wall. But then Adam touches her
cheek, disengages from her arms.

"Where are you going?" She sounds whiny like Bridget.

"To sleep." He smiles and disappears into his lair.

In her own room, Amber can't stay still. She's in a house shaped
like a ship and can almost feel the wind carrying her forward, toward
a new world. She wants to explore this incredible place. And Tali *did*
say they should make themselves at home. So Amber steps out of her
bedroom, closes the door behind her, tiptoes down the hall to the
winding staircase at the center of the house, the one that leads to the
top of the ship's mast.

It's like going up the Grouse Grind. If only she'd kept up her workouts—her calves and glutes ache when she reaches the top. She's met by a closed door. Unlocked. Beyond it, a library.

She could laugh. Kevin's always so paranoid and cynical, makes her feel stupid for trusting anyone. But Geoff Task put a library at the apex of his home. A room dedicated to truth and knowledge. How bad can he be? And isn't the Internet just one big virtual library? Kevin's always saying that the modern world is a tech-autocracy, brutal and uncaring and wildly unfair. But she can't imagine going back to a time before GPS. To a time before she could look up how to start her own kefir culture, make her own shampoo, bench-press with correct form. People like Geoff have provided apps to track her menstrual cycle, to play binaural beats during panic attacks, to tell her when the next bus is coming. And it isn't fashionable to admit this, but she *likes* social media. She often enters an Instagram scroll that feels like a religious trance— cherry blossoms in the spring, yellow leaves in the fall, clear blue skies, pristine beaches. Instagram is a paradise of purity and abundance, a holiday from degradation. And those little hearts truly make her feel loved. Kevin focuses on the negative, and seems to want to save her from the online world, from the world itself—but what if she doesn't want to be saved? She rejected her dad's version of salvation and finds Kevin's equally patronizing. What if Geoff Task isn't depraved and immoral? What if he's a person like the rest of us? A person who loves efficiency, beauty, creativity? A person who doesn't get everything right, but who's genuinely trying to help humanity? A person doing his best.

Also, Geoff Task is hugely successful and Kevin gave up on his dream, so . . . there's that. The world is competitive, always has been—human life has flourished for two million years thanks to competition. Some people win and some people lose. There's nothing immoral about it.

She goes to a shelf and runs her hands along books that, she realizes too late, might be valuable first editions of Jonathan Swift and Nietzsche. The desk is covered in stacks of newer titles that won't be damaged by the oils of her skin, so she takes one at random: *The Sovereign Individual: How to Survive and Thrive During the Collapse of the Welfare State.*

"I thought I might find you here."

She turns, nearly drops the book. Geoff Task stands in the doorway.

"I see you discovered my little crow's nest." He smiles. "Did I startle you?"

"Sorry, I wasn't snooping—"

"You were snooping." He crosses his arms. "But I like that about you. Your curiosity."

"It's a beautiful library. Impressive."

"Isn't it?" He perches on the desk and looks at her with that intensity she can't get used to. "This is my space. I don't even let my wife up here. It's where I get perspective. Privacy."

"God, I'm sorry," she says. "I didn't mean to invade—"

"Not at all. I knew I'd find you here because you seem to have the same craving. For escape. For sanctuary."

"That's . . . I love that." She takes a step toward him. "It's a nice way to phrase it."

"I occasionally enjoy a shot of mezcal," he says. "Can I serve you a glass?"

"I'm not drinking right now. And don't want to impose."

He holds up a bottle. "This label uses solely wild thirty-year-old tepeztate agave plants. Once the mash is fermented, it's distilled in handmade clay pots." He pours them each a shot. "Only sixty bottles are produced a year."

"You're making it hard to turn you down."

He hands her the drink and they clink glasses. "To Mars," he says.

"To Mars." She sips and the liquor is intense, spicy. "Mmm, so good. Ginger?"

"Close your eyes," says Geoff Task. "To fully experience it."

She closes her eyes, takes the mezcal into her mouth, feels it coat her tongue. The flavor comes in waves. At first: soft smoke. Then it's like drinking a garden: mint, honeysuckle, tarragon, wet earth. Then that spicy, biting finish: clove, chile, a kick of ginger.

"I see," she says, eyes still closed. "I get it now."

When she opens her eyes, Geoff Task is smiling. "Sit with me."

She joins him on a red leather couch shaped like a wishbone. He nods toward the book that's still in her hand.

"That's my bible," he says. "Have you read it?"

She shakes her head. "It's about, like, an apocalypse?"

"It was written twenty-five years ago but it predicted this moment. The collapse of liberal democracy in the West."

"So scary. Adam and I talk about this, about how we hope Mars-Now will be a force for good." She sits straighter; maybe this is her chance. "For one thing, overpopulation is such an issue, to relocate some of humanity to another planet—"

"You want billions to live on Mars? I don't think we'll ever have that kind of immigration movement. And the goal is to move beyond Earth-reliance. To become Earth-independent."

"No, but Kevin, my—I guess he's my ex?"

"I'm aware of Kevin."

"He's always going on about how I'm running away from problems, not trying to solve them." Just thinking about Kevin makes her want to rip out her own hair. "But some technologies we need on Mars could change the world here. Recycling CO_2, growing food from waste products, using hydrogen as fuel—"

"I agree completely."

"You do?" She wants to hug him. "I mean, of course you do. I never believed it was just about mining carbon compounds or whatever. That's so stupid. So status quo. You're a *visionary*."

"You give me too much credit." He laughs. "But I think we're very similar, Amber Kivinen. I've always longed for paradise."

"Really? I thought it was just me. I've been so restless, always wanting something else, and thought it was this *flaw*. But maybe the *world* is flawed. Is it my fault everything's so—"

"Imperfect?"

"Exactly." She smiles, a little tipsy. She's barely eaten all day. "I was going to say *fucked up*, but you expressed it better."

"Mars will be perfect."

"It will?"

He holds up *The Sovereign Individual*. "The authors of this book predicted everything. The rise of the Internet, cryptocurrencies, the obsolescence of nation-states. The fact is, Planet Earth is headed toward utopia too."

"Oh . . . yeah?"

"But it will be violent and painful and will take over a century to arrive. Disease epidemics, rampaging AI, collapse of food stocks, resource wars between nuclear-armed states. Total collapse won't be easy."

Amber shifts on the couch, feels those rodents in her gut, gnawing at her stomach lining.

"But on Mars we'll accelerate the process. In fact, we'll skip the chaos," says Geoff Task. "On Mars, right from the start, we'll have a small population made up entirely of a cognitive elite. And most importantly, there won't be any nation-states."

"That's . . . a good thing?"

"Do you like war?"

She laughs. "Of course not."

"Do you like taxes?"

"Do I . . . ? I mean, I like bike lanes and parks and, you know, universal health care."

"You sold illegal substances to make your living before you joined us."

"I'm not proud of it."

"Did you declare that income? Did you say, *Dear inept govern-*

ment of Canada that functions as a cartel, please steal the money I earned with my own inventiveness and intelligence?"

"No, but I hated feeling like a criminal." Sweat beads at her hairline. "If I could have—"

"You had to circumvent the nation-state to do what was right."

"They're actually legalizing—"

"That's why I wanted you here. That's why you weren't kicked off the show when you ran away."

"What?" She stares at him. "You stepped in? On my behalf?"

"It states right in your contract that leaving the set without permission results in instant dismissal." He nudges her foot with his. "Didn't you read your contract?"

"It was a hundred and seventy-four pages."

"I thought you were an academic." He puts a hand on her knee. "Yet a hundred and seventy-four pages vanquished you?"

"I guess I was excited." She can't focus on anything but that hand on her knee. A hand attached to an arm covered with sparse brown hairs. An arm that belongs to Geoff Task. "I would have signed anything."

"None of that matters." Geoff Task's hand moves from her leg to her inner elbow. "What's important is that you're here now."

"Thank you." She catches his eye, then looks away. "For helping me. It means so much—"

"I didn't do it as a favor." He runs his fingers along the skin of her inner wrist. "I stepped in because I recognized you for what you are."

"What . . . am I?"

"You're one of us, Amber." His fingers intertwine with hers. "A sovereign individual."

"That's so." Her throat feels tight, like when she woke to Coach Rodney reaching inside her shorts. "Sweet of you to say."

Geoff Task takes hold of her shirt and pulls her toward him. His kiss is like the mezcal: soft at first, lingering and exploratory, then an intense finish when he bites her lower lip.

BRONWYN COMES OVER RIGHT AFTER OUR PHONE CONVERSATION.
I'm expecting she'll want to *communicate openly* and have prepared some talking points. *In my defense . . .* But she collapses on the Voyager and snuggles against me.

"You okay?" Has she fallen asleep?

"Fine."

"You sure? We can talk about—you know, stuff."

"It's okay."

"I thought—"

"My dad called this morning. Right after you did. Completely drunk, asking if I'd *met a guy* yet."

I think of my own father. A person who might as well live on Mars.

"He's engaged to some woman named Chrissy, who's pregnant, I guess? Said he's not going to screw up this time. Then he started crying."

"Wow."

"Yeah."

Just in time, I remember her go-to line. "How do you feel?"

She buries her face in my lap. "Can we just, like, watch a comedy or something?"

"For sure, let me think." *The Seven Year Itch? Blazing Saddles? What's Up, Doc?* What would be best for a woman in the throes of childhood trauma? To buy time, I find a funny SNL video on You-Tube. But an ad pops up, featuring Amber. Amber for Aveeno: *Get everyone talking about* your *glow-up!* I hit mute. The next ad shows Amber in an air-pollution face mask patterned with stars and comets.

"Ridiculous. She's everywhere." I close the laptop. But Bronwyn must know that YouTube is feeding me Amber ads for a reason, that the algorithm is just giving me what I want. "You know I think you're perfect, right? Bron?"

Thing is, Bronwyn *is* the perfect girlfriend for me—if she'll have me—because she works all the time, at odd hours, and when she's off work she likes to hang at home. Smoke a little weed (which I now purchase like a regular schmuck), watch a movie, go to bed early. Because she's worked in restaurants since she was sixteen, she hates eating in them. Because she and/or her parents don't manage a hedge fund, she's broke like everyone else in this city and never suggests we go to a club or a pub or on a weekend trip. Because she's a stoner, even if she wants to hit the beach or go for a walk, I can usually wait it out until entropy takes over and the couch swallows her resolve.

"Bron? Don't think about Amber." I should take my own advice. "Seriously."

Bronwyn sits up, takes off her shirt.

"Right on." I'm not sure what this is about. "So are we . . . back together?"

"Were we together in the first place?"

"Good point. Who needs labels?"

"Can we just have sex?" She slides down her leggings, and her underwear slips off with them.

"I thought you wanted to watch—"

"Are you not attracted to me?" She unclasps her bra, drops it to the floor. "Is that the issue?"

"What? No. No issue."

"Then what's the problem?" She stretches out on the living room floor, her body exposed. "With sex."

"No problem. With sex." I unzip my jeans, take them off. "You sure you're okay?"

"If you want me, I'm here, Kevin." She gestures to the length of her body. "I'm here."

I'm still wearing my T-shirt and feel strange, unsexy, like a guy in a nightshirt. But I kneel over her, kiss her neck, and she closes her eyes. There is no problem. With sex, or anything else. I kiss the divot between her collarbones. Feel her tremble, hear her sniffle, and realize she might be crying. "Hey. Hey, what's going on?"

Then she goes for it: she *cries*. Tremors rack her thin body. My mom used to sob like this during movies—but not the ones you'd expect, not the tearjerkers. Some innocuous scene would set her going. I'd get the Kleenex box and the crumpled tissues would pile at her feet. It went on and on, this inexplicable female keening that seemed somehow my fault—or at least, I hadn't prevented it. Hadn't been funny or sweet or distracting enough. As a kid, it scared the shit out of me.

Now I get Bronwyn some toilet paper and a blanket from the bedroom. Can't think of a single right thing to say. Can't even touch her. She's entirely naked, sitting on the floor, unraveling toilet paper and pressing handfuls of it to her face.

Finally she judders, catches her breath. "Damn it. So stupid. Sorry."

I pass her more toilet paper. "Don't apologize."

"I get sort of—insecure." She blows her nose. "I shouldn't have done that. Pressured you."

"But I shouldn't have—well, everything."

"I just wonder sometimes, but it's dumb. I know you care about me."

"Of course I do. Care about you." Why can't I meet her eyes? "I think you're awesome." Can't I do better than that? There are some good words, perfect words, I'm meant to give her. An offering. But my throat feels full of sand. "Do you still want to stay over? I mean, everything's cool?"

"It's weird here without the plants." She pulls the blanket around her shoulders. "I almost miss the heat."

"I know. I miss them too."

"Do you know what you want to do?"

"About the plants? I can't get them back. The cops have probably smoked it all already."

"I mean, now that they're gone. What do you want to do? With your life?"

I haven't had to think about *my life* since meeting Amber—didn't even have to think about *our life* because Amber was the one who made plans. My role was to dog-paddle after her, trying to stay afloat.

What do I want to *do*? With my one and only life?

Then Bronwyn offers me a plausible response: "I guess you could write again?"

If she thinks I'm writing, she won't find it strange that I'm home all the time, and moody, and distant—after all, I'll be a *writer*. So I tell Bronwyn that's an excellent suggestion. I say I have an idea for a screenplay. I nod enthusiastically that this is a great time to get back into it, now that I don't have the plants to worry about.

"It won't be easy," I say. "I mean, I might not have much to show for my efforts."

"Just make it honest. Make it real."

"I love that idea," I say. "Reality. Its unbearableness."

She leans into me and says, "I *so* believe in you, Kevin," which nearly breaks my heart. There are endless ways to betray people.

AMBER WALKS DOWN THE SPIRAL STAIRCASE, WANDERS THROUGH
the dark hallway. Except she must have gone the wrong way, because
she can't find her room—ends up near a kitchen that gleams in the
dark. Stainless steel counters like in a restaurant. She takes another
wrong turn, finds herself in front of a small, circular door that's ajar.
A wagon full of cleaning supplies is propped outside. "Hello?" She
half expects to meet a night custodian. "I'm a bit lost?"

No answer. The circular door is made of thick metal, like the
opening to a bank vault or a submarine. She pulls—so heavy—until
it creaks open. Beyond it, a narrow staircase leads downward, into
darkness. She takes one step, then another. Down, down, her hand
gripping the cold metal rail.

At the bottom, she's enveloped in a silence that feels physical—
silence that grabs her by the wrists, presses cold hands to her throat.
She blinks, can't see a thing—this place is darker than the apartment
with its blackout blinds. She touches the cold wall, walks a few steps
by feel. The air smells like bleach.

This is where the world ends.

She turns, runs back toward the stairs, takes them two at a time.
Reaches the top out of breath, heart pounding, but chilled. Shivering.

Retraces her steps, calms her mind enough to find her bedroom.
Okay. Fine. Everything's fine. Seems like a dream now, that circular doorway and underground cold. She'll have to tell Adam about
it, bring him there tomorrow—it'll seem funny and harmless in the
morning.

She brushes her teeth, takes off her clothes in front of the mirrored walls and doesn't even flinch at the sight of her own naked
form. Stands for almost an hour under the rain-shower head, letting

the water run in rivulets down her hair, her back, her legs. Washes Geoff Task's hands from her skin.

Thankfully it didn't go far. There was a moment—he had one hand at her neck, the other gripping her wrist—when she thought the word *no*. Suppressed crazed giggles. It was too much: the mezcal, the flattery, the morbid curiosity. But then Geoff Task pulled back, straightened his collar, cracked his knuckles. Said he'd better check on his wife because she had heartburn.

Either he's loyal to Tali (sweet, pregnant Tali!) or insecure about his equipment—why else would a guy have a big phallic tower in the center of his home? Anyway. Whatever. It was hilarious and gross and kinda cool that *Geoff Task* wanted to make out with her, and hugely awesome that she didn't have to sleep with him. They were leaving tomorrow. Thank god.

She thinks of Kevin, probably getting high with Marcus.

Tamiko and Logan, in bedrooms somewhere in this giant house. Oblivious.

And Adam, sleeping next door; he will never, ever find out. Even though she did it for him. She made out with that billionaire for the sake of the mission. Because if Geoff Task likes Amber, that can only be a good thing for *A-squared*. Right?

When it was over, she tried to stay flirty, made it seem possible that they'd hook up again. "See you tomorrow?"

Geoff smiled, leaned in, bit the side of her jaw so hard she can still feel the imprint of his teeth.

She shivers again. Somehow the shower didn't warm her; she's covered in goosebumps. But when she checks her phone, Pichu has sent a photograph of a pregnancy test showing a pink plus sign and one word: *Positive!*

Everything is working out for the best. Everything happens for a reason.

And she's in paradise. There's the hydrogen-atom bathtub. The Himalayan rug. The king-size bed.

Amber crawls between the sheets with wet hair, starfishes her limbs. Runs her hands along her naked skin. Her body. She's awed by the feel of her muscles, the rhythm of her breath, the power of her pulse. It's been fifteen years since she appreciated this body, since she was the girl people stopped in the streets of Thunder Bay. *You're making us proud! Putting us on the map!* And just as quickly she was defeated and damaged, ignored. Since her injury, she's mistrusted this body, this failure. It's a structure that other people seem to want—to touch, to fuck—yet an entity she hates.

But her body did something good this time. Her body took her *here*, to heaven on Earth, and brought Geoff Task on-side—she's not so naive to think that he's interested in *picking her brain* anymore. But when he kissed her, she understood: Tamiko might be more intelligent and accomplished and beautiful. But Amber is the one people want.

This is real. She could win.

She feels a swell of panic, a rogue wave.

No. No no no. Not tonight.

She's spent too many sleepless nights twisting in the dark, afraid of her own power, feeling the Earth's vengeful weather, the magnitude and heat of its molten core—as though these forces lived inside her, shearing her bones.

Not now. Not anymore.

Everything is unfolding as it should. She closes her eyes, summons the deep stillness of a Mars night, and sleeps.

I WAKE BESIDE A SLEEPING BRONWYN, SLIDE OUT OF BED, AND FILL two bowls with granola, banana, and coconut yogurt. I brew coffee.

Eventually I hear her moving in the bedroom, then the shower turns on.

"You're the sweetest, Kev." She steps out of the bathroom wrapped in a towel, smelling pungent—she washes her dreads with so much tea tree oil and vinegar it makes my eyes water. "Best boyfriend ever."

"It's just store-bought granola." Boyfriend? "Not a big deal."

I find Stephen Colbert on YouTube, and we eat on the couch. All through breakfast I wait for her to leave. As soon as she leaves, I wait for her to come back.

I should be writing. Or reading. Putting some information into my brain. Instead I watch MarsNow, all the blinds lowered. Just me and that glowing light.

The final challenge is in New Zealand. They're in paradise, simulating a Martian disaster: their rover has broken down and they're far from home, with only three hours' worth of oxygen. Countdown clocks are hung around their necks: Get to zero and you're dead. Find your way home, through a natural obstacle course, and you've survived the challenge. They're given three hints: *home is due north, X marks the spot,* and *you can't go around—you must go through.* They're given a lockbox and told that its contents will help them on their mission. But they'll need to find the key to open it.

They walk toward what FirstMan34 swears is due north, and find themselves at the mouth of a cave. They decide to travel deep into the cave—*you must go through*—which contains underground cliffs and rivers. They leap into pools of cold underground water. They slide along muddy surfaces, abseil down rock walls, cross a chasm by walking along a fraying rope, ride black rapids in rubber tires—New Zealand's tourism board definitely sponsored this episode. Finally they reach the end of the cave, find a key, and unlock the box, which contains a four-piece puzzle. They assemble the puzzle, using their headlamps for light, and see that it's a map of the forest that surrounds the cave, with an X indicating where they need to go. They must each carry a piece of the puzzle, the piece labeled with their name; if one of them gets lost or abandons the group, they'll never find their way. The clocks around their necks continue to count down.

Then we see Bridget, in a studio somewhere, her lips so inflated that she seems to slur: "This ultimate challenge tests their ability to work together under life-or-death pressure!"

Great insight, Bridget. Now back to New Zealand, where the Marsketeers get lost even when they do stick together, and Tamiko looks like she's grinding her teeth to nubs. "I told you we were going the wrong way."

Cut to Amber's In the Moment, where she talks directly to the camera: "I'm like, *what?*"

Cut back to the forest scene. Logan says, "Ladies, ladies, we're wasting valuable time."

FirstMan34 ignores them, studies the puzzle map, looks at the sky, then calmly declares: "I know what we need to do."

The puzzle map leads them to Douchebag Billionaire's mansion. Shots of the Marsplorers, dirty and tired, greeted by Geoff Task and Talia Annabelle Lorne. *That* Talia Annabelle Lorne. Her best work, of course, was in the cheerleading dramedy *Three Cheers for Becky Greer!* Canceled after six episodes, it was a precursor to prestige-teen TV and influenced everything from *Glee* to *Friday Night Lights* to *Riverdale*. But I know and love Talia Annabelle Lorne from her starring roles in a series of awful early-aughts rom-coms. There are a lot of reasons why I wish my mom were still alive, and these so-bad-they're-bad films are not at the top of that list, but it still gives me a twinge that Mom didn't live to see Talia Annabelle Lorne's oeuvre. *He's Everywhere, She's Everything*: about a girl who tours Europe hoping to find love, but keeps bumping into her old high school crush from Michigan. *Two's a Pair*: about a girl who works at a shoe store in Manhattan and who sells a pair of Hush Puppies to the man of her dreams. *She's So Real*: about a girl-next-door who steals the boyfriend of a Paris Hilton type played by . . . Paris Hilton. You get the idea. You also understand why Talia Annabelle Lorne decided to pursue her acting dream by taking on the role of loving and devoted wife in that classic vehicle—Hollywood is always remaking this one— *Douchebag Billionaire's Blonde #4*.

Cue *Architectural Digest*-level fawning over Douchebag Billionaire's mansion—it seems clear from the goddamn moat that he plans to retreat there when Planet Earth experiences total environmental/ economic collapse. The house, Bridget informs viewers, is called the Ark, so it must be his future refuge from the flood.

But why doesn't Geoff Task go to Mars immediately, since our own planet is on the brink of disaster and since the space-travel technology is—he assures us all—so very advanced? Why doesn't Geoff Task buckle himself and his pregnant wife into the MarsNow Lander if he's so confident in his "team" and their "innovations"? For the same reasons one wouldn't take medicine before it's tested on lab rats.

Cut to a fancy dinner with Mr. and Mrs. Douchebag. Cut to all the Marsobots, tired and well fed, saying goodnight. Cut to—oh, hello—Amber and Geoff Task alone in what looks like a pretentious library, the kind Douchebag Billionaire fills with books he collects as investments. Shot of Amber and Douchebag Billionaire sitting too close to each other on an oxblood leather couch shaped like a clitoris.

This footage has clearly not been shot with the usual MarsNow cameras; it's grainier and the sound quality is bad. But that's Amber Kivinen's voice saying to Geoff Task, *I've always wanted you.*

Definitely Amber Kivinen kissing Douchebag Billionaire.

I've never seen it before, never witnessed my girlfriend cheating on me. But now I'm watching her cheat on me *and* cheat on the guy she's cheating on me with.

That terrible sentence, the pain it caused you because of its extreme grammatical awkwardness? Maybe that sentence gives you an idea of how it feels to watch Amber make out with Geoff Task.

Can I even continue? Can I live in a world this hideous? And mediocre? And predictable? Of course she let a middle-aged billionaire suck at her face. Of course she was flattered and probably thought he was interested in her *mind*. So uninspired. Did he turn himself on by whispering words like *strategy, revenue,* and *solutions* into her ear? And did she fuck him? Can you imagine having sex with Geoff Task? Or Mark Zuckerberg? Or any one of their soldiers in the tech army, those boys in hoodies and company-branded T-shirts? So bland it would be like making love with conformity itself. Those men are the human equivalent of premade appetizers, the kind that nobody at the party is craving. It would be like fucking a tiny quiche, or a plastic container of hummus, or a half-frozen spring roll.

I've been keeping a vigil for a woman with no standards at all. I've been *waiting* for her. Introducing Kevin Watkins, in the role of dumbest dumbass alive.

A LADY IN A GRAY UNIFORM WITH A WHITE APRON PLACES A SILVER tray at Amber's bedside. Breakfast. The menu is printed on a little embossed card: illy latte made with oat milk and sweetened with Stevia. A smoothie of wheatgrass, aloe, turmeric, macha, avocado, banana, dried reiki powder, cacao, and almond butter.

"Wow." Amber takes a sip of the smoothie—she'll make an almond exception just this once. "This is lovely."

The woman nods, then begins straightening Amber's room. Folding her clothes from the night before and placing them in the armoire.

"Oh shit, is it after ten?" says Amber. "Did I sleep in?"

The door bursts open and Adam is there, open laptop in hand. "You made out with Geoff?"

Her initial thought: calling Geoff Task by his first name sounds unbearably pretentious and they should all stop. Then she wakes up.

"What? No. How did—?"

"How did I find out? The way the world found out. I watched it on TV. I saw you toss yourself at him."

"They were filming?" She sits up. "Wait. You said you never watch the show. That you can't watch yourself—"

"I told a—what's that word? A fib," he says. "But you are a liar."

As if summoned, the MarsNow camera crew comes into the room followed by Slick Nick. "Children," he says. "If you're going to have a lovers' spat, you need to let us know."

"Get out," says Amber. "Now."

"Keep rolling." Slick Nick nods at the crew. "Duh."

Another guy comes into the room, a beast with a brush cut, wearing a bulletproof vest. Amber points at him. "Who the hell is that?"

"This gentleman is a member of Task's security force," says Slick

Nick. "Former Blackwater, got hired after he left Iraq. He's present in case you try anything."

"In case I—?" She wants to scream, punch someone, tear Slick Nick's orange skin from his face. "I didn't kiss him. He kissed me."

Slick Nick laughs. "Semantics."

"Is this a joke?"

"No," says Nick. "But it is pretty funny."

"Hey, Security Force." She turns toward the guard. "Are you loyal? Does Geoff Task treat you like an equal? Like family?" She steps closer, channels one of Kevin's rants. "Or is it impossible to forget that he's your master? And when shit hits the fan, will you and your buddies stage a coup, take over this property, and roast him over an open flame?"

The beast in the bulletproof vest says nothing. His eye twitches. Hard to tell what that means, but Amber takes off. Runs up the stairs, to the crow's nest. Can hear Nick, Adam, Security Force, and the camera crew behind her. She will hunt down Geoff Task and make him confess, on camera—

The library is empty. Peaceful. So luxurious she wants to blow it up.

"You won't find him." Slick Nick catches his breath. "He and Tali flew to another one of their properties early this morning. The private island in the BVIs. Or maybe the Hawaiian island? Or the one in the English Channel."

Amber pictures Geoff in a jet, cutting through the clouds. Careless asshole.

"I was hoping we'd shoot at the English Channel one," muses Nick. "It has a *castle*."

Amber kicks the wall, scuffing the paint job. Then flips couch cushions and smashes the mezcal glasses that are still on the coffee table. Shoves books off the desk—all that neoliberal lit crashes to the ground.

There it is. Above the oak desk. As Security Force lurches toward her, she rips the camera off the wall.

Then her arms are behind her back and Security Force whispers in her ear, "Don't make me tase you, girly."

The MarsNow cameras are loving it.

"You filmed me last night without my permission," she says to Nick, squirming in Security Force's arms. "I never allowed—"

"Did you even read that contract you signed?" Slick Nick opens the liquor cabinet. "We have permission to film you at all times, with or without your knowledge."

"Did you know that?" She turns to Adam. "They can film us anytime?"

"Of course. You didn't read the contract?"

"You did? And signed it anyway?" She stares at him. "So there's some loophole? Some way out? We could sue—"

"No loopholes, baby." Slick Nick uncaps the mezcal.

"That's not like you, Adam." Amber tries to tear her arm from Security Force's grip. "You wouldn't sign that—"

"I signed it for *you*," Adam says. "Because I wanted to be with you."

Amber wrenches free. "That's not true."

"I thought I'd finally met someone who understood me," Adam says. "I don't bond easily with people. You know that."

"Okay, but—"

"It was extraordinary for me, to communicate so openly," says Adam. "I've never been with anyone and thought this was my chance—"

"What do you mean, you've never—"

Adam reddens and turns away.

"Hold on, you mean—?" She shakes her head. *This* is why he won't sleep with her? "But you've—I mean, *physically*—"

"When I left my community, I'd never seen a movie or a television," he says. "I'd only read holy books. I had no idea. Wouldn't have even known where to place my arms and legs—"

"Adam." She wants to press a palm over his mouth, save him from this mortification on camera. "Stop."

He sits on the couch, holds his head in his hands. "I've been with other women, sort of, but never—"

Amber drops to her knees. "Never?"

He shakes his head.

She crawls toward him, over the detritus of her destruction. "Well, you've learned a lot." She tries to catch his eye. "You're great with your fingers."

"I've read manuals."

"I think you'd be good at it." She takes his hands. "I'd definitely like to try. Anyway, it's not like I'm some Casanova. I have a lot to learn too."

"Oh my Lord." Slick Nick drinks the mezcal from the bottle. "Thank you. *Thank you*. We could not have scripted it better. Pathetic and Lonely Virgin, we've been trying to get it out of you all season."

"That's why you cast him?" says Amber. "As the Virgin?"

"You catch on fast, Damaged Slut."

"Fuck you, Nick."

Her phone buzzes. An LA number.

"Answer it," says Nick. "You've broken so many rules already."

She answers and someone named Stefan says he's a crisis manager. "I worked with Martha Stewart." His voice a deep drawl. "Who's now more successful than ever."

"I don't need—"

"Do not try to do damage control on your own," says the voice. "Sex scandals are especially difficult for women—a lot less forgivable than Martha's bit of fraud, obstruction of justice, and jail time. But I can help you."

"A sex scandal? *He's* the one who's married."

"I know for a fact that Geoff Task already had 'sources' speak to *People* and TMZ, suggesting that Talia Annabelle Lorne is a bit of a ball-breaker—she makes him eat very strange health foods, did you know that? It's no wonder he momentarily lapsed. And don't forget that he owns thirteen television stations and forty-eight radio stations, along with the *LA Times.* There's also the fact that you're known to be quite . . . experienced."

Amber hangs up. Logs in to Facebook and Instagram and Twitter. Sees that her pages are covered in thousands of crab emojis—to insinuate that she has an STI?—along with commands from men to *die, whore, kill yourself already and show us your tits,* alarming messages from teen girls—*I used to look up to you!*—and people of every age, background, and gender screaming at her in all caps:

HOW COULD YOU DO THIS TO ADAM, YOU DIRTY TWAT???

I DON'T BELIEVE IN LOVE ANYMORE

YOU KILLED A-SQUARED, YOUR A MURDERER!!!!!!!

When she googles her own name, the first hit is a BuzzFeed article declaring that Amber Kivinen is *the Most Hated Woman in the World.*

IN THE DARK, I GET MEGA-STONED AND WATCH THE AMBER-Douchebag make-out on loop. I field calls from *Us Weekly* and other tabloids, asking me to comment on the situation. A guy from TMZ says, "Buddy, we get where you're at right now. Feeling betrayed? How would five thousand bucks make you feel?"

"You want me to sell out someone I've loved for fourteen years for five thousand dollars?"

"Okay, I've got ten thousand *American* dollars with your name on it, if you give us an exclusive interview and five personal photos of Amber."

I hang up, just in time to get a call from Vivid Entertainment. The offer: a hundred thousand dollars, if I can send them a sex tape of me and Amber. Or Amber and anyone. Amber alone?

"Our sex tapes aren't for sale!" I yell into the phone, because that seems less embarrassing than admitting that we never thought to record ourselves having sex. Of course, as I'm yelling that line, Bronwyn walks in. She heard about the "incident" so she left work early to see how I'm "coping."

"Coping fine." I toss my phone across the room and snap my laptop shut. "Why wouldn't I be? We're not together anymore."

"Let's get some air." She lifts the blinds and opens a window. "I know it takes time to process loss."

"What loss? I never had Amber to begin with." My strategy was to give her freedom, and look where that got me? Then again, she gave me freedom too. Left me alone with my weed and sadness, didn't force me to talk about how I'm *feeling* or what I'm going *to do with my life*. We gave each other privacy. "I don't want to talk about Amber. I'm so over Amber."

I can't quite breathe.

"I took the rest of the day off," says Bronwyn. "Why don't we do something? We could go to Kits Beach? Or English Bay."

"Those are things that people do."

"Exactly." She tickles my ribs. "And we're people. We could do things."

This fucking Canadian obsession with the outdoors. Outside is full of death. Everywhere you look worms are sliced in half by bike tires, drunk guys are looking for a fight, songbirds are swallowed by cats, air pollution decimates lung tissue.

"Doing things, going places," I say. "What a revolutionary idea."

"Come on, Kev." Bronwyn stands and tugs on my hand. "Let's be revolutionaries."

"Or we could . . . not do that. Not do anything."

"It's not even raining." She puts on her jacket. Goes to the doorway and stands there smiling, looking so pretty and kind. "See? We can just walk through this door. We can do whatever we want." She is the epitome of goodness. "We're actually alive, did you know that?"

But a thought has slid into my head. *If Amber is the most hated woman in the world*, my sick brain tells me, *then Amber will get eliminated*. Amber will come home.

Bronwyn stands in the open doorway, offering me the world.

But this world doesn't feel like home anymore, so I say, "Sorry, Bron, I can't. I have to make a call."

ALREADY A REDDIT THREAD CALLED AMBER K SUPER HOAR IS
devoted to deepfake revenge videos, Amber's face superimposed on
the body of a porn star who is being gang-raped and pretending to
enjoy it. Amber's face covered in semen. Amber's voice replaced by
what sounds like a squealing, terrified pig being sent to the slaughter.

Amber, real-life Amber, stands in the stairwell outside the library
clutching her phone—wants to toss it out the tower's window and
watch it smash on the ground, but can't bring herself to stop scrolling
through the hatred.

A text comes in from Pichu: *You made out with Geoff Task? What
was THAT like??*

Boring. He's a bad kisser—does this pointy tongue-thrust move.

Ewwww. Insecure guys are très thrusty. Well, it's a good story anyway.

A good story. Except that her life is over. She's surely lost the competition. She's not going to Mars. And she's lost Adam. The same way
she lost Kevin.

She's exhausted. So tired of herself.

Then she hears a voice like that of God Himself: *Come on, kiddo.
Did I raise you to be a quitter?*

That's it. Of course. She'll call the toughest person she knows.

She dials her parents' house and listens to the phone ring—can
imagine that goddamn landline trilling and trilling. Finally he picks
up.

"Dad, did you see? I'm so sorry, Dad."

"Oh, sweetie." It's her mother. "Your dad's not home right now.
But I saw. Maybe it's a blessing, sweetheart."

"What do you mean, Dad's not home? The show just aired."

"He doesn't watch the show, sweetie. He finds it too stressful to
see his little girl up there, so he goes for a walk."

Amber feels the oxygen leave her chest. He doesn't watch the show? A few months ago, he'd called her a Viking and drunk to her success, and she couldn't understand why it was so easy for him to lose her. But last night she got it: if she makes it to Mars, she'll be his little winner again. His champ. His gold-medal girl.

"You know how sensitive he is," says her mother. "I just tell him what happened when he gets home. What do you kids call that? I give him the spoilers."

"Mom, I need to talk to him. I don't know what to do."

"I don't think you should do anything, sweetie. Remember how they treated that poor Britney Spears? She was just a sweet Baptist girl—"

"So I'm supposed to sit here and take it?" When was the last time they'd spoken? A real conversation. Amber cannot abide her mother's shaky, childish voice. "Not all of us have the luxury of doing nothing, Mom. Of never making a single decision. Or should I do what you did? Just get married and turn off my brain?"

"Amber, I know you're under stress—"

"And don't tell me to pray. Do not tell me to put it in the Lord's hands, Mom, I will lose my shit."

"Amber, disgraceful language—"

"Was it *disgraceful* when Dad disowned me and you went along with it? A year and a half, Mom." They've never spoken of those months when Lydia wouldn't return Amber's calls, wouldn't even reply to emails. "At least I can respect Dad's anger. At least he had balls."

"I have regrets." Her mother's voice drops. "I haven't always acted rightly—"

"I don't need your confession. I've had enough of those to last a lifetime."

"I've prayed—it was a difficult time for me—"

"Difficult for *you*? Is this conversation difficult? Are you going to get a headache and lie in bed for three days? Your migraines were always so convenient."

"You think I faked my headaches?"

"I think you're weak."

"Well, certainly you're just perfect."

"Excuse me?"

"I prayed that my children would love the Lord Jesus Christ the way I do, but since I can't control what's in your heart, I hoped you'd hold on to one value."

"Obedience?" Amber remembers her mother crawling around the kitchen, scrubbing at the bits of jam that had dropped from her husband's toast, then hardened on the floor.

"Charity. I hoped you'd find meaning in generosity."

"Will you tell Dad I called?" It's all Amber can do not to hurl the phone at the wall. "I have to go."

"You're up there on TV now and all I see is greed," says her mother. "All I see is someone who wants, and wants, and wants."

WHEN BRONWYN IS GONE, PROBABLY FOREVER, WITH MY LAPTOP
replaying the moment Douchebag Billionaire slid his pale hand from
Amber's neck to her breasts, I log in to Skype. This is it, my movie
moment, my heroic act. I'm getting my girlfriend back.

Isn't it ironic, as Alanis would say? Here I am wondering if Amber
had sexual relations with a baby quiche who made billions by writing privacy-gutting algorithms, and my solution is to use software
that he probably seed-funded. Maybe it doesn't matter if she slept
with him, because who among us hasn't been negged, seduced, then
fucked hard by those Silicon Valley boys, the ones who wholeheart-
edly value "optimizing click-throughs" and "driving engagement"?
The ones who turn our bodies and spirits into metadata; the ones
who profit off our endorphins and dopamine; the ones who promise
us a paperless and frictionless future while giving neo-Nazis free rein
on their platforms; the ones who use their inflated salaries to take
themselves on tropical tech-detox vacations and enroll their children in Waldorf schools, while ensuring that the rest of us remain
addicted to our own enslavement?

I will not let them win.

If I can save Amber, if I can convince her to drop this bullshit and
come home, maybe I can believe in humanity again. Maybe I can live
in this world—of conspiracy theories and oil spills, jailed dissidents
and clear-cuts, epidemics and exhaust pipes. Maybe I can find some
semblance of hope. Maybe I can save myself.

Breathing hard, I hold the phone and find Amber in my contacts.
Hover my finger over the icon of her face. I have one goal: *the end.*

SHE BANGS HER OWN FOREHEAD AGAINST THE WALL, WHICH IS SO blessedly cool and unyielding.

As a kid she used to look up at the stained-glass window in church, the one depicting the End of the World: flames, melting flesh, souls sucked toward the sky as if by a vacuum cleaner. To be bad was to be doomed; to be good was to be saved. And every single action and thought was recorded in God's ledger. Being a Christian was like being famous—you couldn't get away with anything.

She hears footsteps coming up the stairs—another cameraperson, probably. One guy is filming her from above, but they need to capture her breakdown from every angle.

"Is Nick up there?" Fucking Tamiko. "We're scheduled to do some pick-up shots."

Amber hits her head against the wall again. "Are you kidding?"

"You're still on the show, aren't you?" Tamiko laughs—that's a first. "Only now you're the villain."

Amber wants to shove her down the spiral stairs. "You're enjoying this."

"Incorrect. I think it's absurd." Tamiko leans against the wall. "If you're not satisfied sexually by Adam, you need to rectify it in an open and up-front manner."

Amber slams her forehead again.

"My husband enjoys watching me make love to both men and women," says Tamiko. "Maybe you and Adam would benefit from the swinging lifestyle."

"You're married?"

"To the love of my life."

"And he's okay with you going to Mars?"

"We give each other absolute freedom."

"Good for you." Amber knocks her head into the wall again. "I guess."

"Enough." Tamiko reaches for Amber and turns her away from the wall. "You'll give yourself a bruise and it'll show up in HD."

"Why are you being nice to me?"

"Because I know what it's like to be hated by millions." Tamiko straightens Amber's clothes, then leads her back into the library. "And I don't think a woman should be punished for having a body."

I LISTEN TO THAT TUNELESS SKYPE *DOO-WOP DOO-WOP*, **PRAYING** that she'll pick up. But it isn't her face that appears. It's that Ryan Seacrest look-alike.

"Jesus loves us!" He's grinning. "Keep rolling, boys. It's your *other* boyfriend, baby doll."

He tosses the phone and I get motion sickness as I fly through the air.

"Don't guilt-trip me." Amber's hair and eyes are wild. "I'm getting enough shit over here."

"You made out with that dick?" I didn't mean to launch into it; I meant, this time, to remain collected, to make my points with equanimity. "Did you fuck him?"

"Gross, no, I didn't fuck anyone. And *he* kissed me."

"But you let an evil mastermind douchebag billionaire who almost single-handedly authored our modern-day techno-nightmare *put his tongue inside your mouth*."

"Are you stoned again?" She looks like she might cry. "You're always stoned again."

"And *you* are always going on about how *humanity* has ruined the world. How *we* are responsible for the ecological crisis. It's not humanity, Amber. It's *specific human beings*. It's billionaires and their shareholder friends and the politicians who live in their pockets."

"Will you stop? Please? You're so angry all the time, and I'm sorry, but it's boring—"

"Boring? Because I actually *see*? Because I'm observing reality?"

"Are you? From your comfy spot on the couch?"

"That mansion you're in right now? It's his safe house for when the world ends. His rich man's hideaway."

"I know." She stares at me, eyes wide and wet. "I found the bunker last night—"

"See? I knew you didn't believe in his shit. You know he runs the world with the sole intention of extracting every granule of information, every resource, every dollar. You know he rules over us like slaves."

"Kevin—"

"And yet you made out with him. You said the words *I've always wanted you*. It makes me sick."

"No I didn't." She sits straighter. "I never said those words."

"Your voice said them on TV, Slammer."

"I never—" She looks away. "Nick? I did not say those words."

"You didn't?" I lean forward. "Amber? You sure?"

"Of course I'm sure. I don't want him. I never wanted him. He was just *there*."

"Oh, Christ." I feel so tired. "It's hard being your boyfriend sometimes."

"I mean it wasn't *planned*. I didn't seduce him. I really like Tali."

"Talia Annabelle Lorne?" I can't help myself. "Is she *so* nice?"

"Oh, Kev, she's the best. I wish you could meet her."

"Can we clarify something?" It's FirstMan34 butting in. "Is this person your boyfriend?"

As if he doesn't love this. As if he isn't pursuing Amber for exactly this reason: to have endless men to compete with. To decimate us one by one and prove his alpha status.

"Adam," says Amber, "this is a really high-intensity situation and—"

"He just said he was your boyfriend. And I was under the impression—"

"Oh shut it, FirstMan34," I say. "That's right, I know who you are. I know you've been trying to poach my girlfriend for over a year."

A stupid, manly vein throbs in his forehead. "You have to choose," he says to Amber. "Him, or me."

"Dude, that's bad dialogue," I say. "Also, it's possible to love more than one person at once, so maybe stop being such a fucking fascist."

"Okay, Kev, enough," says Amber.

But I'm just getting started. "Maybe that whole attitude is the problem, FirstMan34. Wanting a thing all to yourself? Thinking you can *own* everything, including other human beings. Isn't that why there's a refugee crisis, and the planet is dying? Because dudes always want to own everything all to themselves?"

Amber's face again. "Kevin, lay off a bit?" She brings the phone close to her mouth and whispers, "He's a virgin."

Am I supposed to laugh?

"I just found out too. It'll be on the next episode. It's not a big deal."

"For real?"

"For real."

"Okay, listen. I hate you somewhat less now, FirstMan34. So I'm going to tell you something." What the hell am I doing? I'm aiming for *the end*, but am somehow on a detour. "Amber, maybe you never said the words *I've always wanted you*—or at least you didn't say them in that moment, or in that order. It's called frankenbiting. Reality TV uses it all the time. You might have said '*I've always wanted* to go to Mars, haven't *you?*' and they just edit the soundtrack to fit the story they've already written."

I can hear Ryan Seacrest's screech-laugh in the background. "News flash! Reality TV isn't one hundred percent real."

"But why?" says Amber. "Just 'cause it's good TV?"

"And the Japanese put in, like, eight hundred and forty million." Budget Seacrest swallows liquor from a bottle. "So Tamiko's going to Mars."

"I find that insulting." Tamiko's voice. "If I win, it will be thanks to superior skill and intellect."

"And Adam is Jewish," I say. "That's a problem—people still

believe in the Illuminati. And Logan's got that white-supremacist, American-hero look. Of course they want him on the ship."

"Correct," says Budget Seacrest. "And there's nothing you can do about it because your contract includes an airtight nondisclosure clause." He leans against Amber and his sweaty face takes up half the screen. "And you better not tell either, Sad Ex-Boyfriend—we will sue you into oblivion." Then he giggles—he's perhaps a touch inebriated. "By the way, this is the same Sad Ex-Boyfriend who told us you have daddy issues."

"You said that? I have *daddy issues?*"

"Was I wrong?" I lean toward the screen. "Amber, he's just trying to distract you."

"Technically you don't have daddy issues anymore," says Budget Seacrest. "We own your daddy issues. We own your whole backstory. You signed that away too."

"You own her *past?*" I might spew. "How is that even possible?"

"I don't need my past. My past is a disaster." Amber looks defeated. "Why didn't they just rig the voting if they wanted me eliminated? Instead of publicly ruining my life?"

"They can't rig the voting," I say. "Trust me, all I've done for months is obsess about this stuff. They can't just send whoever they want to Mars. There are strict laws governing game shows."

"Put in place in the 1950s," says Budget Seacrest.

"Exactly." I sigh. "It's democracy at its best: the people have a voice."

"Well, isn't that beautiful," says Amber.

"So they had to nudge," I say. "To manipulate. It's Brexit all over again. It's gerrymandering. It's the TV equivalent of Russian bots or Trump's Facebook ads. It's a *lie,* fake news."

"That's interesting but doesn't help me."

"Help you what?"

"Get to Mars."

I stare at her through the screen. "You still want to go?"

"I'm the most hated person on Earth, so yeah, I still want to go."

"Jesus Christ, Amber. That douchebag, the one who groped you, he's sending you there to die." How long do I have to do this? How long do I have to try to save her life? "Please. Just come home."

"I can't." She holds the phone too close to her face; all I see are her bloodshot eyes and the top of her forehead. "I can't, Kevin. I just—"

She's crying. Amber Kivinen is crying.

"Slammer, Mars doesn't want you. Mars is a hostile environment. I want you."

"I'm sorry," she sobs. "I'm so sorry."

"Remember when we first moved to Vancouver? How happy we were? *So green it hurts?*"

"I can't go back, Kevin. I don't have any hope. Haven't for a long time."

"I'm hopeless too! That's why we get along."

"And I can't keep hurting you. I won't—" She looks shocked. As if she realizes what's happening, what she's doing—despite never intending to do anything at all. "I won't keep hurting you. I will not."

If I allowed it, a tap would open and tears would pour down my face.

"There's something wrong with me." She wipes at her eyes. "I'm broken. I don't know what's wrong with me."

"You're not broken," I say.

"I'm selfish."

"There's still time." I can't believe the words coming out of my mouth. "People will be voting all week."

"I'm not going to grovel. I'm not going to give some fake celebrity apology."

"You really want to go to Mars? With that humorless FirstMan34?"

She nods, wipes snot from her nose.

"Then do something about it."

"Do what?"

"You'll figure it out." I remember those newspaper clippings I kept tucked in my notebook when we were teenagers. Photos of Amber soaring off the vault, flying free. "I know you, Slammer. You're a star."

KEVIN'S FACE FREEZES, THEN DISAPPEARS. AND SHE'S CRYING, IN public. She's never felt so ugly.

But she's also never felt so important. So observed. *God sees everything.* And now the world has seen her at her worst too. Everyone has listened to her heart and heard its painful pulse: *I want, I want, I want.*

She has nothing to lose.

"They have cameras." She turns to Adam. "But so do we."

"Oh, does Super Amber have a plan?" Slick Nick is sprawled on the floor, cradling a second bottle of luxury mezcal. "Is Super Amber going to save the day?"

She loads EyeSite, that lame social media platform nobody uses. It will be even sweeter, to use his own company to take him down.

"Are you going to start crying *#metoo, #metoo?*" slurs Slick Nick. "Jeeezus."

It takes her three attempts to remember her password and log in. Once in, she clicks *Share Your Drama,* and the screen becomes a video recorder.

"Ready?" she says.

"Ready," says Adam.

She holds the phone so that she and Adam—their bug-eyed, tear-streaked faces—fill the screen.

"We want to set the story straight. We want to be real with you, our fans," she says. "We're in Geoff Task's library, in the home he calls the Ark, probably 'cause he intends to retreat here when the entire world—our environment, social organizations, rule of law, homes, food systems—when everything collapses." She picks up that book he showed her last night, holds it in front of the screen. "This is your bible, Geoff? Instead of reading garbage like this, why don't you pay taxes? Then the world wouldn't collapse in the first place. Then you wouldn't need a security force. Or a moat."

Adam taps her knee; she's off topic.

"I am familiar with hierarchical organizations, and what happened in this room was unethical," says Adam. "There is an enormous power discrepancy between Amber and Geoff Task. He is, in effect, her boss."

"I was confused, 'cause I really wanted Geoff Task to like me. And I was a bit tipsy 'cause I'd barely eaten and he gave me alcohol."

The cyclops-eye of the camera stares her down, commanding her to *confess*. Forget Geoff Task's sin. Give them her soul.

"Okay, listen." She tucks her hair behind her ears. "I let him kiss me. I kissed him back. And it went on for a while." She steals a glance at Adam. "It was disgusting but I also liked it—I felt special and kind of . . . powerful." She takes a breath. "Do you guys ever feel this way? Just so fucking pathetic and scared? Like you're nothing? Useless and weak and the universe doesn't care about you. But then someone wants you, and for, like, five seconds you feel okay? Noticed and valid and worthy?"

"What really matters," says Adam, "is that attempts to smear Amber won't change anything between the two of us. We are still *A-squared*." He takes her hand. "We are a team and that means we practice radical forgiveness. We practice radical love."

She's crying again, clutching his hand. Radical forgiveness. She's longed for it her whole life.

"And we have one aim," he says. "To complete our mission."

"To get to Mars."

They turn toward each other and kiss.

This is probably the end. Also a beginning. *I am committed to nothing.* That was once true, but now she's in it to win. And whatever future awaits, she and Adam will be there together.

She uploads the video and they hold each other. Within an hour, they have over a million views.

#radicallove is trending all night.

卌 卌 卌 卌
卌 卌 卌 卌
卌 卌 卌 卌
卌 卌 卌 卌
/

A WEEK SINCE AMBER MADE OUT WITH CAPITAL-D DOUCHEBAG.
Tonight: a special two-hour finale. Part of the episode was shot in Dallol, Ethiopia, the hottest place on Earth. The sun scorches down from above, heat bubbles up from the ground through volcanic activity, the earth is covered in bright, swirling mineral deposits—it looks like a different planet from the one I know. It looks like the future.

Amber looks different too. They've done something to her hair—it's straighter, shinier, tamer. And they've done something to her face to make it look less open, less natural. Less. She's wearing the unitard thingy with the MarsNow logo over her heart. When she runs through the heat, the unitard shows off her slim, hard muscles. There's a dark, raised mole on her left thigh—a perfect circle, a pristine planet in the galaxy of her long leg. I can't see it on TV, but I know it's there.

Together fourteen years and she dumps me over Skype. Why is tragedy so mundane? Movies and books made me believe that life would be—maybe not exciting and beautiful, but at least narratively gratifying. But when my uncle in Thunder Bay called to say that Mom had died, it was so banal: a gastrointestinal hemorrhage caused by long-term use of ibuprofen and SSRIs. Really? My mom was dead because she failed to notice minute amounts of blood in her stool, therefore failed to see a doctor in time, therefore died from taking Advil. There's nothing redeeming about that story.

But Kev, Amber might say. *Everything happens for a reason.*

I remember hanging up the phone and turning to her. "My mom's dead."

At first Amber laughed. "Wait—you're serious?" Then she sat beside me, put her arm around my shoulder, and I understood that her strength could hold me together. I also wanted her to leave, so I could cry.

The shot changes and they're in the LA studio. The four remaining competitors are onstage, wearing those unitards: Amber, First-Man34, Tamiko, and Logan. One pair will be chosen to go to Mars, one pair sent home. It's an unofficial rule that Amber and Adam are one team, Tamiko and Logan another. People in the studio audience cheer. They hold signs: *Team Tamiko! Adam and Amber 4eva!*

"Tonight two of you will become champions." Bridget pouts her inflated lips. "And two will be eliminated."

Ominous, pounding music. A montage of scenes from earlier in the season plays on a huge screen behind them—lots of running and sweating and hugging and sobbing.

"How do you feel?" says Bridget.

"I feel good," says Logan. "Good to go."

Tamiko is doing some sort of yogic breathing.

Amber holds Adam's hand. "We're ready," they say in unison.

Astronaut Dirk Riley limps out onto the stage to huge applause, and addresses the competitors. "Tamiko, your intelligence and skill are extraordinary—I would be honored to have you on my team. Logan, your calm, focused demeanor is the most essential quality for a future Marsonaut. And Amber, Adam, I can't express enough how much I appreciate your united front. Whoever goes to Mars must have a preexisting and stable emotional bond."

"As you know, we've been tallying votes all week," says Bridget. "People phoned in and logged in from all over the world, and from their votes we discovered who they do and do not want to see on that starship to Mars."

Cheering. Pounding music.

"Now is the moment," says Bridget. "Now we choose our Mars-Now team. Now we choose our Marsonauts."

Commercial break.

I reach for the little glass pipe, the one that used to be the color of Amber's hair, then remember it's gone missing—everything and everyone disappears. I use the clunky replacement I ordered online. Fill the bowl with purchased weed, light it, then inhale like I'm breathing the purest oxygen.

What most people don't understand is that pot isn't a plant or a drug or a habit. It's a destination—a place to travel to. A place between waking and dreaming, between living and dying. I could spend the rest of my life there. And I will too, if Amber goes to Mars. Because who will blame me? And who will stop me?

Then they're back. I hate that MarsNow music, so I mute the sound.

Adam and Amber close their eyes—maybe they're praying—and Bridget says words. Pan to the audience, then close-up on Tamiko's stony face, Logan's devastated shock. Adam and Amber hug so hard they look like lions locked in battle.

The audience is a sea of open mouths. Silent screams.

SEASON TWO

KK, Mars
Is Actually
Happening Now

LAUNCH DAY STARTS WITH DR. LESLIE DABROWSKI, DIRECTOR OF the MarsNow Training Team, shaking Amber awake.

"Up," says Dr. Leslie. "Now. Oh, and the launch might be scrubbed."

"You mean canceled?"

"Postponed."

Amber savors the weight of warm blankets on her limbs. "So why do I have to get up?"

"Because you're a goddamn Marsonaut." Dr. Leslie explains that rain is predicted today—*rain*, in the desert—but a postponement would cost over $4 million, so launch prep will proceed and a game-time decision will be made. "We will launch if it is at all feasible," says Dr. Leslie.

"But will it be safe?"

"Feasible means safe."

This has been an ongoing argument. Dr. Leslie is a former astronaut who was once charged with assault and attempted battery when she kidnapped her boyfriend to prevent him from having an affair. She maced him, tied his wrists with NASA-produced silicone rope, put him in a diaper, and kept him hostage in her guest bathroom. But Amber and Adam are the poster children for #radicalforgiveness, so they can't hold Dr. Leslie's past against her—everyone is allowed to go mental once in their lives. And Dr. Leslie seems fine now: cool and chill and obviously brilliant. But maybe too cool? Maybe too chill? Adam and Amber have had only a little over two months of training, and today they'll be on board the MarsNow Lander, powered by a rocket fully loaded with oxygen and hydrogen. They will basically be strapped to a bomb and blasted upward at twenty-five times the speed of sound.

They don't exactly feel prepared. Training started in a classroom, with crash courses on geology, meteorology, physics, oceanography, and aerodynamics. Then an eleven-day overview of how the shuttle works. A shuttle that contains two thousand switches and circuit breakers, that is made up of more than a million parts.

"It'll all make sense when you're in the simulator," Dr. Leslie said.

Then they were in the simulator, putting the antenna away, opening and closing the payload doors, configuring the computers. Adam was the pilot/commander, so he did a full week of piloting simulation, to practice landing the shuttle on the surface of Mars. Activate the heat shields at 36,000 feet, use friction to aerobrake through the atmosphere, jettison the heat shield while also opening the parachute, power up the retro-rockets, detach the parachute at a high enough altitude to ensure it will not become entangled with the shuttle and low enough that it will soften the landing. But Adam kept starting the auxiliary power units too late, or jettisoning the heat shield too early, or maneuvering the craft so that the parachute lines would cross.

"Your shuttle blew up there." Dr. Leslie made an explosion sound with her mouth. "You're both dead now."

"I need more time to learn the system," said Adam.

"Since you don't have more time," said Dr. Leslie, "what if we simplify that sentence? *I need to learn the system.*"

"Exactly, and I need time—"

"We had this saying at NASA," said Dr. Leslie. *"There's only one thing to do during a landing.* You guys know what that is?"

"Stick to your checklist," said Adam. "Monitor all data."

"That's two things," said Dr. Leslie. "The correct answer is: *pray.*"

"But MarsNow has successfully landed two unmanned rovers and a cargo ship," said Amber. "So he won't actually have to land the shuttle? Right?"

"Nah, it's all automated." Dr. Leslie gave her a wink. "NBD."

No big deal? It feels like a big deal. Historically, half of humanity's unmanned missions to Mars have failed, crashing hard against the planet's surface, or sailing past it altogether—the spacecraft disappearing into the darkness of space. Amber brought up her fears again yesterday, when she and Adam ran laps in the pool. Dr. Leslie stood on the side with a whistle.

"How long was your training at NASA?" Amber dog-paddled to the pool's edge, chlorine stinging her eyes. "Astronauts train for years before they launch."

The pool laps were to prep them for the endurance needed to do a space walk. Which Dr. Leslie assured them they would not do unless something went very wrong. But Dr. Leslie was also always talking about how easily everything could go wrong—with the electrical system, or the shuttle's main engine, or the environmental/life-support system. They could lose contact with their communication team on Earth. They could lose power. Space debris could hit the shuttle—even a pebble would do serious damage if it were traveling at 10,000 miles per hour. And that's before they arrive at their destination. If they are ever exposed to the air on Mars, they will have twelve seconds to get to safety before their lungs explode.

"I think I speak for both of us when I say we're willing to postpone the launch for a few months, even years, if it means greater safety and accuracy." Amber tried to catch Adam's eye as he splashed past her in the pool. "We want to do it right. That's why we were chosen. Because we do things right."

"That's not why you were chosen," said Dr. Leslie. "Anyway, the planets are advantageously aligned for a flight to Mars, and that only happens once every twenty-six months. So."

"But the close approach is almost over," says Amber. "We *should* wait for the next one."

"Reality check." Dr. Leslie squatted and put a hand on Amber's wet shoulder. "We're competing with NASA and SpaceX—Elon is breathing down our necks. If he gets some bro to Mars before us, you see how that would undermine ratings? And let's not even mention China."

"Ratings?"

"Also, whoever gets there first makes the rules. You understand that, right?" Dr. Leslie's face took on a determined, I'm-gonna-tie-someone-up-and-put-them-in-a-diaper look. "If we arrive first, we at MarsNow will write the Martian laws."

"Yeah, but—will we be prepared enough? I mean, to survive?"

"Not if you stand around talking all day." Dr. Leslie blew her whistle. "Twenty more laps!"

Now, in bed, Amber wants to hide under the blankets. It's the same bewildered, reluctant mistrust she felt when she began to doubt the church. "What if we refuse? What if Adam and I decide to scrub the launch until we feel adequately prepared?"

"If you don't go, someone else will," says Dr. Leslie. "Maybe me. Weirder things have happened."

"I'm being serious."

"So am I. You want to be first, right? No one remembers Alan Bean and Pete Conrad."

"Who?"

"The third and fourth people to walk on the moon." Dr. Leslie sits beside Amber on the bed, like a mother about to sing a lullaby. "Listen, at NASA we were always begging for funding. MarsNow has real money. Real resources."

"So money is all that matters?"

"When it comes to space exploration, yes. Don't get me started. Why do banks get billion-dollar bailouts but the men and women at NASA—the ones advancing scientific knowledge and giving the public a deep appreciation for existence itself—they make do with taxpayer scraps?"

"Sure, but—"

"MarsNow has the funds to do this." Dr. Leslie gives Amber's arm a squeeze. "And I'll be down here looking out for you. I will not let anything happen to you."

"Promise?"

"On my life. Which means something to me, because I went to jail, okay? I've stared down death-by-shiv more than once."

Amber burrows under the covers. "Can I have a minute?"

"Don't piss around." Dr. Leslie yanks the blankets off Amber's body. "Let's get this show on the road."

FIVE MONTHS SINCE I STEPPED OUTSIDE—AN AMAZING FEAT? THE
wall is covered with scratched lines. It's like that dream where you
can't scream, can't move your limbs. I'm still on the couch where
Amber and I watched *Guys and Dolls*. The couch where I cried as
Marlon Brando and Jean Simmons sang "I'll Know When My Love
Comes Along." The couch where we played epic games of crib. Where
we napped. Made out. Fought. Conversed cynically about the end of
the world. You know that kind of late-night conversation? When you
tell each other that old, dark story (humanity is shit, everything is
shit) because somehow it makes you feel better? And it did make
me feel better, to know that this woman—this smart, accomplished,
desirable woman—was with me, thigh deep in the flow of feces that
is Existence Itself. Together, we could navigate the everything-is-shit
storm together. *You and me against the world, honeybun.* Without her,
though. Without my copilot, there's just a lot of crap and it slams me
from all directions.

Amber and FirstMan34 were given a couple months of "training"
in New Mexico, then a few staged goodbye scenes with their families
and friends. Caleigh crossed her arms, unwilling to hug Amber, but
her parents wouldn't let go. I refused to participate, but that hardly
made an impact—the MarsNow producers got an even bigger score
when they convinced FirstMan34's family to reunite before his trip of
a lifetime. (Because that's good TV: watching his Orthodox Jewish
mother, wig askew, weep into her apron.) During that month, there
was no time for Amber to come home to sort through her stuff, so
it's all still in the apartment: her clothes, her slippers, her books, her
exercise bands and weights, her jade apple, her favorite Care Bear
mug with its broken handle. No time to sort her stuff or call to say
goodbye, but Adam and Amber did have time to "write" and publish

a book (*Radical Love: How You Too Can Travel to the Mars Within*) after almost a billion people watched the #radicallove video.

You understand what that means, right? It means that hundreds of millions of people joined EyeSite just to watch that clip. It means that the site has officially "scaled" and is now being accessed in 112 languages, by students and moms and businesses and terrorists. A true indication of success: EyeSite has already been implicated in the genocidal killing of two ethnic-minority groups! And you understand what *that* means, right? It means that Amber made Geoff Task even wealthier. Amber handed him the personal data of millions of people, to exploit as he pleases. And he rewarded her by making her the face of the MarsNow Mission Tracker, a wearable prison—sorry, fitness device—that counts your steps, records your heart rate and location, monitors your sleep cycle, dictates your workouts, and shames you regarding your caloric intake in a prerecorded voice of your choice: Betty White or Bob Dylan or Steve Bannon.

If I needed more proof that life is cruel and meaningless, there it is: Amber bought in, fully and intensely and selfishly and stupidly. Amber jumped, feetfirst, into the billionaire's pet project. I loved her for fourteen years and yet I couldn't save her, not from the exploitation-industrial complex, the religion of fame, the consumerist wet dream, the delusion of repairing a dying world through rocket ships. I couldn't save her from the System, the most successful suicide cult humanity has ever invented.

And if I couldn't save one person, maybe there's no point in doing anything. Maybe life is as meaningless as Facebook makes it seem.

I keep thinking about Amber's stash. The painkillers in the shoebox. I don't know what's in there, but definitely enough. Once I asked her, jokingly, if she collected pills with a plan to off herself. She laughed, turned away, then looked me in the eye and said, "There's enough for both of us. If we need it."

"What?" I said. "What the actual fuck?"

"I mean—in case. If shit gets too real."

"What are you talking about?"

"Kevin, we're on track for almost three degrees of warming. That's reality, as of now. And it means refugee crises on every continent, famines, floods—people in the Global North think there's time, but—"

I took her in my arms then, because I understood two things: she was living with such fear, and she loved me so much. Enough that she wanted to die with me, die next to me. Enough that she would never leave me behind—she would take me with her, wherever she was going.

So there's that option. The stash. But I would have to swallow those pills alone.

The other option is for me to buy in too. Or at least give in. If life is meaningless, I might as well launch myself into the System and its Clamoring Void. Practice #radicalforgiveness and start my own YouTube channel and buy a fitness tracker and turn my body and soul into a set of data points. Optimize myself, live my power, be authentic, practice self-care, embody the life I deserve. Post about it.

If you can't beat 'em, join 'em.

It might work. Maybe I'd be "happy." Maybe I'd finally understand her, my space traveler, my interstellar betrayer. It would be a most radical love.

By the way, not to be outdone on the radical front, Bronwyn joined an environmental group and is all over social media posting about her volunteer work at a school community garden. Being with me tends to make women want to go out into the world and get shit done, and I guess her way of coping with anxieties about the future has transformed: astrology became action. She posts photos of herself amid smiling, adorable children—accompanied by the hashtag #hope—and honestly, even I can't shit on that. Can't find the ironic or bullshit angle and just have to click "Like."

That's my update: Amber has been sucked into the neoliberal

void, Bronwyn is busy, and Marcus doesn't come around anymore. Not since I eliminated him. I'm alone and my vigil has failed. So why can't I move?

Mom? Why can't I move?

Who says you need to move, honeybun? Who says you need to go anywhere?

I sit on the couch and drink MarsNow Rocket Fuel protein powder—Amber is the brand ambassador, so cases of this crap were mailed to our address. I could live off this sickly-sweet fake food for months because apparently one scoop contains the equivalent of six servings of greens and twelve grams of protein. I call Bastiaan to tell him that I no longer need grocery delivery. He says, "Sure thing, my friend," then explains that he and Cedar are reunited, living in a "triad" with Freddy. The kids call him Uncle Freddy and the whole family loves riding around in his massive truck. "Crazy what happens when you open your heart," says Bastiaan, and I congratulate him on living happily ever after in permaculture land.

Outside: rain, wind, more rain, and light from that remote star we call the sun. Broken sidewalks, greasy smells wafting from cafés, guys wandering down Commercial Drive asking if you want to buy the shirt they're wearing. I need to move, get my life on track, but outside is too real.

This apartment is okay. This apartment is a museum of our shared life, a reminder that at one time I wasn't alone.

Is this how my mom felt when I moved to Vancouver? Hopelessly abandoned?

Flashback. To my first year in Vancouver, when Mom would call—sometimes multiple times a day. I'd stare at the call display wanting to claw out my eyes. *Leave me alone!* I'd let it ring and ring until she gave up.

My phone sits silent now, so I log in to EyeSite and there's Mars-Now. Launch Day. New Mexico. I could have been there. Director of Casting, Communications, and Commitment Helena Slora offered to save me a seat in the media area. The camera would cut to me while I watched MarsNow steal my girlfriend forever.

No. No thank you. Because there's one last shred of hope, one last shoddy reason to live: I will win in the end. 'Cause I know something Helena Slora doesn't. I know that Amber will never sit still, never settle. Mars will seem great for a while, and so will FirstMan34. But eventually Mars will be as stifling as our basement suite, and First-Man34 will be just like me, the guy who's always around. And I'll be here, on a distant planet she distantly remembers. I'll be the one she wants.

FIRST STOP IS A PREFLIGHT ENEMA, ADMINISTERED BY THE SAME
doctor who once gave Amber an STI test in a hotel. He holds up the
rubber hose and says, "I hate this as much as you do," which sounds
far-fetched. Then Amber showers in the quarantine area, dries herself with a microfiber towel, and stands naked inside the stall while
two women wearing white coats and surgical masks scrub her entire
body with rubbing alcohol. Feels kinda nice. Her skin tingles as she
puts on an adult diaper, then a pair of thermal long underwear, then
is zipped into a rubberized MarsNow launch suit. From there it's
directly to the MarsNow Media Area, where she stands straight-
backed with Adam as members of the press crowd behind glass and
snap their picture. Geoff Task gives a speech in which he calls them
astral pioneers and *humanity's saviors*.

"Christopher Columbus may one day be forgotten," he says, "but
Amber Kivinen and Adam Shnitzer will be remembered for all time."

She looks for Kevin among the invited guests, but he isn't there.
Of course. He couldn't be bothered. But maybe it's better this way—
he would see how terrified she is.

She catches sight of her parents, behind the media fray, and can't
stop herself. "Mom!" She runs toward them, slams against the quarantine glass. "Dad!"

They fight their way forward and her father puts his meaty hand
to the window. Amber presses her palm to the other side, can almost
feel the heat of his skin against the pane. "Do you forgive me? Daddy,
do you forgive me?"

"T-minus ten minutes, Amber." Dr. Leslie is the only other person
inside the quarantine area. "It's time."

They walk out onto the eerie, empty launchpad. No rain. Dr. Leslie helps them climb into the rocket, then buckles them into custom-

molded seats. Amber's helmet is secured, then Adam's. Inside, the shuttle is deafening: pumps, spinning motors, metal that creaks and groans. The ship moves like it's alive.

"Happy flying, guys." Dr. Leslie closes the hatch.

Amber wishes she could turn to see Adam, but her suit is too stiff. Her visor fogs up and she can't read her emergency checklist. But there's her zero-g talisman: the weed pipe Kevin bought for her twenty-fifth birthday. She'd sneaked it into her bag when she went home, like a souvenir—she must have known even then that her old life was over—and requested that the pipe be secured to her dashboard with a string. When they reach weightlessness, it will be the first thing to float.

"T-minus one minute." Dr. Leslie's voice over the comm-set.

They won. They are the chosen ones. Right now, this minute, the Hawaiian tree snail is going extinct, children are starving in Yemen, men are raping women and calling it love—but soon she'll be lifted in a rapture of flame away from this place. And Mars will be a new world, a good world, a perfect world. So why is she crying?

"Leaving on a Jet Plane" begins to play.

Amber can feel Adam beside her, can sense his nervous heartbeat. "I love you." She's never said those words to him before.

"I love you too."

Dr. Leslie's tinny voice: "T-minus thirty seconds, Marsonauts. Are you ready?"

"Ready," say Adam and Amber in unison.

"Ignition," says a static-garbled Dr. Leslie.

At t-minus six seconds, Amber knows, the main engines will roar to life. At zero, the solid rocket boosters will ignite. Then the rocket will heave off the launchpad with 7 million pounds of thrust. In the span of one second, they will go from stillness to traveling at the speed of sound.

"T-minus twenty."

Amber closes her eyes. Allows fear to fall away. Instead, senses that familiar energy-build in her limbs—that full-body anticipation she used to feel in competitions, before she sprinted toward the vaulting table. Bare feet on the mat, hands powdered with chalk, legs burning to run.

"T-minus fifteen," says Dr. Leslie.

Amber couldn't manifest that energy at every meet, but when this presence did alight upon her, she felt pure and clean. All options, all questions, all choices fell away. Nothing existed, not even the audience, not even the judges.

"T-minus ten. Nine. Eight—"

Only her and that vault. Only one aim: *defy gravity.*

THE ROCKET BURSTS FROM ITS CHAMBER AND AMBER AND FIRST-
Man34 are mashed into their seats. I watch them glide through the atmosphere, jettisoning their fuel tank, which will be their final mark on this Earth—it falls to the Indian Ocean, to rust down there like an old ship.

I pack the new pipe with the best-quality blend I could find. Not our own but it'll do. Reminds me of the hours after my uncle in Thunder Bay called to say that my mom had died, after Amber held me. Alone, I took the weed I'd meant to bring home for my mom and smoked it all at once. Let it transport me away from grief, because grief leads nowhere. Grief is a one-way flight to a deadly planet.

"How do you feel?" Bronwyn used to ask as we said goodnight to the moon. How could I explain that I felt nothing? That my aim is nothing.

On the screen, Amber and FirstMan34 hurtle past Earth's atmosphere, then break the grip of Earth's gravity. And there's our pipe. It floats buoyantly, leashed to the arm of Amber's seat. Me, on the other hand. Gravity crushes me to powder.

Speaking of powder, so far my favorite protein flavor is Coconut-Maté-Gogi-Broccoli-Fudge. I guzzle that stuff while Adam and Amber swim like fish inside a tank, puke into MarsNow-branded vomit bags, stumble around like airborne toddlers—their bodies refusing to adjust to zero gravity.

Between episodes, I refresh Amber's social media pages. Before leaving, she promised that her Instagram, Facebook, and EyeSite Stories would give us all *the inside scoop on what it's like to live in space!* But there was only one video, posted to Instagram, taken down almost as soon as it went up. *Vertigo is a thing. And nausea.* She stared at the camera with bloodshot eyes. *Adam's vision has been affected, everything is blurry now. And I've got space-brain, you can imagine what that's like.* Weak laugh. *Edema. Brain swelling. The MarsNow people say it's probably mild.*

But the television show is edited to deliver a more cheerful Amber. Episode three shows her zipped into her MarsNow Sleeping Sack, which is buckled to the wall. *Lots of people want to know what it's like to sleep in zero gravity, and I can tell you it's not easy.* Sweet smile. *Your inner ear thinks you're upside down. The weirdest thing is the cosmic flashes—these bursts of light even when your eyes are closed. Adam says it's radiation striking your retinas. Right, babe? Yeah, so that's freaky. But we both have these incredible dreams! So vivid.*

I fight gravity to stand up. My legs ache; Google informs me that I might be deficient in magnesium, so I drink some of the plant supplements. I lie under the grow lights. I pace. I've got to get my life back on track. I call my agent, a bubbly madwoman whom I call Agent 99 because she looks a bit like Barbara Feldon. Agent 99 always pretends to know who I am, even though she probably represents about a thousand suckers who work as extras.

"Baby, how are *you*?" she screams into the phone.

"Good. Want to get back into the biz. Miss the glamour, you know?"

"Your timing couldn't be better, because they're shooting a post-apocalyptic thing in Burnaby next weekend. Want to be a dead body?"

"I was born to be a dead body."

Then I spend five entire days scrolling through Geoff Task's blog, titled *Move Fast and Break Things.* A place where he can nibble at the edge of stale ideas, the blog details his libertarian "thought experiments," his justifications for sexist hiring practices, his "biohacking" successes, his mishmash of spiritual beliefs, his vision for a "post-human" world, and his plans to use technology to fix the problems technology has created. He's obsessed with AI, which he fears will be a sociopathic force bent on the destruction of the human species; as I understand it, he fears that AI has been created in his own image.

When I finish reading his blog archive, I feel queasy and foul. I take several showers. I intend to clean the apartment, to at least rinse the glasses from which I drink the protein sludge and to scrape the black mold from the windowsills.

Instead I lift the blackout blinds and look out at the rain-soaked street, the majestic spruce stretching into the dark sky, the barely visible stars. She's up there somewhere, like a bird or a plane or a god.

SHE SPENDS HOURS LOOKING OUT THE WINDOW AT EARTH. AT first she can see the turquoise waters of Barbados, the smog over Asia, the golden sands of the Mojave. But the planet retreats, shrinks until it's the size of a tennis ball, then a Ping-Pong ball. Soon there is nothing she recognizes. No Earth, no moon. The sun is shown for what it is: a star like any other.

. . . and the sun became black as sackcloth of hair, and the moon became as blood . . .

She begs Dr. Leslie for updates about Earth and receives a bulleted list: the US economy is flourishing and more growth is predicted in 2020. China will launch a new fleet of mass-produced satellites, assembled by Uyghur grandmothers. Brad and Angelina have yet to split their assets.

Earth's news feels meaningless, but space is impossible. She can't keep food down. Pukes up every meal. What has she done? And *why?* Why Mars? Why now?

A week goes by, then a month. The nausea passes and she gets better at maneuvering her body in zero-g. Better at remembering to attach everything she owns to Velcro. Better at changing her tampon without beads of blood floating into her face.

One thing they haven't figured out is sex in space. Amber and Adam use bungee cords to tie their bodies together so they can make out, but intercourse is logistically difficult. They'd decided to save their first time for when they were in orbit, forgetting that gravity is essential for making love and that the camera-bots would follow them constantly aboard the starship.

So they eat freeze-dried asparagus and shower with wet wipes and pee into urine vacuums. They reconstitute dehydrated eggs and heat irradiated sausages for breakfast. They hook their toes onto rails to stay still. They learn not to floss their teeth too enthusiastically, lest bits of food float through the air for all eternity. They clean mold off the shuttle's inner walls. They take daily samples of each other's blood, and log the changes in their bodies: temperature, glucose absorption, fluid shifts. They quiz each other on the components of the shuttle. They become accustomed to lost objects reappearing: a pair of glasses or a cube of butter or a fork will float by hours or days after it was misplaced. They exercise by strapping themselves to a treadmill on the wall. They meditate. They play Uno.

IF AMBER AND FIRSTMAN34 WERE FIGHTING, SURELY THE PRODUC-
ers would show it for the sake of ratings. So I have to admit that he
makes her happy. In episode six, we see him opening what looks like
a steel cylinder, then reaching for what looks like a plunger. Wild
giggles, then Amber's face. *He's compressing the compost in our toilet.
Ladies, find yourself a guy like this. Find a man who will tamp down the
shit for you.*

During a solar storm, they take refuge in a tiny sheltered area of
the rocket, an aluminum tube that is technically called the HUB
Tunnel but which they rename "the womb." They curl up together
and float in the dark, pressed together. This is where they first have
sex—most of it edited out so that MarsNow can keep its PG rating.
The world cheers for FirstMan34; the world gives him a high-five.
There's a bruise at the center of my chest.

Flashback. Interior. Vancouver – Night. Amber had been disowned, then tentatively re-owned; my mom was dead. We were at a
party, in a dim hallway, avoiding the other people, who reeked of beer
and university pretentions. Both of us drunk on Jäger and Red Bull,
striving to feel nothing. I pulled her into a dark room, and we climbed
onto a stranger's bed, threw the sheet over our heads—created a soft
hideaway, a shelter for two. *I hate these people*, Amber said. *This party
sucks.* Muted music, distant voices. *Can we just go home?*

I call Agent 99 and tell her I won't make it to set. I'm sick; there's
something wrong with my heart.

"A blockage?" she gasps.

"A blockage," I confirm.

Bastiaan would say that male jealousy is just capitalism + misog-
yny, a simple and powerful equation, testosterone making me believe
that I have private-property rights. I put my hand to my breastbone;

the ache fades slightly. Then I call Marcus to apologize for being a dick. He says he thinks we should let "bygones be whatever" but doesn't suggest hanging out. Later that night, Bronwyn comes over, saying she "felt" that I needed her.

"You've been through so much this year," she says. "Amber leaving is echoing the more primal loss."

At first I have no idea what she's talking about, then remember that she thinks my mom died recently. And I almost miss saying goodnight to the moon. The ritual of lifting the blinds, gazing upward, seeing that distant glow. I could do it on my own, I guess, but it wouldn't be the same.

"Kevin?" Bronwyn puts a hand on my sleeve. "You still here?"

"I'm here." I give her a smile. "Thanks for stopping by, but I should really get back to my writing."

"It's going well?" Her kindness feels dangerous—she knows I'm lying. She sees through me, which doesn't seem fair. She was supposed to be my distraction from reality, my temporary asylum.

"The writing's going great," I say. "Two thumbs up."

I remember that Amber hoped I'd write her a story while she did her "Mars thing." And Bronwyn advised me to *make it real*. But what's more real than failure? Than disappointment? Than my inability to find the right words, a new story? My inability to offer them anything at all.

When Bronwyn leaves, I return to my life. And what am I doing with this one and only life? I'm a writer whose work consists of a series of queries punched into Geoff Task's blinking search engine:

> *what do bedsores look like*
> *black mold bad for lungs*
> *cleaning black mold*
> *ammonia bad for lungs*
> *youtube home workout no equipment*
> *youtube cats wearing earmuffs*

california wildfires

california wildfires animals dead

jacinda ardern sexy

public sex amateur

public sex not disturbing

sex outside romantic erotic

sex in space

nasa sex suit

youtube ariana grande one last time

reddit embarrassing taste in music

reddit who would you shame-fuck

amber kivinen boyfriend

amber kivinen kevin

geoff task net worth

geoff task marriage

talia annabelle lorne rolling stone

talia annabelle lorne breasts

how long can you live off protein powder

how often do you have to wash hair

bedsores images

ONE OF THE EXTERNAL FUEL TANKS DISLODGES. AMBER NOTICES IT, tells Adam, then they put through an emergency communication through the Deep Space Network. Eighteen minutes later, Dr. Leslie is on their screen, ready to talk them through the Code Red procedure.

Adam has to do an EVA, as in *extra-vehicular activity*, as in *space walk*.

"You said this was a highly unlikely scenario," says Amber. "You said we didn't need to worry."

"I am here for you," says a pale Dr. Leslie. "Do exactly what I say."

Adam spends an hour breathing pure oxygen from a tank to reduce the nitrogen in his blood, to avoid getting the bends. Then Amber helps him fight his way into the stiff suit—he nearly dislocates his shoulder trying to fit his long torso inside. Amber opens the hatch and Adam jet-propels himself out into the universe. Tethered to the shuttle by what looks like a flimsy cord, he grips the sides of the module and "walks" hand over hand along the rail. The suit keeps oxygen flowing and scrubs his exhaled CO_2, but she can see his glasses slip down his sweaty nose inside the helmet.

"Breathe," says Amber through the comm-device in his ear, her voice a different type of tether. "Love, you need to come back to me."

"My glasses."

"Tilt your head back, if you can," says Dr. Leslie. "You're doing great. And you're looking for handrail 2107. Do you copy?"

"2107. Copy. It's dark out here."

"You'll get some residual daylight in 29 minutes," says Dr. Leslie. "And I have a caution and warning for you when you're ready."

"Ready."

"You're at risk now of fully dislodging the plate."

"Copy."

"I need you to translate slightly further to your right, Adam, yes, that's it, do you see it now?" He must use the pistol-grip tool to tighten four bolts.

"The tool is malfunctioning," says Adam. Then he laughs softly. "Never mind. Just needed to turn it on."

"Good work. Next you'll deploy the gap-spanner," says Dr. Leslie.

"The plate is slightly bent out of shape. There's a piece of upturned metal at the corner."

"Do not snag your suit on that," says Dr. Leslie, and Amber imagines one of Adam's marshmallow gloves sliced open. Instant death.

"Now get a handle on that fuel tank." Dr. Leslie sounds like she's speaking through a cement wall. "Before it runs away."

His gloves make his hands clumsy, but he manages to grip the tank, turn it right side up. "Got it." He sounds short of breath, and Amber wishes she could check his oxygen.

"Just a few more maneuvers, Marsonaut," says Dr. Leslie. "One step at a time."

The maneuvers take four hours. But floating in the vacuum of space, Dr. Leslie instructing him step-by-step, he reattaches the fuel tank. Then he "walks" back toward the hatch, hand over hand, returning home. He survives.

When he enters the hold, Amber can't stop her body from shaking. They hear cheers from the MarsNow people in the background, and Dr. Leslie weeping in the foreground. Amber helps Adam out of his suit, which takes more than an hour, then they hold each other, spinning slowly. His neck smells like space, like burnt metal. She is his sanctuary; he is her shelter. Out here, where each day is a miracle, love will never fade or warp or break.

EACH HOUR IS ELASTIC, STRETCHING INTO WHAT SEEMS LIKE INFIN-
ity. I continue to do nothing, to create nothing, despite the great gifts
of time and privilege—the MarsNow paychecks still arrive in our
joint bank account, because where would Amber spend the money?

I decide to read a book. Woefully old-fashioned, I know. During
my last attempt, I only made it to page 38—I guess my attention span
isn't what it used to be—but I'm determined to reread *The Great
Gatsby*. It's my kind of rom-com. Boy meets girl; boy loses girl; boy
nurtures obsession with girl until it kills him.

I start again from the beginning, and the pleasure of a story well
told makes me wonder if I should use these hours—my one and
only life—to write the Great Canadian Novel, LOL. Because if I
had to write something, it would be a book, which will not monitor
my spending habits or track my location or present me with a "Like"
button. Simple and inefficient, needing only attention and time but
demanding neither, a book is ancient and perfect technology.

Maybe I could write it. My story. Amber's story. Our story. Maybe
it would make me famous.

On the other hand, writing a book sounds hard. An author
embodies the director, cinematographer, set designer, costume
designer, and all the actors. Who has the energy?

I keep thinking about Gatsby on his lawn, reaching toward that
green light. I also think about that conversation with Bastiaan, the
last time he was over. *What does Amber most want?* I should have
built her a paradise.

But didn't I? Our plants, our Garden of Eden. Even before that,
when we had a year or two of exploring Vancouver, before lethargy and busyness swallowed us whole: English Bay, Kits, Burnaby
Mountain. Once we went snowshoeing and encountered a pair of

ravens—not the freaky-ass ravens of literature, but real, alive, oil-slick-black birds.

"They mate for life." Amber leaned against my shoulder. "The male does these elaborate displays, in flight, to win his partner. Then they stay together until death."

"Like us," I said. "Except you did the elaborate acrobatics while I kicked back like a lazy lady-raven."

And didn't Amber and I inhabit paradise even before that? The rambling walk we took when we skipped school that first afternoon—*wanna get out of here?* Along crumbling streets, traffic medians, over the bridge and through the bush until we reached heaven on Earth. Even just Amber's bedroom, which was an escape from parents, school, expectations. A place where we breathed each other's air, under that Milky Way of glow-in-the-dark stars.

For a while, we were the paradise. The two of us together, no matter where we were. Amber and me against the world.

Using Amber's salary, I order thirty packages of glow-in-the-dark stars off Amazon. Thanks to Prime shipping, they arrive within hours, which makes me feel like Zeus—the world awaits my command. I paste stars all over the ceiling, in swirls and loops, then turn off the lights, lie on the couch, gaze upward. Could Bronwyn look at my ceiling and tell my future?

You are destined for long stretches of solitude.

As if she's read my mind, Bronwyn appears. "Are you okay?" She flicks on the light. "You seem so stuck, Kev." She sits beside me. "And that's okay, it happens. Our whole society. We're all longing for the past when really we need to develop new values. More presence. To move forward, to save ourselves, we have to become whole."

"Interesting theory. How long does becoming whole take? A weekend?"

"It's a lifetime project."

"Is now a good time to start a lifetime project? What do the stars say?"

"I'm serious. You need to go deep. Address your grief so you can start living."

I miss the good old days, when she chattered about moon signs.

"When we broke up or . . . whatever we did?" she says, "I was like, *I am not going to rush into another relationship.* I started reading all these books, meditating, watching documentaries. Do you want me to lend you some books?" she says. "Marcus has been reading them."

"I already have a book." I nod to *Gatsby.*

"I'm grateful to you," she says, "'cause you got me interested in plants, and now I've found my purpose. I'm working with kids, we've started a garden and a seed bank. We're growing heirloom tomatoes—"

"I know. I see your posts." Why won't she leave me alone? Literally everyone else does.

"Just—you helped me. You seem to think you're useless or something, but—"

"You've misdiagnosed me. I think *everyone else* is useless. I think the world is monstrous. The only way to cope is to hide away and numb your feelings. Or to throw yourself off a building." I'm on a roll. "Not to get all Freudian, Bronwyn, but do I remind you of your father? Never met the guy but I can tell there's no saving him. Or me. Or anyone. The world doesn't want to be saved."

She sighs like I'm a disappointing child, willfully obtuse. "I brought you something."

From her bag, that huge satchel some toothless woman in Guatemala must have woven, she brings out a tiny potted succulent.

I don't want to cry but nearly do.

"Thanks, Bron. Thank you." I place the succulent on the coffee table beside *Gatsby.* "It's perfect."

"It's not perfect," she says. "It's alive."

"Same diff?" I turn away, try to laugh. And when she leaves, I'm relieved, for both of us.

I lie down to look up at the stars, and put the succulent next to me on the couch, like a girlfriend. I exhale CO_2; the succulent inhales it and releases oxygen into my lungs. Just the two of us, side by side, breathing each other into being.

JUST THE TWO OF THEM, SLOW-DANCING (SLOW-FLOATING?) TO
Leonard Cohen's "Hallelujah." She's as free as she's ever felt, surrounded by blackness. She's now managing to sleep despite the
dizziness. Her e-reader is loaded with books about growing plants
in extreme conditions. Her crickets are thriving, toasty under
their 150-watt bulb and beginning to lay eggs.

Since Adam's EVA and miraculous survival, she's felt certain:
they were chosen.

"This is like the longest, funnest road trip in history," she says.

Adam smiles. "English is my second language and even I know
that 'funnest' isn't a word."

"And that, Commander, is why you're in charge of the mission."

He smells like sanitizer and looks good in his uniform and each
night she lures him to the HUB Tunnel, where they explore each
other's bodies carefully, diligently, uncovering each other's secrets
the way they'll discover Mars's. She likes when he uses one arm to
brace them both against the metal floor and enters her slowly. In
that moment, she misses nothing about Planet Earth. The sun, out
the window, rises and falls each hour. Light flows over them, then
retreats like a tide.

Why Mars? Why now?

Because it was meant to be.

She's seen the Earth from above. She's traveling through an undis-
covered universe, on her way to a place no human has touched. And
when they arrive, she will create a new world, a good world. She
dreams of planetary engineering, of growing her paradise, which will
become possible when the next cargo ship arrives with terraforming

equipment. Huge mirrors to reflect sunlight and heat the ground, to allow frozen water to liquefy and flow.

I have set before thee an open door, and no man can shut it.

Eyes forward.

SOMETIMES I STAND AT THE APARTMENT DOOR, REMEMBERING THE last time Amber walked through it. When I called her a fame whore, which might not have been the best strategy for winning her back. *Let go, Kevin.* I stand at the door, put one hand on the knob, the other on my chest. At the thought of going outside, my heart thrashes.

Maybe I don't have to go anywhere—maybe the world will come to me, if I put myself "out there." I create a profile on Tinder: *Chill, indoorsy underachiever. Looking for love because my last girlfriend went to Mars and all she got me was this lousy broken heart.*

I don't have any recent pics, so post one of me on set, dressed as a zombie, blood running down my chin. Subsequently and immediately, I'm terrified by the women who swipe right—one girl has actual horns surgically embedded in her forehead.

I delete the profile, return to aimless surfing, but every corner I turn online, I run into a MarsNow ad. Geoff Task is constantly on YouTube, expounding the virtues of "living like a Marsonaut." He sits cross-legged in a white, empty room and says, "At MarsNow, we envision a day when we will bring all of you to see the paradise we are creating on the red planet." His tone is aloof, as if there's some indiscernible barbed wire between him and us. "But until then, we are bringing the red planet home to you, with a line of products that can be used both on Earth and on Mars: solar-powered LED lights to improve growth in your garden, weight-loss bars featuring the same nutrition complex consumed by our Marsonauts, and sturdy inflatable Settlement Structures for your camping trips and back-yard parties."

The words *MarsNow: Live like a Marsonaut* unfurl at the bottom of the screen.

I open *Gatsby*: *This is a valley of ashes—a fantastic farm where ashes grow like wheat into ridges and hills and grotesque gardens.*

I close the book. Sometimes novels are too real, so thank god for reality television. When I watch MarsNow, it's just the two of us: me and Amber. I watch what she sees out the windows of her spacecraft. Not the stars or asteroids or dwarf planets. Amber and I stare at the blackness between those things. Infinite, cold, lonely.

Ratings have dropped because nothing is happening. After their successful EVA, Adam and Amber float, and there seems to be no end to it. Space, space, and more space. The show is edited to create as much tension as possible out of this existential nothingness: Will they arrive? Will they reach the promised land?

卌 卌 卌 卌
卌 卌 卌 卌
卌 卌 卌 卌
卌 卌 卌 卌
卌 卌 卌 卌
卌 卌 卌 卌
卌 卌 卌 卌
卌 卌 卌 卌
卌 卌 卌 卌
卌 |||

THEN, LIKE A PUPPY COME TO GREET THEM, THAT SMALL MOON, Deimos, runs by. And there it is: Mars.

First it's just a disk, then a sphere, then a craggy, uneven rock that looks like a potato.

The landing gear is extended, AUX systems engaged. An alarm sounds.

"Tire pressure is low," says Amber.

"Nothing we can do," says Adam. "Keep your mouth open."

"What?"

"So you don't bite off your tongue."

The heat of Mars's atmosphere makes the delicate skin of her lips blister.

The alarm continues to scream.

Breathe. Eyes forward.

The heat shield activates. Then they aerobrake through the atmosphere, the shield is jettisoned, the shuttle's parachute opens, the retro-rockets descend. The shuttle crashes hard on underinflated tires, but they survive the impact.

It's dusk. They've landed in a valley that runs along the planet's equator, a valley that might once have been a lake. There are striated dunes and a giant, extinct volcano.

When they unclip their seat belts and try to move, they nearly collapse—38 percent gravity feels oppressively heavy compared to zero. They need to remember how to walk instead of float.

"Take my hand." Adam pulls her to her feet, presses his heartbeat to hers.

"Didn't swallow my own tongue." She tries to laugh. Then she speaks into her comm-device. "Dr. Leslie? We're here. Alive. We made it."

She feels nothing. No curiosity, no fear. Her legs are shaky, her heart pounding, her eyes dry. They manage to put on their MarsNow suits, check their oxygen levels, secure their helmets, zip their boots. Hold hands as best they can in bulky gloves. Then they step outside, onto dust as fine as flour.

THEY LOOK UP, AND SO DO WE, THE AUDIENCE, OVER FOUR BILLION
of us tuning in to see the first humans walk on Mars. They look up,
and we all look up together. We see a purple sky.

That's when I lever myself off the couch and stumble to my window, pull up the blinds, peer out at the Vancouver skyline. Amber
and I watch the sun set together. I'm so used to seeing through her
eyes that I know she's touching the mystery. It will escape her soon,
but she's touching it now.

"Amber?" says FirstMan34, all business. "You okay? Your vitals
have dropped."

"Hmm?" she says. "Yeah. I'm good."

They climb to the top of a mesa, and decide to marry. Right there,
right then. To survive, they will have to be one flesh.

I remember sending that stupid, lazy text: *Will you marry me?*

"I do," say Amber and FirstMan34 in unison, as micrometeors
slam their suits, as dust particles sharp as glass score their visors, as
the perchlorates in the soil corrode the bottoms of their boots. They
say a prayer, thanking the god they are beginning to invent together.

Then they set about making that strange place home. They build
in Utopia Planitia, the largest impact basin on Mars, where there
is underground ice. A segment featuring a MarsNow "scientist"—
a suspiciously young woman with a platinum bob, crisp MarsNow
lab coat, and teeth bleached Los Angeles–level white—explains that
the volume of water in the plain of paradise is equivalent to that of
Lake Superior. "Water is necessary for survival!" chirps the blonde
scientist, then we cut to Adam and Amber, who use robotic rovers
to inflate their MarsNow Settlement Structure. Inside, they put up
photos of family and friends—my face is there—and revel in one-

third gravity. It isn't much, but enough that they can lie on a bed underneath a weighted blanket. They can kiss without floating apart.

On the seventh day, they stand in their sealed environment and declare it good.

Amber oversees life support, ensuring that she and Adam each get three liters of water per day, 2,000 calories of food, and three pounds of oxygen. Essentially, she's a Martian housewife. She extracts the water from Mars's dirt: heating two pounds of Martian soil to 150 degrees Celsius in a fancy pressure cooker to yield one pint of water. She farms crickets and manages to sprout tomatoes in her hydroponic garden—a solar-powered greenhouse full of LED bulbs that doubles as their emergency radiation-proof chamber. Inspired by photosynthesis, she extracts pure oxygen from the CO_2 of Mars's atmosphere.

FirstMan34 spends his days collecting samples, taking pictures, looking for alien life-forms. He chips away at the permafrost tundra, scrapes salt deposits, digs for fossils in Valles Marineris. He photographs runnels in the dunes that might indicate flowing water. Seeks out trace amounts of methane to discover its origins—was it formed geochemically? Or did microbes create this? Is there life, invisible, everywhere?

ADAM'S TEETH BEGIN TO ROT AND AMBER PULLS SEVERAL OUT with pliers, the bloody holes in his gums threatening to make her weep. But his eyesight is recovering slowly, and she feels strong except for that old, familiar nausea—the nausea she experienced when they first launched into space. It must be the lack of sunlight and fresh air. She hasn't been outside since they inflated their Settlement Structure. Hasn't felt the sun on her skin since she left Earth.

At least she's not puking in zero-g anymore, aiming for a suction bucket that barely stayed still. Now she crouches over the composting toilet, half-digested cricket-slime sliding from her mouth.

"Amber, you're purging a lot." Adam stands above her. "I'm worried about your fluid intake."

"Just need something to settle my stomach. Do we still have that dehydrated pineapple?" Last night she dreamt she was on a beach, with Kevin and Jianju and Brayden and Adam—it should have been stressful, all her men in one place, but it was beautiful. The water warm, the solar rays brilliant as the sun set below the liquid horizon. "I've been craving something tropical."

"We finished the pineapple. And the apricots."

The lack of fruit threatens to make her scream, but Adam kisses the top of her head, disappears, then returns with a glass of water and the last box of gluten-free saltines. She should be used to Martian water by now, but it tastes even more sulfuric and tinny lately. She forces it down. Then chews a saltine that tastes like home, like childhood. Her mother used to sprinkle crackers into her soup. Her mother used to hum as she brought lunch to the table for Amber and Caleigh. *Now you girls find me a word in there. You've got the entire alphabet in your bowl.*

DURING EPISODE SEVEN, FIRSTMAN34 FACES THE CAMERA WITH his newly gaping smile and says, "It is imperative to study how a low-gravity environment affects critical phases of mammalian reproduction and development. Gravity affects cell structure and function, organ system development—"

Amber shoves him aside. "What he's trying to say is: we're pregnant!"

I feel what must be sympathy nausea. Hobble to the bathroom and retch up my protein shake. Purple and green swirl in the toilet bowl like a photo taken by Hubble.

A few minutes or hours later I'm hunched over my laptop when Marcus and Bronwyn come by. Apparently my door is unlocked because they enter without knocking, look at me, and Bronwyn turns to Marcus. "See?"

"Hey, bro," says Marcus. "You look a little rough."

I ignore them, type search terms: *amber kivinen pregnant, amber adam baby*. Click through pages of results.

Marcus says, "We've been worrying about you, man."

Bronwyn says, "We care about you, Kevin."

Then they whisper about me in the third person; I hear their voices as if from a great distance and think: *This must be what it's like to have parents.* They sit on either side of me on the Voyager, hold me like I'm something that might break apart, a meteor that would disintegrate on impact.

"Kevin." Bronwyn puts vitamin D drops in my mouth like she's feeding a baby bird. "Kevin, look at us."

Marcus pulls the computer from my hands and they throw my arms over their shoulders, hoist me to standing. I kick the air, knock *Gatsby* from the coffee table, then turn to Marcus and bite his shoulder.

"Jesus!" he drops me. "He just bit me!"

"I'm right here," I say. "And I understand English."

"What's your problem, man? You're being such an asshole."

I crawl away, crouch in the corner of the room. "You're the asshole, Marcus."

"No. *You* are the asshole. One hundred percent anus."

Bronwyn puts a hand on his shoulder. "Okay, guys. This is getting really conflictual."

"It's *conflictual*," I say, "because you came into my house and you're fucking with my life."

"We're trying to save your stupid life," says Marcus. "Look at you."

"Maybe you should question that embarrassingly colonial mindset. You're like the missionaries who came to 'save the savages' but brought smallpox instead."

"Why does everything have to be so messed up with you? We're your friends."

"Marcus, have you destroyed that many brain cells? My ex-girlfriend just got impregnated by some potent Israeli semen, so you come here, put on a big show of sympathy in an attempt to win over my *other* ex-girlfriend, and I'm supposed to be all, *yay, my friends are here?*"

"Now you're saying I was your girlfriend?" Bronwyn picks up her bag. "We're here for you, Kevin, but you have to, like, rejoin reality."

"Thanks for the wisdom, Bronwyn. Always appreciated."

When they leave, I turn off the lights, look up at the stars. Hold the succulent to my chest. Light a joint and put it in my mouth like a pacifier.

EXHAUSTION. FATIGUE LIKE SHE'S RUN A MARATHON—SIX MARA-
thons. Her breasts ache if Adam even breathes on them; it hurts to
wear a T-shirt. Eating gives her no enjoyment, only quells the sea-
sickness for an hour or so. And there's a bad taste inside her mouth,
as if a wet woolen sock is lodged at the back of her throat.

She tries to walk the treadmill and nearly passes out.

"Focus on the positive," says Adam, whose body is unchanged,
who sleeps through the night and never wakes in a frantic, tearful
state because there is no Hawaiian pizza on Mars—only the desperate, constant memory of Hawaiian pizza. And carrot cake. Bran
muffins. Mint chocolate ice cream. Grapes. Hamburgers drowning
in the yellowest mustard.

She drinks dehydrated cricket smoothies sweetened with monk
fruit. There are not enough calories on this planet. She slaughters
crickets with her bare hands, blends them with the tiny beets she's
managed to grow, adds water, then drinks this sludge with her nose
plugged.

Vomits. Feels better. Or maybe worse.

Her chest, the insides of her arms, the backs of her knees—her
whole body is mapped with blue veins that remind her of Earth's rivers and seas. Her skin erupts in dry, flaking patches. Her hands are
swollen and her feet numb.

Everything happens for a reason. Focus on the positive: her baby
will be only about a year younger than Pichu's little Mohan. "Maybe
one day," she says to the camera, "the technology will be advanced
enough that our kids can have interplanetary playdates!"

She presses her hands to her belly. When she can snap herself
into some form of wakefulness, she can't wait to hold her child. The
baby's weight will be diminished by low gravity, but not its warmth or

laughter. And she can't wait to breastfeed, to nourish an infant from her own body. As a teen, when she began doubting the teachings, when sitting in worship made her feel trapped and sick, when being "watched over" by God felt like being an insect under a microscope, she would stand in the middle of the Sunday service, ignore her parents' questioning eyes, push her way through the stuffy nave and into the hallway, where she could breathe.

Inevitably there were two or three young women out there too, sitting on flimsy folding chairs, breastfeeding their babies. They sometimes glanced at Amber, looking shy or even ashamed. But if she stood still, pretended not to be interested, they forgot about her and smiled at their children. Nurtured them in a silence that seemed to be true holiness.

I'M ON A COUCH IN A CITY ON A FAULT LINE. ON A CONTINENT THAT moves 2.5 centimeters per year.

My legal weed arrives by mail; I have enough protein powder to last through a nuclear winter. If you were to ask me, *What's new?* I could only answer that I've moved on from Coconut-Maté-Gogi-Broccoli-Fudge to Lemon-Vanilla-Buckwheat-Cranberry-Cream. I could only answer: *Amber is pregnant.*

Each day is a smoky haze that turns into a week. Months.

Amber seems tired but giddy as the pregnancy progresses, and puts FirstMan34's hand on her belly, shows him the haunting outline of a tiny moving limb, as if the child wants to break through her skin. *Definitely an A-squared baby,* she laughs into the camera. *This kid never stops moving!*

Meanwhile, here on Earth, the Amazon burns. You can do an image search to see the latest devastation. Glasswing butterflies turn to ash, sloths are asphyxiated, hummingbird eggs cooked alive in their nests.

Now that Amber's gone, now that she's not worrying about the future for both of us, I can't stop thinking about those boiled hummingbirds. But I must be the only one because the biggest news on the planet is A-squared's baby. A pregnant Amber, round and resplendent in a MarsNow T-shirt, is on the cover of *Time*.

Can I go on? How can I justify living at all, being so helpless, so useless? Sitting in my bunker, door shut tight, blackout curtains drawn.

I make another attempt. Stand up from the couch, go to the door. All I have to do is turn the knob. Then I'd be face-to-face with the spruce. The tree that grows, majestic and alone, out of a slab of sidewalk.

I'd rather live on Mars.

So I transition to Mars time, begin to sync my circadian rhythm to the red planet. A Martian day, a "sol," lasts 24 hours 39 minutes and 35.244 seconds. Each night, I stay up thirty-nine and a half minutes later than the night before. The windows are still blacked out, so it doesn't matter that my night stretches longer and longer. I ebb further from my home planet—after eighteen days of sticking to a Martian clock, the beginning of my night is the beginning of an earthly day. Not that I can tell with the windows blacked out, but my laptop still thinks I live in Vancouver, Canada, North America. The Earth.

Every morning, first thing, I refresh the NASA "Insight" page to see the weather on Mars. Study the graphs, memorize the day's wind speeds and air pressure. Today: wispy clouds will release a dusting of snow made from frozen CO_2. Amber will see a shimmer in the sky.

FINALLY THE FATIGUE HAS LIFTED, THE BAD TASTE VANISHED. SHE is creating life. She has a tiny ecstatic dancer inside her—or maybe it's more like a slow-moving amphibian. A creature who swims and swims. "A fish," she says to Adam at twenty-five weeks. "Maybe we're regressing, evolutionarily speaking. Maybe on Mars we'll go backwards."

He hates when she talks like that. He thinks she should eat more. He obsessively monitors her vitals and stats. Doesn't allow her to go outside. He's strict, just like her dad—she sees that now. She almost hates him, especially when he says things like, "Moodiness is a common pregnancy symptom."

"*Moodiness?*" she says. "*Symptom?* As if I have a disease?"

"What if you took more rest?" He strokes her hair. "What if you spent more time on the treadmill too? And use the VR headset."

So she walks through virtual forests, along virtual boardwalks, through virtual cities. Most often she kicks through virtual sand on a virtual beach. That helps. She puts her hand to her belly, feels her tiny amphibian paddling around its habitat. Her amphibian loves the beach.

She tries not to think about the fact that her child won't have friends. Not unless another reproductive-age woman is sent to Mars on the next mission. Amber will have to request that they include toys and children's books in the cargo, though the next launch may be delayed. Something about wildfire smoke that has darkened the sky all summer and made it impossible to test the updated Lander. California is burning; South America is burning. Geoff Task is focusing resources on climate-change mitigation now, particularly the damage done by rising sea levels—the shoreline of his private island in the BVIs is being swallowed.

"The Earth is becoming more like Mars," says Dr. Leslie, in an email that contains a photo of a hazy orange sky.

The Amazon rainforest is burning. So this must be it. The last straw. Amber almost wishes she were there to be part of it. People must be rioting in the streets. Mothers and fathers and grandparents holding hands with children—spending every spare minute marching, writing letters, calling politicians, blockading oil tankers. Fighting for survival as the lungs of the world collapse.

. . . and the third part of trees was burnt up, and all green grass was burnt up . . .

If you got left behind after the Rapture, she'd learned as a child, you had to endure the Antichrist's reign. Wars, earthquakes, plagues, fire and brimstone. The Mark of the Beast.

But she'd made it out alive. She'd risen.

Ironic, because she spends most days lying down. Pregnancy in low gravity: instead of pooling in her feet, the excess fluid migrates to her knees, elbows, sinuses. Her head often feels like it might burst, a balloon attached to her brain stem. Or maybe these are migraines. Maybe she's becoming her mother.

Focus on the positive. Everything happens for a reason.

The first child born on Mars. The baby's skin will be pale and its pupils continually dilated, absorbing sunlight like a sponge soaking up water. The first human made for this place, the beginning of a new evolution. A revolution.

How will she teach this child, this new creation, about their origins? How will she describe Earth? A blue planet that had to be abandoned, a place of weapons and genocide and pathogens. But also a watery, living world—a home like her own womb.

She'll have to explain earthquakes and wars, and atmospheric pressure, snow, prairies, rainbows. It will sound like make-believe. Like stories from an ancient book that the child will have to take on faith.

She puts a hand to her belly, feels her amphibian do a slow somersault.

Maybe she'll never speak of Earth. Better that way. Children always long for what they don't have, they *want, want, want*. In this sterile place, maybe her baby will be the first human to live without desire. To live without pain.

She and Adam were chosen. And now they're creating new life, a new world.

But then. Late in the seventh month.

At first she can't put it into words—it's an absence, a stillness. Is her amphibian more subdued, or is she imagining that? While brushing her teeth, she feels nauseous and grips the side of the sink. Then feels a cramp, like her uterus is an orange that God is juicing in His fist. A blood clot slithers into her underwear.

She calls to Adam and the rest happens fast: she drops to her hands and knees, bleeding onto the inflatable floor. Waves of agony lash her. Then she births a stillborn boy at thirty-one weeks.

With his long limbs and soft spine, he looks nearly invertebrate. His skull is tiny, cone-shaped, squishy like ripe fruit. But he has the same cheekbones as his father, the same curls as his mother. The curls Amber inherited from her own mother. She holds him against her chest. Rocks him until his skin begins to cool.

They name him Aleph Innocence. They stroke his hair, his soft cheek. Adam says he'll bury the baby behind their Settlement Structure, in the place they call the garden even though it's just a barren patch of dirt—but for now, she holds the boy. Stares into his small, ovoid face. He is perfect. The first child born on Mars. Her son.

I CONTINUE TO SIP MY PROTEIN DRINK, CONTINUE TO SCRATCH lines into the wall to measure the passing Martian sols, and manage to read to the end of Fitzgerald's masterpiece. Jay Gatsby lies face-down in the pool around the time Amber loses her baby.

Why do I feel sad? Why do I feel anything at all?

I must be jet-lagged and woozy from living on Mars. And it takes only a couple of weeks of living on Mars for the succulent to die. Its rubbery leaves first turn spongy, then brown and brittle. Maybe I overwatered it. Overloved it.

Which is different from the way I killed my mom. Through neglect. Abandonment. Left her alone, in a world (she knew it all along) that would never be home.

If I'd been there, if I'd stayed in Thunder Bay instead of moving to Vancouver, my mom would still be alive. I would have ensured that she went for her checkups; she was always skipping appointments because she never learned to drive and taking the bus in the winter was tough on her. I could have driven her to the appointments. Such a simple thing, and I would have saved her life.

I want to be held, rocked, soothed.

I google *houseplants*, because I need to fill this place with life. But the problem with life is that it ends.

And it turns out that on the World Wide Web, you can purchase beautiful artificial plants of almost any variety. So I order a taste-ful plastic snake tree. An orbit peacock plant. A few grasses made of silk and succulents of silicone. Then—it's so easy with one-click purchasing—artificial aloe, boxwood, cactuses, a rubber leaf tree, an olive tree.

Some of my purchases arrive within hours. I arrange them

throughout the apartment and they glow a companionable green, these friends who will never leave me. But I want a jungle. An Eden. I order more fake succulents, fake grasses, fake ferns. A fake fiddle leaf fig tree, a fake banana tree, a fake diamond rose bush, faux ivy that I can pin to my walls, golden cane palm, baby's tears.

AMBER NEVER SPEAKS OF THE CHILD. CANNOT LET THIS IN. SHE immerses herself in work: ferments the CO_2 from her own breath inside a fermentation grid she designed herself, based on the structure of a beehive. Grows carrots that taste like soap.

Adam continues his explorations, braving dust devils five stories high, sand traps, and dry-ice storms that lash the windows of his rover. He maps dry lake- and riverbeds, dark dunes that mimic human shadows on the horizon, the rocky and irregular base of a dead supervolcano called Eden Patera. He drills deep into the regolith in the hope of finding water, but turns up only smectite clay that coats him like soot. He puts layers of rock under the microscope, and finds what might be fossilized microbes, long deceased. He discovers that the methane on Mars was formed inorganically. The polar ice caps are primarily made of frozen CO_2, not H_2O. Most of the runnels in the dunes seem to be caused by rivulets of dust, but some probably contained liquid water billions of years ago, back when Mars had an atmosphere. Back when it had a magnetic field.

He tells Amber that he is losing hope. That he may not find signs of life. That his favorite moments are when he comes across *Curiosity* rover's tire tracks or spies Mars garbage, left behind by previous unmanned missions. A shattered CD-ROM in Ultimi Scopuli. A mangled solar panel on the plains of Isidis. Tangled wire coated in the sands of Samara.

"You've seen those things?" She holds the sleeves of his shirt. "Can you show me?"

So he bears gifts. Takes each item home so that he and Amber can wonder at them, hold them, place them on a shrine.

A lethargy overcomes them in the presence of these objects. Amber sometimes doesn't even sanitize them and her hands get covered with golden dust. Even Adam is getting lax. The toxic Martian dirt enters the house in the creases of his suit, the tread of his boots.

Dr. Leslie puts through an emergency call; Adam is reminded of his role as commander. But already the outside has infiltrated their shelter. Dust tints their skin orange, collects under their nails, puffs from their hair, fills their eyes with grit. It's everywhere, always, so heavy with iron that when Amber kisses Adam, she tastes blood.

MY KNEES ACHE. MY HANDS SWELL WITH FLUID WHILE MY TORSO shrinks, my chest becomes concave. My fingers red and sore. Elbow joints hot to the touch. Dizziness. Exhaustion. Fatigue like I've been running for years. From what? Why?

In sympathy with me, Amber begins to feel sick too. At first, it's just a lack of energy, and FirstMan34 quizzes her, wondering if she's depressed.

"Depression doesn't exist here," she says. "Mars is perfect."

But I wonder: Does she long for the outside? For contact? Does she want to forgo the protective suit, walk out into the dunes, feel that foreign air against her skin? Does she look at the door of their Settlement Structure the way I glance at the apartment door—feeling awe and terror at how easy it would be?

Wanna get out of here?

But we stay in our sealed environments. FirstMan34 takes Amber's pulse and temperature, takes blood samples, records everything. Then they see it. We all see it. A tumor that protrudes from her back. A tumor that looks like a human face.

FirstMan34 speaks to the camera. "Amber and I believe she may have contracted cancer from perchlorate or cosmic-ray exposure. Further tests will be needed to confirm the diagnosis."

I stand up, muscles alive, ready to run. Rescue. Then remember: there's nowhere to go.

Fuck her. Fuck Amber, who chose sterility, cold, dust. Who chose death. Who is committing the most dramatic, narcissistic suicide in the history of humanity.

Not entirely different from my mother. When she refused to follow the recommended diet, forgot to take her medication, smoked a pack a day. I was fifteen or sixteen when I finally understood. First, the insomnia—that's how it started. In the middle of the night I'd hear the crackle of chip bags being opened, or the fizz of a pop bottle uncapped. I'd stumble out of bed. *You're making it worse.* And she'd glare at me, a cigarette burning in one hand and the chip bag in the other. *I don't need to be spied on by my own kid.* She'd call in sick to work the next day, spend hours on the couch watching some stupid romantic movie that told nothing but lies, spooning melted ice cream from the container into her mouth.

I didn't kill her. She killed herself.

I stumble to the kitchen and find Amber's Care Bear mug—drop it, watch it shatter on the floor. In the bedroom, I tear her clothes from the hangers, try to rip her T-shirts apart but don't have the strength. Find a pair of scissors and chop up her favorite sweatshirt, shred her jeans, mutilate her bras. Grab armfuls of her underwear—cotton, satin, lace—and her socks, the thick wool ones for hiking, the tiny ankle socks that would seem to fit a child. Dump them all in the sink along with the remains of her bras and panties. Grab my lighter, ignite the pyre. Watch flames lick up toward the counter, smell the fumes as polyester and spandex burn, as the foam inside her bras melts and warps. Everything turns to toxic ash and I might cry. Really? Cry for someone who's getting what she deserved? What she asked for? I douse the embers with tap water. Then head into the living room, grab the olive tree, try to break its trunk—it bends and springs back up. Plants made of fossil fuels, by children in Shenzhen. I find a kitchen knife, stab at the olive tree's trunk—the knife bounces back, hardly making a tear. I use scissors to lop off the aloe's arms. I stomp on the cactus's fake spines—without sharpness, they fold and curve. Try to dump the artificial dirt from the pots, but it's glued inside.

Maybe I need real food. I order pizza, like my mom used to do when she felt bad. Large, double-cheese, triple-carnivore. One bite and my stomach clenches—not used to solids. I fall back to the couch. Land in the imprint my body left in the cushions, deep and lasting like a fossil record.

LIFE EXISTED HERE. BILLIONS OF YEARS AGO. SHE CAN FEEL THEM, the ghosts of Mars—silent and pleading. Life wants to flourish here; life struggles to come into being. And the universe has chosen her, a mother without a child. Through Amber, life will be born, creation will flourish in this place.

And there appeared a great wonder in heaven, a woman clothed with the sun, and the moon under her feet . . . and she being with child cried, travailing in birth, and pained to be delivered . . .

But Adam wants to use the surgical equipment and anesthetic that the MarsNow people provided. He wants to lay her out on a table and cut her open. He doesn't understand that the face is a sign of something—a sign that they are not alone. She lets him perform reiki, but won't let him remove the tumor.

"You're not rational." Adam stands above her, blocking her view out the window. "Your mental stability has been affected by your illness."

She twists her neck so she can gaze past him, to see Earth. A distant crescent, half dark, hardly recognizable. The sky is clear tonight, the dust settled. Two moons and millions of stars. Constellations yet to be named.

"Amber, if you don't comply, I'm going to have to give you an order, as your commander, to allow medical intervention."

But she can feel it inside her, nothing like a disease. It is a presence. Like being pregnant again. A few days ago, she felt a flutter at the base of her spine: the quickening.

"Amber. My love?" Adam is on his knees. "Please."

She can feel the presence moving through her, like water through the veins of a leaf. To her lymph nodes, her blood, her bones.

I CAN'T GET UP OFF THE COUCH; AMBER CAN'T GET OUT OF BED;
but Geoff Task must have gone into emergency meetings, concerned
about the dip MarsNow took on the stock market, because he gives a
press conference, standing in the New Mexican sunshine:

"We knew we might lose our Marsonauts—this is the price we
pay to advance scientific knowledge. Amber understood the risks
when she embarked on her journey, a journey that was her dream.
We at MarsNow know that setbacks are inevitable." Meaningful
pause. "Humans have flown in low orbit. Humans have walked on
the moon. But Amber and Adam's accomplishments are of an order
of magnitude far greater than those of anyone who's come before.
They are pioneers, heroes, Marsonauts." Shout-out to the spooked
shareholders: "And their legacy will continue. We are developing
technology to neutralize the effects of radiation exposure. We are
making our processes more streamlined and secure." Shout-out to
the *Star Trek* fans: "To honor Amber's work thus far, and to honor
the child she lost, we are committed to pursuing our destiny of popu-
lating the solar system, and one day, interstellar space."

Maybe he is mildly dismayed that one of his lab rats is suffering.
Or maybe she's not a lab rat to him—maybe Amber is the equivalent
of Laika the space dog, or a young soldier who headed jauntily off to
the trenches in search of glory.

Can I live here? In a world this cruel?

Stand. Walk to the apartment door. Turn the knob.

I manage to get up the stairs. Surprise myself—I've reached the
entryway. The last time I was here, I was on my knees, begging
Amber to stay.

I open the door. Stay behind the screen.

Sunlight. Birdsong.

All I have to do is walk outside. Rejoin reality.

But the air smells wrong, looks wrong—hazy. Wildfires in California, Oregon, and Washington State. A woman walks down the sidewalk wearing one of those MarsNow masks over her nose and mouth and I nearly laugh—*how dystopian.*

This world might once have been ours, but it's no longer home.

I close the door, walk down the stairs, into darkness.

IT BECOMES IMPOSSIBLE TO GET OUT OF BED, BUT THAT'S OKAY,
because she doesn't need the VR headset anymore. She can walk
through her memories as if they are reality. Her past still belongs to her.

She travels back to when she put her sister in one of their mother's dresses, painting Caleigh's little face with pilfered makeup, saying, *Trust me, trust me. You look beautiful.* Or the endless car rides
to gymnastic meets, the rush of road under the Enclave's tires, the
sun blinding through the windshield as her dad played his Prosperity
Gospel tapes.

*God is promoting you; your faith will be rewarded. You may not be
everything you wish to be, but you are not what you used to be.*

Or those early mornings when he drove her to practice, watched
her from the sidelines, then took her to Tim Hortons before school.
He ordered a cruller for himself, an apple fritter and chocolate-glazed
for her, and they shared a large coffee with double cream. She'd
trained herself, from the age of nine, to accept coffee's bitter taste
because the caffeine kept her awake in class. They sat at the table,
chewing sleepily, and he smelled sour from the beer he'd drunk the
night before. But he was happy; she made him proud. He reminded
her, almost every week, of the Parable of the Talents. "God wants us
to use our gifts, to take risks, in the service of His kingdom."

She'd nod, picking the glaze off her donut and letting the sugar
melt on her tongue.

"Never bury your talents, champ. That's the road to failure and
shame. What happens to the unprofitable servant?"

She sipped the coffee, creamy bitterness filling her mouth. "He's
cast into darkness."

"That's exactly right. He is cast into darkness."

Her memories feel so alive.

Like when the family took a road trip to Prince Edward Island. This was during the summer, on the way from whatever church they'd driven to for some "weekend of praise"—somehow, when Amber was ten, they tacked on this detour that had nothing to do with God, but with the fact that their mother had been reading *Anne of Green Gables* to the girls before bed, the sisters snuggled against their mother's sides as Anne's story unfolded one chapter at a time. It was a family vacation unlike any they took before or after, and it meant that Amber had two weeks off from training. She was free, with time to read and play and sleep. Her parents lounged on PEI's beaches while Amber and Caleigh built complicated castles with bright red sand. Caleigh was into playing SimCity on the computer, and Amber was immersed in an Ursula K. Le Guin phase—pressing the open library books against her knees so her parents wouldn't see the covers—and for once the sisters could combine their interests by inventing whole civilizations to inhabit their sand structures.

Their father wanted photos of them beside their elaborate cities; he was always proud when they built things, whether out of sand, Play-Doh, or popsicle sticks.

"God created the cosmos and commanded us to continue the holy process of making a world." He focused the camera's lens—it always took forever for one stupid photo. *"Fill the earth and subdue it.* Which book, girls?"

"Genesis!" yelled Amber. Then she smiled for the camera, before returning to her God-like task. Building a civilization where no one ever got in trouble. Where you could have chocolate cake anytime you wanted. Where you won every competition. Where sin didn't exist.

It might have been the happiest time of her childhood. Every evening the family attended a fund-raiser at a church, usually a lobster supper, and Amber would pick up the crustacean from her plate, shove it in Caleigh's face, and say, "I come in peace." Caleigh, only six, would scream with laughter.

I MASSAGE MY LEGS TO GET BLOOD FLOWING, BUT THE MUSCLES ache with atrophy. My clavicles protrude. I run my hands along the ridges of my ribs.

I seem to be disappearing. Disintegrating to dust.

Amber becomes smaller too. Her skin goes gray—she looks alien against the bright, swirling mountains of Mars.

Online people blame socialism for her demise, or 5G or China, instead of focusing on the rightful villains: Douchebag and the system that made him a billionaire. MarsNow is already spinning her death into profits: selling Amber T-shirts, Amber hoodies, Amber beeswax candles. Advertising that her face will be the first carved into the Martian Mount Rushmore. There's an industry of magazine profiles, editorials, songs written in her honor.

Geoff Task must be pleased at the publicity. Amber is Princess Diana; she is Jesus; she is dying for our sins and our entertainment.

The story is unfolding as predicted, and I'm supposed to feel—what? Closure?

In episode eleven (they'll drag this out to fill a full season), First-Man34 clutches her to his chest. Sings to her off-key. He's aged, his hair white like the Earth's distant moon.

Amber asks him to tell her a story.

Once upon a time, there was a hummingbird named Amber Kivinen.

In episode twelve, Amber's breath weakens and FirstMan34 murmurs prayers in Hebrew. At one point, she opens her eyes and says, "Do you forgive me?"

And Adam—a better man than me—answers *yes.*

THEN A MEMORY THAT CAN'T BE REAL—AMBER WOULD HAVE BEEN
too young—a memory of wanting, needing. She was in a crib, gripping the bars, crying. But her mother didn't come, didn't pick her up,
didn't hold her. Amber cried and cried, until she vomited on her legs,
and still her mother didn't come. Why? Why?

Then other memories return. Her mother inside the dark bedroom, in the depths of one of those "spells" that were later diagnosed
as migraines. Her mother hunched over Amber's bed, praying. *Jesus,
we ask that you bind the demons inside Amber. The demon of pride.
The demon of self-regard.* Her mother on her hands and knees in the
kitchen, scrubbing the floor. Her mother packing a suitcase, dragging it to the end of the driveway, then standing outside in her night-
gown, weeping in front of the whole street. Her breasts sagging, hair
tangled.

Then the memory of injury returns. Amber's shoulder tearing
from its socket, her failed landing, fainting from the pain.

But right when her talent abandoned her, she got together with
Kevin. She'd been lonely, vulnerable—and he'd made that seem
okay. Her first love feels so real now. She remembers talking to him
for hours on her parents' phone, twisting the cord around her wrist.
And later, in Vancouver, drinking espresso and smoking clove-tipped
cigarettes. Eating salmonberries in North Van. Hiking Lynn Valley.
Watching a drag show in that bar on Main Street. Going out for
sushi for the first time, embarrassed because she and Kev couldn't
use the chopsticks. Smoking hash in New Brighton Park, giggling
at the cargo ships. Sleeping side by side in that too-warm apartment,
their sweat sticking them together.

Most of all, she remembers a Thunder Bay February, minus 42
degrees with the windchill. The first time she noticed him. The day

they should have celebrated as an anniversary. They were sixteen and partying at Marcus's place and it was Amber's idea to try to vaporize water—she'd seen it on TV. "You just bring it to a boil," she said, "then toss it."

She put the pot of water on the stove until it roiled, then tried to rally everyone up off the couch. No one moved. Marcus was playing Mario Kart, and the rest of the crew were too drunk to care. No one wanted to put on boots, tuques, and coats. "Fuck off with your science shit," said Marcus, who was sort of her boyfriend at the time.

"Dickhead," said Amber. "I'll go myself, then."

But Kevin followed her up the stairs. "So what's the deal?" he said. "The water will, like, disappear?"

"It vaporizes." She carried the heavy pot of water, still bubbling. "Instantly."

She liked the way he took the stairs two at a time, to keep up with her. She liked his voice. His interest.

"Does it need to be actively boiling?" he said. "Or just hot?"

"Boiling, I think."

They didn't bother to put on coats or boots. They opened the door, stepped out onto the porch in their socks. The cold was so sharp in her lungs that she coughed.

"Okay," said Amber. "Three. Two. One!"

She dumped the boiling water from the pot. But instead of landing on their feet, it turned into steam.

They said nothing, just stood together, and the water traveled upward like their breath.

THE STASH. THE PAINKILLERS. I FIND THE SHOEBOX IN THE BATH-
room, carry it to the couch.

She left them for me. *In case.* Or maybe she felt she wouldn't need them. She must have been hopeful, stretching her arms toward some imagined green future, some new and better world. A dim, flickering light.

Her belief, her hope, breaks my heart.

With the grainy dregs of a glass of protein powder, I swallow one pill, then another. I think of my mother, letting herself fade away. Couldn't even muster some drama for her final scene.

I wish I could forgive her.

I wish I were braver.

Putting the pills aside, I light a joint. And within a few minutes, I've done it.

I feel nothing.

My plants don't require water or soil or air. I don't require human contact, or real food, or sunlight. I don't exist inside a body. I don't belong to any ecosystem. I'm a pair of floating eyeballs tethered to a screen.

A couple tokes, a couple pills, every couple of hours. The green capsules aren't as good as the white, and the blue ones make my brain feel stale like old bread, but I'm getting the hang of it. Hours pass, maybe days.

Only a disembodied self exists, the self that travels invisibly through this earthbound world: every time I charge my laptop's battery, someone in the Democratic Republic of the Congo dies in an open-pit cobalt mine. Every time I sip that protein slurry, an acre of the Brazilian rainforest is cleared to farm soy. Every time I watch the screen, click on a link, ask Google a question, I am engaging the labor of tons of steel and fiberglass, tangles of wire, satellites that pock the sky like acne across a teenager's forehead.

I tried to be adjacent, to be Nick Carraway. But now, finally, I understand her. I see the Earth from above. This ruined planet is a mass of vibrating industry and technology, and I am the still point. I am the cause of that tsunami in Indonesia, that bushfire in Australia, that hurricane in Mozambique.

I am God.

NEXT SHE REMEMBERS THE LOOK ON KEVIN'S FACE WHEN HE found out about Brayden. When he found out about Mars. When he said: *Tell me you don't believe.*

She remembers her father's voice over the phone: *I don't have a daughter. My daughter is dead.*

She remembers the shark pup, gliding past. Alive, perfect, doomed.

Mars was supposed to be a new world. No elephants poached, no corals bleached, no lovers betrayed. No freedom, no choices, and therefore no losses. *And God shall wipe away all tears . . . and there shall be no more death, neither sorrow, nor crying . . .*

Was that *why?* Her true reason for all of it? Dreaming of Eden, she wasn't brave enough to inhabit reality? She believed Mars would be simpler. A place without grief, a place beyond grief.

But her baby is dead. And her greenhouse grows food she can barely swallow: warped beets, tomatoes with skins so thin that their insides leak like tears. She made a mistake. Left her ecosystem, separated herself from air and water and earth. Because of her pride, her lust, her self-regard. Her fear. She chose this barren place and now she's scraped out, empty, mourning everything. The smell of a red pepper when you cut it open. The pattern of rain on a window. The feeling of water on her skin. She misses birdsong, even a crow's cackle. Her dad's voice. The smell of her mom's hair.

Why won't these details come to her in sleep, in dreams? Instead she sweats through three nights of terrible visions. Sees the concrete her father poured: acres of driveways, shopping malls, parking lots that smother soil. *Fill the earth and subdue it.* Then she dreams, sickeningly, that she is fucking her own father on a bed of concrete, gravel rough against her back. But as he thrusts inside her, her father becomes Geoff Task—biting her jaw, gripping her wrist, sliding his hands inside her shorts. *The goal is to become Earth-independent.*

Then she's kneeling in the kitchen, the linoleum pressing its pattern into the skin of her knees. There's always something to confess. Even if you hadn't done anything wrong, you'd had evil thoughts. Even if you hadn't had evil thoughts, your body had bad urges.

I made a mistake.

She was wrong. Understood, in the moment she held her son, that life isn't competition.

I made a mistake and my baby is dead.

Life is connection.

She understands now. And on the third day, she wakes calm. She has retold herself the stories and she is ready. Unafraid. Because she did this before—took one step, then another, and arrived here. To a place of stillness.

Her ear is against Adam's heart. And she remembers the taste of placenta in her mouth: the sweetness of amniotic fluid, the metallic tang of blood. She knows its taste because after Adam took the baby away to be buried, she lifted the placenta to her lips. Kissed it like a sacred object. It seemed to be alive, and to forgive her, its capillaries spreading like the branches of a tree.

FINALE

MY PHONE VIBRATES AND I RECOGNIZE THE NUMBER. I KNEW THIS was coming, knew I'd get a call from the High Priestess of Capitalism herself.

"Hi, Helena Slora," I say.

Then I hear the voice Geoff Task has hired to speak for him. "Mr. Watkins?"

"Yeah." The fog clears a bit. "I guess."

"I'm sure you're aware of why I'm phoning. You're aware that Amber has passed away."

"No." My lungs seize, tear ducts prickle—my body forgetting, for a second, that it is not a body. That I am God. "I wasn't aware. Her death hasn't aired on TV yet."

Helena falters. "My apologies."

And I understand that none of this is her fault; she probably has a couple kids, a crappy ex-husband, a mortgage. She's like everyone else, chasing the pennies Geoff Task deigns to drop from his pocket.

"My condolences." She regains composure. "I'm only calling today—"

"To see if I'll appear on the show."

"Actually the season finale is already cut. We made an artistic choice to stay with Mars, to let the desolate landscape speak for itself, and of course to look toward the future of MarsNow."

"Okay."

"But we're also putting together an in-remembrance special bonus episode that will air exclusively on EyeSite, and we'd love—"

I hang up.

Can I go on? Can I live in a world this broken?

I want to make Amber laugh one last time. I want to touch her hair.

I want an end to this wanting.

We need new values, more presence, to become whole. Amber asked for a new story. And I should have been able to write it. I should have been able to save her, save my mom. Create a new world, without grief.

Maybe I could write our story. Write it because it doesn't belong to them, the producers at MarsNow. Write it so that Amber can exist in the present tense forever. To feel like she's here, like I'm inside her.

The phone vibrates; Helena Slora again.

They own Amber's past. They stole her future. Should they destroy my present?

I hit "Decline." Then stand, wobble, lean against the wall. Drag myself to the apartment door and rest my head against the wood, catching my breath.

I remember when Amber came home. When she chose me. Fled MarsNow and sat beside me on the Voyager. She was so still. Present and clear.

I'm here.

But that was a lie and we both knew it. She was doing that thing where you float outside your body, looking down at your own life. My girlfriend was already on Mars.

And for a second, I see it: not the stupidity and horror of what she's done, but the beauty and bravery. The ambition. The fulfillment.

She took one step, then another, then another. She made it.

Wanna get out of here?

I haul myself up the stairs, to the entryway. Push open the door. Stand on the threshold.

Sunlight. Smoky air. Dandelions, clover, spruce.

It's so green it hurts.

Just one step, onto the sagging porch, and I'd be outside. One step, and I could launch my emaciated body onto the square of lawn beyond our door. Put myself in the sun like a plant.

I can almost feel it: the grass would make my ankles itch. The soil under my hands would be dry, depleted, built of the same stuff as my own cells: water, microbes, minerals.

I was wrong. I see that now, with the sunlight in my eyes. I'm not God; I'm a pile of dirt.

I take my phone from my pocket and text Marcus: *I'm the asshole.* He texts back right away: *100% anus.* Then: *Crazay to hear from you, bro! Bronny and I are at Clark Park. Wanna join?*

One step.

But the Earth spins beneath me at 460 meters per second and I feel dizzy and afraid and alone. One step, and I'd cry for Amber. Cry for my mom.

I'll try, I text Marcus. *Might not make it that far.*

I think of the stash. The shoebox of oblivion. Can I live here, on this planet with its contaminated air? This planet of sinkholes and clear-cuts and conspiracy theories? War zones and border walls? This place of evil and endless grief. Can I do it alone?

Maybe Bronwyn could find a place for me at her community garden. Maybe my knowledge—Amber's knowledge, which I now carry—could be useful. I imagine myself amid rows of carrots and kohlrabi plants, surrounded by kids who are covered in dirt, who know my name, who clamor with questions. "What's up?" I'd say, when they ask for help. "I'm here."

The phone buzzes again. Slora again. Summoning me.

But I can feel the way the heat of our closest star would warm me. The way gravity would hold me, soothe me, root me to the earth.

Maybe I could write a new story if I made it honest. Made it real.

Maybe I could write it to forgive her.

A jogger sweats past; ants parade along the pavement; a homeless guy rides his bike the wrong way up the street.

One step, and I'd feel everything. I'd cry and I might never stop. There'd be no shelter from the flood—I'd be outside.

But maybe I wouldn't be alone. Because not far away are my friends, Marcus and Bronwyn. Bronwyn and Marcus. I wonder if it's real, if it's love, and feel almost hopeful. Happy for them.

One small step.

Toward my friends. Toward clover and spruce. Toward toddlers on the playground, parents snapping photos on their phones, dogs rolling in fast-food wrappers. And beyond that: people laze on balconies, sleep under cardboard, shoot up in alleys. And beyond that: barnacles and blackberries and sand that can be transmuted into clear glass. Cirrus clouds and seagulls and giant sequoias that grow for three thousand years.

Is this the new story? The revolution?

We inhale, exhale. Breathing this world into being.

Acknowledgments

MANY THANKS TO THE CANADA COUNCIL FOR THE ARTS AND THE Alberta Foundation for the Arts for support while I wrote portions of this book; those grants made all the difference. Thank you to the Stegner House, especially Ethel Wills, for such calm and productive weeks. Thank you to the Hawthornden Literary Retreat for Writers for such a fruitful time of quiet and creativity. Thank you to MacEwan University's English Department Writer in Residence Program, with special thanks to Jacqueline Baker for her support and friendship, and to Jillian Skeffington for extending my residency; in Edmonton, I began to learn how to write a novel. Thank you to the Ventspils International Writers' and Translators' House, and to Ieva Balode in particular; in Latvia, I found the time to complete a first draft. I gratefully acknowledge that much of the creation of this book was done on Treaty 7 territory, where I make my home, and was inspired by time spent in Vancouver, unceded land of the Musqueam, Squamish, and Tsleil-Waututh Nations.

Enormous gratitude to my editors, Jill Bialosky and Nicole Winstanley. Jill, you always get to the heart of things and point me in the right direction. Nicole, you read each draft with such depth and offer such wise advice; I can't imagine going on these publishing journeys without you. Thank you also to Drew Elizabeth Weitman for keeping us so organized, and to Meredith McGinnis and Erin Sinesky Lovett for your dedication to getting this book into readers' hands.

Thank you to Leonora Craig Cohen for her work to bring this novel to UK readers. I'm hugely grateful to everyone at Penguin (Canada), W. W. Norton (US), and Serpent's Tail (UK) for taking a chance on this book. I am enormously grateful to Tracy Bohan and Jacqueline Ko of The Wylie Agency. Thank you for your hard work in support of this book and for your belief in me as a writer.

My reading over many years influenced the ideas in this book and helped me to imagine and understand the novel's world. An incomplete list: *Notes from an Apocalypse* by Mark O'Connell, *Untrue* by Wednesday Martin, *Uncanny Valley* by Anna Wiener, *The Age of Surveillance Capitalism* by Shoshana Zuboff, *The Twittering Machine* by Richard Seymour, *Trick Mirror* by Jia Tolentino, *Thus Spoke the Plant* by Monica Gagliano, *The Uninhabitable Earth* by David Wallace-Wells, *Endurance* by Scott Kelly, *I Didn't Come Here to Make Friends* by Courtney Robertson and Deb Baer, and *How We'll Live on Mars* by Stephen Petranek. The quotes from the Book of Revelation are from the King James Bible and the English Standard Version. Other sources were also helpful to me: the documentary *Jesus Camp*; Daisy Hildyard's concept of "the second body" (introduced to me through the work of Kyle Chayka); Umberto Eco's and Zadie Smith's musings on the perfect technology of the book and the privacy it affords; LaineyGossip.com for an inside look at the celebrity ecosystem; and William Buck's work as the science facilitator at the Manitoba First Nations Education Resource Centre, whose knowledge about Indigenous astronomy informed the scene set in Manitoba. Finally, thank you to the environmental defenders and activists who do such brave and essential labor to remind us that there is no Planet B.

Thank you to Naomi Lewis, who told me that the reader wants only one thing (one's soul) and who generously read this manuscript twice. Thank you to Steve Wahl and Mark Winter for help with the marijuana-bust scene—it's good to have lawyers on call! Thank you to Bryan Milks and Mike Dean for help with details pertaining to Loch Lomond and Thunder Bay. Thank you to Eric Moscopedis, who allowed me to be inspired by his tattoo (how could anyone *not* be inspired by such a tattoo?). Thank you to Sarah Jackson for an in-depth design consultation. Thank you to Rita Bozi for influencing the kind of story I wanted to tell and for helping me to feel the earth under my feet. To my friends who lent their names to characters who are nothing like their namesakes: you know who you are and your name is present as a kind of talisman. Thank you for your friendship.

I am forever grateful to those who read this book in manuscript form and offered feedback: Jonathan Garfinkle, Sarah Jackson, Pichu (the real one and only) Kalyniuk, Naomi K. Lewis, Kat Maine, Rachel Rose, Emily Saso, Barbara Joan Scott, Diana Svennes-Smith, Aritha van Herk, and Samantha Warwick. You each helped me in such individual and essential ways; I can't thank you enough.

Love and thanks to my family of readers: my aunt, Charis Wahl, who always pushes me in the best way and who proofreads like a boss; my dad, Gary Willis, for thoughtful help with the ending and for instantly understanding what this book was aiming for; my mum, Pauline Willis, for inspired suggestions, marathon proofreading, huge encouragement, and support in innumerable ways.

Most of all, thank you to Kris Demeanor—for the concept of the "perfect buzz," the brilliance of "Soccer Mom," for reading many drafts of this book, talking through all aspects of the project, and offering astute feedback at every stage. Living with such a caring, intelligent, deeply funny man, such a sharp and courageous artist, has made me braver as a writer and as a person.

Finally, thank you to Aviva, who was born at the perfect time and saved me from submitting a draft too early. Revising this book during the early months of your life, while you slept in my lap, was challenging, liberating, and magical—your presence made the work stronger and more meaningful to me.